KALVAN
KINGMAKER

JOHN F. CARR

Pequod Press

KALVAN KINGMAKER
A Pequod Press Adventure Novel

Second Edition

Printed in the United States of America
January 2010

ISBN 978–0–937912–06–5

Pequod Press
P.O. Box 80
Boalsburg, PA 16827
www.Hostigos.com

DEDICATION

To Victoria, my Russian Princess,
a lovely Fourth Level, Europo-American bundle of fireseed,
who could pass for Rylla's older sister!
Thanks for the inspiration
and all your loving support
throughout the years.

Hostigos Town

Tigos Mountains

1. Ptosphes' Palace
2. Yirtta's Temple
3. High Temple Of Dralm
4. Hostigos Apothecary
5. Guild Hall
6. Galazar Shrine House
7. Royal Armory
8. Fynos Mill
9. Tranth's Hall
10. The Royal Hos-Hostgos Bank
11. Lytris Shrine
12. Saturday Market
13. Gull's Nest
14. Ptosphes' Almshouse
15. Royal Foundling House
16. Royal Army Barracks
17. Tranth's Temple
18. Red Halberd Inn
19. Silver Stag

Great Kings Highway

Ryphos Road

Priest's Crossing

Tigos Road

Old

Lysra Street

Market Street

Bear Creek Bridge

Prince Zythanes Road

Darro Creek

High Street

Cannos Street

Axyon Street

Great Kings Highway

N

Hostigos Gap

Tarr-Hostigos

14 Xyth Street

15

Styh Street

Ivros Road

Thul Road

Market Street

16

Malthos Road

Coopers

Tanners Way

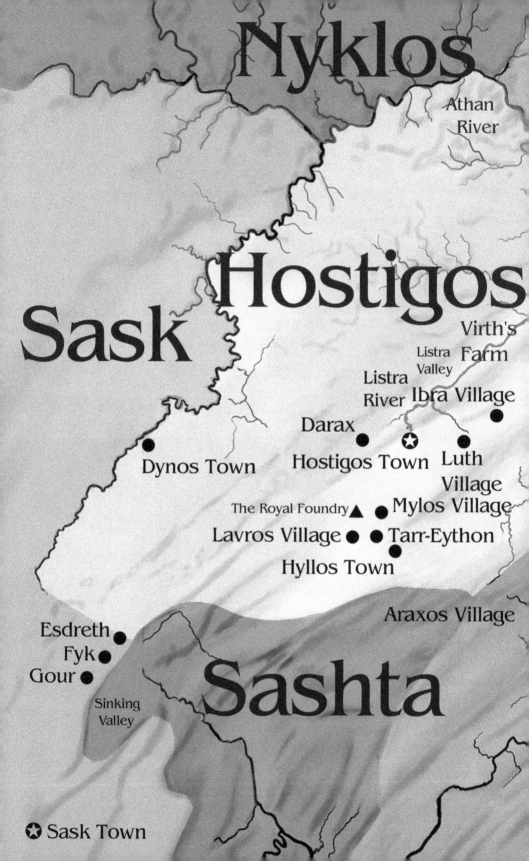

The Saltless Seas

Karphya

Vulthar City

Fryttander

Grefftscharr

Thagnor

Greffa

Upper Middle

Kingdoms

Morthron

Trygath

Tarr-Ceros

Upper Sastragath

Lower Sastragath

Hos-Bletha

Bletha Town

Eryn Town

Hos-Zygros

Zygros City

Glarth City

Ulthor Port

Hos-Hostigos

Hostigos Town

Dyssa

Nostor Town

Hos-Agrys

Agrys City

Lava River

Hyllos Town

Beshta Town

Tarr-Beshta

Tenabra

Harphax City

Mythos

Hos-Harphax

Thebra City

Hos-Ktemnos

Hos-Ktemnos

Balph

Dalthax City

Gythros Town

The Great Kingdoms

Scale: 1" = 200 mi.

1" = 400 Marches

DRAMATIS PERSONAE

Alkides—Officer in charge of the Royal Artillery.

Amasphalya—Hostigos Town Chief Midwife.

Amnita—Princess of Sashta and Sarrask of Sask's daughter.

Armanes—Prince of Nyklos.

Aspasthar—Royal Page and Harmakros' son.

Balthames—Prince of Sashta.

Balthar—Prince of Beshta and king of tightwads.

Chartiphon—Captain-General of the Army of Hos-Hostigos.

Cratos—Highpriest of the Harphax City High Temple of Dralm.

Demia—Princess, Kalvan and Rylla's daughter.

Democriphon—Colonel in Royal Army of Hos-Hostigos.

Ermut—Former Styphon's House slave, now Master at new University.

Gormoth—Formerly Prince of Nostor, now deceased.

Halmoth—Baron and commander of the Old Hostigos Lifeguards.

Harmakros—Captain-General of the new Royal Mobile Force.

Hectides—Head Wolf Hunter.

Hestophes—Captain-General of the Army of Observation.

Kalvan—Great King of Hos-Hostigos.

Kestophes—Prince of Ulthor.

Klestreus—Chief of Hos-Hostigos Internal Intelligence.

Mytron—Highpriest of Dralm and Rector of the University of Hostigos.

Nathros—Captain put in charge of The Great King's Highway project.

Nicomoth—Baron and King Kalvan's aide-de-camp.

Pheblon—Prince of Nostor.

Phosg—Peasant representative on the Hostigi Council.

Phrames—General in Royal Army of Hos-Hostigos.

Ptosphes—Prince of Hostigos and Rylla's father.

Rylla—Great Queen of Hos-Hostigos, Kalvan's wife and co-ruler.

Sarrask—Prince of Sask.

Skranga—Duke and Head of Hos-Hostigos Secret Service.

Sthentros—Baron of Hyllos and Ptosphes' brother-in-law.

Tharses—Uncle Wolf and Highpriest of Hos-Hostigos.

Tythanes—Prince of Kyblos.

Xentos—Highpriest of Dralm and top ecclesiastical figure of Hos-Hostigos.

Xykos—Captain of Great Queen Rylla's Bodyguard.

Zothnes—Former Styphon's House Archpriest, now Baron.

PARATIMERS

Aranth Saln—Study Team Military Expert.

Baltov Eldra—Study Team Historian.

Barton Shar—Deputy Inspector in Charge of Stores and Equipment.

Dalon Sath—Petty-Captain of the Mounted Rifles.

Danar Sirna—Youngest member of Kalvan Study Team.

Danthor Dras—Expert on Styphon's House Subsector.

Gorath Tran—Assistant Director of Kalvan Study Team.

Hadron Dalla—Verkan's wife and Paratime Police Chief's Special Assistant.

Hadron Tharn—Dalla's twisted younger brother.

Lathor Karv—Member of Kalvan Study Team.

Ranthar Jard—Paratime Police Inspector.

Sankar Trav—Medico to the Kalvan Study Team.

Skordran Kirv—Paratime Police head of Foundry Security.

Talgan Dreth—Director of Kalvan Study Team.

Tortha Karf—Former Paratime Police Chief.

Ulton Dorth—Paratemporal Theorist.

Varnath Lala—Study Team Metallurgist.

Verkan Vall—Paratime Police Chief and Colonel of the Mounted Rifles.

Wylant Ordal—Dhergabar University authority on Indo-Aryan Languages.

Yandar Yadd—Prominent Dhergabar City broadcaster and newsie.

Zyldor Lath—Chancellor of the University of Dhergabar.

STYPHON'S HOUSE

Albides—Second in command of Styphon's Own Guard.

Anaxthenes—First Speaker of the Inner Circle.

Aristocles—Knight Commander and second in command of the Order.

Cimon—Inner Circle Archpriest called the "Peasant Priest."

Danthor—Danthor Dras' undercover name as Styphon's House Highpriest.

Dimonestes—Archpriest, one of Roxthar's followers.

Dracar—Archpriest of Inner Circle and Anaxthenes nemesis.

Drayton—Styphon's House Treasurer.

Euriphocles—Archpriest, one of Anaxthenes co-conspirators.

Heraclestros—Archpriest of the High Temple of Agrys City.

Lymachor—Archpriest and one of Anaxthenes' allies.

Neamenestros—Archpriest and one of Anaxthenes' allies.

Phyllos—Highpriest of Harphax Great Temple.

Roxthar—Archpriest and fanatical true believer in Styphon.

Sesklos—Supreme Priest and Styphon's Own Voice.

Soton—Grand Master of the Order of Zarthani Knights.

Syclos—Highpriest of the High Temple of Agrys City.

Theomenes—Archpriest of the High Temple of Hos-Ktemnos.

Timothanes—Archpriest and one of Archpriest Dracar's supporters.

Thymos—Archpriest and one of the Inner Circle's true believers.

Vyros—Archivist of Styphon's Great Temple.

Yagos—Deacon and Anaxthenes' chief lackey.

Xenophes—High Marshal of Styphon's Own Temple Guard.

ALLIES OF STYPHON'S HOUSE

Anaphon—Co-commander of the Royal Army of Hos-Ktemnos.

Anaxon—Co-commander of the Royal Army of Hos-Ktemnos.

Cleitharses—Great King of Hos-Ktemnos.

Demistophon—Great King of Hos-Agrys.

Demnos—Grand-Captain of the Harphaxi Royal Bodyguard.

Leonnestros—Prince of Lantos, sees himself as successor to Mnephilos.

Lysandros—Great King of Hos-Harphax and Kalvan's enemy.

Mnephilos—Lord High Marshal of Hos-Ktemnos.

Phidestros—Mercenary and Grand-Captain of the Iron Band.

Thessamona—Lady of Death, Anaxthenes favorite concubine.

NEUTRALS

Aesklos—Captain-General of the Army of Hos-Agrys.

Araxes—Prince of Phaxos.

Davros—Head Highpriest of the High Temple of Dralm in Agrys City.

Demistophon—Great King of Hos-Agrys.

Eudocles—Grand Duke of Zygros and Sopharar's brother.

Geblon—Banner-Captain of the Iron Company.

Kyblannos—Petty-Captain of the Iron Company.

Kyphranos—Great King of Hos-Harphax.

Lythrax—Iron Company trooper and Phidestros' bodyguard.

Menephranos—Envoy of Prince Araxes of Phaxos to the Court of
    Hos-Hostigos.

Nestros—Prince of Rathon.

Philesteus—Prince and heir apparent to the Iron Throne.

Selestros—Prince of Hos-Harphax and Kaiphranos' wastrel son.

Sestembar—Count and Eudocles' right-hand man.

Sopharar—Great King of Hos-Zygros.

Theovacar—King of Grefftscharr.

Varrack—Prince of Thagnor.

PR⊕L⊕GUE

K night-Sergeant Sarmoth sighed with relief when up ahead he saw the first Kythari watchtower. His oath brother Longshanks was walking behind his destrier, having ridden his own pony into the ground. Steel Hooves was made of sterner horseflesh, but Sarmoth could hear his lungs laboring like a blacksmith's bellows.

"Who goes there?" asked a helmed figure from the top of the watchtower, cradling a crossbow.

Longshanks snorted, as if to say, 'Isn't it obvious we are Zarthani Knights?' After all, Kythar was a garrison town, the garrison to Tarr-Ceros, the biggest and most important of all the Order's castles and seat of the Grand Master of the Holy Order of Zarthani Knights.

"Knight-Sergeant Sarmoth of the Twelfth Lance, reporting. We need new mounts. It is urgent that we see Grand Master Soton at once!"

The guard raised the visor of his helm, revealing a youthful face just beginning to sprout a blonde fringe around the jaw. "Nomad trouble?"

Sarmoth nodded. He didn't intend to give a full report to every guard and under-officer he met.

"In that case, you can use my horse. Leave her at the Old Barley Stable on the first street north of the tannery—you can't miss the smell."

The watchguard's horse was a swaybacked old nag, which snorted and kicked at Steel Hooves approach. Sarmoth was pleased to see that his destrier took no notice of the other horse, except to nip her on the flanks. He tied a rope between the two horses and took off at a canter, with his oath brother riding behind.

Within two candles, after two more stops at a watchtower and a guard shack, they reached the outskirts of Kythar. Sarmoth was pleased to find the city so alert; other towns much closer to the nomad hordes he had passed had been lax about the threat of invasion. He knew that fools ruled their councils.

Kythar was a thriving city, bustling with commerce and industry; half a dozen war galleys were tied up at the docks and dozens of barges and riverboats swarmed the lesser wharves. Twice he saw points of Knights moving through the streets toward the towering castle, perched on a hillside, east of the city. The streets were far wider than those of Dorg, which he had visited with his father many years ago. Sarmoth suspected the broad avenues were to facilitate the movement of troops, since the city had grown up around Tarr-Ceros, not the other way around, as was usually the case.

It took six candles to reach the first barricade; twice he was questioned at the outer works, until he was provided with an escort. Sarmoth was guided across temporary wooden bridges that passed over deep trenches, and through three wooden palisades, the height of the outer walls of Tarr-Syklos! Then came the great stonewalls, eighteen to twenty rods thick, which ringed the foot of the great Tarr. These ring walls would break the heart of any nomad army, thought Sarmoth, as he was led through one gate after another.

He left his mount, escort and the watchman's nag with the Tarr sentry, with orders to have his mount taken to the castle stalls, and the guard's returned to the Old Barley Stable.

Still nothing he had seen so far had prepared him for his first close-up view of Tarr-Ceros, a veritable stone mountain of a fortress, faced with white marble. A great central keep towered over the surrounding buildings like a sentry. The atmosphere was forbidding, as though the great fortress were already under siege. Knights, some fully armored, were coming and going in large numbers through the great portal. Maybe the Order was at siege, he thought, hadn't the Knights fought and lost many of their Lances in far-off Hostigos, where they defended Styphon House, against the heretical Easterners.

Sarmoth was led to a large antechamber with several long benches, holding four or five parties, including that of a yellow robed Archpriest, who was flanked by a bodyguard of Styphon's Own Guard, resplendent in their silver armor and blazing red capes. He suddenly felt shabby in his woolen pants and dusty jerkin, with only a short black tunic emblazoned with the white Holy Wheel to indicate he was one of the Brethren.

Sarmoth was given a scowl by the Archpriest when a Knight Commander in silvered armor every bit as shiny as the Temple's guardsmen approached and called him by name. He followed the Commander into the Great Hall, hung with banners and rich tapestries picturing the Order's great victories. Behind the Grand Master's seat was a magnificent window made of a dozen or more panes of glass, which displayed the Lydistros River and the bustling port. Beneath the window, in a gilded chair that was more throne than seat, sat the Order's commander, Grand Master Soton.

Sarmoth was surprised, when the massive figure rose up from his seat to greet him, he wasn't much taller than he'd appeared seated. Grand Master Soton had a huge head and was clean-shaven but for a mustache. He was also surprised to see that Soton wore a simple tunic, from better cloth, but otherwise similar to the one he wore over his jerkin. The Grand Master's only badge of office was a massive silver chain with a gold representation of Styphon's Holy Wheel the size of his fist. Sarmoth had expected raiment fit for a king; after all, the Knights protected lands larger by two than even the grandest of the Middle or Great Kingdoms.

The Grand Master indicated a chair in front of his desk, saying, "Have a seat. You've come a long ways, Sergeant Sarmoth."

Sarmoth nodded, his tongue suddenly in knots, and sat after the Grand Master.

"What news do you bring?"

The urgency behind his words broke through the temporary paralysis of Sarmoth's tongue and he began to speak. "The Mexicotál have driven the western nomads and Ruthani across the Sea of Grass to the very gates of Xiphlon. The great walled city has once again rebuffed their attempts at siege craft and now the nomads are moving into the lower Sastragath. The Mexicotál have invested Xiphlon and the nomads have nowhere else to flee, but to the east and north. Many of the lower tribes are being pushed into our realms and the Knight Commander of Tarr-Syklos has sent me with this message, requesting additional troops."

Sarmoth removed a folded leather packet from inside his jerkin and gave it to the Grand Master. The Grand Master paused to read the document, his brows furrowing as he read. Halfway through, he rose to his feet and banged his fist on the table. "We will have to put an end to this invasion or we will lose a century of progress!" Then, he muttered some curses damning the Daemon Kalvan and the Inner Circle of Styphon's House for wasting so many of the Order's finest Knights. Sarmoth pretended he didn't hear the curses, since he was not offended: he was no lover of priests, be they for the so-called One God, Styphon, or any other god.

While the Grand Master was busy reading the message, Sarmoth studied the standards and flags hanging from the massive timbers bracing the stones walls. There were old banners, won at battles and wars, from the dawn of history. Many were now the stuff of legend. Wasn't that flag, with a cow skull on a black field, the personal banner of Erasthames The Great? Then he saw the tattered red banner, with the blue halberd-head of Hostigos. He looked in awe; this was the Daemon Kalvan's banner!

"We took that from the Veterans of Hostigos at Tenabra." Soton said, as if reading his mind. Soton raised his head and looked Sarmoth in the eye. "No, it's not King Kalvan's flag, but his father-in-law's, Prince Ptosphes of Hostigos. We had to cut off the banner-bearer's arm to take this away!"

"The spoils of victory."

"Hard won, son. And only after, the traitor, Balthar changed sides in the middle of the battle—the old skinflint." Soton made as if to spit on the floor. Then he paused to load a corncob pipe and light it from a tinderbox. "Balthar found a fitting end at the edge of Kalvan's blade, or so I hear. After Tenabra we chased Ptosphes all the way up the Syphistros Valley and into Beshta. It was a grand chase and we would have caught him, too, if it hadn't been for all our allies straggling behind.

"The Hostigi breed good fighters; I'd be proud to fight by their side and include them in any host."

Sarmoth's eyes opened wide. "They're heretics!"

"Maybe. But before that they're soldiers, and damn good ones at that! We lost three Lances at Chothros Heights and another three at the Battle of Phyrax. And we could use every man jack of them against these nomads, curse and blast it!"

Soton blew out a cloud of tobacco smoke that momentarily obscured his head. "You look like a fighter not a messenger—am I right?"

"Yes, sir. Commander Sytomanes wanted someone fast and I've been called the best horseman in the Twelfth Lance."

Soton looked him over from crown to toe. "I believe you might be. Would you rather return to Tarr-Syklos, or kill some nomads?"

"Kill nomads, Sir!"

Soton gave a wide mouthed smile that showed off the yellowed-wedges of his tobacco stained teeth. "Then I'll see to it that you're transferred to the Fifteenth. You can fight by my side. I promise you more blood than you'll see in any slaughterhouse this side of Balph!"

FALL

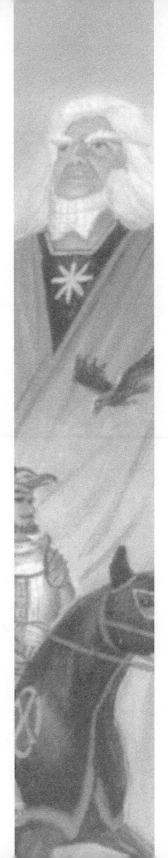

⊕NE

I

Paratime Police Chief Verkan Vall watched while the trees and scrub brush of Fourth Level flickered through the wavering silver sheen of the Ghaldron-Hesthor transposition-field, as the transtemporal conveyer carried him toward Fourth Level Aryan-Transpacific, Kalvan Time-Line. The civilized Second and Third Levels were behind him now. Once in a while Verkan caught flickering glimpses of Fourth Level-buildings, airports, occasionally a raging battle. Fourth Level was the high-probability level of all the inhabited Paratime Levels. There the First Colony had come to complete disaster fifty thousand years ago, losing all knowledge of its origins. It was the most barbaric level, as well as the largest. Its cultures ranged from idol worshippers on Indo-Turanian to the nuclear priesthood on some time-lines in the Europo-American, Hispano-Columbian Subsector.

The conveyer was now entering the low-level probability Fifth Level, where nature not man was triumphant. The only humans were Service and Industrial Sectors proles and their First Level overseers who labored there to keep heavy and light industry off First Level, Home Time Line. On Fifth Level only the mountains remained constant. Occasionally, a large beast could be made out, while several times large pools of water, appeared and disappeared. There was always a bit of variability between time-lines, sometimes nothing more than trees growing in different spots, other times bodies of water flowing in otherwhen deserts.

The Service Sector Proles were not indigenous to the Fifth Level, but were brought from time-lines of near savagery, which they voluntarily left for a better life. The Paratime Transpositional Code limited the colonization of Service Sector time-lines to natives below second-order barbarism. The Serv-Sec Proles were the ones who did most of the administrative and record keeping for Home Time Line. The proles who were dumped in the Fifth Level, Industrial Sectors, where the machines and robots of First Level were manufactured, were at the bottom rung of the Service Sector. Here were the survivors of Paratime screw-ups, when policy or criminal mistakes had made it necessary to transplant entire tribes and sometimes nations to protect them from their hostile neighbors, or to protect the Paratime secret. No matter—it seemed—how diligently the undermanned and overworked Paratime Police worked, there were always new bodies to fill another industrial time-line on Fifth Level.

Few, on First Level, realized the majority of these uncountable time-lines had never been visited by Home Timeliners, even after twelve thousand years of parasitism upon Second, Third, and Fourth level time-lines. First Level Para-topographers had described less than one tenth of one percent of all the 'known' time-lines. In actuality it was an impossible job and most current Paratime theorists did not believe they would ever completely map this near infinity of diverging time-lines.

In theory the transposition field was impenetrable; however when two craft going in the opposite direction interpenetrated, other objects and life forms could and did pass through. It was why unscheduled trips like Verkan's were limited to the highest echelon of the Paratime Police. It was also Paratime Policy to have a weapon drawn just in case the hitchhiker was dangerous or a threat to the Paratime secret. Most human pickups were killed immediately and disposed of back at the conveyer head. Only a few escaped, and even fewer flourished in their new homes.

His friend Kalvan, who ruled an unruly kingdom on Fourth Level Aryan Transpacific, was the exception. There, Great King Kalvan, formerly Corporal Calvin Morrison of the Pennsylvania State Police, had accidentally boarded a conveyer in Europo-American, Hispano-Columbian as a

Paratemporal hitchhiker, and was bumped off on Aryan-Transpacific, Styphon's House Subsector. This was an even ruder and deadlier culture than Pennsylvania, ruled by a mafia of priests who worshipped a god named Styphon. Styphon's theocracy only held their power because they held the secret of how to make "fireseed"—or gunpowder.

Kalvan had not only survived, he had prospered. In less than a year, he'd married a princess, founded an empire, broken Styphon's House's monopoly of gunpowder and more than held his own against the worst that band of priestly tyrants could throw against him. Styphon's House had met him with the unholy Holy Host, the largest army ever assembled on that backward time-line, and he had defeated it.

Kalvan's intervention into local politics had created a new time-line. In many ways Kalvan's Time-Line was unique. It was the first time in First Level history when Paratime observers had been present at the start of a new subsector, identified from the exact point of divarication. The Paratimers had been close before, the President John F. Kennedy assassination, only a few years earlier, had been the critical event in the formation of the Europo-American, Kennedy Subsector. The Kennedy assassination, while newsworthy, had not been considered a divarication event until months later. The Kalvan split had been discovered as it happened: Verkan Vall himself had been on-hand, when the very conveyer that former Pennsylvania State Trooper Calvin Morrison had stumbled onto and exited on Aryan Transpacific, had arrived at the Fifth Level conveyer-head rotunda.

Because of growing instability between the two competing nuclear-powered sovereignties, the Kennedy Subsector was far too dangerous to risk intensive study and monitoring. Kalvan's Time-Line, on the other hand, was technologically backward so there was little danger to outtimers. The Dhergabar University had sent out a Kalvan Study Team to survey Kalvan Prime, as they called it, and other teams to study as many of the nearby Styphon's House Subsector 'control' time-lines as possible.

True, there were some—mostly do-gooders and professors who'd never traveled outtime—who still believed it was Home Time Line's duty to colonize these barren time-lines, even here on Fifth Level. Or worse, that it was their duty to spread the 'benefits' of First Level civilization and Psycho Hygiene. *Worlds without number*, thought Verkan, *only a politician or do-gooder would think they could be tamed in even ten thousand lifetimes.*

Finally the conveyer came to rest outside a white marble villa. Solid mesh appeared overhead, out of the iridescence, and Verkan holstered his sigma-ray needler. He opened the door and saw two lovely prole girls, draped in white togas, tending flowers in the garden. *So much for ex-Chief Tortha Karf's solitude,* he thought!

Verkan watched with amusement as a small brown, long-eared 'beast' scurried through the flowers, causing the girls to squeal in assumed outrage. It appeared that Tortha was losing in his attempt to rid his hideaway, known on Fourth Level, Europo-American as Sicily, of its indigenous rabbit population. He caught the girls' coy glances in his direction, and was glad his wife, Dalla, wasn't along. Jealousy, along with overwork, had brought an end to their first marriage and, while Dalla was less possessive these days, the sight of two half-naked serving girls ogling Verkan would not be taken lightly. A catfight would not be the proper introduction for the bad news he had to share with his former boss and the ex-Paratime Police Chief.

The commotion brought Tortha Karf to the doorway. "Verkan! From your message ball, I didn't expect you for several hours."

"We managed to home-in on the missing Paracop's beacon and were able to extricate him from the Fourth Level mess he'd fallen into. His mission was locating and then extracting French Impressionist paintings from a *gautlatier's* mansion on a particularly nasty Fourth Level, Europo-American time-line. Unfortunately, someone had already removed the paintings and he was picked up by the *Gestapo,* a rather brutal quasi-police force."

"Must have been in the Axis Subsector."

Verkan nodded.

"I remember that Subsector well," Tortha continued, "its impact reverberated across the entire Fourth Level. Adolph Hitler's public works and culling of the regional populations on that subsector makes your Pennsylvania State Trooper's transtemporal interference look like a tempest in a teapot—to use a Europo-American Sector cliché! Remember when the Opposition Party claimed that Hitler was really a renegade Paratime Policeman?"

Verkan refused to be baited.

Tortha noticing his discomfort, added, "Come on in. I've been by myself too long. I've forgotten all my manners."

Verkan gave a pointed look at the girls who were watching them closely.

Tortha shrugged his shoulders in feigned ignorance and led Verkan through the foyer and into the main room, where the rich gold-veined white marble walls displayed Cretan murals. The floor was covered with Fourth Level, Etruscan-Zoroastrian rugs and contained several embroidered purple divans, decked with gold fringe, which appeared to be Alexandrian-Roman in origin.

"So this your 'little cottage?'" Verkan asked.

"Compared to Paratime Headquarters, this place is tiny. And much quieter. So what brings you to paradise?"

To Verkan his ex-Chief looked a little twitchy. *Too much of a good thing?* Maybe paradise was better dreamed about than lived. He was sure Kalvan, in the midst of a war with three great kingdoms, might very well agree. "The Wizard Traders have popped up again."

"Wizard Traders. You mean slave traders, Verkan. We busted that outfit up just before I retired as Chief."

"You weren't so sure a year ago. True, we arrested the obvious ones; those who were passing themselves off as wizards on backward Third and Fourth Level worlds, using their privileges to steal forbidden artifacts and buy and sell people to unscrupulous Home Timeliners. Plus, a couple of First Level dupes, who were manning their secret conveyer heads. Now, we've uncovered evidence that they may be connected to the Opposition Party. Remember how you always told me 'follow the money trail.' I've been following your advice and we've found some evidence that much of it went into the Opposition Party coffers."

"But that doesn't make sense, Verkan. The Oppositionists run on a policy of non-interference and prole equal representation. You're trying to tell me that blood money has been paying for prole equality votes?"

"I think you've been on this big island for too long. Yes, I do. Don't you remember: the end justifies the means. The lesser evil for the greater good!"

"Maybe I have been outtime too long. Could this be the break we've been looking for, Verkan? Get word of this out to our friends in the media and we can break their backs once and for all."

"Break is not the right word. The Opposition Party has been gaining adherents and I'm afraid they may well find a way to point the blame right back at the Department."

"How? We've never been linked to the Oppositionists—just the opposite."

"True, but it did happen on our watch. Didn't it?"

"Don't look at me like that, old son. It's not my watch anymore. I've got some grapes to harvest."

"What should I do about it?"

"What you have to do, according to your commission. You're the top Paracop. Find out who they are, who's supporting them; then root them out. Who's your goat?"

"Hadron Tharn."

"That fatuous prig," Tortha said. "Your brother-in-law's not smart enough to be behind stale bread much less the Wizard Traders."

"He's not behind them, but we've linked one of the Wizard Traders to his University action team."

"You mean that University of Dhergabar crowd that's been crying about Paratime Police barriers to First Level outtime studies?"

"Same group, Tortha. I'd like to hijack the whole lot and dump them on a time-line where the locals have had a brush with the Wizard Traders. The survivors would come back a lot wiser."

"It's too bad they used hypno-conditioning to commit suicide."

"We never got all the trigger words," Verkan said, lighting his pipe. "Everyone of the important Wizard Traders committed suicide, when one of the implanted suggestions froze the Vagas Nerve—instant heart attack." Verkan shook his head. "No two of them shared the same trigger words either; it left the experts at Bureau of Psychological Hygiene in a state of paralysis. The rest of the Wizard Traders were just proles doing a job. I'm still getting bad press over the casualties."

"Not your fault, Verkan," Tortha said, shaking his head. "It does lend credence to the big conspiracy theory, though. That kind of deep conditioning doesn't come cheap. Anything more?"

"Yes, we've traced a new batch of Wizard Traders to Aryan-Transpacific."

Tortha's mouth dropped open. "Already?"

"Yes, they've gotten into bed with Styphon's House on every time-line they've entered. Trading the upper priests weapons technology in exchange for young bodies and precious metals."

"Have they penetrated the Kalvan Time-Line?"

"No. Although, we do have a potential spy on one of the University study teams."

"Why don't you bring him in for questioning?"

"It's a she. And we don't have any evidence other than a family relationship with Hadron Tharn. We do have an agent on the Kalvan Study Team keeping an eye on her. Besides, Tharn is too flighty to set up and run any decent spy ring. We suspect she's a red-herring, as it's called on Fourth Level, Europo-American. Just as Tharn himself is a cat's-paw to lead us astray."

"From what?"

"A potentially embarrassing incident or some other criminal enterprise."

"Good hunting," Tortha said, shaking his head. "Every time I start to think back fondly of my time as Chief, you come along and remind me of why I retired."

"Tortha!" one of the girls called. "It's time for our swimming lessons. Will you be joining us?"

"Yes, of course. Must not neglect my guests. Please, excuse me Verkan, but I've got my duties here to contend with. Let me know if there is anything I can do to help."

Verkan nodded, as Tortha waddled off with a girl tucked under each arm. He wondered whom the show was for, him or Tortha? *It must be tough,* Verkan thought, *trying to have a good time twenty-four hours a day. I'll have to try it sometime!*

II

Warchief Ranjar Sargos watched in red anger as Vanar Halgoth's niece, Althea, was helped into the tribal longhouse. One of Althea's eyes was blackened, her face was covered with scratches and welts, her long blond hair was crusted with blood and her arm was bound in a fresh splint. Yet, despite all the obvious damage and the pain she was in, Althea stood proudly and defiantly as she approached the tribal Table of Judges. Sargos also noticed the admiration shining in his eldest son, Bargoth's eyes, as he sat at his side and watched the maiden—well, former maiden, approaching the Table. She was a comely woman with long legs and wide hips, good for both bundling and bearing many children.

Althea was the last of the Burgdun stragglers who had come into the Raven Tribe's winter camp. The Raven Tribe, who now numbered over two hundred fighting men, was the largest and most successful tribe of the Tymannes Clan. The Burgduns were people of another, but smaller related clan, whose winter camp rested west of their own. Two days ago the Burgduns had been attacked by a large band of Ruthani from across the Great Mother River. According to the survivors, all the Burgdun males over the age of eight had been killed and the women taken captive.

The winter camp had been in an uproar ever since the first survivors had arrived. Many of the Tymannes had kin among the Burgdun Clan and the tales of rapine and murder had impassioned the tribe. Sargos was holding a council to determine what the Raven Tribe's response would be to atrocities committed upon their neighbors. He had already decided upon revenge; now, he had to convince the tribal Elders that this was the best course. He had chosen Althea carefully, knowing full well that having a beautiful young girl as his primary witness would help bend the Elders to his will.

He nodded to Ikkos, who was helping steady the girl. Halgoth, his old friend, came forward. "Warchief, the maiden Althea would like to speak before the Council. May she have your permission?"

"Speak, Maiden Althea. The Council of Elders of the Raven Tribe, First Tribe among the Clan of the Tymannes, will hear your words."

Althea paused, as though to collect her wits, and began to speak, directing her words to Sargos. "As you have heard, our tribe was attacked early in the morning by a large band of Ruthani raiders. Our tribesmen fought well, many of the redmen were killed and sent to Wind. But our warriors were outnumbered"—she paused to hold up her good hand, spreading out all five fingers—"by five times their number. Those who asked for quarter were taken prisoner. Then murdered in cold blood by the Ruthani."

There was a collective gasp among the tribal Elders at this breach of honor. Sargos could see they were impressed by the girl's straightforward and unemotional speech.

"All male children, older than six winters, were also slain," Althea said, tears leaking now from her eyes, but her voice still steady. "The women and girls, even those as young as ten winters, were taken into the longhouses and made sport of."

"Curse, these spawn of Styphon!" one of the Elders cried. All knew that Styphon was not a god of the Ruthani Grassmen, but to the Tymannes, the false-god Styphon—patron of the Black Knights—was a prince among the demons of the underworld.

"Despoilers of young girls; they deserve no mercy!" Another shouted.

Sargos could hear Ikkos—who also had eyes for Althea—grind his teeth, while his son made growling noises at the back of his throat.

"I was taken to the chief's longhouse, the house of my father." Althea was openly weeping, but her voice was strong. She was doing a much better job of telling her story than Sargos had hoped for. All her listeners knew full well what was left unsaid and it further inflamed their passions, whereas an emotional recital would have left them far less moved.

"When my captor fell into a drunken sleep, I found the talisman stone of our tribe."

Sargos was familiar with the Burgdun's talisman, a round river stone the size of a child's skull, painted with the face of a horned owl. He nodded for her to continue.

"I took the stone and smashed it into his head—again and again and again!" Her voice was beginning to rise.

Sargos nodded again and she stopped. He noticed Bargoth's eyes were round in appreciation. Despite her dishonor, he decided, Althea would make Bargoth a good wife and bring forth many strong sons to honor the Raven banner. If such a union were proposed, he would give it his blessing. If not, he would encourage it.

"It was late at night and the moon was gone. I slipped out of the long-house and used the shortcut to the river. They only had two guards on the banks and both were asleep. I used the chief's knife to slit their throats."

There was a rumble of appreciation from the Elders. Few women would have had the nerve or discipline to kill the guards.

Althea continued, "I took one of their canoes, after releasing the others, and went downstream. Then I doubled back and came to your camp. I pray to the goddess that you will avenge our people."

Sargos nodded his approval of her request. He noticed that all but one or two of the Elders had reflexively followed his lead. Althea had made her case, and his, far better than he had expected.

"You are dismissed. We will ponder your words."

She nodded submissively, as was proper, and left the longhouse with Ikkos and her uncle.

Vanar Halgoth, his massive body looming over the Elders, came back into the longhouse and stood before the Council. "Blood of our blood has been spilled by Grassmen from beyond the Great Mother River. My niece has only told you what the others have reported. She has shown honor and . courage; it is our duty to avenge their deaths!"

Several Elders grumbled their approval.

Sargos stood up. "Althea is a brave maiden and has won her honor back by the death of the Ruthani chieftain and her bravery in escaping her captors. I would not expect more from my own daughter. If her uncle, were not already caring for her; I would adopt her into my own family and thereby honor her courage."

The assembled Elders nodded their agreement.

"Of course, my son might not agree with that decision."

Several of the Elders laughed, acknowledging that Bargoth's eyes for Althea had not gone unnoticed. His son turned bright red, but held his tongue—which was as it should be and why Sargos had allowed Bargoth to attend the Council meeting. He could see that the other Elders were pleased with his son's restraint. This would be remembered when he was killed in battle or became too old to ride a horse and heft a sword.

"I say we should gather the warriors of the tribe and avenge our friends and kinsmen. All those in favor of war against the Ruthani invaders raise your knives."

Of the thirty assembled Elders all but three, which included his son who was not yet a formal member of the Council, raised their knives."

"It is done. The Council is dismissed. Bargoth, you and Ikkos, bring the other sub-chiefs to the longhouse. It is time to plan this raid."

TWO ⊕

I

Great King Kalvan looked down from the small window in his war room, at the top of the Tarr-Hostigos keep, watching a company of Queen Rylla's Lifeguard marching in formation. The Lifeguard was an elite bodyguard of riflemen who were supposed to serve as bodyguards for the Great Queen and their daughter, Demia, but Rylla was already talking about the role they would soon be playing in spearheading the spring campaigns. This year, her pregnancy had kept Rylla out of the battle line; next year, Kalvan wondered how he would keep her castle-bound.

Ever since Kalvan's arrival, here-and-now, when he was picked up by some kind of time-traveling flying saucer from a small farm outside State College, Pennsylvania—Kalvan, formerly Corporal Calvin Morrison of the Pennsylvania State Police, had been reacting to events beyond his control. First, he'd had to shoot his way off the flying saucer or whatever it was, then survive by his wits in an alternate Pennsylvania where time had stood still. The local inhabitants of the Princedom of Hostigos, about to be conquered by their neighbors, welcomed any help they could get. Kalvan, with some knowledge—both academic and practical, having fought in Korea—was able to win several crucial battles. After this initial success, Hostigos seceded from Hos-Harphax, forming the new Great Kingdom of Hos-Hostigos.

Kalvan crowned himself Great King and prepared to defend his new king-dom with everything but the proverbial kitchen sink.

The following spring, luck again—and stupidity on his opponent's part—had allowed Kalvan to defeat the more numerous Holy Host at the Battle Of Phyrax. So far, the defeat of their best troops, the fall rains and the illness of Great King Kaiphranos, ruler of Hos-Harphax, had conspired to keep the forces of Styphon at home. Now, he had to learn everything that was known about the history of here-and-now, if he was going to find some angle that could help his fledgling new kingdom survive against the wealth, political influence and all the military might Styphon's House's gold could buy.

From what Kalvan had been able to piece together from oral history, a few old parchments from Tarr-Beshta and local legends, a large group of Indo-Aryans had migrated east into China, rather than south and west into Macedonia, Greece and the Anatolian peninsula. After cross-ing the Asian land mass, some of the migrating tribes had built small ships and sailed their way along the Kuriles and the Aleutians, down the coast of Alaska and Canada, bringing with them their foods, horses and cattle, their iron-making skills, and their weapons, the battle axe and the sword.

From ancient parchments recently discovered amongst the rat's-nest of former Prince Balthames' treasury—which included everything from gold ingots to the former Prince's baby teeth—Kalvan had learned new infor-mation about these early migrations. There hadn't been just one big migration, but a series of smaller ones. The first Indo-Aryan invaders had landed in the Pacific Northwest. Some tribes remained in the northern for-ests, while others broke off and moved into the Upper Plains. The majority continued along the Pacific Coast, the women and children in boats and the men following along on shore, much like the movement of the Sea Peoples in the Mediterranean after the eruption of Thera on Crete. Along the way, they subdued the coastal Indian tribes, while settling in their former habitats.

The majority of these migrants settled along the coast of California, pri-marily around the harbors of San Francisco and San Diego, while building others at Long Beach and San Pedro. There they established colonies of sea trading city-states along the lines of the early Minoan civilization. The

Ros-Zarthani, as they called themselves, exterminated and enslaved the primitive local Indians and began to send out fishing and trading ships. They quickly established trade with their northern cousins, who lived a more tribal and agrarian life. The southern cities traded manufactured products and grains for lumber, smoked salmon and furs.

A thousand years later, a second series of Indo-Aryan migrations followed in the footsteps of the earlier settlers. These new invaders—unlike the Ros-Zarthani, who spoke an early proto Greek dialect—spoke a very early Germanic tongue. Centuries of inter-action and inter-marriage had changed both languages, but the Urgothi still had a separate language.

Discovering the Pacific seacoast already populated and well-defended, the Urgothi peoples moved east and south, some drifting into the Great Plains, known here-and-now as the Sea of Grass, while other Urgothi followed the tributaries of the Missouri and Mississippi into the Great Lakes area and Mississippi Valley, where they founded what were known as the Middle Kingdoms. Following what Kalvan's world had called the Marius Trail, the Urgothi had established trade routes with the major city-states along the Pacific coast. Trade was sporadic until the Great Lakes iron ore deposits were discovered in Grefftscharr about fifteen hundred years ago. Within a century, the Great Trail became a major trade link between the gold hungry Middle Kingdoms and the iron poor Pacific Coast city-states. The Middle Kingdom kings had made treaties with some of the Plains Indian tribes, conquered others and paid tribute only when necessary. Some of the great trade caravans that Kalvan read about numbered hundreds of wagons guarded by small armies of guards and soldiers.

The most recent migration wasn't from Euro-Asia, but began six hundred years ago, when the Pacific Coast civilization, in flux due to a war between north and south, began to crumble. Tens of thousands of migrants poured over the Iron Trail. Not wanting these heavily armed and desperate invaders settling within the Middle Kingdoms, King Chaldorec had decided to help them move into the Atlantic Seaboard. His plan was to use the migrating Ros-Zarthani as a buffer to the quickly expanding Iroquois Alliance in the east. The migrations, which started as a trickle, soon turned into a flood. The war with the Eastern Ruthani, or Redmen, became a war to the death as both peoples realized they could not live in peace.

The conflict ran almost a century and didn't end until the Iroquois were virtually exterminated, with the survivors escaping into Newfoundland and Labrador.

The final migration occurred after the destruction of the Ruthani, and the Ros-Zarthani settlement of the Eastern Seaboard. The latest refugees from the war-ravaged Pacific Coast were forced to make their way down the Potomac into Maryland and Virginia, to what would later become Hos-Ktemnos. The mid-Atlantic Ruthani were far less warlike and organized than their eastern cousins and were quickly exterminated or displaced to the south. It was during the settlement of Hos-Ktemnos that a temple priest of a minor healer god named Styphon discovered the formula for gunpowder, or fireseed as it was called here-and-now. The temple hierarchy had immediately grasped the political implications of this new discovery and made it a church secret. Over the next centuries they dispensed gunpowder to their allies and withheld it from their enemies, using the revenue and their military might to consolidate political dominion over Hos-Ktemnos. They were in the process of moving their tentacles into Hos-Harphax, when Kalvan had taken his cross-time ride and been dropped off into the middle of a war between the independent Princedom of Hostigos and the neighboring minions of Styphon's House.

Kalvan's sudden appearance had turned a sure thing into a donnybrook! Thanks to an improved gunpowder formula and advanced military tactics introduced by Kalvan, the Princedom of Hostigos not only survived the first few rounds with Styphon's House, but had grown to become the nucleus of the new Great Kingdom of Hos-Hostigos with Great King Kalvan at its helm. No sooner was the dynasty founded than it was embroiled in the fight for its life with Styphon's House and its pawns. Primary among these foes was Hos-Harphax, from where the new Great Kingdom had sprung unbidden.

In the last few months, Kalvan had learned that some rather nasty Mesoamericans—related to the ancient Aztecs back home—were stirring things up in the Lower Sastragath, the Mississippi Valley, and pushing the southern tribes north into the Appalachians, or Trygath as they called Kentucky and Tennessee here-and-now. If he could find a way to turn their migration to the southeast, against the Zarthani Knights—the martial arm of Styphon's House and one of the most effective military forces here-and-now—Kalvan might just be able to get a jump on Styphon's House and its allies, keep one step ahead of the headman's axe, and save his family and adopted new home, Hos-Hostigos.

There was a knock at the door and he sighed, pulling his hands away from his face. "Come in." It was probably Cleon with his hot roasted barley, the best coffee substitute he could come up with here-and-now. He didn't like the taste much, but it was better than the sassafras tea everyone else drank. He encouraged his soldiers to drink tea; even if he was convinced that it was the boiling, not the tea, that kept cholera to a minimum in the Royal Army.

A handsomely attired Duke Skranga attempted a grand entrance into the room that was defeated by the way his bony shoulders poked up his ermine cape, like tent poles. Skranga used two fingers to brush a few red strands over his balding head, before bowing and saying, "Your, Majesty."

"At ease, Count."

While Skranga eased himself into the high-backed chair Kalvan reserved for company, Kalvan put some tobacco—at least, that was the same here-and-now—into his pipe, tamped it and used a flintlock tinderbox to light up. It used the same back acting flintlock mechanism that the Zarthani used on their muskets.

"What's the news from Harphax City?" Kalvan asked, since Skranga as Hostigos head spymaster had a number of agents there.

The Duke shook his balding head sorrowfully. "Old Great King Kaiphranos is still lying on his deathbed; the one he mounted when his son led that suicide charge with his lancers and died so gloriously. Ha! It's been going on for moons now. The whole capital is holding its breath, waiting either for the old fool to draw his last lungful, or the Daemon Kalvan to blow down the city walls. Meanwhile, his younger brother Grand Duke Lysandros grinds his teeth down to their gums with impatience, playing off one Elector after another."

"What of his son, Prince Selestros?"

"Visiting fleshpots and gambling dens as though they might all disappear if he lets them leave his sight! No one, including his father, wants him sitting on the Iron Throne."

"What are Lysandros' chances of becoming the new Great King?" Lysandros was one of the few effective rulers and military leaders left in Hos-Harphax.

"The princes of Hos-Harphax have become accustomed to a light hand on their harnesses. Few of them will welcome Lysandros, who's been known to whip his horses on occasion. On the other hand, he has had some military success and is the only Harphaxi leader capable of corralling and leading that gaggle of fools or turning them into an effective fighting force.

"Is there anything we can do to slow his ambitions?"

"Not directly, Your Majesty, but I've got a few ideas."

Kalvan was sure the former horse trader did. Just as sure as Kalvan was that these 'ideas' were going to cost the Royal Treasury more than a few purses of gold.

II

Highpriest Davros did not like the way the Royal Bodyguards were eyeing him. He'd left the Agrys Temple of Dralm early this morning, at dawn, after Great King Demistophon's Royal Page had delivered the Summons. Davros had spent the rest of the morning and afternoon waiting in the anteroom outside the Royal Audience Chamber. Great King Demistophon had not been to the Temple of Dralm or requested an audience with Davros, since Captain-General Artemanes had returned from Nostor where the Agrysi Army had been soundly defeated by Prince Ptosphes of Hostigos. The Captain General had left the field of battle with less than half of his original force; the rest of the Agrys Army left behind, dead or wounded, and most of the mercenaries prisoners were free to join Kalvan's army, when Demistophon failed to ransom them.

Most of Agrys City blamed Styphon's House for encouraging Great King Demistophon's foolhardy attack on Hos-Hostigos. No one knew whom Demistophon himself blamed, since he had stayed holed up in Tarr-Agrys from the moment word of his army's loss had reached the Kingdom. Rumor in the wineshops and alleyways of Agrys City had it that Demistophon was afraid Kalvan's army was going to sack the city in payment for its Great King's treachery—or stupidity.

All Highpriest Davros knew for sure was Great King Demistophon hadn't visited the High Temple of Dralm since his defeat. Then this sudden Royal Summons—Even the under-chamberlain, who was secretly in his employ, had no answers when questioned shortly after Davros arrival at the Palace.

His thoughts were interrupted by the High Chamberlain's voice. "Highpriest Davros, I will escort you into the presence of Great King Demistophon." Davros tried to keep his hands from shaking as he stood up and followed in the wake of the Chamberlain's robes. Great King Demistophon was capricious at the best of times and his sour stomach often made his judgments harsh. Yet, Davros knew there would be some manner by which he could make a profit out of this unexpected Summons.

Davros was most surprised by the Great Kings' appearance. King Demistophon, who had always been heavy, was now obese and barely fit into the Throne of Lights. He had grown a second chin and his jowls were hanging down like dewlaps. His lips were thick like sausages and when he opened his mouth to speak it gaped obscenely. "What is this We hear about a renegade Hostigos priest in the Temple of Dralm?"

He must be referring to Highpriest Xentos, thought Davros, the Highpriest of Hos-Hostigos. Xentos had without fanfare arrived in Agrys City to attend the Council of Dralm. Davros had not yet made up his mind how to use the Hostigi highpriest, but he knew he would come in useful. Davros believed the tales about Kalvan's near divinity were stories told by hayseeds and rubes, but there was no denying Kalvan's military muscle. If allowed the opportunity, he planned to play Kalvan off against the Temple's hated rival Styphon's House, which seemed to fear and hate Kalvan in equal proportions. Not only had Kalvan violated their greatest secret, the fireseed formula, but he had ordered Styphon's temples seized and then stolen the gold right off their roofs.

Xentos might prove useful were Kalvan to march upon Hos-Agrys. But only fools believed that Kalvan could defeat all the might of Styphon's House. Indeed, they would grind Kalvan's army like millstones, if not this year then the next. The one thing Davros did not want to do was give the Styphoni an excuse to destroy the Temple of Dralm when they dragged Kalvan's battered body through the streets of the Five Kingdoms.

Davros had a very good idea of who had informed Demistophon about his presence, Archpriest Haltor of Styphon's House. The Archpriest had spies and informers everywhere.

"Yes, Your Majesty, Highpriest Xentos has come from Hostigos to attend the Council of Dralm and is staying at the High Temple."

"Why was I not informed?"

Davros picked up the anger in Demistophon's voice and paused to answer carefully. "The Temple of Dralm needs him as a witness. There is some question as to the divinity of Great King Kalvan—"

"Great King!" Demistophon had squeezed himself upright, out of the Ivory Throne, his face as red as a beet. "Do not use those words when referring to the Usurper Kalvan who has stolen his titles as well as his lands for his rightful overlord, Great King Kaiphranos. Do I make myself understood?"

Davros felt himself begin to tremble. "Yes, Your Majesty." It would not pay to anger the mercurial Demistophon too much. The King was not in full control of his emotions or habits. He watched as the Great King paused to stuff a gooey pastry into his mouth.

"As far as Kalvan's divinity, bah! He's no more a god than I am. As long as I am Great King of Hos-Agrys, the Temple of Dralm will follow my council. Is that understood?"

"This is not a matter for mere men to decide, Your Majesty. Only the gods can reveal his divinity."

Still standing, Demistophon reached out with his hands as though he were about to strangle the highpriest. "Priest, if you continue to defy me, I will bar the doors of your Temple and put Dralm under the Ban!"

Davros stepped back and gathered his strength; he could not let Demistophon bully him. He was Highpriest of the High Temple of Agrys City, the biggest and foremost temple of Allfather Dralm in the Five Kingdoms. "That would not be a good idea, Your Majesty. A number of your princes and barons, who were not consulted about your attack upon Hostigos, have formed the League of Dralm and I am certain they would not take the closing of the High Temple quietly." Davros prepared himself for a direct assault upon his person. The two bodyguards flanking their Great King looked back and forth at each other nervously.

Instead Demistophon fell back upon his throne, and sat rubbing his eyes. When the Great King continued speaking, Davros had to step close to the throne to hear his words. "Highpriest, I do not have to make a proclamation to close the High Temple. Archpriest Syclos has offered me one million ounces of gold if I allow him the pleasure of closing its doors with Styphon's Own Temple Guard."

The thought of Styphon's Red Hand pouring into the Temple broke Davros out into a cold sweat underneath his robes. He knew his rival, Archpriest Syclos, would be more than happy to clear the Temple and arrest all the temple highpriests, himself included. "Yes, Your Majesty, Archpriest Syclos would enjoy closing our Temple, but what would the people of Agrys City do? Or the League of Dralm?"

Davros had not led a sheltered life, like many of Allfather Dralm's priests, but even he had never seen such naked hatred aimed at himself in another man's eyes—especially one who could order his death. He would have to tread most carefully.

"There are other means," the Great King said, suddenly smiling. "The Throne has always been very generous with Our gifts to the High Temple."

Highpriest Davros nodded. The Temple of Dralm had already been expelled from the Kingdoms of Hos-Ktemnos and Hos-Bletha. The great majority of Allfather Dralm's followers were artisans and farmers so the Temple had little real wealth. Occasional bequests and the generosity of nobles were what kept the High Temple solvent. The Great King's traditional yearly donation of fifty thousands golden Rakmars was very important and he could see where Demistophon was going.

"What if We decided to withhold our support for your Temple and put a head tax on all your worshippers? That is surely within a Great King's rights. What would your princes and barons do then?"

Davros knew the answer—*nothing*. Some nobles might even think Demistophon a wise ruler and be thankful that those taxes were laid on the Temple rather than their lands. There was little glory to be gained fighting tax collectors!

He forced a calmness he didn't feel into his voice. "Then the priests of Dralm would leave their temples and preach in their parishioners homes."

Demistophon reared back his head and laughed. "We don't think so. You highpriests enjoy your food and wine too much!"

Davros felt himself redden. It was true that he had no desire to return to the austerity of his youth, even though his bones had more padding.

"Archpriest Syclos has also asked Us to allow his Temple Guard to storm the High Temple of Dralm and root out all the heretics. However, We have not yet forgiven the Archpriest for his bad council that encouraged Us to attack Hostigos, while his not so grand Holy Host was supposed to be defeating the Hostigi Army. Their failure to defeat Kalvan doomed Our army."

Davros did his best not to smile. Poor leadership, of course, had nothing to do with the outcome, he thought. "I fear, the Archpriest, has once again given you bad advice."

Demistophon stroked his goatee. "You may be right. On the other hand, Archpriest Syclos may be right. I suggest you keep a tight rein over this Council of yours and do nothing that is not in Our best interest. Otherwise, your donation will be gone and the head tax will end your life of ease."

Davros knew he was walking a very thin line here. King Demistophon was both powerful and vindictive enough to do exactly what he said.

"And, as far as the Hostigi rebel is concerned, I want him delivered to Tarr-Agrys upon first light tomorrow."

"This would be a dangerous move, Your Majesty. The princes might well see this as another attack upon Hostigos, and there's no telling how Kalvan might react. May I suggest a safer path?"

Demistophon nodded, a smile playing upon his rubbery lips.

Davros was beginning to wonder if he wasn't playing right into his sovereign's hands? Still, Demistophon left him very few choices; either beggar the Temple or bend his knees. Maybe he could turn this bumpkin Xentos to his advantage. True, Xentos had a native cunning and intelligence, but he also carried the fires of ambition. Yes, they were carefully banked, but with the right encouragement they could burn brightly.

"Your Majesty, I suggest that we use Highpriest Xentos for our own purposes. He has come asking for aid for his master, Kalvan. However, he is an ambitious man, one who has spent most of his life in the provinces. I suggest we make him head of the Temple—"

"Are you mad?"

"No, listen to me. If we feed Xentos carefully, nurturing his pride and ambition, we can use this same ambition to turn him against his own master. Let him risk the fate of the Temple to help the so-called demi-god Kalvan? Davros continued on in this vein for half a candle until Demistophon began to nod his head.

"There is some truth to your words. Try this stratagem. But be fore-warned, if your plan does not work." Demistophon paused. "There will be great changes throughout Hos-Agrys and your temples will be taxed until the stone foundations crumble."

Davros was not happy with this settlement, but he had bought the Temple time. Time to survive until Kalvan's armies arrived? Time until Demistophon died? He didn't know, but—at least—for today the Temple was safe.

For now, he would do as Demistophon demanded, but if circumstances changed he would bend with them. After all, it would not glorify Allfa-ther Dralm if his highpriests were forced to live in the streets as beggars. *Allfather Dralm, damn all the Styphoni to Regwarn and Great King Demistophon, too.*

III

Sargos heard the hand clap of one of his subchiefs seeking entrance to his quarters. Unlike the single men who lived in longhouses, Sargos had his own private hut. "Enter," he said.

Subchief Ikkos, the youngest of his advisors, came in followed by One-Eyed Red and Vanar Halgoth, who appeared to have someone trailing after him. Halgoth was the largest man in the Raven Tribe, for that matter, in the Tymannes Clan or any other clan in the Lower Sastragath. The only men he'd seen larger had been in the Trygath, when he and Halgoth were young and foolish, fighting for now dead and forgotten Trygathi princes. The two of them were the last of the tribe's survivors of those freer and wilder days of his youth.

"Come in, all of you. Who is that behind you, Halgoth?"

Halgoth grinned widely, showing two rows of nubbed and missing teeth. The other subchiefs scooted away from him, as if he were on the edge of a berserk. Out of the shadows stepped Althea. Sargos was surprised to hear his heart skip a beat, but this maiden had a most commanding presence. He disciplined himself by remembering the two wives he had lost in childbirth. After his last wife had gone to Wind, two years ago, he had promised himself there would be no more wives. He had grieved enough for two men, and had no desire to take that path again.

"It is against tradition to bring a woman to a War Council. You know that, Halgoth. Why have you brought Althea?"

"It's her fight, too, Sargos."

The long limbed maiden pushed her way past her massive uncle. "I made him, Warchief Sargos. Do I not have a right to *vergelt*—blood vengeance? It was my family who died at the hands of the Grassmen and my body they used. There are no kinsmen left in my Tribe to redeem my honor. I demand to be included in this party, as my Clan right."

Sargos shook his head. Technically, there was nothing in the Law that said a woman could not seek *vergelt,* but he could remember no other time when a Tymanni woman had claimed this right. The winter Clan Gathering was still a moon or more away, so he could not ask the Clan Elders.

He nodded to show that she was within her rights. Of course, by Law she was not a Tymanni, but he was not one who played the bagpipe of the Law until it squeaked his tune. He had met such men in the Trygath, but he had not enjoyed their company. Althea was of Tymanni blood and the Burgduns were Urgothi, too, a cousin clan to the Tymannes. It was also true that survivors of the Wolf Tribe were now joining his tribe. It would not show proper respect—even in their reduced state—to stop them from seeking vengeance, even at the hands of a woman. And, Althea was correct; there were no men left in her tribe to avenge her, or take *vergelt* upon the Grassmen invaders.

"This is not right—" Ikkos began, before Sargos cut him off.

"Be silent, pup! I am the Warchief and it is I who decides what is right in the eyes of the Law." Ikkos was of the new generation, only four winters older than Bargoth. Sargos knew full well the problems of depending upon untested youth, but the clan needed more war leaders and he and Halgoth already had passed fifty winters. Maybe this Time of Troubles would temper the best of the younger generation. It had to or this Time of Troubles would see the Tymannes go to Wind, like so many clans before them.

Ikkos stood stiffly with a sour expression, which Sargos ignored. Open defiance he would deal with swiftly, insolence—*just don't let it go on too long*—

As though reading his mind, as was frequently the way among comrades who had fought many battles together, Halgoth put his huge hand on Ikkos shoulder, and played gently with the ball of his shoulder. Ikkos looked as if he'd just stuck his hand into a panther's mouth. Sargos had to resist the impulse to laugh.

"Althea, you may join the war party. I will loan you my knife."

The young maiden gave him a look that could have melted stone. "Thank you, Warchief Sargos, but I still have the knife that sent the Grassmen to the Undercaverns of the Dead. I will bring one of my Uncle's bows, as well."

Sargos knew that Halgoth was a master archer; he spent most of the winter teaching the younger warriors how to improve their shooting. He suspected that Althea might share her uncle's gods given gift; if so, she would be a welcome addition to the war band. The Tymannes would be heavily out-numbered in this attack and the Tribe would need any, and every, advantage it could get.

"When do we blood these Grassmen, Warchief?" One-Eyed Red asked. His flame-red hair came out of his cone helmet in two thick braids.

"Tomorrow night. We will avenge our clansmen and fill the Undercaverns of the Dead, with these Grassmen."

"At night!" One-Eyed Red, scrunched his remaining eye. "It's not honorable to attack foes at night time."

If there was one thing a lifetime of warfare had taught Ranjar Sargos, it was, there was no such thing as an honorable war. It was always the victors who pronounced what was honorable, after the war was over.

He addressed One-Eyed Red as though he were addressing a multitude, and in effect he was, since every word said here would be repeated many times this evening over the tribe's campfires. "Honorable war is only for those who would fight with honor. These Grassmen know no honor."

He heard a growl of fury escaping Althea's lips, as she expressed her agreement.

"These grasseaters, who are less than men, are despoilers of our clans-women and the butchers of children. Would you accord them honor?"

One-Eyed Red drew back in alarm. "No, Warchief! Let us butcher them as we do the wolf packs that cross our lands."

An expression that Ranjar would hesitate to call a smile played upon Althea's lips. He would not want to be one of the Grassmen, if she and her knife were within an arm's reach. For a moment, he almost felt sorry for the enemy.

THREE

The chill night air cut through Grand-Captain Phidestros' Greftscharrer buff jacket like a knife blade. He hadn't been back to Zygros City for four years and had forgotten how bitter cold these narrow streets became after sundown. He watched as half a dozen drunken fur trappers staggered out of a nearby tavern, the stench rising off them like steam. One trapper, with a mouth full of broken teeth, eyed him and his mount. Phidestros slowly slipped one of the big horse pistols out of its saddle holster and—by the light coming from the torches framing the tavern door—carefully checked the priming pan.

One of the trappers, with a tilted coonskin cap, saluted him with a flask and shouted, "To Galzar!"

"To the Wargod," Phidestros echoed. On this frozen night he could use all the help the Galzar could provide. Any sane man would have taken Captain Kyblannos' advice and brought a squad of troopers-or, at least, Petty-Captain Geblon, his huge banner-bearer with him. In Hos-Zygros, the northern-most of the Five Kingdoms, a man by himself was not safe on streets of Zygros City after dark—winter, spring, summer or fall. Yet, this night's business was private, between only him and his past. So Geblon was waiting with Captain Kyblannos and the rest of the squad, with a tankard of winter wine back at the inn. And none too happily, at that.

A battle-scarred tomcat screamed and his mount whinnied. Phidestros kneed his horse sharply and pulled back on the reins. He had purchased Grayhawk from a horse trader in Harphax City several moons ago to replace Snowdrift, the faithful destrier he'd left behind—with about half his command at the Dralm-damned battlefield of Phyrax. The horse trader had sworn on his mother's life and Styphon's Wheel that the stallion was battle trained—raised on vinegar and fireseed.

Phidestros swore a promise to Galzar that if Grayhawk shied away from war cries, as he did from cat yowls, he'd fillet that horse trader, from scalp to sole, with his hunting knife.

From farther down the twisted streets, Grand-Captain Phidestros heard the clamor of horse hooves on cobbled stones and rested his long-muzzled flintlock on the saddle pommel. The silver-chased horse pistol, taken from the corpse of one of the Hostigi Royal Pistoleers, had been the sum total of the Iron Band's spoils from the cursed Battle of Phyrax. Phidestros hoped that the more than ten score of soldiers he'd left behind fared better in Galzar's Great Hall.

When the horsemen emerged from the alleyway, he recognized them as members of the watch, rather than some baron's hired bullyboys. They wore cloaks of black wool, with red trim; the city colors. "And what be your business this eventide, your nobleship?" the watch's petty-captain asked, covering himself with the honorific because of Grayhawk's rich trappings.

"An overlong dalliance with a comely tavern wench, my good, sir," Phidestros answered.

"'Tis a frosty night and a good time for a warm fire and willing wench, me thinks." The other watchmen, wearing mismatched bison cloaks around their blackened back-and-breast armor, nodded their agreement. "But, be on your way. There lurks more serious game than sewer rats on these streets."

Phidestros nodded his agreement and urged Grayhawk into a faster pace. The house wasn't but a few doors down, just past the venires, which he knew from past visits—six in the past twelve years. The first had been when he was fourteen, apprenticed to a cabinet master, two moons after his mother's death of the flux. She had been a handsome woman, the daughter of a merchant, who had never married and ran a respectable boarding house. It was there Phidestros had gotten his first yen for soldiering from a retired petty-captain, who'd filled him with tall tales about past campaigns and battles—that is, whenever his mother was out of earshot.

His mother, a woman of unusually stern will, had determined Phidestros' course until her death had set him free. The other children had mocked him as a bastard until his face began to sprout and his limbs hardened like oak. Then he'd paid long-standing debts with broken teeth and blackened eyes.

His father, nor his absence, was ever mentioned. Not by his mother. The earliest inkling that his father was even alive came after his fourteenth winter, when he received an invitation to this same house, here on the Street of Furriers. He'd learned little then about his father, and not much since. Only that his father was a man of wealth and social prominence who was unable to acknowledge his bastard son, but did want to see that said son was provided for. Phidestros had asked more questions, of course, but they'd been met with silence and a purse of gold—even at fourteen winters he'd had the good sense to know when to keep his mouth shut. He had little curiosity left now that he knew the ways of the world and he, himself, had sired two of his own get—un-recognized, but modestly provided for.

In his youth, Phidestros had plotted with his friends to have his father's go-between followed and identified, but finally had concluded that a purse in hand was worth more than a kick in the hindparts. Besides, his life as a mercenary captain was not one to make most fathers puff with pride.

Phidestros saw the familiar portal, a wooden plank door with a boar's head emblem carved into the top brace, and dismounted. He was careful to tie Grayhawk's reins to the thick metal loop in the doorpost. Any thief fool enough to try and steal a war horse would deserve the not so gentle surprise he would receive from his destrier's steel-shod hooves.

He felt his pulse race as he anticipated tonight's purse. His pay chest had been depleted by the Daemon's War and what remained had been quickly emptied re-fitting his troopers, reimbursing their pay chits and mustering them out for the winter. He'd had little enough gold left to do anything more than see after his own lodging. To return the Iron Band to its former strength would take more than one purse of gold, but it was a start. Harphax City was filled to the bursting with returning soldiers and captain-less mercenaries.

The parchment telling him to meet with Count Sestembar had been welcome indeed, despite the half-moon long journey with a merchants' caravan

through inhospitable weather. At least the squad had received a small purse
of silver as payment, earning it twice over when highwaymen sprung an
ambush. Phidestros still grinned at their dismay when they learned it was
the Iron Band, not some gaggle of unemployed mercenaries, they were
crossing swords with. The roads were no longer safe since the war, with too
many soldiers without captains, and peasants without farms or hope.

He hoped there would be enough gold so he could re-outfit the Iron
Band for next spring's campaigns. War with Hos-Hostigos was as certain
now as the morning sun. With Hos-Harphax in the middle of a succession
crisis and the army demoralized, there was little to keep Great King Kalvan
from storming Harphax City itself.

While Styphon's Own Paymasters had indeed paid off the survivor's of
Grand Master Soton's army, contrary to rumor, they had not been generous
with their gold. With no battlefield loot or ransom, there was little left for
any captain's pay chest. Many companies, even those with long serving captains, had been forced to disperse. If Phidestros could obtain a good purse,
there would be no problem next year in raising a full muster. He was sure
Styphon's pay chests would be overflowing gold this spring now that
Kalvan had defeated the Holy Host and was calling himself a Great King.
Having been within spear throwing distance of Kalvan, Phidestros was certain the man was no demon, just a good soldier and a great captain; a man,
had circumstances been different, that Phidestros would be proud to serve
under. If the truth were to be known, he had little love for the flinty-eyed
priests of the fireseed god, Styphon. But their gold was pure and there was
plenty of it.

His sword-hardened fist pounded on the door. Count Sestembar, little
changed except for his baldpate, gestured for him to enter the furnished
room, pointing out a high-backed chair for him to sit in. Phidestros could
remember when that chair had loomed so much larger. The room had
changed in some subtle fashion and his eye quickly added up the contents:
the maple desk at which the Count was now sitting, a large cupboard and
two chests. All stoutly made of quality walnut, he had worked similar wood
as a boy. Everything was the same as always except for the wine-red curtain
at the back corner of the room. Had his father finally decided Phidestros'
reputation was too tarnished to bear, and planted an assassin to see he was
removed from the family's list?

Phidestros casually splayed out his right leg and gently rested his hand on his sword's basket hilt. Should the pistol misfire, with Galzar's help, he would give no man time for a second shot.

Count Sestembar opened, "Even here in Zygros City we have heard of the battlefield exploits of Grand-Captain Phidestros."

Phidestros watched Sestembar's eyes to see if they matched his words. The Count appeared to be speaking sincerely. He swallowed and attempted to relax. "Thank you, my lord. I hope what you have heard has been pleasing to your ears."

"We have long waited for such success for our Grace's son, and it appears our patience has been rewarded. You have done no worse, and far better, than most in the Holy Host."

Phidestros slowly began to uncoil. "I was fortunate to have good soldiers in my employ."

"To survive three battles with the man called The Daemon by the Temple of Styphon takes more than good soldiers or even good fortune. It takes a good commander. One, who having fought the new King of Hos-Hostigos more than any commander yet alive, is now in position to have learned more about his military leadership and strategy than any man in the Five Kingdoms."

Phidestros relaxed a little more, feeling kindly disposed towards Sestembar for failing to mention that the three battles against Great King Kalvan had been losses not victories.

"Now," Count Sestembar announced, "I've got someone who wants to meet you and share your knowledge of the man who has appointed himself the first new Great King in over two hundred years."

The velvet curtains parted and out stepped a tall, long-boned aristocrat, who looked vaguely familiar. The gunmetal blue beard was well trimmed and shot with silver; the aquiline nose looked like the twin to his. *Of course, you idiot! It's the same nose you see every morning in your metal looking-piece when you trim your beard.*

Count Sestembar bowed, saying, "Grand-Captain Phidestros, I would like you to meet your father, the Grand Duke Eudocles of the First House of Hos-Zygros."

Phidestros attempted to rise too quickly and almost tripped over his scabbard.

The Grand Duke motioned with his hand that he should remain seated. "Let me look at you, son. Sestembar, you've been telling me the truth; he does look to be my spitting image—when I was younger, of course. But broader in the shoulders and thicker in limb. Much as I might have been had I lived by the sword rather than by the throne."

"I ... I ... I'm pleased to meet you, Your Grace," Phidestros mumbled. His father was the Grand Duke of all Hos-Zygros, the only living brother to Great King Sopharar. Never in his wildest imaginings—even as a child— had he dared dream of a father sitting so high!

"I must apologize, my son, for the delay at our meeting. But, as you can guess, there are certain political realities that have precluded me from claiming you as my son, or even sharing my knowledge with you. There are men here in Zygros City and elsewhere that might well have profited greatly from that knowledge, or even have tried to harm me through you. The burdens of office and kinship weigh heavily upon our family."

"Of course, Your Grace. I thank you for your kindness all these years," Phidestros answered, his wits and tongue finally untied. *Yes, you old fox, you had plenty of reasons for not letting the world know your by-blow was waiting in the wings. Until the right moment, of course, when said bastard can repay some of his long-standing debt.*

"Since the miraculous arrival a few years ago of the Dralm-sent, or Ormaz-spawned Kalvan, our kingdoms have seen more warfare than at any time in the previous fifty years. With both Styphon's House and the new League of Dralm clamoring for Zygrosi support, we must know more about this man who claims for himself the title of Great King of Hos-Hostigos. Is he a demon, a demi-god-or just a mere mortal? Is he a friend to our House, or an enemy? Will he attempt to raise himself up to be King of Great Kings, as some princes fear, or will he be content with his present crown and lands in Hos-Hostigos? These are just some of the questions that need answering, my son."

Phidestros noticed the coin-sized cold spot under his lower rib that he always felt when facing off against a dangerous adversary. Now he knew the reason behind the long-delayed father and son reunion. He'd had the misfortune—probably the wrong word since he had survived and learned more about Kalvan's tactics than anyone outside Hos-Hostigos—to be bested by the most feared man alive in three different battles.

The question now was how much should he, could he, tell this man who'd never had the time to greet him until now—when it was worth his while? *Yes, worth Eudocles' while it may well be, but the real question was: Was it worth his while?* To feign ignorance of Kalvan would gain him little, and probably cost him a fat purse. A well-crafted answer, however, might raise his value in his father's eyes and possibly lead to future opportunities within Hos-Zygros. A barony, or even a princedom, was not an unknown reward for a valuable son from the left side of the badge. He wondered how word of his parentage might rattle the Inner Circle in Balph.

While mercenary captains were not renowned for their longevity, a significant number were known to live to that ripe old age where both their battle prowess and their wits began to decline. When they reached the age of retirement, there were few Houses or cities that welcomed them, as more than one captain had been known to come out of retirement when it suited his purse rather than his ruler. It would be no bad thing—even for a foot-loose man of the sword, like himself—to have even a minor place in the royal family of Hos-Zygros. Especially, in a kingdom where the Great King had out-lived his two sons and his only grandson was in frail health. *Dare he dream . . . ?*

Of course, he dared! It was the destiny Phidestros had always dreamed of. No, he would not retire to some backwoods village in his dotage! He would rise as high as his ambition, or fill some anonymous grave. It was time to play the dutiful son to his flint-hearted sire. Maybe one day he would rise above even his father's ambitions; the father who had abandoned him to a commoner's life. One day there would come a day of reckoning, when all past debts would be settled. Phidestros, for one, would enjoy each payment—small and large. *Would he ever!*

"Yes, father, I will answer those questions I can. Though no man may see into another's heart, even when he has peered into his eyes."

"You have actually seen this Kalvan up close!"

The hook was set. "Truly, I was as close to Great King Kalvan as the curtain you stood behind." He pointed to the curtain, which appeared to be blood red in the flickering candlelight. "The tide of battle thrust us together on the fields of Phyrax, for a moment, then tore us asunder as the tides of the ocean.

"I saw a man, like other men; but touched by the gods. His eyes burn from a deep inner fire and his laugh is a terrible thing to hear. Still, while a great leader of men and blessed by the gods; he is still a man—like you or me. Not a demi-god as the priests of Dralm would make him, or a demon as the Styphon's priests decry. A man who could be a good friend, or a terrible enemy."

"What of the demon spawned gifts he has brought with him?"

Phidestros slowly brought forth his rapier and demonstrated its point. "This is one of Kalvan's 'gifts.' A sword that not only cuts, but thrusts too. A simple idea, you could say, but one no other man thought to do it. Yes, it makes this sword far more dangerous to my enemies. I say, if this is demon magic—give me more! Like his fireseed that burns smoother and with more blast than Styphon's Best."

Duke Eudocles nodded sagely. "We have tried his new formula here in Hos-Zygros and found it superior to Styphon's Best in all ways."

"He has brought other gifts as well: a special harness that allows him to haul demi-cannon by a team of horses. Cannons that can be taken anywhere on the field and removed in a half-candle. And a musket that shoots as far as a bird can fly, with great accuracy."

"Even here we have heard of these *rifles*, but, until now, I had dismissed them as priest blather."

"I have been on the receiving end of their fire and seen them punch through good proof armor from more than a thousand rods and still knock a man off his horse. I could storm Regwarn itself, with the Iron Band and two hundred of these muskets that Kalvan calls *rifles*."

His father and Sestembar quickly looked at each other. "Could you bring us one of these *rifles?*" the Duke asked.

If I could lay my hands upon such a rifle, *I would have little need for you, dear father.* "I heard a rumor, your Grace—"

"Call me Father."

Phidestros nodded, moving his head down toward his chest, so that the Duke wouldn't catch the unbidden smile that played upon his lips. "I have heard that Grand Master Soton had such a *rifle* and hid it among the gold and silver in the Holy Host's pay chests. I have never seen one close, only at the receiving end, when a company of Kalvan's Mounted Riflemen ambushed us at Chothros Heights. I lost many good soldiers that afternoon."

"If one should fall into your hands, my son, remember your father well. The reward will be far richer than you can imagine."

Phidestros nodded dutifully. He then went on to tell them about his experiences against the army of Hostigos and the many new things he had observed while fighting Kalvan. They seemed particularly interested in how Kalvan had confiscated the gold from Styphon's temples. He finished up with a detailed description of the political situation that Kalvan's victories had created within Hos-Harphax.

When Phidestros was finished, the Duke said, "We have learned a good deal from your answers, my son. I thank you for your forthrightness."

"As I must thank you for yours, father, sir," Phidestros answered with an ironic smile.

Count Sestembar, his face red, started to rise with his hand reaching for his sword hilt, but the Duke pushed him back down.

"The weight of office is indeed heavy, my son, as I pray you might learn some day."

His father had just taken the pot and raised it. Phidestros had to nod in admiration. What new plans brewed in that crafty old skull, and what was his part in them?

"Now, I want your words on a most important matter of policy. How, in your considered opinion, should Hos-Zygros bend before the growing winds of war? As you might surmise, we have no desire to wear Styphon's yoke, or Kalvan's, either. Should we bow toward the Usurper Kalvan, or Styphon's House?"

Amazing, a bastard helping formulate the grand strategy of a Great Kingdom! *Who would have believed it, not me*, thought Phidestros. Still, this was treacherous ground indeed; he would have to answer most cautiously. "Both have great need of Zygrosi blood and treasure and will use them to the last drop of blood and piece of gold.

"King Kalvan is perhaps the greatest general in the history of the Five Kingdoms. He also has weapons of war at his hand that no man has seen before or can truly judge. Yet, he is only one man and Hos-Hostigos is a small Great Kingdom adrift in a sea of enemies. Nor can he depend upon his captains, as himself; thus we learned from the Battle of Tenabra, where First Prince Ptosphes suffered a grave defeat.

"True, Styphon's House has been wounded, but the Temple has many followers and more gold than a company of troops could count in three lifetimes. Hos-Zygros indeed walks a perilous path between these two giants and must walk with care. Yet, if one of these towers must fall; it will surely be Kalvan."

"Then you suggest we support Styphon's House in the coming wars?" The Duke looked as if he were swallowing rattlesnake venom.

"No. I suggest nothing. Even if Kalvan topples, Styphon's House will be the shorter and will never be as it was. I council neutrality for the land of my birth, but armed and prepared neutrality. Support Kalvan with secret gold and Styphon's House with words and promises of soldiers. But give nothing without receiving. Work one against the other and you may stay free of either harness."

"Weighty advice, my son. Well worth consideration. I see now you could have been a courtier as well as a soldier. I will take your words to the proper ears. Now, it is time for us to part. I trust I will see you in good health on your next visit. I will sacrifice to Galzar for your success."

"Thank you, my father," Phidestros answered. The Grand Duke turned and was gone in a swirl of curtains and bows before the words were completely out of his mouth. Phidestros felt as if he'd just watched a street corner gramarye.

His father was not a man to be underestimated, and certainly not the man he'd imagined as his father these many years ago. He was much more and less, too. However, it had been twelve winters since he'd entertained any serious thoughts on the subject. No, this father was not the father of anyone's dreams. He could prove a useful ladder, but only for so long as one kept in mind the rungs could fall from beneath one's feet at the first shake, or misstep.

Count Sestembar stood up and brought forth a bulging leather saddle-bag from underneath the desk. With a grunt of effort, he thrust it into Phidestros waiting arms with a less than enthusiastic expression. "Your father believes that this will be of some help in the coming campaigns."

Phidestros' lips twisted, as he swallowed the glee inside—enough gold to outfit a double-company! And plenty left over for a winter's worth of wenching and drinking.

The Count drew back, as if he'd just witnessed a wolf licking its lips.

"Thank you, Count," Phidestros said, as he staggered under the weight of the saddlebag. "Already, I look forward to my next visit."

FOUR

I

Kalvan blew out the light, waited for the wick to cool, and then twisted the strands of cotton as tight as he could. He doubted it would make much difference to a man accustomed to electric light bulbs, but then it wasn't the light, or lack of, that was bothering him. He sighed deeply and lit the oil lamp. Not so much flicker this time and certainly more light than he was getting from the candles this time last year.

For a moment the light flared, highlighting the lambskin parchment on his desk with the half-completed chart. The chart was the real problem. All afternoon he'd been trying to reconstruct the old Periodic Table, which had taken up a good quarter of the blackboard space in his high school chemistry class in Altoona, Pennsylvania. It was a distance that couldn't be covered by mere time or miles, nor did it appear by memory. Kalvan had been forced to rely on imperfect memory a lot, ever since that cross-time flying saucer had dropped him off in this cockeyed 16th Century world of here-and-now. It was his imperfect memory, in many cases, of college lectures and books he'd read, like Sir Charles Oman's *Art Of War In The Middle Ages* and its companion volume about the Sixteenth Century, that had kept Styphon's House from permanently putting Hostigos out of business.

Besides gunpowder and new military innovations, Kalvan had tried to keep his 'contamination' to a minimum, knowing full well what had

happened in his own world in South America when the conquistadors had
introduced their own 'superior' culture to the native Indians. His only violation of this self-imposed prohibition was the founding of the University
of Hos-Hostigos. And it was for the University, that Kalvan was trying to
recall twenty-year old memories of a chart he had stared at in chem class
every day for two long semesters. He was stuck at element number 37. Was
it Sr, or Strontium, or did that come later in the table? Kalvan closed his
eyes and tried to visualize the chart again. That side of the chart had been
to his left and it wasn't as fixed in his mind's eye. He could see the right
side all the way down to element 86. Even 37 was far beyond the known
elements here-and-now, but it would be important someday.

Which explained why he was kneading his brains until his eyes watered.
Suddenly Kalvan could see it, Rb #37, Rubidium—he couldn't remember
what kind of metal that was and didn't guess it much mattered. He'd never
see any of it here-and-now, nor know what to do with it if he did. Now he
could visualize Sr #38 too, that was Strontium!

There was a knock at the door and Kalvan's wife, the Great Queen Rylla
entered bearing a flask of hot chocolate, a costly import from the south
that they usually couldn't find, but had been looted by Colonel
Democriphon from one of Styphon's House's baggage trains after the victory at Phyrax Field. Rylla, despite the recent birth of their daughter,
Demia, was back to her willowy girl-like figure—just like when they'd first
met—wearing a pale blue dress with tight bodice that perfectly set off her
eyes and curves.

"I like that dress!" Kalvan said.

"Thank you, sire." Rylla spun around like a runway model; it was amazing the things she could do naturally without artifice. It was hard to
visualize this beautiful young woman, with her mane of blond hair in armor
leading troops, but she was a general in the Royal Army and one of his best
strategists. Rylla was just loaded with surprises—most of them pleasant.

"How is Demia?" Kalvan and Rylla's daughter had been up half the night
with the croup.

"She's doing much better. Brother Mytron had just the right herbal tea
for her. She's sleeping now in the nursery."

"Good." He probably worried too much, but then again he knew too
much about how most here-and-now medicine was just one step above

witchcraft and barber doctoring. He also knew about infectious diseases and the high child mortality rate in the Six Kingdoms.

"Ahhh, the spoils of war," Kalvan said as he sipped the dark brown confection, sweetened with honey. "It reminds me of home. Did I ever tell you about Hershey—a town built on the fortunes of chocolate? It's a nice place, for a company town."

"Yes, you told me all about it. Do you still miss Pennsylvania?" Rylla asked, in a wistful tone.

Kalvan wasn't sure whether Rylla wished she could be transported there, or if she suspected he might be homesick. He suspected the latter. "Darling, I would trade all the chocolate in Hershey rather than spend even one night away from you and Demia."

That must have been the right thing to say, for Rylla's face lit up like a beautiful sunrise. She bent over and gave him a kiss that demanded a sequel or two.

"I wish it could always be like this."

"Me, too." Kalvan sighed. "Sadly, our enemies will not leave us alone. Skranga tells me that Styphon's House has plots and counter-plots hatching in every capital in the old Five Kingdoms. It's easier on the battlefield, where your enemies are right in front of you and can be dispatched by sword blade or musket shot."

"We'll get plenty of fighting come spring, my love," Rylla said, her tone brightening. "Never fear."

"Sometimes, I think you enjoy this fighting more than a Blethan oath-brother!" Fortunately, Rylla's pregnancy had kept her off the battlefield most of this year, but it was doubtful anything would keep her away come the spring campaigns. A certain amount of bloodthirstiness was part and parcel of the ruder and cruder life here-and-now, but Rylla at times seemed to display more than her fair share. It wasn't a blot on her copybook, considering the war of extinction with Styphon's House was all Rylla had known since puberty, but sometimes he wished she'd show a bit less enthusiasm for all the fighting and killing.

Rylla looked down demurely, which was so out of character, Kalvan had to choke back a chuckle. "I only serve my Kingdom and my King."

At that, Kalvan could no longer contain his laughter. "How right you are. Our enemies are plotting right now how to overthrow our kingdom."

And, he thought to himself, put your lovely head on a spit. Which was why he had to do the work of ten men, for Rylla and baby Demia, and the fragile entity known as Hos-Hostigos.

"Whatever their plans, you will beat them, my husband. As you always have before."

"Yes, with Dralm's help." Her faith in his abilities was touching, but also worrisome, since one of these days his opponents were going to catch him asleep or off-step and his unwanted mantle of perfection was going to drop off his shoulders with a resounding clang. Even if no one else seemed to realize it, Kalvan knew full well it was only his luck and knowledge of back home military strategy and technology that had kept the headsman's axe from that pretty neck. "We gave Hos-Harphax a bloody-nose last year, which will take a while to heal. Next year, I'd like to catch Styphon's House with its pants down."

Rylla gave a blood-curdling laugh that belied her sugarcoated exterior. Women were tougher here-and-now, he thought, than the ones he'd known back home—had to be to survive. And Hostigi women had to be the toughest of all.

"You have such a way with words, my husband; it's another thing I love about you. Oh, Kalvan, I almost forgot—I came to remind you of the meeting tonight at the University."

"Dralm damn-it, I almost forgot!" Kalvan stood up and pushed the parchment aside. He moved over to Rylla and drew her into his arms. "How much time do we have?"

Rylla smiled, lighting up the room. "It's a rule: Great Kings always have as much time as they want. It's their subjects who must watch the candle burn."

"Well, then subject. I want a full candle of your time."

Rylla performed a here-and-now curtsey, saying, "As you wish, my king."

II

Count Sestembar knocked on the door and waited patiently for the Grand Duke's summons. Two fully armed guardsmen, in the Duke's orange and black colors wearing silvered breastplates and high-combed morion helmets, flanked the door. Sestembar had just returned to the palace from the meeting with the Duke's bastard son. Even knowing ahead of time about the resemblance between father and son, it had still come as a shock to see them together in the same room. They were both blades from the same smith, formed of strong, sharp and well-tempered cold steel.

"Enter."

The Count came through the door and into the Duke's private chambers, taking his accustomed seat. The Duke's face was drawn and his gray eyes were slightly unfocused, as if he'd just spent the past half candle peering into a realm not of this world. As his most trusted advisor and oldest—and only—friend, Sestembar had seen him in this state before, but only once or twice when great things were afoot.

"Well, old friend, so that is my son—I'm not sure Olbia would have approved; she always was a priest lover."

Sestembar chuckled.

"He's a fine figure of a man, but, alas, I saw little welcome in Phidestros' eyes for a father first seen."

Sestembar kept quiet, he could see that this was a question whose honest answer would find no welcome here. The Duke could not expect to receive more than he was willing to spend. Sestembar suspected that this long-overdue meeting had as much to do with a father's begrudging curiosity as a search for information on the mysterious King Kalvan, but the Duke would die before letting such words pass his lips. The son, too.

"What is your measure of this Captain Phidestros?"

"A good captain, as this old mercenary would know. Maybe even a great one, only time will tell. These are the times for it. Were I young and a free companion again, I would follow that one just as I followed his father thirty-five winters past."

"Do you have any regrets, my old friend? Do you feel any dismay for battles missed and glory un-won? Have the years been good to you?"

This melancholy line of questioning was completely out of character for the Duke, meeting his son had unsettled him far more than Sestembar had suspected. Maybe the encounter had been too much like a visit to the past; the Duke seeing himself thirty winters ago with so many paths stretching before him. *Paths, now worn or closed, and each year diminishing them in number.*

"Yes, my Duke. They have been very good years. Had I survived the passing year's battles and treacheries—always the free sword's lot—I would be retired now, a used-up old man. A castaway drifting from tavern to tavern. Here, I am a trusted advisor to the Royal family, a man with his own lands, titled and with coins in his purse and some small honor from his friends."

"Well answered and the honor of your person is held in higher esteem than even you know. But enough of this twaddle," the Duke interjected, shaking his head as if awakening from a deep sleep. "What of this Kalvan? How heavily shall we weigh my son's words?"

"They ring true to these old tired ears. Styphon's House has been hammering chains around the Five Kingdoms like a Sastragathi slave trader. How many times had Great King Sopharar's pleas for more fireseed been turned to a stony ear by the Archpriests? Too many, I say. Now, thanks to this Kalvan—be he demon or man—we make our own fireseed and can use our cannons to cut that chain. For good. I say let them fight each other till both are past this realm. It's not our war. Yet, if Kalvan wins, he may forge bracelets of his own making."

"True words, Sestembar. Your thinking echoes my own. I will whisper these words into my brother's ears. For too long, he has been under the sway of Highpriest Lathrox and if we are not careful Hos-Zygros will become the Council of Dralm's toy. Lathrox has been counseling my brother to renounce Styphon's House and join the League of Dralm. The League may well prove to be Kalvan's device, just as the Holy Host is Grand Master Soton's."

"Denounce Styphon and we may face a war that we can't win once Kalvan is gone, Sestembar said. "That is, if Phidestros is to be believed—and I believe he is. Better to join the League, but not denounce Styphon. Let the League and the Fireseed God work us with promises and gold from their treasuries."

The Duke nodded, his eyes red-tinged pools in the flickering candlelight. "Yes, and we will need a voice in their councils. The Council of Dralm has been yammering at the Agrys Temple for moons now. At court, we get daily harangues from Archpriest Idyol, one day ordering, the next demanding, we gather an army to join Styphon's Holy Host, while Highpriest Lathrox asks for my brother or myself to attend the Council of Dralm and give it Our Blessing."

"It would be a mistake to attend—it might force the Inner Circle's hand against us. But, it might also be a good idea to have a 'secret' meeting with the highpriests of Dralm and woo them with promises of future support and gold. If we can get our voice heard at the Council, we may be able to stop any rash support for the Usurper or the League of Dralm."

"An excellent idea, my friend! You are the only mouth I trust for such a sensitive mission."

Sestembar bowed. "I will make preparations to leave for Agrys City in the morning."

"Not so quick," Lysandros said. "I will talk with my brother this evening and tell him to inform Highpriest Lathrox that we intend to send a secret emissary to meet with the Council of Dralm—of course, he will have to accompany you! Never would Lathrox allow any secret meeting with his fellow priests that he was not privy to."

Sestembar laughed. "Yes, that will please your brother. His ear must be torn ragged from all this priestly jawing. Archpriest Idyol will be happy because he will have King Sopharar's ear to himself to fill with promises of Styphon's gold and mercenaries. Meanwhile, I will accompany Lathrox to the Council and advise them to use caution in their dealings with Kalvan and make them airy promises that we will only fill at our convenience—if at all."

Duke Eudocles grinned. "Your advice and stratagems are worth more than two regiments of cavalry and may save Hos-Zygros more in spilled blood, if we can keep this balanced beam from landing on either side! Let the blood flow in Hos-Ktemnos, Hos-Harphax, Hos-Agrys and Kalvan's false Kingdom of Hos-Hostigos. While they fight, we will build our army and when their wars are over we can resolve some long-standing debts."

Count Sestembar smiled wolfishly. "After Great King Demistophon's poor showing in Nostor, some of the border princedoms in Hos-Agrys may well find it wise to seek sanctuary from the Daemon Kalvan at our breast!"

"We do think alike, old friend. I only hope my son is as lucky in these coming battles as he's been proved to be in the past. My heir, Artiblos, could find many uses for a talented Captain-General when all the smoke has settled."

So this is where Phidestros' pattern was being woven within his father's great tapestry, thought Sestembar. Much, of course, depended upon the health of Great King Sopharar's son, who spent more time in bed these days than he did afoot. And, the Count suspected that if nature didn't take its timely course, the Duke would not be above helping it along its way. So, at last, the great pattern he had for so long suspected was emerging from the murky mists of unrelated incident and deeds.

The Count wondered what his own reward might be. A sizable one he was certain, for was he not the loom? Phidestros might well be a useful design, though not too useful—there were enough ambitions in this family for three dynasties.

"Yes," the Count said, "We shall have many uses for our Captain, though I suspect you do ill in placing your children's welfare before their father's. After all, were Allfather Dralm's sons' Ormaz and Hadron thankful when he put his younger son Appalon up as his successor? No, I think the father should look to himself first, then the sons. Does the old gray wolf turn aside and let his get rule the pack? No, he lets them run on their own until his own time has passed."

"Sestembar, I do believe there are times, even after all these years, when I underestimate your wisdom. Pour me a royal flagon of ale—and one for yourself, too. We have much to work out, as well as a few toasts to make."

"Willingly, your Grace. Most willingly."

III

Styphon's Voice On Earth shivered, tossing and turning on his thick goose down feather mattress. Sesklos' body was covered by a mountain of quilts and furs and still the chill cut through his thin flesh into his bones. He had awoken quite suddenly from a dream where thousands of white-robed skeletons chased after him. His breathing was shallow and he could feel a lump the size of Grand Master Soton's fist inside his chest. Was Styphon Himself reaching out from his lair in Regwarn, trying to revenge himself for Sesklos years of faithless service? "Forgive me, Styphon!" he called out, in a rasping voice.

"What is it, Master?" a querulous voice asked from outside the gilded door.

"A bad dream, Tythos," Sesklos replied. A long and rasping cough shuddered through his thin aged body. What would his fellow highpriests think if they were told that he prayed to Styphon in his sleep? His body shuddered again, this time from revulsion, not cold.

Highpriest Tythos was one of the godless non-believers who had made Styphon's House rich and powerful. He did what he was told, was not bothered by qualms of conscience or belief. Why weren't there more of him? What had happened to the upper priesthood of his youth as a novice, priest and later highpriest, when they were all like Tythos? And how had it changed on his watch? The Daemon Kalvan! It was Kalvan who'd rent the Temple asunder with his heresies and theft of the fireseed secret.

That was where it all had started, when the true rulers of the House of Styphon had been maneuvered into dealing with the true believers! He leaned over the bedside and spat into a spittoon. "A curse on all True Believers!" he called out loud, not even realizing it. *And a special curse on that daemon's spawn Kalvan. Roxthar, too, and his legion of followers!* Sesklos was still awake enough to keep his thoughts of Roxthar to himself. He had heard rumors that some of Roxthar's white-robed acolytes were purging the Great Temple of Balph itself. How could this be? How had this vile True Believer elevated himself so high and so fast? It was true that *even* Archpriest Anaxthenes, the most ambitious and cold-blooded archpriest of the Inner Circle, feared Roxthar's wrath.

And, even worse, Styphon's Own Voice on Earth now feared the sniffing noses and sharp teeth of Roxthar's hounds. After ninety-one winters, had the gods cursed him with so long a life that he would live to see true believers fill the Inner Circle? If Sesklos survived the coming winter and lived through another, he was sure he would. The question that disturbed his sleep tonight was: would he die in the kind hands of old age, or upon Roxthar's unholy rack?

Sesklos had a sudden vision, as though he were a bird, flying higher than any feathered beast had ever gone, peering down below at the Five Kingdoms, boiling with fire and black roiling clouds of fireseed. Bodies lay in courtyards, stacked like cords of firewood. The only creatures alive and moving in all this chaos and destruction were the white-hooded followers of Archpriest Roxthar.

His body went into spasms. *I have to stop this madman.* But how? He curled up, pulling his thin shanks together, trying to keep the chill at bay. There had to be a way to stop Roxthar. *Or, Dralm damn-it was Roxthar really in the service of Styphon! Had they all been wrong about their god?* Sesk-los felt his head spin. If they were wrong and Styphon was a true god, had Styphon sent Roxthar to manifest his anger with his false priesthood?

I must be sick, Sesklos thought, *to even think such thoughts.* If any of the gods were real, this "Investigation" Roxthar was promoting would be like a picnic compared to the rewards he—and all the other non-believers who paraded in Balph as priests—would receive in Regwarn!

"TYTHOS! Bring me another brazier; I need warmth. And call my healer."

FIVE

I

Chief Verkan sat at his horseshoe-shaped desk, watching the viewer replay the takeover of the Memphis conveyer-head on a minor Fourth Level, Nilo-Mesopotamian time-line in the Alexandrian-Roman sector. The Nile delta had been suffering from a famine due to a series of aqueducts built over a period of centuries that had finally reduced the flow of the major river to a trickle. Raising damns upon the Nile river was not unusual; it had been done on First Level and most Second Level sectors, even some of the more advanced Europo-American sectors had completed, or were finishing major dams. The result, of course—regardless of Level—was always the same; too little silt and too little water, leaving the Nile valley an agricultural wasteland. Famine was not the surprise, the real question was: Why had the populace decided to attack the Consolidated Outtime Foodstuffs conveyer head?

The battle was fierce and the prole defenders were disadvantaged by having to employ local weapons. Despite using a motley collection of clubs, cutlery and agricultural implements; the populace extracted numerous casualties among the Paratime staff. A few of the attackers were armed with swords and spears and were probably members of the local constabulary. The soldiers didn't arrive until the buildings had been looted and burned. The Consolidated Outtime Foodstuffs' First Level employees had

gotten out before the doors were blown apart by battering rams. Most of
the proles had died, but five of them had gotten to the conveyer in time.
Verkan made a note that he wanted copies of all the interrogations and
would like to talk to at least one of the surviving proles. As he recalled,
Outtime Foodstuffs had been peripherally involved in the Wizard Traders
case.

Verkan looked up when he heard his secretary's voice announce, "Inspector, Skordran Kirv, too see you, Chief."

"Tell him to come," he replied, wondering why one of his top men had
arrived unannounced.

He motioned for Kirv to take a seat, as he shut off the viewer. "Kirv, I've
got a question for you."

"Yes, Chief."

"Why would half the population of Memphis, Fourth Level
Alexandrian-Roman, attack our local conveyer head?"

"What were we exporting and what were the conditions?"

Verkan answered, "Consolidated Outtime Foodstuffs runs the facility
and there's a famine in all of Egypt."

"Humming bird tongues, ibex steaks, crocodile livers—there's a good
market here for all of that here in Dhergabar. Probably someone got careless and let some of the indigenies watch them bring food into the building.
People are starving in the streets—isn't that one of the sectors where they
built dams on the Nile, or some such nonsense?"

"Yes," Verkan said, enjoying the way Kirv reached almost the identical
conclusion he had after watching the clip.

"It's almost always carelessness that brings disaster. Someday, someone is
going to slip up and one of these more advanced Second Level, or even
Fourth Level, time-lines are going to figure out that they're nurturing a
colony of vampires at their breast and the big bill will finally come due."

The Paratime Secret: the one inviolate Home Time Line secret that had
to be protected at any cost. Not only to preserve First Level society in all
the luxury it had become accustomed to, but also because it wasn't right to
let the poor outtime devils know that they were secretly being taken to the
cleaners, as his friend Kalvan might have put it, by a secret race of parasites.
But sometimes the parasites got careless and mistakes got made and then it
was up to the Paracops to clean it up. This looked like it was going to be

another one of those times. Sure, a few careers might be uprooted at Consolidated Outtime Foodstuffs, but the real losers would be the families of the proles who'd died defending a place they neither built nor profited from.

Verkan shook his head. He'd have to think of a more appropriate punishment for these First Level incompetents; maybe a posting to that new Second Level Ashthor Rammis subsector, where the locals shaved off all body hair, practiced ritual self-flagellation, were strict vegetarians and believed the highest state of being was to forgo all pleasure. That might be just the place for these miscreants to cool their heels for a century or so.

"Good analysis, Kirv," Verkan said. "I've got something pleasant in mind for those in charge, for a change."

"I don't like that look, Chief."

"How does a penal sentence to the Ashthor Rammis Subsector strike you?"

"Just rewards, comes to mind." Kirv said, with a laugh. "But let me change the subject, for a moment. I have news you need to hear: Dalgroth Sorn is getting ready to announce his retirement at Year-End!"

Verkan bolted upright in his chair. "Dalgroth!" The Paratime Commissioner for Security was one of Verkan's and the Paratime Police's staunchest allies. Dalgroth Sorn, was said to be older than time, but Verkan—preoccupied with events on Kalvan's Time-Line—had not considered his retirement, certainly not so soon after former Paratime Chief, Tortha Karf's. It appeared that all the men he'd looked upon as mentors and old friends would be gone from active service by the end of the year. That left Verkan not only feeling alone, but also isolated and with more weight upon his shoulders than any man should have to bear.

Kirv added, "It wasn't unexpected. He is half a century older than Tortha and they are good friends."

"I know," Verkan said. "I should have anticipated this and had a candidate all ready to step forward."

Skordran Kirv winced. "The Opposition Party has put forward Councilman Aldron Ralth as their candidate."

"So fast!" Verkan shook his head in exasperation. Ralth was the Opposition leader who had replaced Salgath Trod—who was assassinated during the Wizard Trader blow-up. "He's a good figurehead and helped rebuild

Opposition after the Wizard debacle, but he's probably the worst person—other than Hadron Tharn—to head the Paratime Security Commission."

"Ralth's sycophants in the Executive Council are saying that it's time the Commissioner was his own man, rather than the Chief's pet stooge! Ralth's been getting a lot of media attention. Everyone knows that Dalgroth is a big Paratime Police booster."

"Sure, he's a former Police Inspector. But he doesn't take my orders. He has always had a very clear agenda: protect the Paratime Secret and keep the Force strong and independent of the Executive Council. I've gotten more than one bawling out from Dalgroth, when he didn't agree with my policies or actions."

"You'll never convince the media nor the Executive Council of that."

Verkan shook his head wearily. For not the first time, nor for the last time, he wondered how Tortha Karf had run the Force for over two hundred and fifty years. "Who do we know that has the right background to serve as Paratime Commissioner?"

Skordran Kirv looked nervous. "We do have one exemplary candidate, Chief."

"And who might that be?"

"Tortha Karf. He's got the best background, great contacts and would back us to the hilt."

Verkan stood up. "Tortha's not about to give up his retirement, besides his nomination—after what Ralth has been saying—would stink all the way to Mars. Is there anyway we can talk Dalgroth into staying in office for a few more years?"

Kirv shrugged his shoulders. "Maybe you could have a talk with him, Chief. I don't know anyone else, other than our ex-Chief, whom he'd listen to."

"Fine," Verkan said, in resignation. He knew when he was beat. "Set up an appointment for later this afternoon. I'll have to worry about Nilo-Mesopotamia tomorrow." I'd better be able to convince Dalgroth not to retire, he thought. Otherwise, this job of policing millions upon millions of time-lines is going to turn into a dead certain impossibility! If Aldron Ralth becomes Paratime Commissioner, it'll be time for me to retire—right to Kalvan's Time-Line.

II

Warchief Sargos led his men stealthily through the saplings that grew along the banks of the Green River. This time the Ruthani sentries had not been asleep and there had been six guards where before there had been but two, when Althea made good her escape. Still, the sentries had not been prepared for a dozen young warriors stealing up the banks from right out of the river. The warriors had killed the guards, leaving only one dead and three wounded, only one bad enough that he might not see dawn.

Althea, her bow in hand, moved like a shadow and he was glad she was at his side. Halgoth was following right behind and Sargos smiled in anticipation of tonight's battle. His warriors had spent the day smoking tobacco and bragging over their prowess; well, tonight they would get a chance to perform deeds that were real, not words. He heard one of the warriors brag about what he would do to the first enemy woman he discovered.

Sargos could see Althea's body stiffen in anger. He put his rough hand over the youth's mouth and whispered loudly, "All Grassmen are to be sent to Wind. All women and children belong to the Clan. Treat them as kinsmen."

Subchief Ikkos spoke up. "It is our right—"

Sargos raised his knife. "This is not a raid, but a blood-debt. Even the Grasswomen and children belong to the Clan. If anyone disagrees, they can argue with my blade."

Not another word was said.

The saplings were beginning to thin and Sargos could hear the distant cry of keening women, mostly captives, but some cries were coming from the throats of the victors' women as well, since they too had dead to mourn. The presence of so many women only proved the wisdom of this attack. If they left the Grassmen in peace, they would either attack the Tymannes next, or wait until more of their kinsmen had crossed the Great Mother River. Either way would bring death or migration to the Tymannes.

Warchief Sargos brought his warriors to the edge of the copse. They could see that most of the campfires had burned down. *This is good*, thought Sargos, *they feel safe.* He counted less than forty sentries, most of them grouped around a hastily built corral that was easily twice the size of the

Grassmen's encampment. Already, some of the warriors were spreading around the edge of the wooded thicket.

Sargos called Ikkos over and gave his orders. "Capture the corrals first. Then kill any Grassmen who escape and try to take their mounts. Keep the horses inside the corral, if you can. Take these men with you." It was a group of handpicked warriors Sargos knew would fight to the death.

Subchief Ikkos nodded. "We will win, or die, Warchief." He, too, was aware of how much wealth this many horses represented. There appeared to be many hundreds of horses.

Sargos next placed his prized horsepistol, after checking the load, into Ikkos' hands. The horsepistol had belonged to some long-departed nobleman and was chased with gold and silver. It was used infrequently, since fireseed was as expensive as gold dust in the Sastragath. While its sale outside of the Five Kingdom's was under Styphon's Ban, pouches could be bought for the right price.

The younger man looked up in surprise. This was one of three working firearms owned by the Raven Tribe.

"Use the pistol only if there is any trouble. Otherwise, I want you to shoot it when the corral is secure. Either way, we will attack the camp when we hear it fire. Remember, it has only one load. And, I want it back, too!"

Ikkos grinned, showing his long canines. He, like everyone else in the tribe, had heard the stories how Sargos had won the pistol almost twenty years ago in a battle against a Trygathi king. Sargos had taken the pistol from an armored nobleman he had slain with his battleaxe.

As the wind changed, Sargos could smell the enemy campfire smoke and privies. It was all he could do to keep from coughing. The Grassmen were unclean as well as savages. He watched as his scouts fanned out and dispatched the outer sentries. By the time the pistol shot broke through the still night, there were less than half a dozen guards left alive in the camp.

The forward warriors were already breaching the longhouses, while the main body attacked the hide huts the wandering Ruthani used as homes. Sargos saw a Grassman run from a tent, spear in hand. The Grassman tumbled to his feet, when an arrow from Althea's bow struck him in the chest. Sargos nodded his approval. Then they were at the first hide dwelling; he used his knife to slice through the deerhide. There was a small fire and he could see a Ruthani stumbling around, trying to pull up his trousers, when Sargos split his skull with his axe.

A younger enemy, probably the older man's son, rose out of a bearskin blanket, a saber in his hands. Althea put an arrow through his left eye; he twirled around and then dropped like a stone. An older woman screamed, then brought up a knife. Sargos knocked her out with the flat of his axe. Althea looked over at him and smiled; it was both beautiful and ugly.

They left the dead and wounded and went to the next dwelling. There was already a small fight inside, four Grassmen—two badly wounded—were fighting three Tymannes. Althea's bow made quick work of one, while Sargos buried his axe in the leader's back. There were screams and shouts, then the quicksilver flash of Althea's knife and all was quiet.

By the time they emerged from the wreckage, the battle was over except for some skirmishing on the outskirts of the camp. There were a few muffled screams, but many more war cries. Subchief Ikkos, surrounded by a bodyguard of young warriors, approached, shouting, "We've taken the horses!"

"Good!" Sargos replied, as he took back his horsepistol. After pausing to reload, he asked, "How many Grassmen have escaped?"

Vanar Halgoth, showing a long cut on his face, from forehead to chin, that would make a most honorable scar, said, "Less than a dozen. We will hunt them down with the dogs in the morning."

"Very well. How many prisoners."

"All the Grassmen are dead. We took more Grasswomen captives than I could count. Less than a hundred Burgdun women and fifty or sixty small children still live."

Althea's face was as mobile as a statue, but her eyes welled.

Sargos growled. "Strip the dead of all clothing and jewelry. Then throw them into their own privy pits."

"It will be done, Warlord."

"Halgoth, send messengers to all the tribes of the Tymannes. Tell them of our great victory and warn them about the treachery of all Grassmen. Tell them it is time for the Clan Gathering. We will meet at the winter campgrounds. It is time for the clan to gather around the Raven banner!"

A chorus of shouts and war cries split the night air. Then someone started a chant of "Warlord Sargos! Warlord Sargos!" Soon two hundred

throats repeated the words over and over. "WARLORD SARGOS! WAR-
LORD SARGOS! WARLORD SARGOS!"

Sargos felt a surge as the words entered his body, like a lightening bolt—
much like the power of the berserk, the warrior madness. Althea's eyes were
upon him, glowing in the firelight of burning huts and longhouses. At this
moment, Sargos knew he could out-wrestle the sun and the moon and sit
astride the world!

III

Danar Sirna, lowliest member of the Kalvan Study Team, left the swelter-
ing foundry to walk to the well for a drink of fresh water. She still wore the
leather apron that protected her from arrant sparks. Her hands were
scabbed and torn from working the primitive tool that passed for scissors
on Kalvan's Time-Line. Also, she had a message ball to release for Hadron
Tharn, the man who had arranged for her to become a member of the most
celebrated study team in recent history.

For twelve years Sirna had labored in the Outtime History Department
without spending an hour outtime; until Hadron Tharn had talked to a
few of his friends. Now she had the dream assignment that everyone in the
Department had been talking about. And, the opportunity to work with
some of the Department's top scholars, like Danthor Dras.

Later, at one of the interminable academic parties, Tharn had asked for
a favor. She had heard stories, from her former husband, Ulvarn Rarth,
about how bad things happened to people who refused Hadron Tharn's
favors. Besides, she rationalized, she did owe him in return for this career-
making assignment to Kalvan Prime.

Once again, there wasn't any real news to relay; just that Sirna hadn't
observed any Paratemporal Contamination by the Paratime Police, or much
of anything else during the last moon at the Royal Foundry of Hos-
Hostigos. In fact, there wasn't much of anything happening, other than the
constant bickering between the different academic factions on the Study
Team. The constant tension was leaving her exhausted: how could these
people talk night and day, yet, never say anything?

Despite the boredom and in-fighting among the Kalvan Study Team, Sirna had to admit she was enjoying her first outtime posting. Kalvan's Time-Line was a fresh new world with different smells and full of people who lived their short lives to the fullest. The Hostigi foundry workers and farmers she had met had a 'freshness' about them that was unlike anything she'd ever encountered on Home Time Line or at Dhergabar University. They knew their lives were short and brutal, but that didn't stop them from enjoying them to the fullest. Or maybe that was why.

It was also true Sirna had lived a sheltered life, since both her parents were Dhergabar professors, with a long record of dedication to various idealistic causes. To them, she'd been a not very pleasant distraction; born during the second century of their marriage in a brief moment of social responsibility—'if intelligent citizens with our superior genetic gifts don't reproduce, who will be left to maintain future academic standards?' The actuality of child rearing had almost terminated the marriage and resulted in Sirna, essentially being brought up by the Dhergabar University Crèche. The few times they got together as a family, usually on Year-End Day, her parents were as familiar with her as they were with new acquaintances.

Sirna supposed it was her search for surrogate parents that had pushed her right into the arms of her much older first husband, Ulvarn Rarth, one of Hadron Tharn's staffers. Their companionate marriage had floundered, almost from the first day. Rarth was a man who loved humanity, but did not like people—which soon included his young wife. After her divorce, Sirna had returned to what she knew best, university life and had majored in Outtime Studies.

With her student status—she was still working on her Scholar Degree—it was no wonder Sirna had been surprised when Hadron Tharn had contacted her about joining the Kalvan Study Team as the junior member. He had promised his support if she returned his favor with updates on the Study Team's work on Kalvan Prime. She had not really taken the offer seriously, and had been as nonplussed as her Department head, when she'd been selected for the Kalvan Study Team.

Now, having been outtime on Kalvan's Time-Line for half a year, Sirna was beginning to regret her initial decision. She liked the Hostigi people she'd met and was impressed by how hard Kalvan was working at protecting his new subjects. Sirna knew that whatever Tharn had in mind for the former Pennsylvania policeman; he was up to no good. Unfortunately, she also understood that if she stopped working for Hadron Tharn, he would take her refusal as a betrayal. Having Hadron Tharn as an enemy was the here-and-now equivalent of a rattlesnake bite—with local Aryan-Transpacific medical treatment.

Sirna reached the well and pulled up the pail. A cool late autumn wind blew through her red hair, whipping her long dress against her legs. Soon it would be winter and she would be locked inside with these bores. Sirna found herself envying the outtime foundry workers who could leave at nightfall and return to their families. For the first time, she thought about going 'Outtime' herself, or native, but dismissed it quickly. A single woman in a low technology, patriarchal-centric society would be easy pickings for the first man who passed by.

She would just have to work out her term of duty, send Hadron Tharn his message balls about events in Hostigos, write her Scholar's thesis during the long winter nights and wait for her freedom from Tharn when she returned to Home Time Line. Gorath Tran, the assistant Study-Team leader, had already made several obvious passes, but she would rather spend the long nights with Archpriest Sesklos, Styphon's Voice on Earth! He probably had sweeter breath and a livelier personality than the spindly faculty administrator.

While very cold, the water she drank from the dipper was refreshing. She put the dipper back into the pail, looked around to make sure no one was watching, and then threw the message ball into the sky. It disappeared with a flash that if observed, would pass for a meteorite. She was halfway back to the foundry when Eldra approached. "Getting some fresh air?"

"Yes," Sirna answered. "I've had enough hot air for one lifetime."

Baltrov Eldra laughed out loud, with her deep rich laugh. Eldra was a complex woman, full of life, yet quick to anger. Eldra also carried a sense of tragedy that was often belied by easy laughter. She was not an easy person to know. Sirna found her to be a role model and the single most interesting person on the Kalvan Study Team.

"I have to get away sometimes, myself," Eldra said. "I have this wonderful Fifth Level outtime ranch where I can race my horses as far as the eye can see. I think you would enjoy it there."

Sirna smiled wryly. "As you may have noticed, I'm not much of a horse person. I'm actually looking forward to returning back to Dhergabar City!"

"Not me," Eldra said, shaking her head. "I've had it with First Level stuffed tunics! If I hear one more of Varnath Lala's discourses on the Repression of Patriarchal cultures and its effect on females' sexual mores, I think I'll wring her scrawny neck!"

Sirna laughed. "If she wasn't the University's top Pre-Industrial Metallurgist, I doubt she'd have gotten such a plum assignment."

Eldra's brow wrinkled, showing a stern side that made Sirna pull back. "I agree that Lala knows her stuff when it comes to metals, but if I ever got my hands on the University administrator who confused knowledge with ability to get the job done, I'd personally geld him."

"I'm glad Varnath wasn't around to hear you say that. Your assumption that it was a man who made that decision would be more evidence that you've been 'contaminated' by our prolonged stay in the male dominated Zarthani culture of Kalvan's Time-Line."

Eldra reared back in mock horror. "Please, I beg you. Don't breathe a word about my breach of proper gender assumptions!"

Sirna laughed. "You've got my word. I've heard Lathor Karv, our sociologist make that same breach of etiquette—and the results were not pretty!"

After Eldra stopped laughing, she stared up into the star bright evening sky.

"Not to change the subject," Sirna said. "But what do you think will happen to Hos-Hostigos now that Kalvan has defeated the Holy Host?" She knew that Eldra, despite the Study Team and general University anti-Kalvan bias, was one of the few Kalvan fans.

"It's difficult to tell. To use a boxing metaphor from Fourth Level, Kalvan won the first round with a technical knockout: Styphon's House went home with a bloody nose. While poor Prince Ptosphes is down for the count, Kalvan himself is ready for another match. Styphon's House has more gold stashed in its treasuries than Kalvan has bodies, more soldiers than he has guns. But, if Styphon's House doesn't quickly press its advantage, Kalvan will revolutionize Hos-Hostigos and win. If they press Kalvan hard, it is anyone's guess. It's really up to the priests now."

"What do you mean?"

"Styphon's House has declared war on the other gods, as well as Kalvan, even if the priests of the various gods on this time-line don't know it yet. All this talk of the Styphon's Holy Warriors sounds like the Crusades again, back on Europo-American, Hispano-Columbian Subsector eight hundred years ago. If Styphon's House wins this war, all the other gods will disappear in a generation. I'm not sure the non-Styphoni priesthood understands just how dangerous the concept of one, and only one true god, can be."

Sirna nodded. All First Level children studied the horrors and destruction brought about by the Religious Wars on Home Time Line—it was an abomination not to be repeated, but they were ancient history. As a freshman at Dhergabar University, she'd spent a full term studying the end results of outtime religious fanaticism. Actually having to watch some of those gory battles in three-dimensional color, as they happened, had been much more real. The class had left Sirna with awful memories that still haunted her dreams.

"From what I've heard from our man in Agrys City," Eldra continued, "the highpriests of Dralm are under the misconception, that this is a mere disagreement over who is or who is not top god in the Zarthani pantheon, and don't want to stir the waters. I think some of the Princes realize how dangerous the one-god concept is and how that could turn the Six Kingdoms into a kingdom-wide theocracy. This is why they formed the League of Dralm. But the League can't come out in support of Kalvan without the blessings of the Council of Dralm.

"With the armies of League of Dralm behind him, Kalvan would be almost invincible. I just hope the highpriests of Dralm stop worrying about propriety and who's going to chair the table and get down to 'brass tacks'—as they call it on Europo-American. Otherwise, it's Hos-Hostigos against the richest and biggest military power on this time-line, Styphon's House. And that's not going to be good news for Hos-Hostigos, or for those of us who 'appear' to support Kalvan by working in the Royal Foundry of Hos-Hostigos."

Eldra rubbed some goose bumps on her tanned arms. "Let's get back to the Foundry, it's getting chilly out here."

"Good idea," Sirna said, picking up a sudden chill of her own. If things went bad for Kalvan and Rylla, who knows how nasty they might get for the Study Team; after all, they were far away from First Level help. Unfortunately, Dhergabar University—in an attempt to assert its authority—had stopped Paratime Chief Verkan from keeping enough Paratime Police on Kalvan Prime to protect the Study Team; she just hoped that the University people in the field wouldn't have to pay in spilled blood for this bit of backroom political maneuvering.

SIX

I

Verkan flew his aircar through the corridors of Old Town, the last section of Dhergabar City, that still housed ground-hugging buildings, some dozen square blocks of densely packed ground level residences and commercial facilities. There were even a few buildings that could trace their history back to First Level PP (Pre-Paratime), but most only went back four millennia to the Religious Wars, when most of Dhergabar had been leveled. Years later it had taken its present shape of tall anti-gravity towers and spires. Old Town was where the infirm, those who found it difficult to live in townhouses only reachable by aircar; the indigent—even the Bureau of Psych-Hygiene hadn't been able to root out all the bums from First Level society—the out of work Proles and a small criminal element that not even the most determined Psych-Hygiene techniques could eradicate, nor the Metropolitan Police sweeps take captive.

Sticking straight up and out of the middle of Dhergabar City was the Paratime Commission Building, a two hundred-story edifice, protected by a next to impenetrable collapsed-nickel shield. Verkan parked his green aircar on Chief's reserved landing port and took the lift down to the hundred and eightieth floor. From there he walked to the office of the Paratime Commissioner for Security, where he was quickly ushered into Dalgroth Sorn's office.

"Chief Verkan, nice to see you," Dalgroth said, "please, take a seat."

Dalgroth Sorn was a tall, thin man with the air of a scholar, which was belied by both his piercing black eyes and raspy voice. There were still a few Paratime Police veterans who could recall, when during his term as an Inspector, that voice could peel collapsed-nickel. Dalgroth was more formal than usual and Verkan wondered if it was because he already knew why Verkan was visiting.

Verkan paused long enough to remove his pipe, load the barrel and light it. "This is not easy, Commissioner—"

"Verkan, you get right to the point. It's one of the things I like about you. But this time, I know what you're here to ask. The answer is yes."

Verkan blew out a lungful of smoke. "Thank you, Commissioner—"

Commissioner Dalgroth held up his hand to stop him again. "I hate to keep interrupting you, Verkan, but I've got some things I need to tell you."

Verkan nodded this time.

"I'm going to keep my job as Commissioner, but not just because you need my help. But, because, there are some serious problems facing First Level society, and I think I can do a better job right here at the Paratime Commission than I would be able to do as head of the First Level Social Stability Project. The job I was going to take after I resigned as Commissioner of Paratime Security."

"I'm very relieved by your decision, Commissioner. I believe I heard something about this Stability study on the evening news."

"What you heard, Verkan, from some newsie was just window dressing, as our friends on Europo-American call it. The real subject and purpose of this Project is not for public consumption."

Verkan braced himself. "I know I've been spending too much time on Kalvan's Time-Line and outtime in general, but—"

"Don't apologize, Vall. I'm one of the few people who completely understand how demanding the Paratime Police Chief's job truly is. I doubt you know this, but once—thirty years before Tortha's reign—I was offered the position of Paratime Chief. Oh, yes. I turned it down flat; I saw what it did to the man they wanted me to replace. Remember, back then I was Chief Inspector. I've seen four Chief's in my lifetime and Tortha was the only one who resigned without a physical or mental breakdown."

Verkan realized that he had never really known Dalgroth; he'd just been another useful ally who knew how to tell a good story. Verkan was beginning to realize that even with five times the normal human lifespan, there was still not enough time to do everything that needed to be done—much less what one wanted to do.

"I think your sojourns to Aryan-Transpacific are an excellent way to get away from the pressures and demands of a job that is simply too much responsibility for one man. Unfortunately, it has come to my attention, and that of several other highly placed persons that something is fundamentally wrong with our First Level culture. This is the reason behind the Social Stability Project."

"By fundamentally wrong, just what do you mean?"

"Vall, this time-line stinks! Maybe it's the accumulated sins and bad debt of ten thousand years of living off the labor of other human beings, but—whatever it is—it's beginning to manifest itself here on Home Time Line."

"I haven't noticed anything unusual. Well, maybe crime is up a little."

"That's just one of the many symptoms. Did you know that First Level population has been dropping for the past fourteen centuries?"

"No. It certainly isn't obvious, Commissioner. There appear to be just as many Citizens as ever."

"True, but only because of the large increase in Prole citizenship—even as hard as the tests have become. The Prole problem is another part of this issue."

"I have noticed there is more actual Prole prejudice in Dhergabar than I recall growing up."

"You're right, the prejudice is growing worse. As Scholar Elltar has proposed, the Prole in our society has assumed a place quite similar to that of the Negro in the Europo-American, Hispano-Columbian Subsector, in the political entity still known as the United States, during the period they call the Reconstruction—after the War Between The States."

"The Civil War, I remember that. I did one of my first University Outtime Studies there while the War was still going on. I can see the parallels. The Civil War, in a lesser part, was about freeing the slaves. Separate, but not equal. The threat of slave rebellion."

"Exactly. As you've noticed in your Europo-American Quarantine proposal, this situation has been exacerbated with the passage of time. A number of observers believe there will be large-scale race riots on Hispano-Columbian Subsector in the next few years. There are a number of parallels to what's happening here on First Level."

"The Proles aren't slaves, but I do see similarities. So you believe that this is a threat to First Level Security?"

"Not now, but it could be. Are you familiar with a man who calls himself The Leader?"

"No. Should I be?" Verkan paused to re-light his pipe.

"Not really. However, the man—and we don't know who he is—that calls himself The Leader is becoming more and more influential amongst the youth and the politically disenfranchised Citizens. Those who most feel threatened by the former Prole Citizens and by society as a whole. He's even encouraging his followers to wear a uniform of sorts, blue shirts and pants."

"That sounds similar to the fascist black shirts in Italy, and brown shirts of the old Nazi Storm Troopers on Europo-American." Verkan shook his head in disgust.

"You're not the only one who has come to that conclusion. There are some frightening parallels."

"Commissioner, as long as I'm Chief, I will not tolerate the harassment and murder of Proles on First Level Time-Line."

"I don't think it will come to genocide here, Verkan. We have a completely different situation here on First Level. No one here wants to eliminate the Proles, just keep them from becoming Citizens."

"Well, the whole idea of allowing outtimers to become Citizens is fairly new. Less than three hundred years old."

"Yes," Dalgroth said, "that's when it was first brought to the Executive Council's attention that the population decrease was going to continue no matter what laws were passed. To counter the steady population decline, a program was set up to administer citizenship to the best and brightest of the outtimers. It's been one of the last millennium's few successes. But the Proles are not the real problem, just a symptom. The problem is with the Home Time Line Citizens and their growing malaise."

"How bad do you think this problem really is?" Verkan asked.

Dalgroth's brows furrowed heavily. "Bad. Bad enough that I believe it is the biggest problem facing the survival of the Home Time Line."

"More dangerous than the possibility of the Paratime Secret being uncovered?"

"Yes, because it threatens the very core of our society. The fact is, Verkan, our society is crumbling before our eyes. There's enough social and commercial momentum that it might last another millennium, certainly a few more centuries—but it is dissolving. That is why, for right now, I have decided it is more important for me to continue on as Paratime Commissioner to help stabilize your stewardship as Paratime Police Chief, than it is to delve into First Level social problems. Because, if you fail as Chief, the results will be so catastrophic it will no longer matter what the problem was or is. The Paratime Police is First Level's most stable institution and if the Force collapses, because its Chief has been forcibly removed. Well—the fact is—this whole time-line will go up like a thermo-nuclear blast!"

For the first time that he could remember, Verkan Vall was so nonplussed he was actually speechless.

II

Kalvan walked quickly down the stone staircase, his boot steps echoing behind him. In his mind he still heard baby Demia's coughs—or croup as his Aunt Harriet used to call it when he was growing up. He remembered his younger cousins having it a lot, but then they had sulfa drugs and cough syrup. Now, of course, there was penicillin, which was the best of the antibacterial medications. Here-and-now there were a few potions and poultices, but nothing he'd risk his daughter's life on—if he had any other choice.

Note: Do research on penicillin molds, starting with common bread mold.

Of course, if he wasn't spending most of his time in weapons research and building here-and-now's version of the military industrial complex, he might get some of these less dramatic inventions out of his head and into their lives. Of course, every time he 'invented' another device, this changed the future in directions he wasn't sure were for the best.

Kalvan passed the Great Hall and went down the long corridor past three doors to Rylla's private audience chamber, stopping suddenly when he realized she had company. He was about to go in anyway; after all, he was Great King—but the note of urgency in Rylla's voice stopped him in his tracks.

"Why isn't he answering our letters, Mytron?"

"Queen Rylla, do you remember Xentos' last missive, where he stated that the Temple's business held priority over any worldly realm—including that of Hos-Hostigos?"

Rylla's voice sounded a petulant note Kalvan hadn't heard very often. He remembered Xentos' last letter, which had arrived at least a moon ago, and Rylla's white face after he read it aloud. She had left the room quickly before he could read her face. He hadn't realized just how badly she had taken Xentos' lack of support—or betrayal—only time would tell.

It bothered Rylla enough that she was still fretting over it. "Mytron, doesn't Xentos realize that he only attended the Council of Dralm on Our sufferance?"

"You know Xentos better than that, Your Majesty. He suffers no one. He has ruled the Temple of Dralm in Hostigos with an iron hand."

"I never saw that side of him, Brother Mytron. He was always my 'Uncle' who came with presents and funny stories to cheer me up, whether in the tiltyard or in the music chamber—although not so much when I sang!"

Kalvan could hear them both laughing.

"I fear that has changed, now that you have a husband and a kingdom to run. Xentos has a very stern side; I remember when he would wake us novices before daybreak and put us to work scrubbing the stone paving of the temple floors. Even now, as a grown man, I walk softly when I hear his voice rise. He never shouts, but he does get his words across and woe to those who do not listen."

"How strange, Mytron. It's almost as if we are talking about two different people."

No, thought Kalvan, just two different roles—palace sycophant and temple bully. He himself wasn't very happy about Chancellor Xentos' reluctance to help Hostigos win its needed allies in the war against Styphon's House. Kalvan had expected some act or word of encouragement from Agrys City long before now. It also hurt him to hear the plaintive little girl voice come out of Great Queen Rylla's mouth.

"I had such a wonderful life at Tarr-Hostigos growing up. Maybe because I didn't have a mother, I always had all these 'uncles' to take care of me."

Spoil you is more like it, thought Kalvan. That was one mistake they wouldn't repeat with Princess Demia.

"Bring me presents, play with me and share their knowledge. There was old 'Uncle' Chartiphon, 'Uncle Harmakros' and my favorite—'Uncle' Xentos. I never thought he'd betray my trust like this—Her voice broke.

Kalvan could almost see young Brother Mytron's fluttering hands, since the cherubic priest had little or no experience dealing with the opposite sex. Kalvan took pity on him and, after making noise with his boots, walked into the chamber.

"Oh Kalvan!" Rylla said, brushing at her eyes. Mytron, red-faced, bowed and bolted from the room as quickly as his stubby legs would take him.

Kalvan tried to wave him back. The poor little priest probably thought Kalvan suspected something was going on between the two of them.

"I didn't expect you until lunch, husband."

"I heard little Demia coughing in the nursery and I thought I ought to talk to her mother about it."

"It's just the Baby Cough; all the babies get it. Nothing much to be done about it either. Brother Mytron's bloodroot tea is too strong for babies."

Kalvan wondered about the little ones who contracted pneumonia and how their parents dealt with that. Well, he knew the answer here-and-now: it was stoically and with great resignation. There were few alternatives, since the various gods and their temples offered little religious consolation for a grief-stricken parent. He suddenly realized, as he saw the worry in Rylla's eyes, that there could be far greater losses than even those on the battlefield. Some half-remembered aphorism about children being their parent's hostage to fortune came to mind and he resolved to beef up security measures in the nursery. He doubted there were many Styphoni sympathizers in Hos-Hostigos, but all it took was one . . .

III

Hadron Tharn heard the portal alarm go off and looked over at the privacy screen, seeing the face of his older sister, Dalla. He tapped the release code and the door opened.

"Long time no see, Sis."

Dalla winced. She was still playing mama—a job their birth mother had rejected. They had been close during their youth, until she met the future supercop, Verkan Vall. Actually, he rather admired Verkan's single-mindedness and lack of squeamishness. Verkan's, problem was that he still retained too many of the ideals of the old nobility that he'd been born into. Whereas, he had cast off all those old-fashioned ideas when Herr Goebbels and his philosopher friend, Martin Heidegger, had introduced him to the works of Friedrich Nietzsche. 'The overman is free because all his own values flow from his own will.' He remembered those words well and lived them.

"I haven't seen you in a half-year, where have you been?"

None of your business, he wanted to shout, but Big Sis still had her uses. Without her influence, the super Paracop might be taking a closer look at his wanderings and financial dealings. That would not do, at least, now while events were still percolating. "I've been overseeing some of my outtime business affairs."

"I understand from cousin Falro that you've been causing quite a stir in First Level financial affairs."

Falro was in banking and it was useful to know that he still owed his loyalty to Dalla, who he'd unsuccessfully tried to romance—pre-Verkan era. "It keeps me occupied. And, as you know Dalla, the only things our parents left to us were credits." That was a sore spot, he knew it and smacked her with it whenever Dalla tried to play mama. The truth was mother had left the family for outtime adventure and it had been no great loss to anyone but Dalla. He'd been too young to even remember her. He saw mother once or twice every twenty years and ohhed and ahhed while she treated him like a distant friend.

"So what really brings you here, Dalla? I've been a good boy; no more visits to Fourth Level, Europo-American Axis Subsector." He'd been fortunate to make his first visits there, while a student at Dhergabar University, secretly ferreting out future business as an agent with Consolidated Outtime Foodstuffs before the Big War in Europo-American, when the entire Axis Subsector had been declared off-limits to all First Level commercial and travel bureaus. He still had his contacts, but no one knew of them but Warntha, his personal bodyguard, the only person in the universe he completely trusted.

Dalla blushed fetchingly. She was as beautiful without make-up as most women were with it. She could have been a film star on any Europo-American time-line. If she weren't so useful, he might have been tempted himself. She was so good at protecting him, protecting him from everyone and everything—but himself. It was good to know that she still felt guilty about telling Verkan about his little Axis excursions; fortunately, she hadn't known the half of it.

He decided it was time to punish her some more. "Have you told my esteemed brother-in-law about the Hadron family secret."

She gasped. "No! No one outside of the family knows about that."

"Supercop hasn't even made a guess. I'm disappointed; maybe he's more smitten with my elder sister then I surmised. Isn't it ironic that your husband's toy policeman—Kalvern, isn't it—drops off rather conveniently on the same time-line created by our esteemed great, great, uncountable great grandfather. Don't they still have some devil god named after the old fossil—rather like the family name? Must be the family curse."

Dalla nodded listlessly.

Hadron laughed. "Good old Arnall. It wasn't enough to violate the Paratime Code, but had to create his own time-line by scaring away the natives! Now, it's Kalvan—that's his name, right? —who's getting all the attention. The first Paratime time-line observed from the moment of divarication— ha! Maybe it's time we set the record straight. Told them about how 'ol Hadron Arnall arrived on a Fourth Level time-line a couple of thousand years ago and played god to one of the tribes. How he used to ride around in a big aircar taking the prettiest young girls with him and how he killed and tortured any of the tribesmen who 'objected.'

"Of course, he never brought the girls back—alive. He made such an impression on the primitives that they actually changed their migration route and created a whole new Subsector—Aryan-Transpacific, if I remember. To this day, they even remember him as some sort of an underworld demon. Now, that story would get good old Kalvan off the home screens, but I doubt it would enhance the old family name."

"Now, that's enough, Tharn. That story is not the least bit amusing!"

"It's not a story! I forgot what a prig you turned into when you are around me. Does Supercop get to see this side of you, too?"

"Shut up about him!"

"I see the family temper has bred true."

For the first time since the Big Fight, he saw tears in her eyes. He wondered what nerve ending he'd struck. Maybe Verkan wanted to breed—now there was a frightening thought—little Verkans running around with toy needlers.

"Why do you strike out at the people who love you?"

Oh no, he thought, Big Mama's coming. Time to change the conversation again. "So you still haven't told Supercop the family secret. I bet he already knows."

"What do you mean? That file was purged from the records thousands of years ago."

"And you believe that! Oh no, I guarantee you that in some secret data base in the Paratime Police supercomputer there's a flagged file with our shameful family secret. Probably only accessible by the Chief. Maybe the reason Supercop hasn't brought it up is: he's waiting for you to tell him. Maybe he does love you, after all!"

"Of course he does. You don't mean that really? There can't be any such file."

"Oh, yes I do, Dalla. True, it cost the family a few million credits to keep the story away from the newsies, but I didn't think you were gullible enough to think the Parafanatics buried it as well."

There were worry lines creasing Dalla's forehead and he wondered if anyone cared that much about what he thought. Probably not. Big Sis included.

"Enough of your verbal sparring, Tharn. I came hear to warn you that the Paratime Police know all about your little spy."

For a second he was worried, but little was not a description that would describe his real agent in any manner. "She of the big mammaries. Yes, I admit she's working for me. One of my co-workers daughters who needed a job; I sponsored her for the Kalvan Study Team. I still have friends at the University, even if they couldn't stop my expulsion. After my Axis studies; though I did receive a *lot* of moral support for what the Paracops did to my fledgling academic career."

"You still don't see the danger in what you did?"

"I wasn't telling the natives about the Paratime Secret, if that's what you mean, just soaking up some local flavor and finishing my studies on Great

Men in history. A little firsthand research never hurt anyone; not that most of the University professors would agree—it's too much like work. What I want to know is, why do they always proscribe the 'interesting' subsectors and time-lines? And, how, in Zirppa's Foodtube, was I to do original research on Great Men without any subjects!"

"There are great men all over Fourth Level; the one you picked may have been a catalyst, but by no other definition could he be called great—especially in regards to height, or any other adjective."

"You're wrong there, Dalla, but we could argue over these minor philosophical differences for days. What brought you here this time?"

"I wanted to warn you to be careful. Your tame little spy could get you in serious trouble if she's caught tampering on Kalvan Prime. Verkan and I both like Kalvan and Rylla and I wouldn't be able to stop him again if he caught you involved in some outtime contamination."

"I'll keep that in mind, Dalla. Now I know the end point of sisterly devotion. I have no intention of contaminating Verkan's toy soldier's field of play. And, as much as I do admire, the priestly scoundrels in charge of Styphon's House, I really have no interest in the outcome of their little war. I do like to keep an eye out for any slip in the old family secret. After all, the Zarthani do have written records and who knows what oral history some priestly scribe might have heard around the campfire and saved for posterity."

"You don't think?"

"I really don't. But anything is possible and it's best to have a 'friend' on hand to help contain the damage, so to speak."

Dalla blanched.

"Sorry to upset your placid existence, but someone has to protect the family name." It was hard to keep from laughing at that lie. His sister was too preoccupied to notice his change of expression; it was amazing how love could screw up your life.

"Oh, at the risk of upsetting you further, I just thought I'd let you know that word of the Kalvan's contamination of Aryan Transpacific has some University scholars quite upset. They propose the novel hypothesis that every time Kalvan introduces another piece of military technology the risk of exposing the Paratime Secret grows more real. Some are even asking why Kalvan's not been dispatched for the good of Home Time Line and all that other patriotic self-serving nonsense. Of all people, they're asking why the Paratime Police aren't doing their job. Your husband might want to consider the ramifications."

Dalla's face, if possible, grew even whiter. He enjoyed that, even if he didn't give a fig over the Paratime Secret being exposed. How could some barbarian from Europo-American teach a bunch of savages enough to uncover a technological marvel that had taken three geniuses in three different fields to concoct and had been the life's blood of First Level for ten thousand years. The probabilities were so low they weren't worth thinking about.

"I'm sorry, Tharn, I don't feel well. I've got to go."

"Sorry to hear that. Be sure and give my best to Supercop." For a moment he was bothered by the thought that almost all their meetings ended this way, with Dalla either in tears or feeling sick—sometimes both. Maybe there was something to the family curse. After all, even father had succumbed in his third century and was now a permanent resident of some Psych-Hygiene house of horrors. No, madness was the escape route of lesser men—not an overman such as himself. Not with all that he had left to accomplish.

SEVEN

I

Kalvan followed Rector Mytron, who was wearing the university robes of green and maroon, instead of the blue robes of Father Dralm, to the massive plank door. The large room had formerly been the lesser hall of a baronial mansion belonging to his former aide, Baron Nicomoth, until he took a bullet in the eye at the Battle of Phyrax. Dying without wife or issue, Prince Ptosphes had claimed it for the Throne and presented it to Kalvan as the permanent site for his new University of Hos-Hostigos. It was an ideal place, situated just outside of Hostigos Town, close to the Royal Foundry (near State College in otherwhen), with a mansion as solid as a castle keep, a city-block of grounds and a dozen or more outbuildings.

Mytron led Kalvan through the hall, out another door to the outside, where the former stable barn turned Artificer Workshop stood. Both doors were wide open and half a dozen forges, with varlets working the bellows, burned cherry red. On anvils the size of tree butts husky smiths pounded out splints of steel, turning them into three and four foot bayonets. Along the far side of the Workshop, apprentices sorted bayonets into groups, while others honed their blades. These were nasty Napoleonic spear-like bayonets, not the stubby knives of Kalvan's Korean War days.

Phylo, the Chief Artificer, took a musket and one of the newly made bayonets, which were hafted with tapered plugs instead of handles, and put the bayonet into the end of the firearm. Then a student approached him with a cloth and wood dummy and he proceeded to charge it with the musket and bayonet. When the student had proved that the bayonet could strike with reasonable impact, without becoming dislodged, Phylo dismissed the apprentice and took apart the musket and bayonet.

"Very nice, very nice," Kalvan said, "but what about the sockets we talked about?"

The gray-haired Chief Artificer shook his head. "Your Majesty, we did a complete inventory of every firearm in the Royal Armory and found that of the twelve thousand or more firearms, including muskets, arquebuses and calivers, no more than a few hundred shared the same bore or outside muzzle diameter. Our master gunsmiths believe that it would take more than a year to provide half the Armory's firearms with both socket and outside bushing for the bayonets. And that is only if we halved production of bayonets and produced only sockets and bushings."

That figure, of course, didn't include firearms already issued to the Royal Army. Winning five out of six major battles had over-stocked the Royal Armory on firearms. This wealth of firearms had had an unforeseen consequence; it had made a shambles of Kalvan's attempts to standardize musket barrels and bores. On the other hand, it did make possible Kalvan's plan to replace the Royal Army's pikes with muskets. Most here-and-now infantry were a combined arms army of pikemen and firearms, usually in equal proportion. It didn't take a genius to figure out the advantages of turning all those pikemen into musketeers; for one, it would double the rate of firepower in one fell swoop.

In actuality, Kalvan was finding it wasn't easy to get those proud pikemen to drop their sixteen-foot shafts in favor of a little five-foot musket with a four-foot blade. Nor had it been easy to convince them that what they saw as a drop in status was in reality a jump in military effectiveness, since the pikemen were convinced that any fool could point a stick and pull a trigger. Pike drills took real coordination and strength. Nor had they wanted to give up their breastplates and taces, armor which he knew would only be in the way and weigh them down as musketeers. The pikemen thought it would make them more vulnerable to enemy shot. They were both right, but as Great King, he won the argument. Morale, though, had suffered.

"Chief Phylo will you be able to outfit the entire Royal Army with your plug bayonets by spring?"

"Your Majesty, we can provide enough of the new bayonets for about half the Royal Army; the other half will have to make do with converted knives and short swords."

"Here's what we'll do then. Give all the new bayonets to the pikemen, which will help their morale. Make plugs for the musketeers; who'll be happy to have anything at all to help protect them from rampaging cavalry."

"A good plan, Your Majesty. That should halt some of the grumbling."

There was no easy way to reverse a lifetime of thinking and conditioning, but they were going to have to try if the Kingdom of Hos-Hostigos was going to survive and flourish. If only he had more time—even just two or three years, but time was one advantage Styphon's House wasn't about to relinquish.

The next stop was the former barn turned University auditorium or Great Hall. Kalvan noticed that since his last visit, over a month ago, the walls had been plastered, whitewashed and wainscoted with dark wood. At the head of the hall, above a large desk, were the Hos-Hostigos national flag and the University coat-of-arms, a retort crossed with a quill pen.

According to Rector Mytron the University enrollment was up to sixty-two students, not counting the part-time students in the Department of Military Science, which was primarily an adjunct to help quickly train the new Royal Army officers in what they called Kalvan-style, military tactics. Captain-General Harmakros of the Royal Army was the Department head of Military Science in all his copious spare time.

Rector Mytron sat at one of the tables and indicated that Kalvan was to sit at the other. His broad cherubic face beaming, he said, "Now Master Thalmoth will give his report on progress in the Department of Sappers and Engineers."

Master Thalmoth, weathered by age and hard work, but unbent, remained standing. Thalmoth was a former Hostigi artillery officer brought out of retirement by the war. He had a natural talent for engineering and had done a little bit of everything during his two decades as a mercenary artillery captain. He was a colonel in the Royal Army as well as head of the engineering department; his eighteen students were soon to be the nucleus of the first Sapper and Engineers Company.

Thalmoth had been experimenting with gun carriage design and had come up with improved trunnions for some of the big twenty-four pounders There was also, at Kalvan's suggestion, some work being done on pontoon bridges. Thalmoth was highly animated and already talking about the spring campaign against the Great Kingdom of Hos-Harphax. He planned to have another fourteen of the four-pound sakers, or light cannon, cast during the winter and with his new carriages. Thalmoth claimed he could take them into the Trygath backwoods if necessary.

This was far better than Kalvan had expected and he praised the old engineer for his good work. With the new four-pounders, plus the twelve he already had, and the six and eight-pounders already in service, Kalvan would be approaching the kind of mobile artillery force that Gustavus Adolphus had used so successfully in Germany during the Thirty Years War. He was going to have to talk to General Alkides of the Royal Artillery about training some additional gun crews. Maybe he couldn't out-number his opponents but, By Galzar, he could out-shoot them.

Master Ermut, a big man with a fair beard, was the last to speak. Ermut, a former Styphon's House temple-farm slave, was living evidence of Kalvan's positive effect in his new world; Ermut was hale and hearty and even well dressed. Independently of Kalvan, Ermut had re-discovered the experimental method, while working in Kalvan's proto-paper mill and was the first real here-and-now scientist. Mytron had wisely made him Master of Alchemy.

"Your Majesty, I was hoping today to present you with some of our new paper, but we have still not determined the best clay for sizing and it is still too porous. I should have some of the new paper for your inspection in about a moon half."

Kalvan sure hoped so. He was running out of parchment, some of which had been scraped so often it could pass for lampshades, and he'd collected enough pine boards to create a fire hazard. If it got any worse, he was going to have to re-invent the Sumerian clay tablet

"I give you Tranth's Blessing, Master Ermut," said Kalvan, referring to the god of guilds and craftsmen, "because there's not a lambskin left in the Kingdom and the shepherds are threatening to mutiny if we butcher anymore of their sheep!"

Everyone laughed.

Ermut answered, "Yes, the Great Queen tells me you use parchments up as fast as you use up Styphon's troops, Your Majesty." Mouths gaped at Ermut's effrontery, but Kalvan laughed. A good leader wouldn't remain one for long once his confidants feared to speak their minds, and Master Ermut had come a long way from his days as a temple-farm slave to be able to make an open jest before his Great King, even one as feeble as that.

As Kalvan laughed the tension level dropped. "Speaking of Queen Rylla, she wanted me to ask you for more soap. Her ladies-in-waiting are 'losing' it faster than you can make it!"

"I'll see that you have a basket full of soap before you leave. Production is way up, now that we have a good source of lye."

Ermut's perfumed soap, another of Kalvan's ideas, was catching on quickly among the nobility and upper middle class, especially now that Queen Rylla was now bathing daily. Soon it would be an export commodity; Kalvan was gifting every ambassador and head of state with a basket of soap before they left Hostigos Town. He was making little progress among the lesser townsfolk, but they had little disposable income.

Ermut began to speak again. "While our paper project lags behind, one of our other projects has born surprising fruit." Ermut motioned to an apprentice by the door holding a large jug. The apprentice approached the table and at Ermut's direction filled a flask with a deep burgundy colored liquid.

Ermut carefully held up the glass flask so all could see the liquid's rich color. Glass was in short supply and made only in far-off Hos-Agrys. Kalvan thought, *Note: Work out a rough formula for glass and give it to Ermut to work on.*

Ermut brought the flask over to Kalvan and indicated he should drink up. Kalvan hesitated for a moment, then thought, when the time came he needed a food-taster to take a drink among friends, he was long overdue for another trip on a cross-time flying saucer. The first sip tasted like strong winter wine until it reached his throat and then he knew full well he'd just tasted the first here-and-now brandy.

Kalvan took another longer sip and that clinched it. "Master Ermut, you're a genius! How did you do it?"

The big man blushed to the roots of his blonde beard, while wiping his hands on his green robe. "Your Majesty, it was your idea and his," pointing to his apprentice, "device. I was listening to Apprentice Antros talk about the distillation of petroleum spirits for heating oil—he's only arrived several months ago from the Princedom of Kyblos to join the University—when I recalled something you had said about the strong spirits of wine, berries and corn mash you called *liquor*. Since you sounded quite fond of these spirits, I thought I would keep my experiments to myself and see if I could come up with this *liquor*. I suggested some ingredients and turned Antros loose; these are the results."

"Well, in truth," Antros broke in, momentarily forgetting that he was in the presence of his Great King, University Rector, and several masters, "these liquor spirits are much easier to conjure, because they don't require the high temperature of the oils we make in Kyblos. Oh, excuse me, Your Majesty!"

"You're excused, Antros. It's not everyday someone brings me a miracle such as this!" Kalvan took another long drink. "It even tastes good!"

Antros blushed so deeply he had to hide his face. He quickly began to pour goblets of brandy for all the assembled masters and in moments their words echoed Kalvan's.

"I think we might want to change the University coat-of-arms to include the noble grape vine," said Master Phylo.

"That may be going too far," said Kalvan, "but I would like to make a toast with the first fruit off the University vine. To the University of Hos-Hostigos, long may it prosper!"

"To Great King Kalvan, without whom there would be no University—or Hostigos!" toasted Rector Mytron, his fair skin turning red as he quaffed another goblet of brandy.

"To Pandros, God of Wine and Song," said Master Thalmoth, whose red nose was now burning like a hot coal.

"To Pandros!" echoed Phylo and several others.

After a dozen more rounds, two of the masters were slumped over the table and Thalmoth had wandered off singing ribald songs in search of less coarse company. Gasphros, a troubadour who had been attracted by the noise, had found a lyre, of some sort, and was strumming along in accompaniment to a song about marching into Hos-Harphax. It was a good thing the University wasn't coed yet, thought Kalvan, shaking his head.

As Antros re-filled his flagon, Rector Mytron said, "I am glad to see our labors bring pleasure for a change. I grow weary with all this talk of war and machines of warfare."

"Yes it's nice just to relax. Enjoy the fruits of your labor!" Kalvan started to laugh, until he noticed no one else got the allusion, but, of course, it was not a here-and-now bromide.

"Come here, Mytron. Sit next to me. Antros, pour us both another glass."

"By doing Galzar's work at the University, we are making the world safer for Dralm and the freedom to worship all gods. Here, have another drink."

Clearly not used to strong spirits, Mytron's head bobbed like an apple on a stick. "Maybe you are right."

"War is a terrible thing, but a necessary thing if people are to live their own lives instead of being enslaved by some tyrant—like Styphon's House, or Prince Balthar. You've seen the lash marks on Master Ermut's back."

Mytron's face blanched, and not just from strong drink. Ermut was a former Styphon's House Temple slave and his back was living proof of Styphon's House's corruption and cruelty.

"There is a lot of truth to your words, my Great King. Let me toast your health and say a prayer to Dralm that you may continue your reign for many years!"

II

Dalla walked into the smoky bar at Constellation House, looking for Tortha Karf's comforting presence. She was still exhausted from her visit with her brother, Tharn. She paused to take out a cigarette and three different men approached her to light it. She smiled graciously and used her own lighter. Verkan would have been proud.

"Over here, Dalla." She heard Tortha's familiar and comforting gravely voice.

She sat down at the booth and asked the robot bartender for a bourbon and cola. Unlike most First Level citizens, Dalla preferred the unobtrusive mechanical servants to the status enhancing proles that many of her contemporaries preferred. Possibly, it was because her adopted Sister, Zinganna, was a former prole, but she liked to think it was that she had more respect for outtime people than to use them as personal servants, no matter what the cachet.

Tortha was wearing breeches and a well-filled civilian tunic; his hair was streaked with gray and thinning in front. He was too practical and too much a stick-in-the-mud to have a hair treatment. He reminded Dalla of a big old cross bear, with a soft heart. She offered him a cigarette and was surprised to note that instead of a lighter he used one of the peculiar Kalvan time-line flint tinderboxes to light it. She wondered if it was significant, he probably missed hanging around with Verkan and the other boys.

"Thanks, Tortha, for coming to see me on such short notice. I know you just arrived from Fifth Level, but Verkan's so busy and I really need—"

"It's all right, Dalla. You can stop blathering. I take it you've just come back from another visit with your lovely younger brother."

"How did you know?"

"Hadron Tharn is the only person I know, besides your husband, who can break through your impenetrable good humor. And, since I've stopped my meddling, you and Verkan have been happier than I can ever remember."

"That wasn't all your fault, Tortha. I could have turned down some of those assignments. In those days I was younger and didn't realize how rare it is too meet a man of Verkan's caliber. I do now and I don't ever intend to forget it, or chance losing him again."

"Good. I don't have to tell you that I agree with you wholeheartedly. Now, tell me, what's the problem with Honorable Hadron Tharn?"

"I don't know, he's nastier than ever. I've overlooked his tantrums and mean behavior for years. He was always jealous of Verkan, you know. Before Verkan, he was such a sweet boy."

"Whoa. Now, wait a minute, Dalla. Is this the same Hadron Tharn I know? The one who burned your house down? And that was years before you met Vall."

"Yeah, well, maybe I exaggerated a bit. But, his personality took a real nose dive after Verkan came into the picture."

"Dalla, that might be because Verkan was the first man you really fell in love with."

"True," Dalla said, trying not to blush.

"I think Tharn's problems are deeper than mere sibling jealousy. Yes, I know you both were left to fend for yourselves, after your mother went outtime. Your father was always too busy to spend any time at home. He bedeviled the Department as Chief of the Opposition Party. It may sound horrible, but I was neither surprised or disappointed when the Bureau of Psych-Hygiene decided to put him in 'protective' custody."

Dalla felt her eyes begin to well again.

"Sorry, Dalla, damn this tongue of mine. I didn't mean to stick a soft spot."

"It's not father I'm feeling bad about; it's Tharn. Today, I finally saw him for the spoiled, mean, horrible little man that he's become. He's not a boy anymore, flirting with danger and oddball cults. He's a devious and—sadly—unprincipled grown-up, who I really don't know at all. If anything, I think he's . . ."

"You don't have to say it. I know all about your family."

"I know," Dalla said sadly, "Insanity runs through our family."

"Yes, and no." Tortha replied.

"What do you mean?"

"It always begins in the early thirties after the first longevity treatments. The longevity serum may well be the trigger."

"How do you know?"

Tortha looked very uncomfortable. "After your first compionate marriage with Verkan went sour, I decided to do a deep background check when I learned you two were getting back together. I also learned that the Psych-Hygiene people told this very thing to your brother and he disregarded it. It happened while he was at the University just before he got involved with those awful Axis people and got expelled for going outtime without a proper Paratime Permit. He knew that subsector was proscribed—"

"You don't have to defend yourself to me, Tortha. It was Tharn's decision to spend time with those terrible Nazis people. It wasn't your fault he got caught! He still looks up to them, you know; that's one of the reasons I believe he's insane himself. There, I've finally said it—admitted it to myself. He's as mad as grandfather and it scares me."

"That's not all that scares you, is it?"

"Tortha, you can see right through me! This is a secret I've never shared with anyone, not even Vall. Promise you won't ever tell."

"I promise, Dalla, you have my word."

"Good. There's no better bond. I'm worried about my own children becoming like Tharn or my father or his grandfather, well—you get the picture. I love children, but I'm afraid to have any of my own. Look at the horrible choice I have to offer: be sane and die soon, or live long and go crazy!"

Tortha shook his head. "That's not what I was expecting. I thought you might be worried about yourself."

"No. The family curse only strikes the males in our family; probably one reason why they marry so badly."

"That I didn't know. You could always adopt, and there are ways to guarantee birth sex."

"Sure, and give my daughters the same terrible choice I'm having to make! I won't do it."

"You could adopt, or get a surrogate mother, or clones of you and Verkan. Today on Home Time Line there are lots of choices."

"Yes, I know. But I want children from me—like Rylla and Kalvan are having. Still, the clone idea isn't bad. It would be nice to have a little Verkan around, one *I* could actually house train."

Tortha laughed. "Good luck. You can see how successful I was with the original."

Dalla laughed, too, feeling as though a terrible weight had moved from her shoulders. It was almost like having a father, talking with Tortha. "If you've made a study of the Hadron family, I guess you know the family secret too."

Tortha nodded, not saying a word.

"Does Verkan?"

Tortha shrugged. "I've never brought it up. I always believed if anyone should tell it, it would have to be you."

"Thank you, you old bear!"

Tortha actually blushed when she reached over and kissed him on the cheek.

"Should I tell him, Tortha?"

"That's for you to decide. It won't change his feelings for you that I know. Or I'm a complete romantic idiot."

Dalla laughed. "I will, I promise. But not now; poor Verkan, already has more problems than any three people I know; well, except for Kalvan and Rylla—and poor Ptosphes, of course. He still blames himself for the defeat at Tenabra."

"Not his fault; he was up against Styphon's heavy troops; and he's no Kalvan. But, my advice to you, young lady, is, don't wait too long. Secrets are burdens and no one understands that better than myself."

Dalla nodded. Tortha had spent almost half of his life protecting the Paratime Secret, and many times from the very people he was trying to protect. Now, her Verkan held the same untenable position.

To change the subject, she asked, "What are you doing here so far away from your farm?"

Tortha shook his big head. "It was getting boring, maybe I'm not cut out to be a farmer. And those rabbits!"

Dalla smiled mischievously, "That's not what I heard from Verkan. He told me about your nieces and their swimming lessons!"

Tortha blushed right down to his hair follicles. "Dralm damn-it! That blabber mouth!"

"Don't blame Verkan, I weaseled it out of him. Why did you really come?"

"Oh, you want the real reason as opposed to the fit for broadcast story. The truth is Dalla; I'm bored out of my skull. I'm tired of trapping rabbits and gophers. I'm tired of grapes and silly young girls. I'm tired of myself, I don't wear well; just ask any of my six former wives! I've spent the last three hundred years of my life doing important work and I'm still too young for the scrap heap. I came back here to help Verkan, if I can, or just help myself, if I can't."

"I understand. And, really, Tortha, Verkan needs all the help he can get. I've never seen him so 'involved' with an outtimer as he is with Kalvan—not that I blame him, I adore Kalvan and Rylla is already my best friend. Now he's fretting because he's stuck dealing with this Europo-American shut-down project of his! I've been going to all these meetings and I can tell you it's going nowhere. Can you pump him some sunlight on the issue, Chief?"

"Ex-Chief—really Dalla," Tortha said, trying to hide a big grin.

"Sure, but you'll always be Chief to me. Anyway, Europo-American has become the public 'Sector;' it's been that way since they brought back jazz and flappers. You know how these outtime fads run; everyone was Indo-Turanian crazy when I was a girl. I still remember practicing yoga, wearing a turban and those tantric exercises, although those still come in handy with Vall."

Tortha turned pink again.

She smacked him on the shoulder, playfully. "You've been with those nieces of yours for too long, Tortha. Anyway, it's gotten worse ever since rock and racket became popular. Remember when every nightclub had to have their own 'Elvis?'"

"What a headache for the Paracops! They were hi-jacking them from every subsector where that crazy noise was still undiscovered. For a while we had to guard that dumb hillbilly truck driver on a thousand time-lines. I'm still surprised we never designated an Elvis Subsector!"

"Verkan's really never paid it any attention, because he doesn't hear or see what he doesn't like. I can't get through to my husband, because he's a snob—and I mean that lovingly—he just doesn't realize that everyone on Home Time Line doesn't have his class or taste. Well, it's worse here now, since the Beatles. Not the insects, it's another noisy Europo-American singing combo. They're even noisier and louder than Elvis, if that's possible. And then there are the flat screen films and film stars—Marilyn Monroe, Clark Gable, Humphrey Bogart, and now James Dean—and art deco and all sorts of nonsense. Europo-American is—to paraphrase one of their aphorisms—the "cat's pajamas" and if Verkan doesn't quit this silly crusade of his he's going to derail his job and possibly the Paratime Police along with him."

"Wow!" Tortha replied. "Dalla, you've just given me a needler shot of reality. Maybe we have the wrong Chief! I'm even worse than Verkan, when it comes to these crazes. And I never had any children, except you two—by proxy, of course—to teach me any different. I'll try to talk Verkan into holding off on this shutdown for a few decades until all this Europo-American sheep-dip becomes old hat. It will; I've seen half a dozen of these crazes just since I've been Chief. Meanwhile, you stay on top of these committees and study groups."

"Good. I need something to keep me occupied while Verkan's glued to his Chief's chair. But what about you? What are you going to do?"

"Dalla, I don't know. Hang around the office, I guess, until Vall throws me out."

"Well, I know some other people who need some help. And you would definitely be an asset to them."

"Really. Who?"

"Rylla and Kalvan."

"I'm an ex-Paratimer. I can't deal in contamination—"

"Oh, stop being so huffy, Tortha. Hear me out. Sometimes you remind me so much of Verkan. The two of you! Anyway, you could give them moral support and be a Dutch uncle. I'm sure Verkan could come up with a suitable disguise. And don't tell me you're not interested—I see that smile."

"Dalla, that might be a very good idea. I'm curious about Kalvan and his lady, Rylla, that I've heard so much about. I would like to meet them. And, with this Styphon's House Crusade, it sure won't be boring!"

"Tortha, you've just said a mouthful!" They both laughed.

EIGHT

I

The great stone walls of Balph rose up all around him, while the air was torn apart by the boom of cannon fire. Kalvan was shackled and bound with gold and silver chains. Dozens of yellow-robed Archpriests of the Inner Circle were carrying him toward a giant hopped-iron bombard. It wasn't until they reached the barrel that he realized they meant to stuff him inside. He broke one of the golden shackles and attempted to force his escape, but the Archpriests only gripped him tighter.

Where were Rylla and baby Demia? He tried to scream but they stuffed wadding cloth deep into his mouth. The air was filled with the yells and screams of a great multitude, all chanting, "Kill the Daemon Kalvan! Kill the Daemon! Kill the Daemon!"

Again he tried to wrestle away, but the Archpriests manhandled him into the giant bombards borehole. Outside everything was suddenly still and he could hear the crackle of the burning fuse—

"Kalvan, Kalvan! Is everything all right?"

He opened his eyes to a throbbing headache and a blurry view of Rylla leaning over him. "Where am I?"

"In bed. You must have come home at dawn, my husband. It's almost mid-day and Duke Skranga is here for his audience."

Kalvan fell back into his goose down pillow and groaned. "Help me, Dralm, I have the murthering mother of all headaches, and the father, brother and sister, too. Where was I last night?"

"You were supposed to be at the new University," in a tone-of-voice that hinted if he hadn't been there, he would soon come to more than wish he had.

"Ahhh. I remember now. Master Ermut's new brandy. It must have had a higher proof than the Hostigi mint! I must warn him about over distillation. Not that I could fault the smoothness. Rylla, please bring me my pipe."

"Yes, my darling. How about your crown, too?"

"Ouch! No . . . thank you. I don't think it would fit. Can I cancel the audience with Skranga?"

"No. You've put him off twice already. Do it again and he'll think there's something amiss."

"Yes, and that man could read larceny in tea leaves. As usual, you're right. Maybe if I had another spot of that brandy, it might help."

"I wouldn't begin to know where to look," Rylla replied, "nor am I about to fetch and carry for his Most Debauched Majesty!"

Kalvan tried to grin, but it hurt too much. "You're only jealous because you missed out."

"It wouldn't be the first time," Rylla said, her wrist pressed back against her forehead in a pose of a long-suffering wife—something Rylla would never allow to happen. "I'll get Cleon and he can fetch you some winter wine."

"Thank you, darling." Kalvan said, as he tamped down the bowl of his pipe and then used his gold tinderbox—a gift from Rylla—to light it. "Now is Harmakros about? I'd like to have him attend this little meeting."

"Last I saw, he was waiting patiently in your private audience chamber."

"Dralm-damn it! I never thought I'd say it, but there is such a thing as being too contentious. Back home we give people like Harmakros and Prince Phrames halos. Ermut, well, the Master might win a forked tail—for the introduction of spirits, at the least, by the Temperance League. I'll have to talk with Master Ermut about shortening the distillation period of his brandy."

Rylla rolled her eyes, paused to light one of her silver-inlaid redstone pipes, and added, "Or maybe tell him to pour smaller portions."

"Hush, woman, hush. I've got to get dressed. Cleon get in here!"

After a goblet of winter wine and with his hose and breeches on, Kalvan almost felt human again. He sucked in his stomach as Cleon pulled the stays and tied up the cords to his doublet. Kalvan had been totally against having personal body servants, until the first time he'd had to put on one of these jacket-shirts, or doublets, all by himself. Rylla had laughed so hard she'd fallen to the floor and Kalvan had realized that he was going to have to have his own personal servants or face a total loss of dignity in the Royal Bedchambers.

Now Cleon was as indispensable as his sword's scabbard and he didn't know how he got along without him for so long. Kalvan tottered to his audience chamber and found Harmakros and Duke Skranga, the former horse-trader turned intelligence chief, deep in conversation. They both stood as he entered. "Sit down, sit down, both of you,"

They both waited until Kalvan was finished lowering himself into the chair behind his desk before sitting down. "Is His Majesty all right?" Harmakros asked, with concern written all over his face. Skranga sat there with a knowing grin which told Kalvan that either his intelligence gathering network was better than he knew about, or that Skranga had been in his boots so often he could tell a fellow sufferer at first glance.

"Nothing serious, just a bit more of Ermut's new spirits than necessary and a spot of indigestion. Now, Duke Skranga, what's this news that's so important I had to leave my sickbed to hear it?"

"As I was just telling Captain-General Harmakros, Your Majesty. Great King Kaiphranos of Hos-Harphax is dead. He died in the bed he hasn't left since the fateful Battle of Chothros Heights, where his eldest son died of sheer stupidity. I don't doubt they had to burn the bed in the royal chambers since it positively reeked of noxious vapors, or so the rumors go."

Considering the general bathing habits of here-and-now, or lack thereof, Kalvan didn't doubt that for a moment. Still a Great King should go out with a bang, but it appeared that Kaiphranos the Timid had gone out with barely a good sneeze. Kalvan had hoped the old king might have stayed bed-ridden for a few more years, thereby leaving Hos-Harphax in a permanent succession crisis and Kalvan free to wage war directly on Styphon's lesser lieutenants.

Kalvan mentally reviewed the Harphaxi line of succession. Kaiphranos's only remaining son was Prince Selestros, a whoremonger and slave-of-the-flesh, who had already lost all the love of the Prince Electors and would be lucky to get the position of Royal Slop-Catcher. Next in line was the late King's brother, Duke Lysandros, who was so far into Styphon's pocket that even the debauched Princes of Hos-Harphax, spoiled by too many years of Kaiphranos's light rein, were revolted. After those two, there was a gaggle of greedy cousins emboldened by Kaiphranos's mismanagement and their own venal natures.

"Duke Skranga, who do you think will come out on top in the race for Great King of Hos-Harphax?"

Skranga picked at the fringe of his sparse red beard for a few moments. "If I were a bettin' man, I'd place my gold on the old fool's younger brother, Grand Duke Lysandros. Yes I would. He's got all of Styphon's gold he can carry and a natural gift, that unfortunately his older brother was spared— the gift of leadership. It'll take him six moons or so to whip the Princes and Electors into shape, but for my money there's no doubt he will be the next Great King. The rest of the Harphaxi are curs fighting over a bone too big for their greedy mouths."

"What's your opinion, Harmakros?"

"I agree with Duke Skranga, Your Majesty. Duke Lysandros is the only high lord they have who can lead an army. Before he can claim the Iron Throne, we need to move our siege train into Hos-Harphax, invest Harphax City and once the city is taken, put forth Your Majesty as Great King of Hos-Hostigos and Hos-Harphax. Prince Selestros and Lysandros can be drawn-and-quartered for the whoresons they are." Harmakros paused to rub his hands together. "And that, Your Majesty, will end the Harphaxi Succession issue."

Harmakros was a brilliant tactician and a fine military leader, but he was still a little too atrocity happy. Phrames, now Prince of Beshta, had taken off some of Harmakros's sharp edges with his almost too-good-to-be-true character, but with Phrames in Beshta, Harmakros was reverting a little too much to type.

"This is something We will have to consider. What are your further thoughts on the matter, Skranga?"

"If there's no coronation by spring campaign time, I say go for the Throne. It can't make you any more enemies in Hos-Harphax than you already have and it will neutralize a great many more than you will gain.

Although, I don't suspect it will be seen with great favor in Hos-Agrys and Hos-Zygros; in Hos-Ktemnos, *nothing* you do will ever be seen with any favor. I say you might as well be shot for a wolf, as skinned for a lamb.

"But more importantly, Your Majesty, it depends upon how fast the Electors make their decision. If they elect a new Great King before spring, then it might not be worth your coin to invade Hos-Harphax. We do know that after last spring's whippin' it'll be a year or two before the Harphaxi can muster enough troops to fill a parade ground."

"I would like to go into Hos-Harphax next spring," Kalvan said, thoughtfully, as he refilled his pipe. "If we could knock Hos-Harphax out of the war that would leave us with only one major front to worry about. That would also put the lid on Great King Demistophon's ambitions and keep him in Hos-Agrys where he belongs.

"On the other hand, I don't think it would be wise to go for the Harphaxi crown, since it would give Styphon's House more ammunition than I would gain. It was shock enough when I went from Lord Kalvan to Great King Kalvan. Great King Napoleon made just that mistake, back where I came from, and he found himself in a war every time he walked to the latrine.

"What I need is a Prince I can trust and make him Great King of Hos-Harphax."

"How about Prince Phrames," Harmakros said. "Look at how well he's doing in Beshta. With very little help from Your Majesty, he's raised and bought enough grain that there'll be porridge in every farm and hut in Beshta this winter."

"An excellent candidate, Harmakros. Although he's not seasoned enough as Prince to satisfy most of the Harphaxi nobles."

"Yes, better an unknown Prince for King, than one they know all too well, Your Majesty."

"True. It worked well in my case. All that leaves is conquering Hos-Harphax! Our first objective must be to stop the Electors from electing a new Great King, especially Grand Duke Lysandros since he's firmly in Styphon's House's hip pocket."

"That might not be as difficult as you imagine, Your Majesty," Skranga said, with a wolfish grin. "When Your Majesty formed the Great Kingdom of Hos-Hostigos last year, you took with you eight of the Harphaxi Princedoms and five Electors, the Electors of Sask, Nyklos, Ulthor, Kyblos, and Nostor. That takes the original number of Electors down from thirteen to eight, which means there is no way they can split a tie. Already they are divided as to the means of replacing the five missing Electors, the minority position, or just creating one new one. This is compounded by the succession crisis in Thaphigos, brought about when Prince Phrames killed Prince Acestocleus."

Kalvan had almost forgotten about that crisis, since he had so many of his own. Acestocleus had been the only son of the man who usurped the Princedom of Thaphigos twenty years ago. Since Acestocleus had died without issue, that had brought forth more than half-a-dozen claimants from the old Princely House, who had been driven into Hos-Agrys. Two of them had ties by marriage to the Agrysi Royal House, which had always wanted to add the border Princedom of Thaphigos to Hos-Agrys.

It was a real mare's nest, in many ways reminiscent of the conflicting claims made by Medieval France and Austria upon the duchy of Burgundy after the death of Charles the Bold. It appeared to be fertile ground indeed for the cunning talents of his former horse-trader turned Chief of Intelligence, Duke Skranga.

"This means," Kalvan said, "that the Harphaxi Electors have to solve their problems of membership before they can decide who will be the next Great King."

"Yes, and my agent in Harphax City said that this Election could take two or three moons."

"It would be even better if it took them until next spring," Kalvan said, "then they could let the Army of Hostigos solve their dilemma. Skranga, I think you're just the man to make sure they don't make that decision, or any other."

Skranga rubbed his almost bald pate vigorously. "This comes as quite a surprise, Your Majesty. I've got a few odds and ends to tie up before I can leave Hostigos and I have neglected my estates in Nostor."

Kalvan had heard about some of Skranga's ends, most notably the wives and mistresses of several noble houses. Despite his plucked-chicken body and homely face, Skranga was a deadly cocksman, and had cut quite a swathe through the war widows during the spring campaign. In fact,

Kalvan might be doing the Duke a favor by getting him out of the capital before his luck ran out.

"It's going to be expensive, Your Majesty. I'll need to purchase a good townhouse in Harphax City, a new noble patent—I know just who to buy one from, and a score of courtesans."

"Courtesans!" Harmakros cried. "Hos-Harphax is filled with war widows."

The Duke tried to look insulted, but couldn't pull it off.

Kalvan responded before an argument ensued. "Here, Skranga, I'll write you out a requisition from the Royal Treasury for ten thousand ounces of gold and fifty thousand ounces of silver."

Skranga all but rubbed his hands with glee. Then his face dropped as he remembered some local business that had to be brought to conclusion. "May I be dismissed, Your Majesty, I have many things to do before I can depart?"

"Dismissed. And give the Baroness Phania my love."

Kalvan saw a sight he had never expected to behold: Duke Skranga blushing cherry red from the top of his bald crown to his fingertips.

Harmakros looked at Kalvan in wonderment. "Who would have ever thought—the Baroness Phania? How do you know such intimacies, Your Majesty?"

"Don't give me all the credit, Harmakros. You can thank Great Queen Rylla. There isn't a belch or baby she doesn't know about two minutes after gestation anywhere in Tarr-Hostigos and Hostigos Town, my friend. That woman is a wonder to behold."

II

Count Sestembar followed Highpriest Lathrox through the High Temple of Dralm's back entrance, into a small vestibule and down a long hall to a closed plank door. Lathrox rapped his knuckles three times in succession and the door squeaked open. Through the smoke and candlelight Sestembar could see a hands-count of priests in blue robes. "Follow me," Highpriest Lathrox said.

The Count was given a seat at the foot of the table, as Lathrox introduced him, "I will not give any names, but our emissary is highly placed at the Court of Great King Sopharar. He speaks for the Royal family."

Sestembar stood and bowed, then dropped a large saddlebag full of gold coins on the table. It landed with a resounding thud. "A small donation for the High Temple. Count Sestembar, at your service."

The clank of gold coins brought smiles all around the table, except upon the face of the Highpriest of the High Temple of Hos-Agrys, who Sestembar identified by the eight-pointed golden star he wore suspended on a thick gold chain around his neck.

The Highpriest pointed a finger at him, asking, "Why do you ask us to meet like thieves? If your Great King grants his support to Allfather Dralm, let him do so openly."

Sestembar groaned to himself. "Not all his princes share the Great King's belief in Allfather Dralm."

Highpriest Lathrox nodded piously, indicating these words were true.

Of course they were, Sestembar thought, *all the princes of Hos-Zygros collected together couldn't agree on the color of the sky.* "Many of them argue that the Ivory Throne of Hos-Zygros should support Archpriest Syclos and Styphon's House."

There was the hiss of indrawn breath. One highpriest began to cough.

Highpriest Lathrox added, "Highpriest Davros, I do not see Great King Demistophon attending services at the High Temple."

Davros frowned and started to speak.

Before any words were spoken that could not be taken back, Sestembar said, "Of course, my master does not intend to follow the false god, Styphon." That got their attention. "His worry is that the Council of Dralm will prematurely support the Usurper Kalvan, who calls himself Great King of Hos-Hostigos."

"Why shouldn't we support Kalvan?" the elderly Highpriest asked.

"Kalvan shows proper piety and offerings toward the Allfather," another added.

Sestembar smiled to himself. "True, this Kalvan outwardly makes the proper motions of respect. But really, who is this man? I have heard he is a demi-god sent from the Cold Lands?"

He could tell from the tittering murmurs that he had hit a sensitive subject.

"How do we ascertain that this is true?" Sestembar shrugged his shoulders. "What if Kalvan were one of Hadron's demons, come to lead us astray with false promises and devotions?"

"Old Xentos has met Kalvan," a younger priest said. "Xentos tells us many good things about him; Kalvan has proper piety and shows respect for all people, not just the nobility."

"Wouldn't a demon in human form do such to disguise his true intentions? Styphon himself was said to be a Daemon sent from Hadron's Hall at the bidding of his snake-headed master. Where else could have Kalvan learned the fireseed formula, but in Hadron's Hall?"

Everyone at the table was talking now. Highpriest Davros pounded his fist on the table to demand quiet. "These questions of yours have no answers. We do not know what Dralm's Will is concerning Kalvan. If he were a demi-god, I do think Dralm would have given us a sign or portent. Yet, I doubt that Kalvan is a devil. The Council must find out what he truly is before we declare him a demon, or pledge our support. Otherwise, we risk becoming Hadron's tool, may Dralm forgive us!" He quickly circled the eight-pointed white star on his chest, as did several of the other highpriests.

"What do we tell Xentos," the younger priest asked. "He has come to the High Temple requesting the aid of Council and the princes of Hos-Agrys for Great King Kalvan."

"Xentos is a pious priest, but—truth be known," Davros said, "he has never before been outside the small Princedom of Hostigos and still has straw in his mattress."

Several of the highpriests laughed out loud.

"Do not laugh. I have noticed that many of our simpler brethren, those who live in the provincial towns and villages, have great respect for his simple words and strong belief."

"This is true," the younger priest confirmed. "As do many who attend the Council."

"I have also noticed that as the moons have passed his protestations upon Kalvan's behalf have become fewer and fewer. I suggest we offer him a high post that he cannot in good *conscience* turn down and let him make our decision for us."

"What if he offers the Temple's support to his friend Kalvan?" Sestembar asked.

Highpriest Davros laughed. "Xentos is a good horse, when we lead him to the right grass he will chew it up, even if it cuts his tongue."

"This is good news," Sestembar said. "I would not like to see Allfather Dralm's Temple torn apart as Styphon's House has been by different factions. Although, Praise Dralm, it is good work to sow discord among the false god's supporters."

This time everyone nodded and circled their breasts.

NINE

I

Grand Master Soton, ruler and highpriest of the Zarthani Knights, jerked hard on the reins of his destrier as ten to twelve thousand shouting warriors advanced out of the forest on the other side of the Odra Valley. He'd had to ride his last warhorse into the ground during the retreat from Phyrax Field and his new destrier was not as battle hardened, as he liked. Blasted Fireseed War was harder on the horses than the men!

Below the ridge, where Soton himself was commanding the Fifteenth Lance as a reserve, were five Lances of Knights drawn in a line four ranks deep. The Urgothi barbarians, from across the Great Mother River, were unfamiliar with the Knight's tactics or they would have never been so easily goaded into an attack. It would have been next to impossible to coax such a suicidal charge from a Sastragathi warband, who had cut their teeth fighting the Knights and their allies.

Knight Commander Aristocles, Soton's aide-de-camp, turned in his saddle, and asked, "Can we trust Commander Lestros to set the noose on these barbarians, Grand Master Soton?"

"Commander Lestros has a good battle record with the Eighteenth. I wanted to see firsthand how he does on his own since we need a replacement commander for Knight Commander Geox, formerly of the Third Wedge."

"Yes, he died at the Battle of Chothros Heights."

"With too Dralm-damned many other Knights," Soton answered. "Good men wasted trying to stiffen the Royal rotters of Hos-Harphax. We wouldn't be in this mess today if we had our full complement of troops. Not that I haven't enjoyed being in the field myself; especially after three moons of listening to Archpriest Roxthar's endless harangues in Balph before I escaped to the Fortress and a mountain of documents. I fear that upon my return to Tarr-Ceros, there will be another storeroom of parchment waiting—most of it from those Balph blabbermouths!"

"I find it difficult to believe, but wasn't it Archpriest Roxthar who saved you from being the Inner Circle's scapegoat for the defeat at Phyrax Field?"

"Yes, but at the cost of my eardrums! And, I'm sure, Roxthar's price will be steep. Someday I may wish I was boiled in that barrel of tallow that Archpriest Dracar had set to bubbling."

"Blast the Inner Circle and all its machinations!" Aristocles cried. "The fools would boil alive the only commander in the Five Kingdoms who has defeated the Daemon Kalvan in his own lair. Next time we'll show this Usurper Kalvan the sharp points of our lance-heads. Although, first, we ought to smoke out that wasp's nest in Balph!"

"Watch your words, Aristocles! I've grown fond of your tough hide and there's Styphon's Own Ears everywhere—even among our own ranks. The Inner Circle trusts no one, not even its own Holy Arm. But, speaking of the Usurper Kalvan, he is why we need a commander for the Third Wedge who has fought in the Northern Kingdoms. The Third hasn't been north of Tarr-Odra in a hundred years. Before he took his vows, Lestros served as a mercenary captain in Hos-Agrys."

"Then you plan to return to Hostigos, Grand Master?"

"Yes, but not this year. Of the four Lances that fought the Hostigi at Chothros Heights, only one returned. The others have their banners hung in the Hall of Heroes in Tarr-Ceros. At the Battle of Phyrax, we left enough Knights on the field to man three Lances more along with three thousand dead Order Foot. Even with all the new recruits, it will take years of training before we can muster at our former strength again; that is, if we don't spend the next three winters fighting nomads!"

"Never in my lifetime, Grand Master, has their been such a stirring of the nomads as we have seen in these times. It is as if the Daemon Kalvan has loosed all of Hadron's demons and imps upon their backsides!"

"This is no demonic visitation, unless you count the devil priests of the Mexicotál—who dress in human skin—as demons, which surely those who live in Xiphlon do," Soton said. To advance their siege at Xiphlon, the Mexicotál had pushed the fierce desert Ruthani tribes into the Sea of Grass, thereby shoving the Urgothi, Zarthani, and Ruthani tribesmen living there both north and east. Those tribes, in turn, had put pressure on the clans living near Xiphlon, Wulfula and Dorg, forcing many of them to cross the Great Mother River and move into the Lower Sastragath. Now all the Sastragath was a boil, with only the Knights between them and the Lower Kingdoms.

"Look, the Urgothi warriors draw closer!"

The warband was now completely out of the forest and almost halfway across the valley floor. About a third of the tribesmen were on horseback, armed with lance and sword, while the rest were on foot with their great swords and buffalo-hide shields. The deep-toned Zarthani war horns sounded and the two end Lances began to move out, a movement that would only be complete when they had encircled the warband. The five hundred mounted auxiliaries, mostly armed with bow or arquebus, on each side would form the glue between the Lances as they pressed the encirclement home.

In answer to the bellow of the Zarthani war horns, a loud roar went up from the Urgothi, who were screaming and beating their swords and spears against their shield hides. As individual warriors, thought Soton, the Urgothi were without peer: brave to a fault, fearless with the intoxication with their own battle prowess and anger, strong as bulls and able to fight without pause for hours. Fortunately, for the Knights—who were outnumbered in this battle at more than two to one—when the Urgothi fought as a unit, it was as a mindless rabble, each warrior fighting for his own glory and fame.

This, century after century, had always been their undoing.

The Urgothi were a handsome people, big, blond, and fair skinned, much like the Zarthani race, except taller and more bellicose. Their defeat here would be sorrowful, at least to Soton, who had grown up in a border village with its menials and field slaves. He had seen all the guises of slavery, and the Urgothi men, being too spirited and warlike for peaceful labor, would be sold as galley slaves or used as Styphon's House temple-farm slaves. The women would be sold, the fair ones as concubines, their uglier sisters as household servants or drabs to fill soldiers' brothels. A sad end for an honorable and warlike people.

There was another bellow of the Zarthani war horns and the Fourteenth and Seventeenth Lances began to move forward, linked behind to the Thirteenth, Eighteenth and Ninth. The warband was still in one great mass and it looked to Soton like the encirclement might well succeed. A coup for Lestros if it was successful and almost certain promotion to Knight Commander.

The Urgothi army was now within spear-throwing distance of the Knights now crescent-shaped line. There was a loud roar and the sky darkened with flying spears and arrows. A score or two of horses went down, toppling Knights out of their saddles, but most held the line protected by both the distance and their armor. As a rule the Knights were very heavily armored, with the leading hundred Brethren Knights of each Lance in full armor, the following two hundred Confrere Knights in three-quarter lobster-armor, and the next two hundred Sergeants in back-and-breast. Only the oath-brothers, the blood-sworn brother of each Knight, were lightly armored, with cotton-padded gambesons and chain mail shirts.

Soton heard the first screams from the wounded horses and felt his stomach wrench. Even after thirty years of warfare and two score battles, it was the cries from the wounded horses that bothered him most.

Blast and curse the Mexicotál priests who released these heathens upon his lands and domain like a plague of locusts. Let the Archpriests claim it was demons' work, a curse brought upon the land when the Daemon Kalvan gave the fireseed secret to all without Styphon's Blessing. Soton knew that for the poppycock it was; he didn't believe in demons of any sort, or gods, for that matter. Styphon himself was a fraud engineered by priests greedy for their own profit and comfort.

It was not Soton's belief in any god that bound him to Styphon's House, but the undeniable fact that the Temple had raised him from a simple peasant boy to the most important military leader in the Five Kingdoms. The Temple was his family, and, because of this, they owned his loyalty and his life. He knew that in great part it was his innate ability that had lifted him so high; yet he could never forget that Styphon's House was the instrument of his elevation.

The Urgothi nomads were now close enough to the Knights' line they were drawing stray pistol fire. Soton mentally cursed those fools who fired precious rounds before the enemy was within pistol range. Some of the shots were coming from the Urgothi ranks as well, since the ban on fireseed sales to the tribesmen was as much violated as honored—often by the Temple's own priests. Twice he had had to go to Balph in person to have the Inner Circle reprimand highpriests who were selling fireseed to the tribesmen. It was bad enough the Temple had sold fireseed in secret to the Mexicotál for many years, a secret—that if it got out—could do more harm than all of Kalvan's armies. The Inner Circle had finally stopped all fireseed sales to the Mexicotál, after the invasion of Xiphlon— even the most corrupt upperpriests realized that if Xiphlon fell, the Mexicotál would next move into the Sastragath and from there into the Five Kingdoms.   •

The front ranks of the Fourteenth and Seventeenth Lances were almost to the rear of the Urgothi warband, when Soton saw the first of several dozen war chariots leaving the forest. "By Ormaz's beard!" he cursed, slamming his fist against the saddle pommel.

"Aristocles, tell Lestros the nomads have forty to fifty war chariots coming his way. Order him to hold the line with the Eighteenth reserve— no matter what the Urgothi throw at him!"

Aristocles nodded and quickly rode down the grassy embankment. The young Sergeant, who had brought the news of the invasion, was chomping at the bit as he waited beside Soton and his bodyguards. It would temper his mettle. Soton was not displeased by the younger man's desire to cross swords with the enemy. Sarmoth would see action soon enough. He had sent Knight Commander Aristocles, instead of the Sergeant, because he knew Lestros would have to listen to a superior officer, and thus not hare off in some wild glory charge.

Soton had fought against chariots a few times in his career and that had been across the Great Mother River, where the ground was more level and less forested. He could only guess at the price the Urgothi had paid ferrying those big war chariots across the river and the swamplands that bordered it.

The Urgothi line was now so close to the Knights, that from where Soton sat, the two lines appeared to merge. Then the first salvo rang out.

A ripple of falling men and horses suddenly ran along the front of the Urgothi warband like a wave. There were two more big salvos of pistol and musketoon shots before the two lines merged. With all the pre-loaded guns fired, it was now hand-to-hand combat; sabers against flesh and rawhide, spears against armor. In a static fight the Urgothi were doomed unless they could disorder the ranks of the armored horsemen holding firm against their front.

Soton watched with mounting apprehension as the warband parted in the center to let the war chariots reach the front ranks. The Fourteenth and Seventeenth Lances had completed their encirclement of the warband, but that would mean little if the chariots punched a hole in the front ranks of the Thirteenth, Eighteenth and Ninth Lances.

With King Commander Aristocles at the front with Commander Lestros, that left him in command of the Fifteenth Lance.

"Dress ranks," he shouted. There was a creaking of leather and steel as the Fifteenth assembled into battle formation. "Move out!"

"Sound the charge!" he ordered, moments later the great warhorns sounded. As the Fifteenth Lance, trotted down the ridge, Soton could see that the chariots were much larger than he had thought. Big four-horse drawn war chariots, with leather armor and steel bosses, each one holding four to five warriors and a driver. The first line of chariots hit the Knights' center at an angle in a tangle of flying chariots, horses and men. The Thirteenth held, but it was wavering. Lestros's Eighteenth, the reserve, was rushing to fill the gaps. The Ninth Lance, not having taken the full brunt of the charge was holding firm.

Soton's Lance had now reached the bottom third of the ridge. "Charge!" he cried, as the second line of chariots broke through the Eighteenth's thin line of reserves, stretched to its limits to cover both the Thirteen and Sixteenth's rear. Soton was racing down the bottom of the incline at the head of the Fifteenth; a foolhardy place for a commander, he knew, but where his Knights needed him. Only his presence and the reinforcements behind him would stop the Thirteenth and Eighteenth Lances from routing, as well as give them the heart to reform ranks and charge again into the mad scythe of barbarian spears and swords.

In less than a few heartbeats Soton had reached the furthermost chariot and he emptied both of his horse pistols into the face of a red-mustached chieftain, with blue tattoos all over his face. Then he was using his war-hammer to ward off a long thrusting spear, when a Brethren lace-tip caught the barbarian under the armpit.

The young Sergeant had his hands full with a nomad chieftain, with a golden torc encircling his neck.

While the shock of impact was great upon a stationary line, the chariots did not fare so well against charging Knights armed with lances and pistols. But, unfortunately, when the last chariot was halted and its crew butchered, the chariots had done their job. The break in the Order's line was now a flood as thousands of barbarians escaped the encircling ranks. By the time Soton was able to re-form the tattered Thirteenth and Eighteenth Lances over half of the warband had already escaped. Soon the majority of the encircled Urgothi, realizing they were trapped, threw down their weapons and shields in surrender. The rest were spitted like ducks in a net and pro-vided about as much sport.

It was a victory of sorts, but not the total victory he preferred. To Soton the fun of war was the strategic pitting of his men and will against that of his opponents. The slaughter and butchery afterwards was the business side he didn't like, although, he realized its necessity. Kindness and mercy were always viewed by the barbarian mind as a sign of weakness and resulted in more warfare. Only strength and ruthless power were understood and prop-erly feared. Soton had spent a lifetime teaching both respect and fear to the various tribes and clans of the Lower and Upper Sastragath and, until now, there had been more peace under his reign in the Sastragath than there had been in the previous century.

Now it appeared he was going to have to tame them all over again, if the war with Kalvan allowed him time and the men to do the job. Why couldn't the gods have released this plague of barbarians on Kalvan and Hos-Hostigos? Why not? Why not indeed!

Soton sat on his horse as if he were a statue, his mind awhirl, until Knight Commander Aristocles rode up and broke the spell. "Grand Master, are you all right?"

Soton shook his head to clear his thoughts. "Yes, I'm fine."

He saw fresh blood all over the Knight Commanders' black tunic, and asked. "What about yourself?"

Aristocles looked down in surprise. "Not mine! Only a few bruises and minor cuts, nothing serious. From the way you sat, Grand Master, I thought you'd taken a blow to the head."

"More of a bolt, than a blow, Aristocles. I think I may have found a way to stop this slaughter and maybe stop Kalvan as well."

"You would win Galzar's Blessing, were you to accomplish such a wondrous thing. Also, my Lord, another messenger from Balph is here to see you."

"Bring him here," Soton said, with exasperation. *Where else can a man find peace, if not in the middle of a battlefield, from meddling priests?*

The messenger was dressed in a travel-stained gray tunic trimmed in orange, indicating he was an Archpriest. It must be a powerful message indeed, thought Soton, to bring an Archpriest this far from his lair. Since Roxthar's ascension, the Temple seemed to be breeding a tougher line of priests. It was too bad that Roxthar was crazier than a sun-struck Sastragathi rattlesnake priest with a viper in each hand.

"Master Soton, I am Archpriest Prysos. I have a message for you from the First Speaker, Archpriest Anaxthenes."

"It is *Grand* Master Soton, you are speaking with priest," he said, marking each syllable with a swing of his gory warhammer.

The Archpriests face paled, draining the hauteur and arrogance, as each swing of the warhammer ended only a finger-joint away from his hooded face.

"Yes, Grand Master, I . . . I . . . I have good news. Good news for all of Styphon's House. The traitor Kaiphranos of Hos-Harphax has died in his bed."

"Great King Kaiphranos dead!" Soton said, feeling as if one of the pillars of the earth had fallen. Kaiphranos had been King of Hos-Harphax since he'd been a child, longer than Supreme Priest Sesklos had been Styphon's Voice.

His warhammer was stilled and the Archpriests' color was returning. "The First Speaker wants you to return to Balph at once for a private audience."

Soton's warhammer rose.

"At your convenience, of course, Grand Master Soton. But it is most urgent. With the traitor Kaiphranos gone to Hadron's realm, Styphon's work can go on unhampered and with the help of his servant Lysandros."

"Kaiphranos was a doddering old fool, but never a traitor. His eldest son died fighting for Styphon! Remember that, priest."

The Archpriests eyes were riveted to Soton's warhammer. "Yes, Grand Master."

A year ago Great King Kaiphranos had been Styphon's friend and ally, until he lost his beloved son in the war against Kalvan and went into seclusion in his bedchamber. Now he was a traitor and fool. Soton wondered how his own epitaph would read. The Inner Circle of Styphon's House had all but branded him a traitor, for having the bad fortune to lose the Battle of Phyrax against Kalvan. Since that experience, he had much more sympathy—even be they fools—for the Kaiphranoses of this world.

"Yes, as soon as this business is done," Soton stopped, to direct his hand at the slaughter of the encircled and bottled Urgothi in Yargos' Pasture.

"A great victory for Styphon!" cried Archpriest Prysos.

If he was Anaxthenes tool, Soton was certain this was no true believer he was dealing with. "I have business of my own to discuss with Archpriest Anaxthenes. The timing is good." Yes, he would need additional men and gold if his plan to drive the barbarians up the Sastragath and into Hostigos, and Kalvan's lands, were to work. By the Mace of Galzar, this would be one job he would thoroughly enjoy. Let Kalvan dull his swords on the barbarian's thick hides, while Soton and the Knights sharpened theirs for the battles to come.

II

"It's beginning to appear, Vall," Paratime Commissioner Tortha Karf said, "that you're more interested in playing Colonel Verkan of the Hos-Hostigos Mounted Rifles than you are in being Chief of the Paratime Police,"

"That's hitting below the belt, Tortha," Verkan said, running his fingers through his blonde beard. "I know I haven't been back on Home Time Line for more than two ten-days, but it's imperative that I establish my cover in Greffa as Verkan the trader. If I don't, one of these days some Grefftscharrer merchant is going to arrive in Hostigos Town and someone's going to ask him about the merchant prince Verkan, and he's going to answer,

'Verkan who?' Then, not only will two years of hard work be plunged down the drain, but also the Paratime Secret itself will be endangered, along with Great King Kalvan and his family. You know how those Dhergabar University Professors would like to get their hands on a 'noble savage' like Kalvan and pick him apart in one of their Mentalist labs."

Tortha nodded his head in agreement.

The Paratime Secret was the keystone of First Level civilization. The only inflexible law concerning outtime activities was that the secret of Paratemporal Transposition must be kept inviolate. Life had been grim on Home Time Line twelve thousand years ago, when his ancestors had just about worn the planet out. Then the Ghaldron-Hesthor Transtemporal Field was discovered and First Level civilization was allowed access to an uncountable number of parallel time-lines. Before Paratime Transposition, First Level had a world population of half a billion and it was all they could do to sustain that small number. Now the population had stabilized at ten billion and most Home Time Line Citizens lived a life of ease and luxury, with both mechanical and outtime human servants to answer every need and desire.

It was the ultimate parasite culture, secretly drawing off the resources and population of millions of other time-lines. A little here, a little there, but not enough to really hurt anyone. But unfortunately, maybe even tragically, that secret would be discovered on another time-line someday, just as Kalvan had brought an end to Styphon's House fireseed secret and monopoly by re-inventing gunpowder and then telling everyone about it—even his enemies! Which made him many friends and the nemesis of Styphon's House. When the Paratemporal Transposition secret—a thousand times more complex than the fireseed mystery—was broken; well, it wasn't an exaggeration to say that the fate and welfare of ten billion Home Timeliners would depend upon the reflexes and ruthlessness of the Paratime Police.

"Verkan, it appears to me you've got a bad case of Outtime Identification Syndrome. As you yourself know, it happens to the best of Paratimers. First Level civilization depends on being able to secretly draw upon the resources of millions of alternate time-lines and we can't afford to let any one man—not even the Paratime Chief of Police!—put our way of life in jeopardy. One of these days you're going to have to make a choice between loyalty to a friend and your natural loyalty to the Home Time Line.

"If it ever comes to the point where King Kalvan or his people comes between you and your job as Paratime Chief of Police, then I'll be the first to recommend the Paratime Commission that you be cashiered from your job." Tortha removed a cigarette from its pack and had to will his fingers to keep them from trembling as he lit up.

"Tortha, you know me better than that. You're the one who talked me into taking over as your replacement! My duty to the force comes first, before everything. Yes, I admire Kalvan; he's taken the tiny Princedom of Hostigos and turned it into a first class outfit. Without any real help from me, I might add. And, as much as I admire and like Kalvan, Rylla, Ptosphes, Harmakros, and the rest; I have no desire to go native and throw away three hundred years of longevity just to live a simpler, more honest way of life."

The wistful tone Tortha heard in Vall's voice indicated to him that on some deeper mental level Verkan might be quite willing to do just that, but Tortha couldn't see that there was anything to be gained by picking at that particular scab. He'd just have to keep a closer eye on Verkan, try to help take some of the pressure off and then be ready to jump in whenever it appeared that the Chief's judgment was going awry.

"I'll accept that for now. How is Dalla's work with the Fourth Level Europo-American Study Group going?"

Verkan laughed. "To listen to my wife talk you'd think she'd been shut up in the Inner Circle at Balph and been forced to listen to one of Archpriest Roxthar's tirades for a year! She's not sure what's worse, listening to the representatives from Tharmax Trading and Consolidated Outtime Foodstuffs pleas for open 'trade' lines, or the University cliques talk of the inevitability of outtime social interests conflicts with Home Time Line politics until First Level civilization embraces the benefits of post-industrial socialism, or some such garbage."

"Good, it's going just about as we expected. As long as they keep arguing semantics and ideology they'll never get down to what the Study Group is all about, a full embargo on Fourth Level, Europo-American. That will leave you and the Paratime Commission free to do what has to be done, if or when that time comes. Although, I want to tell you that I hope it never comes. Without a Code Red situation, or all out nuclear slugfest, shutting down Europo-American, it may not be politically feasible—"

"You, too, Tortha? I get enough of that from Dalla."

"Well, maybe in this case, it might not hurt to listen. We get a lot of everyday products from that Sector, for example, the Camel cigarettes I'm smoking.

"True, it would be inconvenient to relocate our sources of supply, but it could be done, Verkan answered. "I can't think of anything critical to First Level life or civilization that comes from there."

"In a strategic sense you're correct, but the Europo-American Sector has caught the public fancy—like nothing else this century. They're behind the flat screen film craze and are the suppliers of that hideous 'rock and roll' music that's been jamming the airwaves."

Verkan's eyebrows shot up. "The first time I heard that jangle of atonal sound waves, I thought I'd tuned into a cat fight."

"Verkan, just listen to yourself! You sound just like me: it must be that crazy horseshoe desk. Or the responsibility of protecting ten billion contrary Timeliners who don't always know their own best interests."

Verkan shook his head. "I don't know how you kept going for so long."

"Maybe because I thought I was doing really important work."

"That doesn't sound like you, Tortha. Getting tired of that Fifth Level rabbit farm in Sicily already?"

"Actually, it's been so dull there this past year I've taken to watching Fifth Level prole soap-operas."

Verkan shuddered in mock horror. "The only two things worse than prole soap-operas would be either attending an administrator's conference at Dhergabar University, or one of the Kalvan Study Team's argue-fests at the Royal Foundry in Hos-Hostigos."

Tortha laughed. "Actually, I wanted to talk to you about a cover story for a trip to Kalvan Prime."

"That's a wonderful idea, Tortha. Kalvan and Rylla can use all the help they can get."

"Well, I'm not a military genius, or engineer—"

"I didn't mean that kind of help, Tortha. They need a good shoulder to lean on now, especially since Prince Ptosphes took a mortal wound at Tenabra."

"I didn't know he was shot?"

"Not that kind of wound—it's worse, he's stopped believing in himself. And that's the most terrible thing that can happen to a man like Ptosphes. There aren't a lot of people in Hostigos Kalvan can really talk with and you might be the best medicine he could get. I know how you've helped me over the years."

"Just my job, Vall." Tortha pulled a pack of Camels out of his pocket and reached for Verkan's tinderbox.

"We both know better. It wouldn't be wise to make you a Grefftscharrer merchant, too. Xiphlon's far enough away that no one in the Northern Kingdoms knows much about it, and it's in a bit of a bind. Another of those Aztec empires—the Zarthani call them the Mexicotál—that crops up on one Fourth Level time-line after another is trying to move their cannibalism racket into the Middle Kingdoms. Somebody's been selling them 'fireseed'—another local term for gunpowder—and last I checked they had some huge slave trains dragging these antiquated hundred and two hundred pound siege guns, old hooped iron bombards, to try and blast through the great walls. The Mexicotál are not familiar enough with gunpowder weapons to know that those stone balls will do about as much damage to the walls of Xiphlon as their ceremonial obsidian blades do on plate armor!

"Xiphlon, is one of the most 'civilized' cities in the northern hemisphere. The city reminds me of Byzantium on Fourth Level, Alexandria-Roman. Hugh outerworks and walls as thick as the Great Wall of China and almost as tall, made of quarry stone that must have been transported by river barges for a hundred years. Very sophisticated inhabitants, they've done it all, seen it all and know it all. The city has been besieged a number of times; they've got fresh water cisterns and provisions enough for a ten-year siege. Right now Xiphlon's biggest problem is all the trade and portage business they're losing. I wouldn't be surprised if, after the Mexicotál have picked up their pieces and gone home, the High King of Xiphlon doesn't hire Kalvan to take his army into Mexicotál and teach those heart-stabbers a thing or two about gunpowder diplomacy!"

Tortha blew a series of smoke rings. "Sounds like my kind of place. I'll make a covert visit to Xiphlon, first, so I can familiarize myself with the city layout and find a place to set up my cover story."

"Great idea. I'll get Kirv to send in a team to help you. After you leave, they'll stay behind and establish a deep cover. Fortunately, these Middle Kingdom merchants do more traveling than a Paratime Policeman."

Tortha smiled. "This sounds like fun. Do you know how long it's been since I went undercover outtime? No, don't even try to answer."

Verkan laughed loudly for the first time, Tortha could remember, since he'd become Paratime Chief of Police.

TEN

I

As Grand Captain Phidestros walked down the long stone hallway to the new Captain-General's office in Tarr-Harphax, he felt the dampness in his hair right through the helmet padding. The recent, but long-anticipated death of King Kaiphranos the Timid, had left the capital city in an uproar. Kaiphranos was in his grave less than a moon-half before the Regency Council had been formed, because the Electors were at an impasse on electing a new Great King. Four of them had voted for Lysandros; the other four Electors had voted for anybody else, but. Still, someone had to run the Kingdom and the Council was 'trying' in a manner of speaking. This Regency Council did not want to rock the Harphaxi ship of state and was so crippled by the infighting between Duke Lysandros and the other candidates that it dared to do nothing.

Rumors of a revolt led by Prince Lysandros had been talked and bandied about in every wineshop and tavern in Harphax City for the past moon. Meanwhile, the Regency Council dithered, until finally, in a surprise appointment, it made Lysandros Captain-General of the Royal Harphax Army—a move that has astounded every bar-chair 'captain' in Hos-Harphax.

The truth, as Phidestros heard it, was no one else wanted the job, not after the ruinous end of the last Captain-General who'd faced Kalvan in battle. Besides, as everyone knew, Lysandros was the ablest Harphaxi

General still alive. Phidestros, knowing full well the decrepitude of the Royal Army, thought the Regency Council's motives might have been more cynical. Putting the Royal Army back into fighting shape was a job that would daunt even Kalvan, with all his Dralm-sent help!

What bothered Phidestros was: why did the new Captain-General want to see a mere captain of a mercenary band? Phidestros didn't know of any other mercenaries who had been accorded a private audience with Lysandros, who, if rumors were to be believed, would someday be crowned Great King. Had he committed some infraction of Harphaxi Law that he knew nothing about? Or had he been followed to Hos-Zygros? He didn't have any idea of what Lysandros' actions might be if he learned that one of his mercenary captains was a bastard son of Grand Duke Eudocles, only two knife blades away from the Zygrosi throne.

The two halberdiers guarding the Grand Duke's chamber were wearing Lysandros' red and black livery and design, a black felt ragged staff, over their silvered breastplates. After unbuckling his sword and handing it to the Captain of the Guard, Phidestros was announced and escorted into the Captain-General's chamber. Lysandros was working, quill pen in hand, on a small mountain of documents.

Lysandros continued writing for a few moments before looking up and giving Phidestros leave to sit down.

Phidestros took off his morion helmet, set it in his lap, and tried to find a comfortable spot on the high backed wooden chair. To take his mind off his discomfort he studied the Grand Duke's countenance. Lysandros was sharply featured, like a ferret, and his piercing blue eyes reminded Phidestros of his father's eyes. Lysandros was wearing a dark ruby-colored robe with a silver-fox fur collar, a vestment that alone would have kept the Iron Band in ale and fireseed for a moon-half.

The Grand Duke set aside his quill pen and said, "I wanted to satisfy my curiosity and take a closer look at the man who has faced the Hostigi Usurper three times and lived to tell about it."

Phidestros felt a clammy chill.

"Is Kalvan god-sent by Dralm as the priests say? You've seen him, Captain, what do you think?"

Phidestros weighed his options carefully. Lysandros was known to be a devout follower of Styphon's House; yet, not so devout that it interfered with his kingly ambitions, or so Phidestros had been told. "My opinion is that Kalvan the Usurper is like other men and puts his hose on in the morning one foot at a time. He is comely and a great captain, but in all other aspects he is the same as other men."

"But what of his miracles?"

"Miracles are often confused with great deeds. I have seen Kalvan's horse-drawn artillery up close and it is in all respects like our own except for the ingenuity of the carriage, which gives it its mobility. It is not god-made, but manmade."

"I understand that these gun carriages, as you call them, are being duplicated here in Hos-Harphax?"

"Yes, Your Highness. Unfortunately, they are inferior to those of the Usurper. I have one of my petty-captains, Kyblannos, a former wainwright, working with Master Systhos of the Harphax Foundry working to improve their design."

"Excellent, Captain Phidestros. I see you have initiative, too." Lysandros pushed away a stack of parchments and pulled out a half-section of a musket barrel. He handed it to Phidestros, asking, "What do you think of this?"

Phidestros moved over to the window slit and peered closely at the inside of the barrel, where he saw a series of small raised ridges. "What is this? I've never seen a musket with such markings inside the bore."

"This is a half section of one of the Usurper's *rifles*."

"May Galzar be Praised! I would give a chest of gold for a whole one of these *rifles!* Where did it come from?"

"While the battle at Chothros Heights was lost, a few things were won such as this rifle and three others like it. I gave an award of five hundred silver Rakmars for each. The Royal Gunsmith has taken apart two and they both have identical spiral grooves inside the barrel. He has promised to wrest its secret and produce a sample rifle in two moons."

"A few hundred of these rifles and some mobile cannon would have put us on more equal footing with Kalvan and his army."

Lysandros grinned evilly. "And better leadership, though my nephew did the kingdom a favor when he led his Lancers into Kalvan's guns. These rifles, as the Hostigi call them, will help, but I fear that the Usurper has already stolen a two-year's march upon us. We need time to raise a new army and train the soldiers we have in these new tactics. How much time do you think the Usurper will give us?"

"If I were the Usurper, I would be mustering an army of conquest this moment to march into Hos-Harphax the moment the roads are dry and the rivers are no longer swollen. The Harphaxi Royal Army—even after reinforcements—is at half strength. We have less than four thousand mercenaries and little prospect of getting more until spring, which would give us no time to organize or train them to meet Kalvan's army, to say nothing of his new style tactics. To this we can add two temple bands of Styphon's Own Guard, neither at full strength, for another six hundred foot. Kalvan could besiege Harphax City with an army four times the size of our own with all the mercenaries he's added to his army."

Lysandros hunched over and rubbed his forehead vigorously. "These are my worries, as well. Yet, all my waking hours are consumed by palace intrigues." He banged his fist on the table, knocking two candelabras to the floor. "Curse the Usurper Kalvan and all his spawn!"

Phidestros, like all the other mercenaries on Royal pay, had listened closely to the rumors about the Harphax Succession Crisis. Former Prince Selestros, the debauch, had renounced any and all future claims upon the Iron Throne and had 'retired' to a luxurious manor house as far from the capital as distance would allow. Rumor had it that the manor was paid for with Styphon's gold. Right now the tavern odds were split between Lysandros and Prince Soligon of Argros as to who would be the new Great King. Phidestros had wagered his purse of gold on Prince Lysandros.

"How do you see the Succession Crisis?"

That was a loaded question if ever Phidestros had heard one. Now that it appeared he was not about to be called up on charges, there was little to be gained in complete honesty. Yet, so far it had served him well, and there was more at stake on this table than musket barrels and parchments. "The word on the street is that the Electors are split down the middle between you and Prince Soligon. The Council gives you half its votes, but the other half is lost. As Prince of Harphax, since Selestros has renounced all claims on the Princedom, you have twice vetoed new Elector candidates, since both were members of the League of Dralm. Of the other candidates, Prince Necolestros is Soligon's cousin, so he will never yield to reason or Styphon's gold, while Valthames lost both his sons at Chothros Heights and blames you and Styphon's House. I would recommend a tavern accident for Valthames, except that upon his death there will be more claimants upon the crown of Xanx than there are for the Iron Throne. This might delay the Royal Succession for years.

"Of the other candidates, Prince Bythannes of Thaphigos would appear to be the weak link in Soligon's chain, even though his daughter is promised to Valthames, who hopes for more than any man at his advanced age should dream—unless he wishes to die upon the bridal bed. The nobles of Thaphigos have lent their Prince far more gold than any prudent Prince would sanction. I suspect that a few of these men might have old scores to settle against their Prince, or failing that, have private debts of their own. Debts that Styphon's gold might recover and move into hands less approving of Prince Bythannes policies toward Soligon than his current advisors. Finding himself in great need of gold, Bythannes might very well find it prudent to renounce his support of Soligon—after his appointment as Elector, of course. I understand all you need is one vote."

"Most interesting, Captain Phidestros. You blow a fresh wind on a subject that has been obscured by the fog of my own advisor's stale air. I will share your words with Archpriest Phyllos when we meet this afternoon. I must say that this talk has given me more confidence in the decision that I came to earlier in the day."

Lysandros took the parchment he had been writing on earlier and handed it to Phidestros. He was struck speechless when he saw it was no ordinary parchment, but a commission to make Grand-Captain Phidestros the Captain-General of the Royal Army of Hos-Harphax! Phidestros could hardly believe his eyes.

It took a few moments to collect his wits and trust his voice to speak without breaking. "A great honor, Your Highness. I . . . I never expected—I will follow your commands and prove worthy of your trust in me . . ."

"As I am sure you realize, this commission means I am passing the gold chain of command from my shoulders to yours. I do not do this easily, but my advisors have convinced me that I cannot both run the army and woo the Elector Princes at the same time. The Regency Council suggested older and wiser captains than yourself, but all were either too old to change or did not understand this new kind of total warfare that Kalvan the Usurper has brought upon the land. I wrote to Grand Master Soton and he gave me your name—not without reservations, but he thinks well of your general-ship, and much less well of the others I mentioned in my letter. The Regency Council gave their approval of your appointment this morning."

Phidestros could see that Lysandros was highly displeased to have to get permission from the Regency Council, but he would not let that pour rain on his festival! Praise be to Galzar, Soton and Styphon, too—or at least his gold. Phidestros felt so light-headed it was a miracle he hadn't floated out of his chair! "Thank you, Your Highness, for your trust and faith in my—"

Lysandros raised his hand. "Before you continue, let me make you aware of certain conditions regarding this commission."

Phidestros felt his spirits sink back to the ground.

"Because I am placing so much trust upon untested shoulders, I will expect more than I might from an older, more experienced Captain-General. My opponents, too, will see much in your appointment to use against me as well. If you lose, I will lose. Therefore, you must win."

Phidestros got the message all right: *Fail and we both lose our jobs.* But not even this warning could dampen his spirits on the day he became Captain-General. This promotion, if played in the right manner, could lead to a fortune in gold and lands of his own. And much, much more. And succeed he would, even if it meant beating Kalvan at his own game. "Yes, Your Highness, I do understand."

"Good. When we have defeated the Usurper, I will grant you a charter to the Princedom of Beshta, and those lands formerly belonging to the Prince-doms of Beshta, Sask and Hostigos, now falsely known as Sashta. You will officially have the title of Prince, and all the benefits and lands traditionally held by former Prince Balthar, as well as all of the former territories of Sashta as your own estate, in the Princedom that will be known from that point hence as Greater Beshta. When the war is won, you can retire to your estates to enjoy your title."

Phidestros couldn't believe his ears—Prince of the Great Princedom of Beshta. This day would stay in his memory as the best day of his life. Now, all he had to do to claim these rewards was to claim victory over the never-defeated Kalvan in his own backyard!

"Word of this appointment, of course, will go no farther than this chamber."

Phidestros who didn't trust his voice to speak out loud, without sounding like that of a frog's, nodded his agreement.

"I take it we are in accord."

From almost any other Prince, Phidestros would have worried that this 'gift' might be withdrawn after Kalvan's defeat, but Lysandros, who was a hard taskmaster, was known to be a man of his word. Now his future was truly in his own hands, and in those of Kalvan, too.

II

Archpriest Dracar sat in his high-back chair, with a bearskin covering his waist, watching his fingers twist and squirm across his lap like a clutch of snakes. With deliberate concentration, he forced them to straighten and lift the golden idol of the god Styphon from its altar shelf and hold it up to his eyes. In the flickering candlelight the statue blazed like molten bronze and through some play of the light it appeared as if the tiny mouth twisted into a sardonic smile.

It sent a chill straight to his heart and he almost let the statue slip through his numb fingers.

If only you were real, he thought, *I would curse you for what you have done to me!* They were all against him now: Supreme Priest Sesklos, who had promised him the highest post the Temple had to offer, First Speaker Anaxthenes, who coveted the power that had been sworn to him, and all the other Archpriests of the Inner Circle who were laughing at him in secret. They all knew that Sesklos's promise to make him Supreme Priest was a lie. Otherwise, the Supreme Priest would have already announced his decision by now. Curse and blast him!

Not that he hadn't told his share of lies as he made his way up through the Temple hierarchy—maybe that was why the other Archpriests hated him. Why had he allowed his ambition to blaze so high? He had been safe before; yes, the others had laughed at him in private and mocked him, but they had left him in peace.

Now the Archpriests praised and honored him in public, while damming him in their chambers. He could feel their cold contempt, when they thought he wasn't looking and he saw their stony faces. Now he was afraid to sleep or eat, as he waited for one of Roxthar's Investigator's to violate his bedchamber, or one of Anaxthenes's deadly little vials to be poured into his drink. Oh, what price power, when food lost its taste and sleep no longer soothed?

Yes, if he now spurned the office he had sought for so long, the other Archpriests would rend him as the Mexicotál priests butchered their sacrificial victims before the screaming multitudes upon their pyramidal temples.

A knock sounded at the door and his heart lurched. Now he was forced to entertain the most dangerous of Styphon's wolves in his own chambers in an attempt to salvage something out of this disaster. "Yes," he cried out."

"You have a visitor, Archpriest," said his steward, his voice trembling. "It is the Archpriest Roxthar."

"Come in, come in," he knew it was said too hastily, as he ran his fingers through his thin gray hair.

The door opened and Roxthar entered like a shadow. Roxthar, who was composed of sharp angles and long bones, was the self-appointed Guardian of Styphon. He was a man of deep secrets and known to follow a dark pathway. He frightened Dracar on a subterranean level that even the most vicious and venal Archpriests of the Inner Circle could never hope to reach. Roxthar wore the white robe of the novices that marked him and the Peasant Priest Cimon as the holiest of the True Believers. They were the only outspoken True Believers of the thirty-six members of the Inner Circle; although recently disturbing rumors had reached his ears that their ranks were beginning to swell. Styphon Be Praised, no more of them had yet reached the Inner Circle.

Roxthar was a tall, thin man with wiry strength that bordered on the miraculous, if the tales were to be believed. But if his physical attributes were startling, his spiritual presence was like a hammer blow. In the semi-dark room his eyes burned like red coals and Dracar felt as though he were in danger of being smothered.

"I have answered your call, Dracar. Now I must know why you have interrupted my fast." He sat down across him, his eyes holding Dracar's in an unblinking gaze.

Dracar repressed a shudder and said, "I wanted to confer with you and see if I could count on your support for my elevation as Styphon's Voice."

Roxthar made a hacking laugh and raised his head back, which in the dim light took on the appearance of a hatchet.

It was a terrible sound and Dracar's heart pounded like a Sastragathi drum.

"My support! HOW DARE YOU LITTLE MAN! The only man worse than you for that exalted position is Sesklos, who blasphemes the red robe of primacy. Or his marionette, Archpriest Anaxthenes. And you've already bought their support."

Dracar fell back in his chair, his bearskin slipping off his lap unnoticed. "I . . . I . . . I only did what I had to in order to stop Anaxthenes. It was not for myself, I swear, by Styphon's Great Wheel!"

"You scurrilous unbelieving dog! How dare you swear by the Holy Wheel! Arrrgh! Your tongue should be ripped from its offending orifice!" Roxthar rose up as if he contemplated doing the deed right there.

"No, no, Archpriest. You have me wrong. I believe, I believe. But under Sesklos those who followed the true path were exiled or sent to the Temple Library. I knew that if I spoke my heart, my days would be short in the Inner Circle—I lack your fiery faith, Father."

Roxthar sat back down. "Is this possible? Tell me more."

"Thank you, thank you," Dracar cried, unable to bend tongue to his will any longer. It was as though it had a mind all its own. Maybe he truly did believe? Is that why his mind was so divided, always at war with itself? What to believe, what to believe?

"Father, I have always disdained those who only thought of the temple offerings and turned their hearts away from the One Faith. But I have not had your courage and strength. Yet, I believed that if I could rise to a high enough office, I would be able to do much for our god Styphon and His House Upon Earth."

"Archpriest Dracar, your confession has taken me by surprise, but is good news indeed if your words are spoken in truth. Should I learn otherwise, however, you will quickly rue the day you were born.

"It is true, it is the truth," Dracar said, surprised as Roxthar at the words pouring forth from his throat in a torrent. He felt like a rabbit transfixed by a snake. Oh why had he invited Roxthar into his own bedchamber?

"It appears that Styphon's Will works by mysterious means indeed." Roxthar said, dryly. "As he brought the Daemon Kalvan, as a purgative, to restore His Temple to good health, Styphon now speaks through your worthless mouth. Was this why you called me to your chamber?"

"Yes," Dracar said nervously. "I need your hands and those of your supporters added to my ranks so that we can defeat Anaxthenes at his own game."

"How many of the Inner Circle can you count as standing by your side now?"

"Twelve for sure, and two more who are leaning towards my ascendancy. Anaxthenes has promised his support and Sesklos his blessing, yet neither have been given openly and Sesklos' days grow increasingly shorter."

"If your words are spoken in truth and your heart is pure, you will have my support."

Archpriest Dracar had to stifle a loud sigh of relief.

"If, as you say, Styphon has truly claimed your heart, in turn, you will support my new Office of Investigation."

Dracar felt his heart sink. "Office of Investigation? What could this be?"

Roxthar leaned forward so that Dracar could almost feel his astringent breath. "Styphon's House is a-rot with the worms of unbelievers, ravenous ne'er-do-wells, corrupt leeches, and all manner of blasphemers. It is our Holy obligation to root them out and restore the Temple to those who treasure her. The corruption has dwelt too long and bored too deeply within the Temple to be dealt with other than by the most stringent of measures. I will need your help to convince the Inner Circle—as corrupted by decay as the Temple itself—that we must purge even the lowliest acolyte to prepare ourselves for the war with Dralm and his minion, the Daemon Kalvan."

"Would you investigate the faith of the Archpriests of the Inner Circle itself?" Dracar asked, his face blanching.

"No. It is not necessary, now. First, we must attend to the foundation and walls of Styphon's House on Earth. When they are cleansed and strengthened, the roof will be trussed from the inside."

Dracar let out a breath he hadn't even known he was holding. "That is wise, Father. I fear that faith in Styphon is so lacking among the Brethren of the Inner Circle that they would turn aside your request, if they suspected they themselves were to be questioned." Not that he would like those steeling eyes searching out his beliefs, beliefs he was unsure of himself. Let the underpriests, novices, and temple-farm priests fend for themselves.

Roxthar made a strange barking noise that Dracar finally identified as a laugh. "You know our Brethren quite well, Dracar. They will much prefer the witnessing of those below them rather than undergoing an investigation of their own. I believe we will work together fine. You will have my blessing and support as Supreme Priest."

Dracar's head bobbed up and down. "Yes, Father, as you will have mine for your Investigation."

When Roxthar had finally left, Dracar walked over to his bed as if wading through a fog. He fell upon his bed and slipped into the best sleep he had had in over a year.

ELEVEN

Highpriest Xentos looked out the window, made of real glass, at the busy Agrys City streets down below. Through the wavy glass, he watched as a caravan of flatbed wagons, chased by dogs, passed by. The barking reminded him of home; he missed Hostigos; not the bustling, preparing for war Great Kingdom of Hos-Hostigos he had left last summer, but the pastoral Hostigos of his youth and adulthood. Sadly, change was in the air and the winds of war were blowing in every direction. Some of them were changing the Temple, too. For several moons, the Council of Dralm had been meeting to discuss these changes and to set new policies for the Temple, but always they had skirted the most important issue—Kalvan's divinity.

Now, at last, in the Grand Hall of the Hos-Agrys Temple of Dralm, Xentos was meeting with all the highpriests of Hos-Agrys, Hos-Harphax and Hos-Zygros, who were about to decide whether Great King Kalvan was, as he claimed, only a man from the Cold Lands; or if he was a demi-god sent by Dralm and the other gods to save mankind from the evil inequity of the Fireseed Demon; or if he was a devil in man's guise from Regwarn to lead the followers of Father Dralm astray? The decision reached today, at the First Council of Dralm, might well decide the fate of not only Allfather Dralm's worshipers, but the Six Kingdoms as well.

Xentos not only wished he had the answers to Kalvan's divinity, but most importantly whether or not the Temple of Dralm should commit its precious, and pitifully small, resources to what might well prove to be a long and fruitless struggle. Few outside the Temple realized just how far the Temple of Dralm had declined, as Styphon—formerly a minor healer god—had risen to prominence among the gods worshipped in the Eastern Kingdoms. Allfather Dralm, once the primary god of the Pantheon, had fallen as Styphon's followers persecuted and drove out Dralm's priests from Hos-Bletha and Hos-Ktemnos. The Styphon's priests claim that Dralm was the priest of slaves and farmers was now more true than not.

Should the Temple of Dralm commit its precious resources to the future of Kalvan and the new kingdom of Hos-Hostigos; there was a good possibility—that should Kalvan lose the war—it would mean the end of Dralm as a major religious figure and the destruction of his Temple On Earth. Allfather Dralm would truly become the god of outcasts, the poor and slaves. Already, half the princedoms of Hos-Harphax had raised Styphon above all other gods, and this practice had already gained a foothold in the northern Kingdoms of Hos-Agrys and Hos-Zygros.

Today another letter had arrived by messenger from Hos-Hostigos. Queen Rylla was, once again, asking why the Council had not come out in support of their new Kingdom of Hos-Hostigos. Sadly, there was no answer he could give her that Rylla would want to hear. He turned to the massive bronze statue of Father Dralm, dressed in an enameled blue robe with an eight-pointed white star on his breast, but no answers were forthcoming there either. He bowed down to pray, *Father, I beseech thee. Please answer my prayers. My heart is torn asunder between my duties to my Lord and my duties to thine Temple.*

As always, the bronze idol was silent. Maybe that was acceptable for a god, but men wanted, no needed, answers. Soon there would be more questions from the assembled highpriests, who were now just beginning to fill the room and take their seats at the massive walnut table. In the alcove, next to the altar, were two of the small terra cotta idols of Dralm, their robes painted white emblazoned with a blue star on the breast. The smaller figures were painted in opposition to the actual robes of the Allfather, because the peasants often broke the clay statues and in this way only the backwards image was destroyed, not the true reflection of Allfather Dralm.

Xentos turned away from his god and walked to his seat at the head of the table. As the only priest of Dralm to have seen and talked with Kalvan, he was offered this great honor, but on days like today it seemed more a curse than a blessing. He was a simple man with few answers.

As before, Xentos made the opening invocation to Father Dralm. After his prayer was finished, Davros, the Highpriest of High Temple, who sat at the foot of the table, rose to speak.

"Well, done, Highpriest Xentos. Today is the day we have all been anticipating—some with fear, others with great hope. The time has come to assay the official Temple position on the new Great Kingdom of Hos-Hostigos and its ruler, Great King Kalvan. We must cast aside those voices from the outside, like those of Great King Demistophon, who lost many soldiers in his unwarranted attack upon Great King Kalvan. We beseeched him to wait, but he was convinced by the agents of the Devil known as Styphon to do their will. Nor will we try to curry favor of those rash Princes who have, without our blessing and forgetting that Dralm is the God of Peace, formed the League Of Dralm in support of Great King Kalvan. Praise Allfather Dralm, we have been able to convince them to hold back their offers of soldiers, armaments and gold until after the Council makes its decision upon the divinity of the man, or demi-god, known both as Lord Kalvan and Great King Kalvan.

"Now, I shall ask Highpriest Xentos, Chancellor of Hos-Hostigos and Highpriest of Hostigos, the only one among us who has met and talked to King Kalvan, to give us his judgment. Highpriest Xentos."

Xentos rose and tried to formulate answers that might please the assembled highpriests, but none were forthcoming. "True, I have met the man known as King Kalvan. He came to us in strange clothes with no knowledge of our language. He carried with him a miniature tinderbox and a pistol the likes of which I had never seen. He told us that he was sent from another time, a thousand winters in the future. He had a great enemy, an evil wizard, who tried to kill him. Another wizard who was his friend sent him far away from the Cold Lands, so not to be sorcerously slain. Thusly, Kalvan was sent far back into the past and into our own time, landing in the Princedom of Hostigos.

"I do believe he is not like other men. Whether he comes from the future, past or is Dralm-sent, I do not know. Kalvan has never shown fear and is at all times filled with great curiosity. He arrived not knowing our tongue; yet quickly did he learn to speak and even write."

There was a collective sound of in-drawn breath at that announcement. It was most unusual for anyone past the age of puberty to learn the runes and how to decipher them. This alone marked Kalvan as a special and unique personage.

"He has always acted with the highest regard in his relations with women and children. He is friendly to everyone, irrespective of rank. When the Princess Rylla accidentally wounded him in battle, he quickly won her heart and then her hand. Kalvan's fearlessness in battle is beyond reproach. All the great lords of Hostigos quickly fell under his spell and he was given the title Lord Kalvan."

"All this is known and documented, Highpriest Xentos," the Highpriest of Meligos City said. "What we need to know is whether he was sent by Dralm, or the Undergods."

"I do not have any sign from Dralm that tells me Kalvan was sent from the Cold Lands at Allfather Dralm's direction. However, I do know for certain that he is no friend to the Undergods, neither Hadron, Ormaz, nor Styphon. I believe, from the first, when he gave away the Fireseed Secret, he proved that he is an enemy of Styphon, the Devil god, and his false priests. He has not to my knowledge, or that of anyone else in Hostigos, made devotions or sacrifices to the Undergods.

"What are you telling us?" Highpriest Davros asked. "That there are no earthly means to determine how or why Kalvan was sent to our lands?"

"Yes. In my heart, I want to believe that he is Dralm's son, but belief does not make truth, nor does Kalvan claim to be god-sent. Yet, he shows the proper reverence and respect to the gods, including generous donations of silver and gold. The only aspect of Kalvan that is worrisome is his mastery of Galzar's tools and his love of war, but then it could easily be said that he is Galzar Wolfhead's son. And there is much evidence for that."

Highpriest Davros' voice rose in pitch. "Then what of the people whom Great King Kalvan counts among his family and friends?"

"I know them well. First there is Prince Ptosphes, a reverent believer in the true gods and a beloved ruler. He is fair and honest. No better man has ruled Hostigos since his great, great grandfather's time. His daughter Rylla is as beautiful and radiant as the summer sun, and as hot tempered."

The last statement brought a few laughs.

"Rylla was brought up without the benefit of a mother, when the Princess Demia died in childbirth. Perhaps, not having a son, Ptosphes not only spoiled the girl, but also encouraged her in manly arts. I have known her all her life; she even calls me Uncle Xentos. Still, I have been dismayed on numerous occasions by her quick temper and violent nature. It is said that she laughs with glee upon the battlefield. And shows little mercy to the vanquished. We have shared bitter words over this fault."

There was a collective drawing of breaths.

"I fear she encourages her husband in the battle arts, rather than the ways of peace, may the Allfather forgive her. I have pointed this out to both of them on numerous occasions to little result. I fear that the Great Queen's influence on Kalvan is not for the best."

"Are you saying that she is under the spell of the Undergods?" asked an elderly highpriest, with a white, tobacco-stained beard that coursed down to his waist.

"No. I believe she means well, but her nature was tainted by her father's desire for a man-child to continue the line. I pray for her every day."

"This is disturbing," Highpriest Davros said. "If Kalvan is Dralm sent, why has he picked this woman as his consort? I fear that we will not be able to declare his divinity until the will of the gods has manifested itself. True, he has worked miracles, defeated large armies and done well for the common folk of Hos-Hostigos, but yet he is still besieged by the Devil Styphon's spawn and their armies, and even legitimate rulers debate his qualities. Until these matters are resolved, we cannot recommend that the rulers of the northern kingdoms and princedoms supply Kalvan with gold, weapons or fireseed."

The Highpriest of Glarth stood up. "I do not understand this reluctance to support and aid the one man who has many times over defeated our greatest enemy, the false god Styphon and his corrupt priesthood. Those of you in the north have not yet seen the false-priests of Styphon buy their way into your provinces, as we in Glarth have seen. Styphon's agents grow bolder day after day. Those nobles who cannot be bought directly with the False Temple's gold, are seduced with loans from Styphon's banking houses and led into debt whereupon they are beholden to Styphon's money lenders. They are then encouraged to leave the Temple of Dralm and worship only at Styphon's altar. What say you to that?"

Highpriest Socratos, former Highpriest of the Harphax City Temple and now in exile, stood up and spoke. "As you all know, I was fortunate to escape from Harphax City less than a moon ago, after Great King Kaiphranos left us to ascend into Allfather Dralm's Court. Now, since his leaving, there is open persecution of Dralm throughout Hos-Harphax. Never before have Temples been sacked and burned in the Northern Kingdoms until the Usurper Kalvan arrived! I lay this all at his feet."

The Highpriest of Glarth, his face blood red with anger, cried, "Are you saying that Kalvan is now burning and destroying Dralm's Temples?"

"No, but he has angered the Archpriests of Styphon's House and nobles and prince of Hos-Harphax, turning them against Allfather Dralm. Were Kalvan still in the Cold Lands, I would be safe in my former Temple and on the avenues of Harphax City. Yes, we have had disagreements with Styphon's Archpriest before, but they were always resolved amicably; until this Usurper Kalvan arrived!"

"Styphon's House is buying their support with gold and their Temple Guard. We need to support Kalvan, not vilify him! He is the only ruler in the Northern Kingdoms who dares to defy Styphon and his minions."

Davros stood stiffly. "Anyone whose beliefs can be bought with gold and silver is not worthy to worship at Temple of Dralm. I do not fear Styphon's moneylenders, what I do fear are Styphon's armies. And before Great King Kalvan, they stayed home in the south; now they threaten us all. As Highpriest Socratos has so clearly explained, Kalvan—be he Daemon or demi-god—has brought Styphon's armies to our lands.

"Will the Temple of Allfather Dralm support the man who calls himself Great King Kalvan, or do we recommend that the northern kingdoms hold back their gold, arms and soldiers? How do you vote? Yea or Nay."

"Nay," came the almost unanimous voice of the Council of Dralm. The Highpriest of Glarth and few other northern Harphaxi highpriests voted yea. Xentos, because of his friendship with Kalvan and Rylla, did not vote.

"It is done!"

The Highpriest of Glarth and a few other highpriests stomped out of the Temple, shaking their heads.

"Xentos, you are to take our judgment to Great King Kalvan and council him to have patience. Tell him when the auguries are right; we will reconsider our decision. I will talk to the leaders of the League of Dralm and council them to prepare for war, but refrain from any alliance with the Kingdom of Hos-Hostigos until Allfather Dralm has spoken."

Xentos felt his stomach drop. There would be no celebration upon his return to Hostigos. In truth, there would be much recrimination—not the least amount from Rylla. Yet, how could he council otherwise?

"Finally, in recognition of the Unholy War raised against the True Gods and their head, Allfather Dralm, we will need someone to lead the high-priests of Dralm. A Primate, first among equals. And for that position, I nominate Highpriest Xentos, who has shown no favoritism towards his home and friends, thereby proving his devotion to the Father God. How do you vote? Yea or Nay."

"Yea," thundered the assembled highpriests throughout the Great Hall of Dralm.

Xentos looked down at the table to hide the tears in his eyes. First Primate of Dralm, never had he—a simple highpriest—dared dream so high. But how would this appear to Kalvan and Rylla? Would they think him a traitor to Hostigos, coming home with a title and empty hands? Yet, it was his devotion to Allfather Dralm that had won these accolades. He would take their punishment and recriminations; his duty was to a higher master. Praise Dralm, they would understand in time. And, if Kalvan were truly Dralm's chosen one, he would make his presence known to all men. If not, he had made the right decision.

TWELVE

K alvan stopped writing with his quill pen, set it aside and began to massage his temples. He stood up, stretched and walked over to a narrow castle slit, where he watched the First Royal Regiment of Foot practicing their musket drill in the outer courtyard. The musketeers formed ranks, assumed positions—with the first ranks dropping down to their knees—and 'fired.' Had they been really firing the noise would have been loud enough to wake baby Demia, but these dry runs were essential for teaching the musketeers shot discipline.

Kalvan's study was on the third and top floor of Tarr-Hostigos, along with the Royal bedchambers, the Royal nursery, the solar, and the upper chamber, which acted as the Royal Army's Chief-of-Staff operations room and meeting hall. The second floor contained the dining hall, Prince Ptosphes's quarters, the guardroom, the common hall, and the Great King's audience chamber. The first and largest floor held the Great Hall, the kitchen, the servants quarters, and the Royal Armory.

From the third story, Kalvan could see the First Regimental colors, a red flag with a blue square containing the royal double-headed gold axe in the upper left-hand corner. The officers and their guards were outfitted with red plumes, while the enlisted men wore red sashes over their breastplates or leather jacks.

A year ago Kalvan had seriously thought of using his own colors, maroon and green, for the Royal Army until Rylla had made a convincing case for sticking with the traditional Hostigi colors of red and blue. Now only his bodyguards, King Kalvan's Lifeguard and the First and Second Royal Horseguard, used his flag—a maroon keystone on a green field— and colors. He knew that these small details might appear trivial to the non-military mind, but to an army on the march, with dozens of distinct flags and banners, it might well mean the difference between fighting its own advance guard and reconnoitering the enemy before they came within artillery range.

At this height the standard Royal Army battalion, consisting of two one hundred and ten men companies, and a small headquarters unit, appeared awfully small. These undersized battalions had also been difficult to maneuver *enmasse*. Now was probably the time to double the battalion strength, by adding two additional companies of shot. This would then make each 'New Model' battalion almost the same strength as last year's regiment and with twice the number of arquebusiers, since he planned to convert all the pikemen in the Royal Army to shot weapons. That should put a bee in Grand Master Soton's burgonet.

This would give the Royal Hostigi Army the advantage of concentrated firepower without depriving it of the flexibility of small unit movement, since each company would still have its own sergeant, or petty captain— he was still working on getting the new titles accepted—and chain of command. *Note: Make a 'New Model' army more along the lines of Gustavus Adolphus than Maurice of Nassau.* Then, if they were facing tercio-sized units, like the Hos-Ktemnos Sacred Squares, he could form up two or three of his New Model regiments into Gustavus's famous 'Swedish Brigades.'

The Royal Army of Hos-Hostigos was growing faster than Styphon's temple bureaucracy at the Holy City of Balph. Thousands of new recruits, many of them captured mercenaries from the spring campaigns, were swelling its ranks. Now as winter approached, thousands of free companion, from all over the Trygath and Northern Kingdoms were arriving daily, eager to sell their services to a Great King who paid them year around rather than only during the campaigning season. Another of Gustavus's innovations that Styphon's House was sure to pick up on once they realized the great mercenary leak into Hostigos had grown from a trickle to a stream.

The net result was that Kalvan needed a new source of income; by Dralm's Beard, make that several sources. The Royal Treasury was still making vast sums selling excess Hostigi fireseed, mostly to Hos-Agrysi Princes, but soon most of the Hostigi production would have to go into powder depots for next spring's invasion of Hos-Harphax. Kalvan had already spent over half the gold looted during last year's campaign from Styphon's temples in the Harphaxi princedoms' of Dazour, Balkron, Arklos, and western Syriphlon—almost two hundred thousand ounces of gold and six times as much of silver!

At this rate, not even Prince Balthar's Great Hoard, taken after the Siege of Tarr-Beshta last year, would last more than another year or two. There were times when Kalvan wondered if he were the Great King or Great Robber Baron of Hos-Hostigos. They were definitely living on borrowed time, and borrowed income as well. Eventually, there would have to be an accounting. The cost of year-around mobilization was forcing him into war as much as Styphon's Holy Crusade; even if Styphon's House were to sue for peace, he would still have to go on the offensive or risk demobilization. He hoped no one in the Inner Circle was smart enough to come up with a here-and-now version of the Cold War!

When it came to cash reserves, Styphon's House held a full deck; they owned most of the great banking houses. This was why he had taken the here-and-now unprecedented move of attempting to corner the market on all the uncommitted mercenaries in the Six Kingdoms by promising the unprecedented offer of year-around wages. This had opened the floodgates; mercenaries of every stripe had poured into Hos-Hostigos from every part of the Six Kingdoms, and the Middle Kingdoms as well.

In order to understand the here-and-now history of mercenary troops, Kalvan had spent the last year, going over old records and histories. The original Zarthani settlers had moved by boat down the Great Lakes, or Saltless Seas as they were called here-and-now, to the Niagara River, where they were halted by Niagara Falls. Here, the migratory wave split up into three different rivers, one landing at the natural harbor at Ulthor (Erie, Pennsylvania); the second going ashore in upstate New York, moving down the Mohawk and Hudson Rivers to New York Harbor where they founded Agrys City; the third portaged Niagara Falls and moved down the Saint Lawrence, founding Zygros City at the site of Quebec.

The Ulthori branch portaged to the Allegheny River, went down the Allegheny, using one of the short portages to the tributaries of the Harph (the west branch of the Susquehanna River). Since the Zarthani had metal tools, they could build bigger and better boats than the Ruthani, or Native American Indians, could even though they had little or no natural advantage over the Ruthani in woodcraft. Therefore, the early Zarthani settlers kept to the river valleys as much as possible until they reached salt water at the mouth of the Harph where they founded Harphax Town, which later became Harphax City.

Harphax Town may have originated as a fishing village, but it quickly became a naval base, since a fleet of Great Lake galleys based there could drive the Ruthani canoes off Chesapeake Bay and dominate all of Tidewater Virginia. Isolated from the rest of the major landmass by Zarthani boats and a line of fortifications roughly along otherwhen Chesapeake and Delaware Canal, the Ruthani in the Delmarva Peninsula were soon exterminated.

The Ulthori Zarthani left the western shore of the Chesapeake alone, since the Ruthani there could retreat into the Piedmont, safe from Zarthani naval vessels, and make raids into the Tidewater. So the Zarthani proceeded to colonize the flat land of the Delmarva Peninsula. Within a few years they began producing a surplus of corn, which meant for the first time the settlers in the Harph Valley were something more than subsistence farmers in a perpetual combat zone. Later a second wave of Zarthani migrants moved down the Harph to Delmarva, this population increase meant more farming, hence more food in storage, more ship and wagon building, and more young men to be soldiers. The result was that sizeable Zarthani armies, with the infrastructure to support them, were now available to carry the war to the Iroquois.

Erasthames the Great was not so much a Napoleon as a Carnot who could organize the Chesapeake watershed into a war machine that could grind down the Ruthani by sheer staying power when it couldn't beat them in battle. Erasthames did not resort to conscription. Instead he levied heavy taxes on farms and boat and wagon operators, using the proceeds to pay soldiers. Eventually, he had a large supply of mercenary soldiers, which meant that the profession of mercenary, at least in the Northern Kingdoms, became an honorable profession, if only because so many sons spent a year or so at it. Undoubtedly, Erasthames the Great had lavishly subsidized the priests of Galzar. By the end of the Ruthani wars the profession of mercenary was not just honorable—it was traditional.

The shipyards of Harphax City had a boom time from the beginning, first producing war galleys. Later small merchant vessels to carry settlers into the Chesapeake and north, then coastal vessels to trade with the Carolinas. Harphax City turned into a prosperous seaport. In a few generations the ship builders and ship owners and ship captains turned into shipping magnates and became considerably wealthier than the upstream boat and wagon train operators. This meant that Harphax City, and likewise Agrys and Zygros Cities, developed the economic muscle to dominate their upstream relatives and before long the oligarchies/monarchs of the seaports began to throw their weight around upstream, if for nothing else, to protect and encourage their trade routes back to Lake Erie and Grefftscharr.

So it was the seaport city eventually became the capital of a Great Kingdom, whose unity was more economic than political. As long as an upstream Prince behaved himself and paid appropriate tribute—while above all keeping the trade route running smoothly—the seaport kings had no problem with letting him do as he pleased. Styphon's House didn't invent this local autonomy; it merely encouraged it to keep the political power of the Great King low and the fireseed burning.

Kalvan's discussion with Skranga and Harmakros about conquering Hos-Harphax and placing Phrames in the throne was more than just talk. If the Great Kingdom of Hos-Hostigos were to have good trade relations with the rest of the Five Kingdoms, it was imperative they either made friends with Hos-Harphax or beat-her-up militarily and install a friendly King—the latter being the easier of the two possibilities if Lysandros were crowned Great King. The merchants of Hostigos hadn't yet begun to riot in the streets; they were too busy dealing with the smugglers who were anxious to share some of the Hos-Hostigi Styphon's House temple loot. When that treasure ran out, Hos-Hostigos would begin to look like Spain in the Eighteenth Century, when the South American and Mexican gold and silver mines began to peter out. Already inflation had halved the value of the Royal Hostigos Crown in one year.

There was much more to being a Great King than winning battles and robbing temples—the latter, thankfully profitable work!

Kalvan heard the door open and turned to see Rylla, dressed in a gorgeous blue gown, walk inside. For a moment, he sat transfixed—Rylla looked every inch a queen, in fact, in that outfit she reminded him of Princess Grace of Monaco, with a sprinkling of freckles across her cheeks and a well-turned nose. Being married to Rylla was the best part of being Great King of Hos-Hostigos. If Styphon's House would only leave them alone, he'd be content to play consort for the rest of his days.

"Did I disturb you, darling?" Rylla asked, coming into the study.

"No, my love. I'm just going over the muster roles of this year's recruits for the Royal Army." Kalvan gently laid the piece of tan, crumbling-at-the-edges paper on the silver tray and pushed the tray across the table toward Rylla. "Try picking it up and reading it. If it starts to fall apart, leave it on the tray and read it there."

"After all this time, I'd almost stopped believing . . . And if I can't read it?"

"Then we don't charter the Royal Hostigos Guild of Paper-makers this moon."

Rylla nodded and reached for the paper as cautiously as if it had been a newborn kitten with the mother cat watching. As she lifted it up, the edges where she held it started flaking like a too-thin slice of army ration bread. She hastily put it down and started reading:

ROYAL ARMY OF HOS-HOSTIGOS

CAVALRY

Light Cavalry	— 800 pistoleers, 300 mounted crossbowman
Dragoons	— 1000 with musketoons, pistols and sabers
Heavy Cavalry	— 800 lancers and 3,600 Cuirassier with pistols

INFANTRY

Arquebusiers	— 1,600 with arquebus and sword
Musketeers	— 2,200 with musket and sword
Pikemen/Billmen	— 2,400 with pike or bill, and sword
Sword-and-Bucklermen	— 900 with sword and buckler
Halberdiers	— 1,800 with halberd or poleax

ARTILLERY

Artillerymen	— 700, including boys and servants
	— 26 guns (2 siege, 24 field, with 13 already mounted on carriages)
Sappers & Combat Engineers	— 500 engineers and support troops

"What are *Combat Engineers*?" Rylla asked.

"You can read those words!" The Zarthani runes were unusual looking first and it had taken Kalvan a few months to make the proper phonetic substitutions for the Roman characters. Because, like English, Latin, and most European languages, Zarthani was an Indo-European dialect, most of the sounds were familiar. It hadn't hurt that he'd had Greek—which was closer than English to spoken Zarthani—drummed into his head by a most determined Professor during the first two years at Princeton.

"Would I be asking what they meant if I couldn't read them?" Rylla asked.

"Combat Engineers are soldiers specially trained and equipped to build or destroy bridges, roads, and earthworks."

"Like the sappers who helped with the siege of Tarr-Beshta?"

"Exactly. You remember how I had to be in three places at once during the siege because I was the only man who knew how to lay out the trenches. The officers of the combat engineers will do that work the next time we have to lay siege to a town or castle. With Dralm's help, they'll have a chance to perfect their craft on Harphax City. After all, I can't do everything and be everywhere at once even if Lyklos seems determined to keep throwing new balls my way faster than I can juggle the ones I already have."

Rylla took his hand. "You can juggle better than any other man in the Six Kingdoms, Dralm be praised!"

"I'll gladly praise all the true gods at once, but they won't make me twins, or give me two extra arms!"

"I suppose not. What weapons will the combat engineers carry?"

"Pistols and swords and half-pikes. They'll usually be working close to the main army, so they'll have lots of infantry support. I was thinking of making Captain—what's his name, the one with the red hair that sticks out—the captain of the Ulthori fishermen. . . ?"

"Kybanthos."

"Captain Kybanthos—I was going to suggest him as Captain-General of the Sappers and Engineers. Master Thalmoth would be the ideal candidate, but he says he's too old for any more campaigning. I think he just doesn't want to leave the University, which is just as well because he's indispensable there, too.

"Another of the Sappers and Engineer's jobs will be building boats and rafts when we have to cross a river where there's no bridge."

Rylla frowned, obviously a little out of her depth at the idea of crossing a river too deep to ford anyplace except at a bridge. Kalvan wondered why, if this was standard military doctrine here-and-now, nobody had thought of blowing up or burning bridges to foil an enemy. Probably because every Prince or King had to reckon on fighting on his own real estate sooner or later and didn't want to set a precedent for demolishing things as expensive and hard to replace as bridges. In fact, the whole idea of carrying the war to your enemy had been rarely done, until the Dralm-sent/demon-serving Kalvan I of Hos-Hostigos proved that this strategy could knockout an opponent so thoroughly you didn't have to worry about his doing anything to you next year.

Of course, it would have been even better if there hadn't been people serving Styphon's House who could learn that lesson too: Grand Master Soton. Grand Duke Lysandros of Hos-Harphax. Archpriest Anaxthenes, who wasn't a soldier but could almost certainly hand pick generals and teach them. It would have been much more convenient if all his opponents could have been of the caliber of Prince Philesteus—who'd died a glorious and futile death at the head of the Hos-Harphax Royal Lancers—or even the late Prince Gormoth of Nostor.

For a while, he'd even begun to convince himself they were all that hapless, but he'd learned otherwise by now, and perhaps he should have always realized that Styphon's House must have something going for it to survive five centuries as the ruler of rulers here-and-now. One of the problems of being an agnostic dropped into a world of believers: you weren't used to the idea of how much work people would do on behalf of their god.

Rylla was still frowning.

"Yes, darling, what is it?"

"Kybanthos might not be the best man for Captain-General of the Sappers and Engineers. He's not a nobleman and the other Captain-Generals are. If you give him a title, some will say you are ennobling too many commoners too quickly. Also, those Ulthori are not well thought of in Hostigos.

"The Ulthori don't fight by Galzar's rules, I'll admit," Kalvan replied. "But—no, you're right. Kybanthos hasn't done nearly as much as Alkides or Hestophes. And a very important rule for Great Kings as well as for Ulthori fishermen is 'Don't rock the boat if you don't have to.'

"We will need a Captain-General for the Engineers sooner or later, to give them status. Right now, we can just organize an Engineer Regiment and put their Colonel on the Great King's staff. That will honor him without needing to give him a title." The way Rylla beamed told Kalvan he'd hit on the right solution, and for the fiftieth time he wondered what in the name of all possible and impossible gods he would have done without her.

Rylla traced the figures on the paper with her finger. "That is 6,500 cavalry, 8,900 infantry, 26 guns, and 500 engineers you will be adding to the Royal Army. Add these to the 5,000 men of the regiments we already have, and the Great Throne will have better than 20,000 men in its pay, ready to march. That *is* truly an army worthy of a Great King!"

"We have Styphon's House's temple treasuries and Balthar of Beshta to thank for being able to pay that many. Also the two armies we smashed last year for being able to arm them. In the armies of Hostigos it had become a point of honor to glean the battlefield for any useable piece of abandoned equipment, from an artillery-piece down to a thrown horseshoe. Of course, this meant bore-standardization was not only out the window but also on the trash heap for years to come, which would doubtless make those Dralm-damned gunsmiths happy.

"You have not divided the men into regiments yet?"

"No. That can wait until spring. I want to see which captains do the best work, so I can make them Colonels."

"You will need more Generals with so many new regiments. A General cannot give orders to twenty Colonels all at once in the middle of a battle."

Kalvan nodded. He explained his plans for doubling the size of the Royal infantry regiments, by increasing the number of musketeers in each battalion. They'd gone as far as starting to work out a model Royal Army Brigade, when a royal page arrived to announce that an outrider sought audience with the Great King.

"Thank you, Aspasthar. Bid him enter, then go to the cellar and order some beer brought up." Even Kalvan, who'd had a giant adolescent growth spurt himself, was amazed at how much Harmakros's left-handed son had grown since spring. Already his ankles and wrists were showing on his Royal livery.

"The courier must have been waiting outside the door because Aspasthar had him inside the study before Kalvan could finish his thought. The messenger was obviously bushed, his jerkin and trousers were still wet from his horses lather and he reeked worse than an infantry soldier after a long day of latrine duty.

"Your Majesty, Great King Kalvan, I have come from Vygon Town in Ulthor. A large body of cavalry, with the colors and flag of the Princedom of Eubros, has just left Eubros Town and are said to be journeying to Hostigos. Their captain is Duke Mnestros, son of Prince Thykarses of Eubros. They are said to be representatives of the League of Dralm."

"At last, the other shoe drops!" Kalvan exclaimed.

Both the messenger and Rylla looked at him in confusion. "What I mean is, after all this waiting, we shall finally learn the intentions of the League—good or bad."

"Their news will be good, Xentos would never forsake his homeland." Rylla answered with a confidence that Kalvan wished he shared. "Soon we will have even more soldiers and gold."

"I hope you are right. I just wish we'd get word of that from the horses'— I mean—Xentos' mouth."

"His last post said he would be here in a moon-quarter. I'm sure Chancellor Xentos will have wonderful news for the Kingdom."

If so, why didn't he even hint at it in his last rather cryptic and short letter, Kalvan wondered to himself. For the time being, it was best to keep his doubts to himself; Rylla didn't need to have her hopes dashed. He just wasn't as sure of their Chancellor as she appeared to be.

THIRTEEN

I

Hadron Tharn knocked at the door, the peephole opened and a gravelly voice asked, "The password?"

"Death to all Paratime Police."

The voice answered with a booming laugh. "That's a good one boss. Your 'friend' is already waiting in the privacy booth, like you requested."

Hadron, followed by Warntha Thul his personal bodyguard, entered the Blind Pig—one of a chain of mock speakeasies he owned—patterned on illegal bars on a Europo-American Sector that had once attempted the 'apparently' noble, but futile, effort to prohibit the consumption of alcoholic beverages. The prohibition had barely lasted two decades, glorified a group of sub-moronic gangsters and opened up the Hispano-Columbian Subsector to serious penetration by a number of First Level outtime firms.

The loud racket of some new outtime music called rock and roll washed over him. He grimaced, but noted in satisfaction that almost a quarter of the gyrating young people were wearing the blue shirts and trousers uniform. He could imagine their surprise if only they knew that the man 'they knew' as The Leader was present! He felt a wave of pleasure, knowing that they were at his beck and call should the need arise—although with Warntha at his back it was most unlikely.

Hadron motioned for Warntha to wait, while he tapped in his private access code on the privacy booth's terminal. The door opened to show a frightened, middle-aged man in a wig and some dark make-up. A passable, but pathetic disguise.

"Tharn, are you crazy!" the man known as Ladon Darl, Vice President of the Opposition Party, shouted, as soon as the door closed. "If the Metropolitan Police ever found us together—"

"Shut your yap!" Hadron shouted, he liked to use the appropriate slang of whatever milieu he was in. It showed his uncanny ability to adapt to any period or background that he deigned to enter.

Not used to disrespect of any kind, Ladon Darl did just as he was told, Hadron noted to himself. He was not surprised; most First Level citizens were used to giving orders, not taking them and were easily intimidated. Especially, those like Ladon who were stay-at-homes and had never worked outtime.

In a loud whisper, as though they might be overheard—which was a laugh, Darl continued. "Tharn, this is dangerous meeting in this part of town in a 'joint' that you own."

Tharn choked back a laugh at Ladron's pathetic attempt to fit in. "This is just what the Metros expect from the eccentric Hadron Tharn. You should know, Ladon, isn't that why you and the Party used me to act as your bagman for the 'Wizard Traders,' as my brother-in-law so colorfully described the Organization? Not to mention, any pull that I might have with the Paratime Police through my sister. Now, there's a laugh!"

Hadron could tell from the sweat beading on Ladron's forehead that he had hit a nerve. He wasn't surprised; he'd spent most of his life cultivating his harmless, slightly mad image. If they only knew what really went on behind his masks—Well, someday they would. He had found his true calling almost two decades ago on a major off-shoot of Fourth Level Europo-American, when he met, using his disguise as the son of a wealthy South American German expatriate industrialist, Reinhard Heydrich, one of the major architects behind the Third Reich. Heydrich had recognized a soul mate and introduced him to the real minds behind Adolph Hitler—Goebbles, Himmler, Eichmann and others. That day, despite Lathor's misconception, was the birth day of the Organization and his own incarnation as The Leader. He, too, knew his role: to bring order out of chaos and to keep the outtime vermin in their proper place.

Misinterpreting Hadron's silence as intimidation, Ladron's voice grew more confident. "We told you to cut off all connections with the Organization, after the Paratime Police scoop. We can't afford to have our former ties with them come out in public; it would disgrace—if not destroy—the Party."

"Party be damned!" Tharn thundered. He enjoyed the shocked expression on Ladron's face; it secretly amused him the many ways others saw him. Only a chosen few—like Warntha—recognized and saw the real leader behind the facade. "The Organization wasn't created to fill the Party's coffers, despite you and your friends misconceptions. Truth be known, I've skimmed far more money for myself than ever went into the Party's open hands."

"Why? How!" Ladron looked like a man in a state of Post-traumatic Paratemporal Shift Syndrome, as the Bureau of Psych-Hygiene would call it. "That money was for the Party so that we could finally evict Management from power and control the Executive Council and bring truly enlightened government to the First Level."

"Please spare me your Party cant, I've heard enough of it over the past decade! It's time you and your cohorts learned a few hard realities. "First of all, the Wizard Traders are still in business—"

"What! Are you trying to destroy us all? The Paratime Cops are onto the Organization; they've already captured several key figures. Half the Council members who disappeared or discorporated were Opposition Party members. What if they find a way around the narco-hypnotic blocks? Chief Verkan is no fool!"

At the mention of his hated brother-in-law, Tharn felt his blood beginning to boil. He took several deep breaths. *Focus on the moment,* he told himself. "That's not your concern." He neglected to tell Ladon what it was that stopped the captured operatives from talking, a narco-hypnotic command that stopped their hearts, when facing immanent capture or detainment. The operatives, of course, knew nothing about the death command. Doctor Vermor claimed it paralyzed the Vagas nerve, which controlled the heart, or some such thing. All he knew was the demonstrations worked perfectly; dead men did not talk. "There will be no leaks from the Organization, I guarantee that."

Ladon didn't look convinced.

"However, I'm not so sure I can count on the Party."

"We know how to keep our mouths shut, even if the Metros were to suspect us. Men in our position do not get interrogated."

Tharn laughed! "Then you don't know my brother-in-law! In fact, as much as I hate to admit it, Verkan does possess some admiral characteristics, when compared to weaklings such as yourselves."

Once again Ladron's jaw had dropped; it was getting to be a habit, Tharn thought. Maybe, after all this was over, he could find useful employment on some post-apocalypse Second Level world as a flycatcher! "As I was saying, the Wizard Traders are still in business. We still need more credits, not only to fund your corrupt friends but to help finance The Leader."

"The Leader—you know how he is? He's doing more to destabilize the youth of our city than Verkan Vall himself, and this King Kalvan the media have made a folk hero out of!"

Hadron put on his mask, although he felt like screaming; *Who do you think The Leader is you spineless jellyfish?* Instead, he said, "The Leader is but one more piece of the coalition to unseat Management Party and restore the Home Time Line to proper authority."

The familiar words seemed to calm Ladron's fears as the color returned to his face. "Tharn, your rashness endangers all of us. However, the Party could use additional funds in the upcoming Dhergabar municipal elections. And, if as you say, the Organization is still in operation, we could use a 'donation' of half a million credits."

It never ceased to amaze him how quickly political types could restore their equilibrium once they were on the familiar grounds of elections and credits. "It can be arranged. However, I didn't call you here just to arrange for a campaign donation. It's time to put some political and public pressure on Chief Verkan. Kalvan Prime is overflowing with outtime contamination. Verkan is endangering the Paratime Secret by protecting his friend King Kalvan—"

"That won't work, Tharn. The public is in love with this Great King Kalvan—he can do no wrong, at least, for now. If his ratings ever slip, then we may have some leverage. Right now every public station is broadcasting the latest Kalvan nonsense."

"Then hit Verkan from another angle. Log how much time he's personally spending on Kalvan Prime and show malfeasance of duty. I don't know; I can't do your job for you. YOU PEOPLE ARE THE OPPOSTION

PARTY—"Hadron didn't realize how loud he was yelling until Ladron put his hands over his ears.

"Do something, or you'll never see another credit from me—for this election or any other. And don't even think of threatening me, I'll take the whole Party down with me."

Hadron was pleased at how his remarks affected the Party hack; he was cringing with each word, as though he were wielding a nerve whip. He could see that his true self, The Leader, was at last beginning to emerge. The Opposition Party would not take him for granted again.

II

Grand Master Soton, disguised under a green cloak and wearing his special elevated boots, entered the King's Head Tavern. Despite its proximity to Old Balph it struck Soton as an odd name for a tavern in the Holy City. Inside the tavern was filled with mercenaries and Temple soldiers. He was instantly aware of two tables full of Styphon's Temple Guard, decked out like popinjays in their bright red cloaks and silver-plated armor. Soton wondered if they bothered to take their iron breeches off, even when they took one of the wenches to an upstairs room.

Soton had never been fond of elite units, even the Order's Holy Lancers; it struck him they were usually more worried about dirtying their fancy armor with blood and gore than they were about getting the job done. But, after the Battle of Phyrax, when several Temple Bands died to the last man, he would admit that Styphon's Own Guard took a lot of killing on the battlefield.

Archpriest Prysos arrived moments later. Soton had identified him as a man in a brown cloak leaning against a livery stable on the opposite side of the cobble stone street.

He walked passed Soton, saying, "Follow me."

Soton followed Prysos into the back of the tavern, up a flight of rickety stairs. The Archpriest's subterfuge passed muster, because no one bothered to give them a second look. Soton suspect it was not unusual to see guests arriving and going upstairs for assignations. In the new Balph, inquisitiveness was not rewarded for the lower classes. Soton's throat tightened at the heady odor of ripe beer and ale that followed them to the top of the stairs. There he followed the Archpriest into a darkened hallway, where Prysos made three rapid knocks on the second door to the left. Soton had his hideaway pistol half drawn.

The door opened quickly to reveal Archpriest Anaxthenes, wearing a floor-length traveler's cloak like Soton's. The Archpriest's clean-shaven face was pale and there were droplets of perspiration covering his forehead. "Come in, come in. Prysos, good work. I will meet with you back at my private chambers."

There were two rickety chairs and a lumpy straw covered pallet in the corner. Soton picked up one of the chairs and set it next to a small hearth and started warming his hands. Anaxthenes appeared not to notice and was pacing back and forth in the small cell-like room.

When it appeared that Anaxthenes was not going to start the conversation, Soton began to speak. "What is so important you called me to Balph, away from killing barbarians in the south, First Speaker?"

Anaxthenes looked at Soton as if he'd just popped out of the woodwork. "I'm sorry, Grand Master. My mind is a tangle."

If the Archpriest called Styphon's Mouth—so cleverly did he manipulate Styphon's Voice, Supreme Priest Sesklos many strings—was this distraught, clearly Kalvan and his army was marching on the Holy City of Balph with all his troops, and those of the Great Kingdom's of Hos-Harphax and Hos-Agrys besides.

"Have you seen the bands of priests in white-robes, emblazoned with Styphon's device, crowding the streets?"

"Yes. I was wondering if it was some special festival for all the village and under priests." Truth was Soton had never seen more than a few white-robed priests in Balph, and only then as lackeys for some out-of-town Temple highpriest. The underpriests, novitiates, village priests, and temple-farm priests, had never been very welcome in Balph; it was as if they were an affront to the upper priesthood.

"No festival. And these are no ordinary temple farm underpriests, raking cow dung for saltpeter. They are Archpriests Roxthar's—the new Holy Investigator's—special Investigators. Blast his slippery hide! They are here to rake the temple priests in Balph for blasphemers and non-believers."

"Investigators? I've never heard of such priests."

"You will now."

"Please explain this puzzle, Anaxthenes? I have been gone from Balph little over two moons and mood of the entire city has changed."

"It's that fiend, Roxthar. I had heard word, from Sesklos, of his plans for an Investigation of Styphon's priesthood to root out the unbelievers, but I understood that he would not make his move until the Council had met at Ktemnos City."

Soton had little sympathy for Anaxthenes; yet, for all of his treacherous ways, Styphon's House had prospered under his and Sesklos' hands. And to be so quickly undone by a man unknown outside the Inner Circle until Kalvan's mysterious arrival. Oh, how it must gall.

Yet, look how successfully the two unlikely musicians were now beginning to play—Kalvan and Roxthar—polar opposites, yet both catalysts for great change. It appeared they were both playing the same melody—the corruption of Styphon's upperpriests—but on different lutes. The rot had been there all along but no one had really noticed until Kalvan and then Roxthar began to harp on it.

"How could this thing happen?" Soton asked.

"Archpriest Dracar! That sniveling swine of a man. When Sesklos didn't immediately shout to the rooftops of Balph that Dracar was to be his successor, he saw treachery. If he had but come to me, I would have told him the truth. Instead, he called Roxthar to his private chamber, I'm told, and there sold his birthright. The fool. Now that Roxthar's set his fangs, they will never be withdrawn. May Styphon curse the lot of them!"

Ahhh. Everything became clear. Anaxthenes had sold his right to be Styphon's Voice to Dracar in exchange for Dracar's support at the Seventh Great Council and had then expected to pull Dracar's strings as he'd pulled Sesklos, when the time came for Dracar to become Supreme Priest. Dracar was at heart, a timid man, who'd only risen so high in the Inner Circle because his fear gave him purpose and that certain ruthlessness that was necessary to ascend to such heights in Styphon's Priesthood.

But Roxthar had cut Anaxthenes's strings and put his own on Dracar. Yes, Dracar would well fear Roxthar—and for good reason—as the Investigator's fanaticism burned like a house fire. Now that Archpriest Roxthar had new powers as Holy Investigator, Dracar would have even more reason to fear him. There was nothing about these new developments the First

Speaker could do, except bide his time—but the art of patience appeared to be no longer one of Anaxthenes's virtues.

"What about the Inner Circle? Dracar's wits must truly be addled if he let Roxthar Investigate those who wear the yellow robe."

"No, he's not completely undone. According to the writ the two of them had the idiot Sesklos sign, the Inner Circle—being the highest manifestation of Styphon's Will Upon Earth—is exempt from any Investigation. Praise Styphon! But who knows what evil designs lurk within the dark cavities of Roxthar's skull."

"I am thankful that you saw it necessary to inform me of these developments, but why was it necessary to call me to Balph, when a special envoy, like Prysos, would have done just as well?" Yes, what new scheme was cooking in the First Speaker's mind? And Anaxthenes was talking so rashly; one would hardly recognize that he had been raised on Sesklos' knee. Soton had never forgotten the old peasant proverb, 'In Balph, even the planks have ears.'

Anaxthenes, for the first time, lowered his voice to a whisper. "I need your help, Styphon's House needs your help. You are the only man who can stop Roxthar before it's too late."

"Me? How?"

"Mobilize the Knights. Tarr-Ardros is not far from here and a full Wedge is based there. Bring them into Balph and arrest Roxthar and the Investigators. My supporters will help you find them all. We will deal with them after you've put them into our care. Any blood will be upon our hands."

Soton could hardly believe his own ears. Was Anaxthenes asking him to bring in Knights to arrest Styphon's own priests? Madness, surely. Could he even command the Knights to do such a thing. Well, yes he could, but the repercussions . . . And what would Styphon's Own Guard have to say?

"Once the boil is lanced, only Styphon knows how much blood will spill."

"Leave the thinking to me," Anaxthenes replied. "Sesklos will do whatever I tell him, now. And I've got him beyond Roxthar or Dracar's reach. All you have to do is bring in the Knights."

"Perhaps this Investigation is not such an ill thing. Styphon's House needs purpose and unity if it is to defeat the Usurper Kalvan."

"Grand Master, had you been in Balph these last two moons, you would not think this way. You are the pillar of Styphon's House on Earth. You are the only one who can deliver us from this scourge. I plead with you to heed my words. Before it is too late!

"Now I must depart before someone notices my absence. We have only days to decide. I'll leave you alone with your thoughts. Prysos will join you soon and take you to a safe house where you can stay until you have digested my plans."

"Anaxthenes, I cannot support this plot. Such a split in the Temple would weaken the fight against the Usurper and he surely would use it against us. We must not let our enemies know our weaknesses—"

The First Speaker slipped out the door before Soton could finish, leaving him with a splitting headache and too many questions he could not and did not want to think about.

F⊕URTEEN

I

It had been Kalvan's idea for the entire party to retire, less any ladies, to the Crossed Halberds tavern for some of Ermut's new brandy. He'd been spending way too much time in the audience chambers of late, dealing with guildmasters, merchants and landlords. Everyone else, but Prince Ptosphes—who didn't know what fun was anymore since Tenabra—was having a good time. Today the delegation from the League of Dralm had arrived, in the person of Duke Mnestros, eldest son of Prince Thykarses of Eubros.

Kalvan had taken an instant liking to the straight-talking big duke, probably the tallest Zarthani—other than Rylla's bodyguard Xykos—he had seen here-and-now. Mnestros would have made a good prospect for the NBA back home in otherwhen. The only thing Kalvan missed back in Pennsylvania, besides hot showers, was baseball season. While he'd never had much truck with the Phillies, he'd been a big Pirates fan—even on occasion traveling to Forbes Field when they had a weekend home game.

Kalvan had also noticed the Duke's stolen glances at Rylla—not that he could blame the prince-to-be; he would have done the same had their positions been reversed! However, they hadn't heard any good news from Hos-Agrys since Highpriest Xentos had left for the Council of Dralm and Kalvan wanted to hear what the Duke had to say, minus any distractions.

He took a drink of Ermut's brandy, now called Ermut's Best. The University brandy was now appearing in inns and taverns all through Hostigos, soon to go kingdom-wide, he suspected if the harried barmaids at the Crossed Halberds were any indication of its popularity. Which was fine with him, since it was turning into a blessed source of revenue for the exchequer—and without any taxation, either! Once production was up, they'd start exporting Ermut's Best to Hos-Agrys and Hos-Zygros.

"As I was saying," Duke Mnestros paused to take another drink from his goblet. "By the way, King Kalvan if this "brandy" is any example of your demonic talents, why I'd like to take your Ermut back to Eubros with me as the Prince's Distiller." That got a few laughs and another round of drinks. "Seriously, the highpriests of Dralm have chewed their jaws for moons: Praise, Dralm, I mean no disrespect to the Father God, but his priests do not know how to use one word when ten will do. And, after all this babble, they still refuse to bless the crusade against Styphon! Priests, what do they know?"—Mnestros nodded his respect to Tharses, priest of Galzar, indicating that the priests of the Wargod were not included in what he was about to say. "To these highpriests of Dralm, life's biggest headache is how much corn, beans and squash the peasants will bring for the fall offerings. And, while they ponder these weighty matters, Styphon's Archpriests are planning on how to cut off their heads and stick them on poles upon Tarr-Agrys battlements!"

There was a big "Hear, hear," from Prince Sarrask, who was already half in the bag and, if possible, even more bored than Kalvan with the endless rounds of parchment shuffling. "Another round, for Duke Mnestros. A man destined to go far in the Six Kingdoms!"

Kalvan was already feeling a little light-headed, but if a man couldn't have a few drinks with good friends, what did it all mean anyway? Kalvan cleared his head long enough to ask the question he'd wanted to ask all afternoon. "Do you think the Council of Dralm will bless Hos-Hostigos and lend us their support?"

The Dukes arrival with a cavalry band of around five hundred troopers had been heartening indeed.

Duke Mnestros sobered right up. "It's still too early to tell, but I wouldn't be anticipating much in the way of gold or guns from the League of Dralm or Hos-Agrys. Great King Demistophon, who has become the Great King Whom No One Has Seen—ever since Prince Ptosphes' victory over his forces at the at the Battle of Lycostt—has been trying to walk a tightrope between his Styphoni creditors and his Princes' exhortations of support for Hostigos. He has even called upon the Electors to disband the League of Dralm. Of course, we have pretended not to understand his emissaries, since we know that he is still in hiding. Since when has Demistophon heeded our cries of troops or a portion of the royal treasury!"

"All Great Kings are skinflints," Sarrask slurred, "present company excluded." He bowed in Kalvan's direction. "Duke, you appear to be a man of soldierly virtues. I will tell you this, By Galzar, you will not find a better ruler to serve than our Great King Kalvan." He sat down his goblet and held up a scarred and callused hand, the size of a baseball mitt. "He has given us a hand's count of great battles, with more to come. What more can a Prince ask for in this life?" Sarrask paused long enough to pat the rear of a busy barmaid, then winked. "This war has made me so popular among the wenches I haven't had to pay for their favors in a year! Is Kalvan a great king or what? Another round, Sysis."

"A toast to a real Great King!" Mnestros ordered. This time Sysis brought two rounds of Ermut's Best.

"If it's not impolite," Chartiphon interjected, "has Hos-Agrys become so dangerous that her princes have to bring along four troops of cavalry just to bring a diplomatic pouch?" The Captain General appeared uncomfortable in the present company. Kalvan figured it was probably some remaining animosity with Sarrask; after all, when Calvin Morrison had been dropped off here by that cross-time flying saucer, they had been mortal enemies.

"Not at all, Grand Captain-General. I was unable to bring the charter of support I had hoped to win from the League so instead I got myself appointed League advisor. Of course, along with such a prestigious appointment, comes the necessity of a proper guard. So I brought with me two companies of the Eubros Household Guard and two companies of my own pistoleers. Truth be told, I'm hoping that King Kalvan will make his long-awaited advance into Hos-Harphax this spring and allow me to accompany him," he paused to wink at Kalvan and Chartiphon, "as League advisor. Of course, my troopers will not be bound by the same rules."

Now it was Kalvan's turn to make a toast. "To Duke Mnestros, who—for once—brings us deeds, not hot air from Hos-Agrys!" A chorus of voices echoed his words. "Five hundred horse are welcome indeed. I welcome your support, Duke." Even Chartiphon had a smile, instead of his usual grimace. "And, I promise, by all the gods, you will get more fighting than you ever dreamed!"

"By Galzar's Mace," Sarrask shouted, rising to lean over the table and give Kalvan a bear hug, "Is this not a great life?"

II

Soton sat in his chair for another quarter candle trying to see the patterns in all that Anaxthenes had laid at his feet. His head felt as if it were in his helm and someone was banging on it with a battleaxe. These impious Inner Circle priests with their plots and counterplots . . .

There was a knock at the door.

Soton pulled out a pistol from his belt, checked the priming pan, and set the lock. He walked over to the wall on the other side of the door and flung it open, following it with his pistol.

The barrel was set level with the red design, Styphon's Great Wheel, upon Archpriest Roxthar's chest. "My apologies, Your Holiness"

"It is naught. These are trying times for gods and mortals. Please set your pistol aside, Grand Master Soton."

Archpriest Roxthar being diplomatic; had the stars fallen from the sky? It took a moment before Roxthar's request registered full upon his mind and he lowered his pistol.

"Come in, Your Holiness."

"No need for titles, this white robe is enough. Call me Roxthar."

They both sat down and Soton tried to hide the tremble in his hands while he waited for the Archpriest to speak. His talents lay on the battle-field, not in Temple machinations.

"You know why I'm here?"

"I assume that a certain Archpriest has more than one master."

Roxthar's smile was a heart-stopping sight; Soton decided he'd rather shoot his way out of Balph than face an Investigation. Now he knew the walls did have ears.

"My Holy Investigators and I were in the next room listening to your conversation with the First Speaker."

For a moment Soton wondered if Roxthar did have diabolical powers and could read his mind. No. He just had a better intelligence system than Anaxthenes—surely this demonstrated the First Speaker's star was in decline. How many times during an interrogation had he played the same sorts of tricks upon Sastragathi headmen.

"I was not displeased with your handling of the First Speaker. He is losing his grip upon the reins of power, and for the moment his wits as well. But this will pass, Styphon's Will Be Done. He has uncommon sight and soon his vision will clear again; Styphon's House still has need for men of his talents for the battles to come—against the Daemon Kalvan, the vipers in our own nest and the damnable spawn of the False God of Dralm."

For the first time since Roxthar had entered the room Soton felt his pulse return to a beat approaching normal. It appeared he had his place in Roxthar's schemes as well as Anaxthenes. So be it. As long as they left the Knights in his command and did not interfere with his orders, he would leave them to their Temple plots and ambitions.

"There is much work to be done," Roxthar continued, "and Styphon will need his sharpest tools to separate the wheat from its chaff. You and your Knights are one of Styphon's finest blades and we cannot allow your purpose to be dulled. Do you derive my meaning?"

"Yes, you don't want the Knights involved in Temple affairs."

Roxthar grinned, reminding Soton of one of the alligators he'd seen while doing a tour of the forts in the Great Peninsula a few winters back.

"It is a pleasure, unfortunately, all too rare in the Holy City, to parry words with a man of intelligence. Yes, that is exactly what I wish." Roxthar pulled a parchment out of his robe with a flourish. "You might want to look at this."

It was a long list of names of prominent Zarthani Knights, including most of the Commanders and Knight Commanders. His trusted friend and aide's name, Aristocles, topped the list. "What is this?"

"This is a list of men under your command who have taken Styphon's name in vain, or who have not shown proper respect to the True God. I fear that there are many of your companions on that role. The ears of the True God hear everything."

"You've been working on this a long time," Soton replied in a monotone, his pistol inching its way upward.

Roxthar appeared oblivious to the pistol's trajectory and continued to stare into Soton's eyes. "Styphon's work must first begin in the fields."

Soton tapped the parchment with his pistol barrel. "And just how do you propose to walk into our forts and carry out these arrests?"

"In the next room sits Captain-General Xenophes, commander-in-chief of Styphon's Own Guard. They will gladly submit to Styphon's Will."

Xenophes, Styphon's head butcher, was head of the infamous Red Hand of Styphon. He would welcome—nay relish—such a confrontation with the Knights. And, the great forts taken tarr by tarr, with little warning, he might catch the Order unprepared and do his bloody deeds. In the end, all the Zarthani of the Five Kingdoms would pay when the barbarians learned of this infamy and poured through the gaps . . .

It appeared Roxthar had him by the privy parts. There was a slight possibility he could shoot the Archpriest, fight the inevitable guard outside—and *maybe* reach and kill Xenophes, but what would be the end result? Surely he would die and who would command the Knights then—to say nothing of Styphon's House. He could feel the tension flow out of him; his pistol dropped into his lap.

"I see you are amenable to reason, Grand Master. I will take back that list. It will stay on my person, hidden from my Investigators for as long as you do your job. Is that understood?"

Soton nodded his head slowly.

"Now let us forget this unpleasantness and talk of things vital to our cause. How fares the Order's war with the nomads?"

"Slow. But we are pushing them back towards the Great Mother River. There are more barbarians on the move than have been seen since the time of Telcides the Terrible. On the other hand, the Holy Warriors of Styphon have swelled our ranks, since the arrival of the Usurper Kalvan, and we are beginning to replace our losses at Chothros Heights and the Battle of Phyrax."

Roxthar nodded his head as though he were actually listening, instead of bobbing his head as most Archpriests did when talk turned to the tools of war and strategy. "Will the Knights be ready to lead another offensive against Kalvan in the spring?"

"No. Too many new recruits, and we dare not strip the tarrs because of the barbarian threat. We might be able to spare a Wedge, but no more."

"This is not good. The Elector Princes of Hos-Harphax are dragging their hind-ends on selecting a new Great King. Instead, they have appointed a Regency Council and it turns in circles chasing its own tail. Yet, in the end, Prince Lysandros will win out, as none of his challengers have his birthright or access to our gold. And the Union of Styphon's Friends is still building its membership."

"Styphon's Friends? What is this Union?"

"A counterweight to the False God's League of Dralm. Already Great King Cleitharses has joined along with most of the Princes of Hos-Ktemnos. In Hos-Harphax the Princes of Hyphax, Syriphlon, and Pindar have joined the Friends and several others in Hos-Agrys as well."

"Hmmm. Can we count on them for troops as well as support for the priesthood?"

"Soon. It will take a few moons for these ideas to be presented and accepted."

"Is the League of Dralm openly supporting Kalvan now?" Soton asked.

"No. Our spies report that they yet withhold their support for the Usurper. Their highpriests say let the Usurper use his soldiers and gold to fight Styphon's House." Roxthar grinned.

"Good news indeed! I would not have dared hope for so much. The gods intervene on our behalf."

"The God wills it. Styphon's Will Be Done."

"If I were Kalvan," Soton said, "I would make my move this spring while the Electors are still debating in Harphax City. If he takes Hos-Harphax, we may never defeat him. I'm sure he knows this. We must give Lysandros *all* our support in Hos-Harphax. He is the only man there who has a prayer's chance of building an army that can defeat the Hostigi."

"Yes, he will make a devout Great King and a fine tool for Styphon. But how can we stop the Daemon before Lysandros is elected and can re-build the Army of Hos-Harphax?"

For the first time that afternoon, Soton smiled. "I know a way."

"Then out with it!"

"The nomads. We will drive the barbarians northeast, up through the Upper Sastragath and into the Trygath and Hos-Hostigos. Those Princes sworn to Kalvan, who live on the Trygathi border, will demand his aid, as they have every right to do. Then let Kalvan dull his blades on the barbarians' shields."

"Most excellent, Grand Master! Styphon will have you by his side in the next life. I will present your plan to the Inner Council myself. Request what victuals and gold you will need to aid your endeavor."

Soton knew he should have felt some triumph at getting everything he wanted from Roxthar, instead there was a cold lump in his stomach. If Kalvan thought he had troubles before Roxthar's ascension, he didn't know the meaning of the word trouble. Soton—as a fellow soldier—could only feel sorry for Kalvan the Usurper, who might well be master of the battlefield, but, when it came to men's souls, had met his match in Roxthar—or worse.

III

The small boat banged against the stones of the Greffa pier so hard that Verkan Vall, under the guise of Trader Verkan, heard the timbers creak. He grasped the brass rungs overhead before the boat could rebound, then hauled himself swiftly up the ladder before the boat could strike again. Behind him he heard the sailors shouting as they hooked the net holding his baggage to the rope being let down from the pier. Verkan hoped that the rope and net were good and stout. He needed a moment or two to recover every time he came ashore after traveling by boat.

Because of the lateness of the season, the usual two week sea and overland journey from Ulthor Port to Greffa had taken twice as long as usual. It had almost been too late in the season to hire a boat and he'd had to pay the captain a big bribe to get him to make the journey. When he reached the top of the stone pier and got his footing, Verkan looked back at the gaff-rigged galleass, with oar banks on both sides, riding the swells inside the port. Never again, he promised himself. The sea was gunmetal blue and every so often he heard an explosion as a swell whacked against the pier.

First Level mental disciplines and First Level medicine kept his stomach under control; Verkan had never been seasick and never would be. He also had never been, and never would be reconciled to being, bounced around a small cabin like a cork in a baby's bathtub. Nor would he be completely reconciled to the idea of long trips by waterborne vehicles. A short moonlight cruise on a calm bay with Dalla beside him was one thing; actually traveling all the way from Ulthor to Greffa by ship was something entirely different.

This wouldn't be the last such trip he'd have to make, either, although it would be the last one he'd make during the winter. The Middle Kingdoms of Kalvan's Time-Line lived by water transportation—on the Saltless Seas for Greffa, on the (Mississippi and Missouri) for Dorg, Wulfula, and the Southern Sea for Xiphlon. Verkan's own work for Kalvan also depended on it. Although, in the future, he would have his own ship and it would ply the seas with a Paratime Police crew, but no Chief. It was a blessing his critics didn't have a camera on board!

Someone was calling his name. Verkan turned to see his baggage on the pier, sitting in a puddle of water and dripping more. Dralm be thanked for oiled leather, plus the concealed layers of First Level waterproofing!

Beyond the baggage, Kostran Galth and his wife, Dalla's adopted sister Hadron Zinganna—Zinna on Kalvan Prime—were hurrying toward him. Zinna stopped to tie her scarf more tightly around her long dark hair, to keep it in place in the brisk wind, so Kostran arrived first.

"Welcome home, Verkan." Kostran, normally a Paratime Police Inspector, wore a buffalo robe over clothes that supported his tale of being a journeyman clerk who'd married a cousin of Verkan's wife.

"Greeting, cousin. How go our affairs?"

"Well enough," said Kostran, making the hand gesture that told Verkan there were untrustworthy ears too close at hand. "Did you have a good voyage? What news from the Great Kingdoms?"

"The voyage could have been better. Have these storms done any damage to the sea walls?"

"In a few places, yes," said Zinna. "But the City Sea Watch has been diligent with their repairs."

"Good," Verkan said. In Greffa when the Sea Watch went well it meant that the city's largest bureaucracy and lobby was quiet, and that the various city, merchant, and noble factions within Greffa were at peace. King Theovacar was proving himself to be a strong and able leader, which was good for business and might inevitably be good for Kalvan who needed staunch allies.

"As to news from the Eastern Kingdoms—Prince Selestros has now publicly abdicated his claim to the throne of Hos-Harphax."

The surprised expressions on Galth and Zinna's faces were a tribute to the Paratimers' acting ability. Thanks to Verkan's radio message, they'd known it almost as soon as he heard it from the agent in Harphax City.

"All claim to the Iron Throne?" Galth asked.

"Selestros made both Lysandros and Soligon swear to provide him with suitable estates and revenues when they are on the throne. Also to take care of his bastards."

"All of them? Well, that will still be cheaper than having him on the throne. I'm surprised he was sober enough long enough to think this up."

"I don't think it was his own idea," Verkan said. The look on both faces said "Styphon's House?" as plainly as speech. He shook his head.

"I don't know whose advice he took. Still less do I know who is likely to reign in Harphax now that the nearest heir has abdicated. Soligon always had one virtue—he was not (He searched for a polite alternative to 'fanatical.') an ardent worshipper of Styphon."

"I wonder how the Regency Council will take this announcement?" Galth asked.

"With a great sigh of relief! Even that bunch of corrupt youngest-sons, know that if the Council had placed Selestros on the Iron Throne, they might as well have been offering it to Great King Kalvan. Former Prince Selestros has never been on a battlefield, much less fought an enemy."

"The Inner Circle will surely throw all their silver behind Lysandros," Zinna said.

"They won't if they're wise," said her husband. "If they too openly try to buy the Iron Throne for Lysandros, many Harphaxi nobles who care little about the gods but much about their independence will turn to Soligon. A king who can rule without the consent of his nobles is—a man to whom the gods will give enemies," Galth amended for the sake of discretion. Since

King Theovacar was widely suspected of aspiring to reduce his nobles to what he considered a proper state of submission, it was politic not to make any sweeping public comments on the rights and wrongs of such a policy.

By this time, the porters had come up and loaded Verkan's baggage onto carrying poles. With Verkan bringing up the rear, the party climbed the stone steps from the pier to the top of the great mole, where Kostran's servants waited with a cart and horses.

At the head of the stairs the near-freezing wind caught Verkan so that his cloak flew out like bat's wings. Fountains of spray shot into the air on the north side of the mole, as waves beat against the granite blocks facing it there. The wind carried some of the spray into Verkan's face and the stone underfoot was slippery with it.

The great mole ran half a mile out into the lake from the north side of the mouth of the Greffa River, then turned south for a quarter of a mile. It gave Greffa a sheltered harbor for the entire navigation season on the Saltless Seas, and the guns on the batteries set every quarter mile all along it made the city too tough a nut for the hardiest pirate to try cracking.

The foundations of the mole were laid in the days of Grefftshcarr's great trading empire of the Iron Route, fifteen hundred years ago. It had been growing ever since, a shipload or more of stone a year, with every king trying to leave his mark on it. King Theovacar's plans were ambitious, like Theovacar himself—he wanted to completely rebuild the lighthouse at the elbow of the mole, which had been in ruins for eight hundred years, raise its beacon fifty feet higher than it had been placed originally, and replace all the batteries' old bombards with Kalvan's brass new-style long guns.

While Zinna supervised loading the baggage into the cart, Kostran Galth drew his Chief aside. "I had problems getting the audience you requested. It may be a couple of moon halfs before I can set it up. Since we're not well-known here, I'm having to use intermediaries and I don't want to pay enough gold to attract the wrong kind of attention."

"Good thinking, Galth."

"Time for a civilized breakfast, then." Verkan normally didn't care what he ate as long as it didn't eat him first, but four weeks of rock-hard bread and salted fish had whetted his appetite for real food. Verkan was disappointed about the interview with Theovacar taking so long to arrange, but now that they had a conveyer-head in Greffa, he could slip back and forth between Dhergabar and Greffa as events allowed. It was too late in the season to bring the cannon and arms that Kalvan needed, so there was no damage done.

"Yes, Zinna will go on ahead and see to it. Did your best finery survive the voyage?"

Verkan made a Zarthani gesture of averting bad luck and looked Kostran a question. Kostran nodded. "I think we're about to receive our charter, or at least an explanation of why we can't be granted it at this time. A messenger from the palace had an escort of six Companions. I haven't heard of that happening to anybody Theovacar wasn't planning to favor, or at least anybody whose good will he didn't value."

Since the Royal Charter would give them a legitimacy no one in Greffa or on Kalvan Prime could doubt, that was good news. The eight hundred Companions were the elite bodyguard of the Kings of Grefftscharr, descended from the household warriors of the tribal chiefs who'd founded the kingdom over two thousand years before. They were crack lancers but carried (and used) musketoons for palace guard duty, swore blood-oaths to the King and at least twice had died to the last man rather than outlive a fallen King. They weren't a likely choice for messengers to anyone King Theovacar didn't wish to honor.

The Palace Seneschal usually conducted the interview and an appropriate 'gift' was expected. He wished he'd had a cask of Ermut's brandy that Ranthar Jard had told him about; he suspected a purse of gold would do as well.

Verkan swung himself into the saddle and urged his horse up to the head of the little procession. Kostran brought up the rear. Verkan noted with approval that he had one hand effectively, but not blatantly, close to the butt of his pistol, just in case the teamster might be in league with—or an agent—of Styphon's House, since ordinary robbers would hardly dare operate in broad daylight in the best-policed area of Greffa.

If the Styphoni were able to work effectively in Greffa, it would be through local allies too powerful for Theovacar to suppress, allies bought with gold or hopes of it. The Middle Kingdoms had always regarded the gods of the Five Great Kingdoms as socially inferior to their own war and thunder lords. The incomprehensible act of mere mortals calling a council to demote Allfather Dralm had sowed further confusion. Now that the fireseed secret was free to all men, there was hardly reason for more than common politeness to Styphon's House, if that.

Correction: King Theovacar and the nobles had no reason for more than politeness. The merchants who lived by trade along the Saltless Seas might think twice before risking having the Great Kingdoms barred to them if Styphon's House won its war against Hos-Hostigos. Since Theovacar was trying to win the favor of the great mercantile houses as a balance to his unruly warrior nobility, he might turn a blind eye to their dealings with Styphon's House—even if those dealings led to moderate breaches of his peace.

Verkan wondered if his information from the east could be traded for information about Styphon's House activities in Greffa. A pity to have to use strictly local resources and methods on such a vital matter, since it would surely involve him more deeply in Greffan politics. It couldn't be helped, though—there was an old Paracop saying: 'A little bit involved is like a little bit pregnant; there's no such thing.'

Also, the only way he could make himself independent of local resources and methods was to bring in many more Paracops than he could justify devoting to what was after all a glorified hobby—he'd be cutting his throat *and* Kalvan's if he did that!

FIFTEEN

I

Kalvan was in the audience chamber, where Captain-General Harmakros was telling him and Rylla, about the problems he was encountering in getting the former Hostigi pikemen to embrace their new-bayoneted arquebuses, when a royal page arrived to announce that Chancellor Xentos had just arrived in Hostigos Town and sought audience.

"Thank you, Aspasthar. Bid him enter, then go to steward and order some wine to be brought up." He'd save Ermut's brandy until he saw if any celebration was in order; Rylla was hot enough under the collar without adding any fat, in the guise of brandy, to the fire.

Queen Rylla, who looked magnificently regal, announced in chilly tones, "I hope the Chancellor brings us better bones to chew on than those brought by Duke Mnestros."

There had been few letters and even fewer encouraging words from Xentos since his leave taking last summer to attend the Council of Dralm in Agrys City. What little Kalvan had learned about the new League of Dralm had come from Duke Mnestros who was openly dissatisfied with the Council's lack of progress. The League's un-stated goal was to act as a counter to Styphon's House's growing secular and priestly power. Any such gathering of princes, before Kalvan's dissemination of the Fireseed Secret, would have resulted in Styphon's Ban and no more fireseed, which meant their greedier neighbors would have rushed in with their armies to carve out big chunks of territory.

To Kalvan, without whom there would be no League of Dralm, not even being invited to join the League was a bitter pill indeed. Their snub did not bode well for monetary, or any other kind of Council of Dralm sponsored support for Hos-Hostigos. He had not counted upon going against Styphon's House all by himself, either, for even moral support would have helped Hos-Hostigos' cause.

Kalvan, who was familiar with the Evangelical Union (The German Protestant equivalent to the League of Dralm during the Thirty Year's War), hadn't exactly expected them to send him great sums of gold or muster large armies to come to his aid. On the other hand, he hadn't anticipated a cold shoulder from the Council of Dralm either. Rylla, who'd been bounced on Xentos' knee as a child, was even more surprised—and hurt, too. Kalvan saw his primary duty during this meeting as defusing Rylla's temper so he could prevent a full-blown church and state conflict on top of the religious war Hos-Hostigos was already fighting.

Aspasthar returned with a large amphora of wine and Chancellor Xentos, who was still brushing the dust from his journey off his blue robe. Aspasthar set down the amphora and returned to the kitchen for a tray and some goblets. Last year's grapes had produced wine that mostly reminded Kalvan of South Korean homebrew, which a fellow enlisted man had described as "certified pure goat piss." However, it was all they had for celebrating right now, and Xentos' return did call for a celebration—of sorts.

Note: Have Ermut send over a cask of his best Brandy for the Royal Pantry.

They both rose to greet Xentos as he entered, walking slowly but easily. The rheumatism, which had flared up during the Winter of the Wolves, didn't seem to be troubling him yet despite all the hard travel. But, up close, there were bags under his eyes and hard fatigue lines running through the surface wrinkles that creased his face. It was said that a week's fast travel across the roads of the Great Kingdoms could take a boy right through youth and into middle age.

Seeing the tight-lipped grimace that passed for a smile on Rylla's face, he decided to side-step the issue on everyone's mind and move into neutral territory. "Greetings, Chancellor. Let me show you the first piece of paper ever produced in Hostigos where something can be read after it's written down." He pointed to the curling brown sheet that laid like some precious object on a gilded platform.

Xentos smiled thinly, bent over the table, and read off the roster of mercenary recruits. Then he made a quick circle around the eight-pointed white star emblazoned on his chest. "Let us pray to Dralm that such a host will not be needed this coming spring."

"I will make many such prayers," Rylla said evenly. "And also to Galzar, for the host to be ready, trained and armed, if they are needed."

"As the gods will it," Kalvan joined in, trying to keep the peace. "Don't touch it, yet. The paper is too dark and it turns brittle after a few days, so we still have much work to do. Master Ermut thinks he will have a sizing for the papers to that will not turn brittle by spring."

"Let us hope so," Xentos said. "This *is* good news, Your Majesty. With paper to spread the word of Dralm's truth to the world, Styphon's House has just lost another battle. I met Brother Mytron—I mean Rector Mytron—in the Great Hall and wondered what had brought him here at night in such a hurry. He smiled and said it was the Great King's secret. He was carrying something in a large saddlebag and he still had the dust of his journey on his cloak."

"Is it another batch of *paper* for you to examine?"

"Indeed it is, but I have no secrets from you, Xentos." Praise Dralm this stays the truth, and also that Mytron doesn't put his foot in his mouth again. Had the younger priest really decided to change his loyalties from Dralm to Kalvan or was he simply getting carried away with the thrill of scientific discovery? He'd have a talk with Mytron to find out where his true loyalties rested.

"I am sure of that, Your Majesty, and likewise that Mytron has the wisdom to know how to serve both the Great God and his Great King. May it always be so."

Kalvan murmured a politely pious agreement, mostly to keep Rylla from saying anything. Several moons with his fellow highpriests at the Council had brought out a new side of Xentos personality, one that Kalvan wasn't sure he liked. Rylla's face showed more than her normal dislike of verbal fencing. He put a hand on her shoulder and after a moment felt her relax.

"I do have a complaint about the way you have been feeding Mytron. He appears to have lost weight since my leave taking. Is the kingdom still rationing food to prepare for the winter?"

"No. We had an excellent harvest and have bought additional stores from Hos-Agrys and Ulthor."

At this point Aspasthar returned with the pewter goblets, and they all drank toasts to the papermakers of Hostigos—about as neutral a toast as Kalvan could come up with under the circumstances.

Xentos set his cup down after one swallow and said, "I wish that I could have come to bring good news as well as to hear it. Dralm has willed otherwise. Great King Kaiphranos of Hos-Harphax is dead."

"We know," Kalvan said. "Duke Skranga informed us of Kaiphranos's death a moon quarter ago."

Xentos wrinkled his nose as if he'd just had a whiff of a particularly bad odor.

Kalvan said nothing. He'd exhausted his supply of polite pieties. Rylla poured herself another goblet of wine and took a healthy swig, then grinned. "Kaiphranos was dead long ago, if he ever lived."

"That is unseemly said—" Xentos began, then sighed and sipped his wine. "That is unseemly," he continued, "but it is also true. Kaiphranos had few gifts for kingship, and those few he lost many years ago. When his eldest son died there was not much left of even the man." He circled his breast-star again and seemed lost in thought.

"Prince Selestros is Kaiphranos's only surviving son," Rylla amended. "I don't think Kaiphranos had enough blood in him to get more than two. And who would fight for Selestros? The madams and winesellers, perhaps. They'd have to be loyal to their best customer. But who else?"

Xentos face whitened at Rylla's coarse words and he gave Kalvan a look that said, 'what are you going to do about it.' Kalvan wisely decided not to light that firecracker. Xentos didn't used to be such a fuddy-duddy, perhaps too much time spent with his pious associates in Agrys City. Kalvan wondered what other 'sensitivities' the Chancellor had recently acquired.

"Have the Electors made any decision on Kaiphranos's successor?" he asked, to keep the conversation afloat, it was listing badly.

If Selestros's character outweighed his blood in the eyes of the Elector Princes, there were only two other candidates, the formidable Grand Duke

Lysandros and Prince Soligon of Argros, Kaiphranos's cousin and brother-in-law, who apparently had at least the negative virtues of being neither a fanatic nor a drunk.

"At this time, Prince Soligon is the man whose election would offend the smallest number of those who should not be offended," Xentos finally answered. Kalvan refrained from asking for a list of "those who should not be offended;" Xentos doubtless had it down in such detail that it would take an hour to recite. "Grand Duke Lysandros has taken the title, Prince of Harphax, since Selestros has renounced his claim as both Prince and Great King. It is said that this was in exchange for enough gold from Styphon's House to pay all his debts. With Selestros not in the line of succession, Lysandros is closest by blood to the crown of Harphax. Since Hos-Harphax is now without a Great King, the Electors have appointed a Regency Council to rule Hos-Harphax until the Harphaxi Succession Crisis is resolved.

"The Council of Dralm has recently 'learned', from friends in Harphax City, that the Regency Council has appointed Lysandros as Captain-General of the Royal Army. It is said that the Regency Council is so crippled by the infighting between Lysandros and the other candidates that it dare not to do anything decisive."

That sounds a lot like the Council of Dralm, Kalvan thought to himself. As he shot daggers at Rylla with his eyes to keep her from saying such out loud.

"It is hoped by the Regency Council that re-training and re-organizing the Royal Army will keep Prince Lysandros too busy to do any effective politicking. Styphon's House is supplying him with gold, fireseed and arms to buy the goodwill of the captains of the mercenary companies and the Princely levies."

That was new news and not so good at that. Lysandros had a reputation as a savvy commander and as Captain-General of Hos-Harphax he could place his captains in key leadership positions and pick up good will where it counted the most. The unanswered question was still whether Lysandros was planning a *putsch* or not?

Xentos doubted it. "The laws of succession bind all candidates for the Iron Throne to avoid intimidating the Electoral Princes. To be sure, laws of such a nature are often the least obeyed, but in this case I think Lysandros will be cautious. He would not care to have those who fear his devotion to Styphon also able to call him a usurper."

Men of Lysandros's character with loyal armies at their back tended not to fear very much of anything, but Kalvan was sure Xentos knew this himself. "If we're able to march against the Harphaxi in the spring, we may be able to take a hand in the succession. Any Prince who pledges not to vote for Lysandros will be treated as a neutral, his lands left unmolested, his fireseed restocked, and so on."

Rylla grinned. "Yes, and then Prince Lysandros would have to stop playing Captain-General and come out to fight a battle. We could make sure he got home with his tail between his legs, if he got home at all."

"Can you be sure that the new Royal Army will be ready for the field, and that it will have no other enemies to fight?" Xentos asked.

"The answer's no on both counts," Kalvan answered, "but if the nomads come this far east, we can send the Princely levies to hold them while the Royal Army knocks out the Harphaxi. After the licking we gave the Holy Host at Phyrax, Great King Cleitharses of Hos-Ktemnos will be in no hurry to invade Hos-Hostigos again!"

"If the Princes will stand content with being given the less honorable of the two wars to fight, I suppose you could."

"And I suppose you could tell us what you're trying to hide," Rylla said, with an edge of steel in her voice. "Has the Council of Dralm refused to recognize Kalvan's title?"

To Xentos' credit, he met their eyes as he nodded. "It is the judgment of the Council of the Dralm that the resistance of Hostigos and its allies against Styphon's House was lawful, for Styphon's House has become the sworn foe of all those who worship Allfather Dralm. This blessing has been extended to include last spring's invasion of Hos-Harphax, for the Harphaxi took the field not solely in defense of their rights but as allies of the false god Styphon."

How magnanimous of you and the Council! thought Kalvan, as he practically bit his tongue to keep from speaking out loud.

"Such a blessing would *not* be extended to another invasion of a lawful Great Kingdom, until that kingdom has committed further offenses beyond the ones for which they have already been punished. We also understand that the Regency Council would like to declare a state of truce with Hos-Hostigos until the Succession Crisis is resolved."

Half of Kalvan couldn't believe what he was hearing, the other half was not surprised at all. Who was Xentos working for now, the Council of Dralm or the Regency Council of Hos-Harphax? Kalvan wondered cynically, if he conquered Hos-Harphax and all the Regency Council princedoms, would the Council then consider that legal? Might, might not make right, but certainly the victors wrote the histories and defined what was legal and what wasn't. "Wouldn't the election of Lysandros be a sufficient offense to justify an invasion?"

"Is it your wish to find justification for a war that you have already decided to wage?"

Fortunately, for future relations with the Council of Dralm, Rylla's jaw dropped too far for her to say anything. Kalvan managed to fill the silence with, "Her Majesty and I have *decided* on nothing, Xentos. Unlike the Council of Dralm, we *try* not to give judgment before we know all that there is to know. Now that we have answered your question, would the Lord Chancellor care to answer ours?"

"Lysandros would have to commit some recognizable act against Hos-Hostigos at the bidding of Styphon's House to give further offense," Xentos answered, smiling thinly. "Considering how much he is likely to owe the Godless by the time he ascends the throne and how ready they are to call in debts, I do not think he will be slow to commit such an offense. Then the Council of Dralm may not give its blessing but will certainly withhold any protest. If you cannot be free to march within a moon of Lysandros's succession, I will be amazed."

"Also, he might not be elected," Kalvan replied. That was sounding more conciliatory than he felt. A month could be Styphon's own lot too long, if it meant facing an extra ten or fifteen thousand men, perhaps including Zarthani Knights under Grand Master Soton. He was tempted to quote Napoleon's maxim about time to Xentos, but decided that would only start the catfight all over again.

Kalvan also decided not to ask Xentos how much he had done as Chancellor of the Realm to persuade the League of Dralm to declare Kalvan a Great King instead of a usurper with a legitimate grievance against

Styphon's House. Xentos might not have done as much as his Great King was entitled to expect. From the look on Rylla's face, it would be better if that didn't come out in the open for now. She would certainly insist on Xentos' resignation yesterday at the latest, when his experience was badly needed for establishing the Hos-Hostigos bureaucracy *and* keeping peace with the priesthood of Dralm. Mytron was the only possible successor who wouldn't be a slap in the face to the temples, and he was up to his eyebrows making paper and running the new University.

"The Royal Army of Hos-Hostigos will be mustered as I have written it down," Kalvan said, tapping the paper. "If the Council of Dralm opposes that, we shall consider them hardly less our enemies than Styphon's House."

The look on Xentos' face almost matched that on Rylla's.

"However," Kalvan continued, "we shall not use the Royal Army except as a lawful ruler may always use soldiers, against his enemies. The greatest of those is Styphon's House, and those who do not march with Styphon's House need not fear us."

"How do your Princes agree with this position?"

"They must abide by Our decision," Kalvan said, "for whether or not the Council of Dralm recognizes Our title or not, We are the Great King of Hos-Hostigos." Rylla gave him a smile that at any other time would have brightened his day.

Kalvan would be Dralm-damned, if he'd give his princes the right to veto their Great King, even to keep Xentos on as Chancellor of the Realm! As long as the Council of Dralm refused to call him 'Great King,' instead allowing him to be called 'Usurper', and as long as his title wasn't recognized by those who *should* be his allies, whomever sat on the Iron Throne of Hos-Harphax would be encouraged to think he could win back what Kaiphranos had lost.

As long as the Great King of Hos-Harphax thought that, he—whoever he was—would be willing to make nice with whomever gave him gold, guns and fireseed fight to fight Kalvan. And until Hos-Harphax was completely overthrown, that was going to be Styphon's House. The Harphaxi and the Styphoni might just be sleeping together instead of actually married, but that wouldn't make any difference to the Hostigi dead in the next war. Kalvan would have given his right hand to have it make no difference to the Council of Dralm.

And to think he'd actually thought that not only would he have gotten political legitimacy from the Council, but troops and gold as well—another triumph of hope over wisdom. Maybe it had been a mistake to send Xentos to the Council in Hos-Agrys as the Council's representative from Hos-Hostigos, but whom else could he have sent? When all was said and done, Xentos was the Highpriest of Hostigos. He would have to be replaced as Chancellor of Hos-Hostigos, but carefully. Very carefully.

Rylla poured more wine, and they all drank to "a just peace," which everybody carefully avoided trying to define, as well as "to the overthrow of Styphon's House," which didn't really need any defining.

II

As Archpriest Anaxthenes gazed out the panes of glass into the pastoral scene outside, where his gardeners tended his lawns, it was hard to believe that Roxthar and the Usurper Kalvan had turned the world he had known all his life upside down. What kind of world was it where True Believers persecuted their brethren in the name of the false-god, Styphon?

Anaxthenes turned, as he heard the soft swishing of Thessamona, his favorite concubine's, gown. She had been his mistress for over twenty years and she still possessed much of the freshness and beauty that had attracted him all those many years ago at the court of Hos-Ktemnos. While some of his younger concubines were lovelier, none had shared Thessamona's incisive mind. These days she was the only living person with whom he dared share his true thoughts. If Roxthar were to ever get her on his rack, they both would 'ride the flame' as so many of the Investigator's victims had in the last moon. The stench of Roxthar's 'cleansing fires' hovered over Balph like a cloud of Ravens at one of Kalvan's battlefields.

"Are you worrying again, my lord?" Thessamona asked.

Anaxthenes nodded. It was such a relief to be able to actually voice his thoughts without thinking of plots and counterplots, treachery and disloyalty. "Our world is on the verge of destruction."

"Surely, you exaggerate. Roxthar does not dare move against you openly."

"He dares, he just doesn't find it politic. He is trying to use me, as I used Sesklos all those many years. But I was not speaking of our simple palace here and our life together. He will be the death of Styphon's House, if the Usurper Kalvan does not destroy us first!"

"I don't understand," she said. "Has not Roxthar's Investigations raised Temple donations to an all time high?"

"Yes, but that's part of the problem. We want people to respect Styphon, not live in mortal dread of his Investigators. Now they offer their gold to prove their piety to Styphon! That's the entire problem; how can there be heretics of a Temple that has no god?" There he said it out loud, the unbidden thought that had long plagued his mind.

Her laugh sounded like the tinkling of bells. "He is a madman, of course. We've discussed that many times. He is looking for air in a rock. But doesn't Styphon's Treasury need more gold to pay for her armies?"

"Yes, but we already have more than enough. Roxthar is creating a climate of fear, and, if it continues, it will break out in a thunderstorm—and who will take the brunt?"

Thessamona nodded. "The Inner Circle and Highpriests. Roxthar will say it was their corruption that has incensed the mobs. When it is the fear of his Investigation that has driven the multitudes out into the streets."

Anaxthenes nodded, squeezing her shoulder, in an unusual display of affection. "You understand what my fellow highpriests do not. Sesklos now fears Roxthar more than Hadron's demons! The old priest has at last outlived his usefulness."

"What about one of your vials?"

"I was tempted last winter, but that was before Roxthar's ascendancy. No, it might prove too convenient. Too many fingers would point my way."

"Someone has to take the helm of your rudderless galley, before a rock rips out the belly."

"A most apt metaphor, Thessamona. What the fools of Inner Circle don't realize is, Styphon's Temple was doomed the moment Kalvan"—he hissed the word—"learned the Fireseed Mystery. Of course, the Temple had anticipated such an event. In the past hundred winters, we have killed two other alchemists that 'learned' the Mystery. Kalvan was not known to us and worked in secrecy in a small princedom that had escaped our eye until Styphon's gold was discovered in one of their valleys. It's not a common substance, like the other ingredients of the Mystery, and smells of Regwarn's Caverns."

"Then why are we still here? You have enough gold for a prince."

Anaxthenes smiled. "And leave a lifetime's work! I am no voluptuary, who can sit and drink myself insensate or lose myself in the weaknesses of the flesh. My pleasure is in bending men to my will and changing their lives."

"Yes, it is hard to imagine you sitting still for any length of time."

He stopped his pacing to laugh. "You know me too well, Thessie."

"I still do not understand why the Temple of Styphon is doomed, as you say. The Temple owns more gold than all the Great Kings combined, it owns the Great Banking Houses, it commands a huge trading fleet and war fleet, as well, and owns more land than is contained within the borders of Hos-Agrys."

"All of what you say is true, and more," Anaxthenes replied. "The Temple has wealth like a farmer has manure. Unfortunately, our greatest weapon—the Mystery—has been pillaged. Some think this Kalvan is a former Zygrosi Temple underpriest who joined the Temple to steal our Mystery. It may be true, although he takes to command like one born to it."

"As does, my lord," Thessamona replied.

Even after all these years, she was still in awe of his noble birth. Yes, he was of the nobility, the fifth son of a penniless baron, who left the family tarr to make his own fortune. Years later he had bought the family estate, kicked his older brothers out and put their former seneschal in charge. That the estate had thereafter shown good profit had amused him to no end.

"Yet," he continued, "without the Mystery to hold over the barons and princes like a club, we are no more useful than a merchant. The day some Great King decides to tax our Banking Houses or put duties on our cotton our time is ended—maybe not that moment in time, but shortly thereafter. Outside of the Temple underpriests, how many true believers of Styphon are there? Archpriest Roxthar. And Archpriest Cimon, the one they call the 'Peasant Priest,' who is so rare a bird that he was elevated to the Inner Circle so that we could display his piety to those besotted worshipers of Dralm! How many 'real' converts has Roxthar's Investigation brought? Not one whose faith in Styphon will last one day longer than Roxthar's last breath!"

Thessamona sighed. "I have never seen you so heated. Why do you not use one of your vials upon—?"

"Don't say it, don't think it! That wolf-in-man's clothing will smell it, I tell you. He breathes in thoughts. If Roxthar were to die, his followers—mostly ambitious underpriests who hang upon his robes to further their own careers—would turn upon the Inner Circle and kill us all. These are no longer men of restraint: they have tasted human blood and suffering and now they gorge themselves upon it. Roxthar feeds them and thus he owns them. The Investigators are outcasts to all humanity."

"You are not thinking clearly, my lord. Who is it that owns the Temple? Not the old fool they call Styphon's Voice. Nor is it Dracar for all his plots and counter-plots. Nor is it Cimon, for all his piety. Nor is it Roxthar for all his terror. It is you, my lord. You who know the Archpriests and their appetites. You who know their secrets and where they are buried. It is time you made some plans."

Anaxthenes nodded. "You are right, as always, Thessamona. I must or the Temple is doomed."

"If Roxthar is made Styphon's Voice, even the peasants will throw rocks at the priests of Styphon!"

"Yes, the devil must know that. That is why he uses others in his place. Sesklos is not worth the candle it takes to light his chamber, since it will be snuffed out soon. Dracar is the key."

Thessamona smiled as if she could read his thoughts. "Do you want me to boil the roots upon the next full moon?"

Anaxthenes shook his head. "The time is not right. I will let you know when the time has come for Dracar to join Hadron's Realm."

SIXTEEN

Danar Sirna, Outtime Historian and one of the political peons of the Second Kalvan Study Team, listened to the rain on the roof and to the argument in the Foundry common room, wishing earnestly that one would grow loud enough to drown out the other. Sirna didn't much care which; both the argument and the rain had gone on much too long and she was growing more depressed with each passing minute.

The argument was the latest round in the endless feud between Aranth Saln, the Teams' only military specialist, on the one hand and Varnath Lala and Lathor Karv on the other, over the Study Teams' attitude toward the 'true gods' when they reached Nostor to set up a new foundry there. Varnath and Lathor saw this as the ideal opportunity to introduce rational patterns of thought into Kalvan's Time-Line by, at the very least, not mentioning any of the gods as they taught the new foundry workers.

A blatant violation of the Paratime Code's anti-contamination act, thought Sirna. *Too bad I'm not spying for Chief Verkan.*

Aranth saw his colleagues' proposal as pointless at best, likely to expose the Study Team to a charge of heresy at worst. Both sides had long since ceased to come up with any new arguments; neither was so far gone that they carried on the argument in the presence of any Fourth Level listeners.

"The Council of Dralm hasn't developed the concept of heresy," Lathor Karv was saying in what, for him, passed for a reasonable tone of voice. "Therefore how can you argue that we'll be in danger of being charged with a crime that doesn't exist?"

"That doesn't exist now," Professor Aranth replied rather grimly, Sirna thought. She wondered if what bothered him was the strength of the opposition, possible danger to the Team or simply that an argument he'd probably begun to cure his own boredom was now making it worse, now that the professional nit-pickers had gotten into it. "We have no idea what the highpriests of Dralm may eventually decide is appropriate, in the face of Styphon's House and what is on the verge of becoming a full-blown religious war. Kalvan can't do a Dralm-damned thing to stop them from inventing heresy if they want to, either, so don't give me your usual song-and-dance about Kalvan, Eldra."

Baltrov Eldra just sighed and looked bored.

"You're showing a typical male reversion pattern, Aranth," Varnath Lala said. "The minute men get into a patriarchal culture like this one, they seem to soak up its attitudes with the air they breathe and the water they drink. If they can't do anything else, they are rude to their female colleagues. You've gone completely out of sight on oath-bonding as well."

"You call yourself a pre-Industrial Specialist—even if it is Metallurgy, Lala. Then actually have the gall to say oaths aren't taken seriously? Guilds that work metal take oath's especially strong." Aranth Saln's voice held honest incredulity. Sirna had to admit that once again Varnath Lala had left herself wide open in an effort to ruffle a man. That wasn't the first time for that, either, or the twentieth. In part, brought on by the attempt to pass for 'free' women among Fourth Level foundry workers, who didn't believe the term free applied to women in any sense, the rest because of her irascible personality.

"I don't think it can honestly be said that we've sworn any oaths that require us to mention the 'true gods,'" Lathor Karv said, in his lecture-hall tone of voice. "Therefore I don't think we will be considered oath-breakers as long as we observe the appropriate rituals and don't break taboos or interfere with the priests."

Even over the rain and crackle of fire in the next room, Sirna heard Varnath Lala's hiss of indrawn breath, then her tight-voiced reply.

"I'm afraid I lack your enthusiasm or your talent for hypocrisy, Lathor. Kalvan himself didn't mince words calling fireseed the result of 'simple mechanic arts' any child could learn. Why shouldn't we follow in the Great King's own footsteps?"

"I, for one, lack enthusiasm for wet rugs," Baltrov Eldra said, "and in case none of you has noticed, the roof is leaking again."

Sirna listened to the names of a number of gods being taken in vain in the next room, the thump of a rug being rolled up, the clatter of a bucket being set down and the steady plink-plink-plink of the leak dripping into it. Sirna would have invoked the weather goddess herself, except that this weather seemed more likely to have been a gift of Lyklos, god of lies and practical jokes.

To do Lyklos as much justice as the Trickster ever deserved, it wasn't entirely the fault of the rainy weather that the University Study Team hadn't long since been on its way to Nostor Town. If they'd just had to transport themselves and their personal possessions, riding horses and pack mules would have done the job well enough. Sirna's buttocks and thighs ached at the mere thought of long days in the saddle, but she had to admit that only a few of them would have taken her and her companions to Nostor.

However, the University had to transport not only their nearly complete set of blacksmithing tools, but their specialized Zygrosi foundry equipment, too. That meant a load running over a hundred tons, which in turn meant a fair-sized train of wagons and carts, since at best the Zarthani covered wagons could transport about twenty tons each. They also had food and clothing and provisions for the Foundry workers and teamsters. All that meant waiting until the roads were passable—sometime next spring. No number of draft horses and ox teams that the Great King could spare would be able to haul the foundry train to Nostor over roads knee-high in mud, and in another moon or two snow.

If the Foundry crew traveled light, they would arrive sooner but would need four to five moons to build everything from scratch. Due to massive unemployment in Nostor, Kalvan wanted the new Foundry built there, rather than expanding the old one. It was Eldra's opinion that Kalvan wanted it closer to the Harphax City, where he would need it once the city fell.

There the matter settled—and the University Kalvan Study Team as well, trapped ten miles outside Hostigos Town and trying to fight boredom and cabin fever without drinking too much or interfering with their Hostigi workers.

Sirna decided that she was in the mood for some fresh air, before anybody missed her and came looking to dragoon her into a floor-mopping brigade. She knew the fresh air would be at least half water and the ground more than half mud, but she didn't care. She slipped past the half-open door toward the wardrobe in the outer hall where the outdoor clothing hung.

The mud was even deeper than Sirna expected, and it took her nearly half an hour to make one circuit of the entrenchments around the foundry and storage buildings. By then the rain was beginning to soak through her outer clothing. Oiled leather was better than nothing, she admitted, but it was as heavy as a suit of armor, prone to crack and leak, foul-smelling wet or dry and not really all that waterproof. If she stayed out here much longer, she'd pay for her fresh air by being soaked to the skin. It would be just her luck for the Team leader to decide that one of the University team members should come down with a cold so as not to arouse suspicion of sorcery by undue immunity to disease!

At times like this Sirna sympathized with the idea of playing god-sent-teacher-to-the-unenlightened; at least one could wear sensible clothing and use First Level medicine.

In her half year on Kalvan's Subsector she'd reported no conditions of outtime contamination by Kalvan, yet Tharn—who sent her regular letters as Uncle T.—seemed inordinately happy with her posts. She couldn't figure out why. Most everything she'd reported could have been taken from a standard University Kalvan Study Team press release.

Why should she feel so obligated to follow Hadron's orders? True, if it hadn't been for his pull she never would have gotten such a high-prestige assignment, but he could hardly report her to the University for that. On the other hand, he could make trouble with her parents—who would certainly put politics above mere 'anarchistic familial ties'—as well as stifle her future career at Dhergabar University. Even though Hadron had been expelled after some sort of outtime fiasco involving the Paratime Police that nobody—even his supporters wanted to talk about—but his grants to the University were a major source of funding for outtime research.

And there was one more reason she would follow Tharn's orders until her assignment to Kalvan Prime was over—Hadron Tharn scared her to death. There was something in those dead eyes of his that told you he'd no more regret ending your life than that of some insect that happened to get in his way.

All her life Sirna had been dominated by men. First her father, who had really wanted a son, but lacked the will to defy her mother and who'd settled for a daughter who would follow in his footsteps. Then, when she became 'inconvenient,' dumped her into a University crèche when her mother went outtime. Next, there was her husband who had wanted the appearance, but not the actuality of a wife. Now by Hadron Tharn, who wanted her to do his dirty work against Verkan Vall and the Paratime Police.

She wished she had the courage to say To Styphon with the entire lot!

Sirna had nearly completed the circuit of the foundry entrenchments when a broad figure in a woolen cloak and high-combed morion helmet loomed out of the darkness ahead of her. She froze, cursing herself for going outside without a pistol as well as her dagger.

Then, remembering the odds against a flintlock's firing in this kind of downpour, she shouted, "Who is it?"

"Master Aranth, of the Royal Hostigos Foundry," the figure answered. "Who are you?"

Sirna sighed with relief, while wondering what brought the military man out on a night like this. "Sirna, Mistress Pattern-Maker. What are you doing out here, Master Aranth?"

"The same thing you are, Mistress," he said, pointing to the Foundry quarters. "Escaping the bedlam of too much talk about too little. And call me Saln."

"Me too, Saln. I think I'd rather attend one of Xentos' prayer meetings for deliverance from Styphon's House at the Temple of Dralm than spend another five minutes in there."

Aranth Saln laughed, exposing a mouthful of well-formed and broad teeth. "Right, Xentos is back from the Council at Agrys City. No one seems too happy about it. Ranthar said it had something to do with the Council refusing to recognize the Sixth Great Kingdom and its ruler. No one at the palace is talking, but the Paratime Police have established agents at all the capitals and big cities."

Finally, Sirna had something to report and it came from a reputable source even; however, it was less than significant, but would at least show she was doing her job.

"Trader Ranthar seems like a good man, even if he is with the Paratime Police."

"They have a lot of good men, another year on this time-line and you'll lose a lot more of your University prejudices."

"It looks like the rain has stopped for a time," Aranth said. "Would you like to accompany me to Hostigos Town? I'm going to the One-Eyed Owl for some good company."

Sirna had heard Varnath Lala go on about how the One-Eyed Owl, a tavern where mercenaries and the King's regulars liked to do their drinking, was a cesspit of male supremacy; well, the company would have to be pretty bad before she'd miss the bickering and one-ups-manship here at the Foundry.

"Sure, Aranth, I'd love to go."

Sirna followed Aranth Saln to the stable where he helped her bridle and saddle a gentle bay mare. By the time they'd left the stable, a full moon was casting a silvery glow over the hills and the rain had come to a complete stop. Thank you, Lystris, she said under her breath.

As they slowly made their way through the muddy path leading to the Great King's Highway, Sirna noticed that beneath his cloak Aranth was wearing a back and breast with taces.

"Why all the steel?" she asked.

"Footpads. Even the Great King's Patrol and the weather won't convince them to keep their distance any better than tempered steel. Despite the calm of the past few moons, there's still a war going on here and I wouldn't be the least bit surprised to learn that a few stragglers from the Battle of Phyrax are still skulking around."

"After all this time?"

"Yup. Tuad, the chief carpenter, was telling me that about a ten-day ago someone stole half a dozen chickens and a bushel of turnips from the Foundry garden."

A lone wolf howl echoed through the hills and Sirna shivered. "Are we going to have troubles with wolves, too?"

"That's the first one I've heard this fall. Kalvan had his wolf hunters stake out the battlefields this year and thin their ranks. He's kept the bounty high enough that the only wolves you're going see this winter are the two-legged variety."

Aranth slowed down his horse. "Be careful getting onto the highway. This would be a nasty place for a fall." Aranth paused and added, "Your own hands are properly dirty."

Sirna laughed and said, "You mean my shoes are muddy."

"No. I mean your hands. Student Sirna, I happen to know that you were added to the Study Team only because you are the niece of that two-faced politician Hadron Tharn."

"I'm not his niece," Sirna replied. "My parents work for him."

"No difference. You were a political appointee, a pipsqueak version of Varnath Lala, and I stay clear of such. Then came the Battle of Phyrax, and you volunteered to stay at the Foundry when Varnath and Talgran both cut and run. Spoiled brat or not, I decided you had what it really took to be an outtime researcher. We're comrades now, veterans of Phyrax together, and what say we team up for a good bar-room brawl."

Sirna was stunned by this fairly accurate capsule description of herself; she was about to pull a Varnath Lala and lose her temper, when she burst out laughing. "Am I that easy to read?"

"For someone of my age and experience, yes. I doubt most of the other Study Team members will remember your name a week after you leave."

"Praise Dralm, then!" she cried.

A moment later, the horses were clomping along the stone roadway of the Great King's Highway.

"Dralm Bless King Kalvan!" they both said in unison and then started laughing. "And bless the Great King's Highway," Sirna added.

"Did you know, Sirna, that Kalvan had half the Royal Army prisoners-of-war and displaced peasants working on this highway during the summer. Twenty-eight miles worth. It's what they'd call on Kalvan's Europo-American time-line a two-lane highway; not too impressive there, but a major engineering feat on Kalvan Prime. From what Captain-General Harmakros was telling me, Kalvan plans to run this road from Hostigos Town north along the Listra River and then west through Nyklos and into Ulthor Port at the Saltless Sea. He's had less success with the semaphore stations, which someday will reach Beshta. It may take him a lifetime, but these innovations of Kalvan's will change trade patterns like nothing this time-line has seen since Styphon first discovered the fireseed secret."

"You know Captain-General Harmakros!"

"Yes, I do. Met him at the One-Eyed Owl with Captain Ranthar. He's a quick wit and very down to earth. It's no surprise he's one of Kalvan's top generals; Harmakros would be a chief-of-staff or head constable on any time-line where talent took precedence over birth, and on quite a few where it doesn't—like this one! You may get an opportunity to meet him yourself tonight."

The horses were moving at a respectable trot now that they were on solid ground and Sirna began to see more farmhouses as they approached the outskirts of Hostigos Town. The fields were covered with small lakes of rainwater and she was surprised to see how peaceful everything looked despite the war. "It looks like the farmers managed to harvest most of the barley and corn this year."

"Again, you can thank Kalvan. He had his University artificers knocking-out primitive reapers through most of the summer. As a result, they had a bumper harvest throughout all of Hostigos and Sask, and reaped enough of a surplus to feed all of Nostor and Beshta, too."

"Why do I get the idea that you're pretty impressed with our Great King Kalvan?"

"Simple, Sirna, it's because I am. He is doing the kind of job here that I would like to think I would do under similar circumstances. He is doing a tough job and doing it well. And, he's the underdog of all underdogs."

"Most of the other Team members just think he's lucky, but you don't. Why is that?"

"Because, I am watching what Kalvan is doing, not what I think he is doing or my sociological theory tells me he is doing. And, from where I sit; he's doing a Dralm-damn good job. Look at Kalvan's army; there are more men under Hostigi colors than there are farming, smithing, and crafting. How is this possible in an agricultural pre-industrial economy? Easy. When there's work to be done, everyone pitches in—including Great King Kalvan. Did you know that Kalvan himself went into the fields this fall and helped pick corn for two solid weeks!

"The Hostigi economy, which would have been a disaster for a lesser man, became a triumph of public relations for Kalvan. You can Dralm-damned be sure that the soldiers quit their grumbling about 'serf's work' after that. I would just like to know how damn many of Styphon's House upperpriests were trampling through the ruined fields of Hos-Harphax!"

"Not a single one," Sirna responded, "nor upperpriests of Dralm either."

"Of course," Aranth said, "after all, priests have to keep their hands clean in this world as preparation for the next."

As they approached Hostigos Town, Sirna turned her horse to the side of the road to let a big canvas covered wagon go by in the opposite direc-tion. Then they were over the slight rise and she could see Hostigos Town down a dip and spread over a series of rolling hills. Right below the Gap and Tarr-Hostigos was the Royal Army encampment, which looked to be about a quarter the size of the town.

"That's a big army camp," Sirna said. "It's more than doubled in size since last year."

"Sure it has. Kalvan had half the army working on this road, another quarter billeted all over Hos-Hostigos and the rest drilling and marching. Now that it's almost winter he wants them where he can keep his eye on them. Other than the Army of Observation, which Captain-General Hestophes is commanding, the rest of the Royal Army is right here. Look at his defensive perimeter! He's got a series of earthworks all around with gun batteries, too."

"Hostigos Town looks to be growing as well," Sirna said, trying to divert their talk from things military, which she knew very little about, and cared even less.

"It has been growing almost weekly. When Kalvan first arrived over a year and a half ago, there were only about ten thousand people living in Hostigos Town, now the population's grown to over twenty-five thousand, not counting military personnel. It's hard to get a reliable census since there are so many transients."

"Why so fast?" Sirna found it interesting that the Team's military expert knew more about the Town of Hostigos than all the Study Team sociolo-gists put together. Of course, the idea of mingling with actual Hostigi was unthinkable, to the sociologists, and reeked of Outtime-Identification Syn-drome. Sirna was beginning to think it was because they didn't want to confuse their theories with facts. Or, Styphon forbid, actually get to know the people they studied. Of course if they had to bug-out in a hurry, as Ranthar put it, it could hurt to have to leave friends behind. Still, she'd rather face that pain, than adopt the studied indifference of the University 'professionals.'

"Because Hostigos Town—soon to-be City—is now the capital of a Great Kingdom and the headquarters for the largest standing army this time-line has ever known. It's a military boom town, engineered by King Kalvan and paid for by Styphon's House temple loot."

"What happens when Styphon's gold runs out?"

"Kalvan has a saying, which I learned from Harmakros, I will try to paraphrase, 'while gold can't always get you good soldiers, good soldiers can always get you gold.'"

"But doesn't that just make Kalvan a Great Pirate, rather than a Great King."

"Sorry, I was just being amusing at Kalvan's expense; though there is more truth to that maxim than the military layman would understand. I think if Styphon's House would just leave Kalvan alone the economy of Hos-Hostigos would take care of itself. Turn that University artificer crowd of his loose and you would see more action on the Street of Coopers than you see now on Army payday at the Street of Lamps."

Sirna was glad it was dark out so that Aranth wouldn't see her blush. There was little prostitution on Home Time Line where Citizens had a chance to freely express their naturalistic impulses; Sirna found it a rather unseemly statement on the condition of women's rights on Kalvan's Time-Line. Not that she thought it was her duty to personally lash out at any male who appeared to disregard those rights as Varnath Lala did.

A few moments later they trotted off the Great King's Highway, which in town turned into the single lane of Tigos Road. They passed one of the new roads, Princess Demia's Street, and across Tanner's Way down into Hostigos Town proper where most of the inns and taverns were located. The One-Eyed Owl tavern was right across from the Crossed Halberds, another Royal Army favorite or so she'd heard.

Even in the rain, which had started up again, there were carts and wagons moving through the streets and a steady stream of cloaked men and armed guards. "Make way, make way," cried one group of armored men, wearing the blue capes of the Hostigos Town watch. They also carried sharp-bladed halberds and a foot long oak club at their belt securely tied by leather thongs.

As they boarded their horses at a nearby stable, Sirna said, "It's strange to think that on most every other Aryan-Transpacific, Styphon's House Subsector time-line most of these people are dead and Hostigos Town is in ruins or a shadow of its former self. Is this right?"

"Don't know," Aranth said, "but these people are very much alive and plan to continue on so."

"I just wish there was more we could do to help them. Is it right that we keep the secret of longevity from Outtime peoples, too?"

"Don't know about that either. I'm not at all convinced it's the length of a life that counts. Look at most of that University crowd out at the Foundry. If I had my choice between a long lifetime with that gang, or a much shorter lifetime here; you wouldn't need to be a gambler to predict my pick."

"A lifetime with Varnath Lala and Lathor Karv would be torture indeed!" Sirna laughed.

"Most truly spoken, Sirna," Aranth said, as he paused to whisper something into the ear of a very young girl less than half his size. The girl was provocatively dressed and her painted mouth dropped open at Aranth's words. She ran off in haste, her clogs banging on the wet cobblestones, as he opened the door to the One-Eyed Owl.

Sirna asked, "What was that all about?"

"An under-age soliciter—actually not very common in Zarthani towns, but especially rare here. I just reminded her of Kalvan's punishment for solicitation. He's a bit of a prude on these matters."

And so am I, thought Sirna, even though she was a neophyte when it came to outtime studies. She supposed she had a lot to learn, but was sure that no degree of experience or sophistication would allow her to accept the practice of children selling themselves on the street.

Inside was a score of overburdened and undersized tables with about half of one of Kalvan's Royal regiments in attendance. There were shouts of greeting from more than a couple tables, which showed that Aranth's trade was well known here. Aranth pointed to a table where two soldiers and several—for lack of a more polite term—harlots were sitting.

With a quick side-step here and there Sirna managed to make it to the table with both dignity and skirts intact. Aranth introduced her to General Alkides and a Colonel Democriphon, a dashing young soldier with flowing golden locks and a handsome face worth writing home about. After additional chairs were obtained by the tavern keeper, she listened with more fascination than she would have ever believed possible to Democriphon's tale of King Kalvan's charge into the Styphoni right wing at Phyrax.

Maybe Aranth was right; there was more to outtime travel than University inter-disciplinary shoot-outs and inter-departmental feuding.

SEVENTEEN

I

Sitting in a circle with a dozen tribesmen, Ranjar Sargos was shaking all five of the knucklebone dice for one last roll. He made his throw, hoping his luck would change and he would win the pile of silver coins and quarter-cut ingots spread before the campfire. While the dice were still in the air, his youngest son, Larkander came crashing into the clearing, knocking over wine bags, mead kegs, silver coins and dice alike.

Before Sargos had time to raise his voice, his son began to talk excitedly, his voice breaking with both eagerness and the first changes of manhood. "Father! The Badger Tribe has arrived! Many of the warriors are hurt or missing. Old Daron sent me to tell you that it's time for the Clan Council. Come, father!"

Vanar Halgoth placed his hand gently on Larkander's arm. "Calm down, son. There can be no meeting without the Silver Fox Tribe."

Larkander shook his head. "Old Daron says the Silver Fox Tribe is no more. They were driven from their lands by the Grassmen from across the Great Mother River. The few survivors have joined with the Badger Tribe. So the Council is going to begin as soon as everyone arrives. Can I go? My initiation is only a few moons away!"

Sargos shook his head. "You are still not a man. When you are, you will have a place at the Clan Council."

Larkander looked down at the ground.

Another tribe lost, thought Sargos to himself, that made two this season. The Clan had shrunk from nine tribes to seven since last winter. Eight tribes, if you counted the Burgduns, who had lost all their men, except for less than a single handful of warriors, two of whom were permanently crippled from the injuries taken when their tribe had been attacked by the Grassmen.

"Come with me," he told his tribesmen. "Larkander, you find your brother and send him to the Council." Bargoth had spent most of his days, since arriving at the Clan Gathering, sitting outside the maiden's longhouse, trying to gain Althea's notice. So far he'd been rebuffed, along with half a dozen other young bucks, but it hadn't lessened his determination to win her favor. Occasionally, Sargos had found himself stealing glances over at the maiden's longhouse where she resided. Once they had met accidentally at the river and he couldn't tell who was more uncomfortable when their eyes met.

The Clan Council, which included all the adult males of the Tymannes, met in a large hollow in the shape of a cup. The shape reminded Sargos of the Rathon amphitheater, where he had spent all his gold after two years of hard campaigning in the Trygath. He had only gone to the Games twice, and for the most part had found the staged sword fights between criminals unworthy. Not only did they have no honor, but also few had any skill with weapons other than the knife. Most even died badly.

Only one of the staged contests had been entertaining, but in an unexpected manner. That day the Games had featured wild animals and in one event, he witnessed a remarkable contest, a mother bear and her cub were set on by a small pack of wolves. The bear, trying to protect her cub, had taken the worst of the initial attack, until one of the larger wolves had gutted the baby bear. The mother bear had gone berserk, turning into a killing machine and dispatched the wolves as though they were cubs. Then, when the pack lay dead around her, their blood dripping from her snout, the bear had jumped—without warning—over the inner wall and into the crowd! The wall had been taller than Halgoth and Sargos had never seen a bear jump so high, nor had he seen so many people move so quickly. Even those nowhere near the bear stormed the tunnels to leave. He and Halgoth were laughing so hard they had fallen out of their seats, as they watched the city people in all their finery scramble every which way to escape the bear they had been taunting moments before.

The bear had finally been hunted down and killed by guards, but not before it had killed two score of revelers. Not having lived among so many people before, Sargos was surprised to find that ten times more of the city dwellers had perished in their blind flight to safety, than had been mauled to death by the mother bear. This had sworn Sargos off towns and cities and he had returned to the Raven Tribe never to leave again.

As befitted his station as Warchief of his tribe, Sargos stood near the grassy bottom, where the carved-stone Judgment Table stood. His sub-chiefs and the rest of the Raven warriors stood to his rear. He was shaken when all the Clansmen arrived and he saw with his own eyes that several of the tribes had shrunk by half their number. He had realized many old friends were missing, but not this many. The Raven Tribe was larger by three than any of the other tribes.

The Clan Chief stood before the Judgment Table, and, when the last few stragglers had arrived, he said, "Welcome men of the Tymannes." He gave a sharp look toward the Raven Clan and Sargos wondered why, until he turned and saw Althea standing behind him with her uncle Halgoth. Her unwavering eyes met his and he shrugged his shoulders. Althea had earned her place, woman or not, at this Gathering.

"Clansmen, look around at your fellow clansmen and you will see these are Times of Trouble. Many clans and tribes and all their multitudes have crossed the Great Mother River and it is said that many more wait behind! Two of our tribes, the Horse Tribe and the Silver Fox Tribe are no more. May the gods watch over them! The Horse Tribesmen were ambushed on a hunt by bandits, hundreds of tribeless men brought together by the lust for loot and battle. All but two of the Horse Tribe were killed and the women and children were taken by the lawless. The Silver Fox Tribe was attacked and run off their lands by Grassmen, who hunted them down like cattle! Other tribes of the Tymannes, as you can see by their thin ranks, have taken their own losses. Another bad year like this and the Tymannes will be no more!"

There was a great moan from the assembled warriors.

"It is time to fight, or leave these lands for new ones. We need a Warlord now to lead the Clan. I call Chief Mordar of the Longhorn Tribe to the Table."

Chief Mordar limped up to the Table. Mordar had been a tall, large man only a few years ago, but now, over sixty winters old, he was shrunken by age and the flux. It had been fifteen winters since the Tymannes had called upon a Warlord and much had changed since then, including the former Warlord.

Chief Mordar stood before the Judgment Table, trying to stiffen his bowed back. "I have served before as Warlord in the Time of Troubles, when the Vargox Clan invaded our lands. I will give the Clan the benefit of my many years of war and soldiering among the Lower Sastragath—"

One of the clansmen, from the Dog Tribe, yelled out. "When was your last fight old man? The Longhorn tribesmen hid in the hills when the Grassmen came!"

"Yes, truth," cried several others.

"We want Sargos!"

The Clan needs his war magic!"

"Warlord Sargos!" All two hundred warriors of the Raven Tribe, including the sole woman at the Gathering, quickly joined the chant.

"Quiet!" the Clan Chief shouted. "Who will make the claim for Ranjar Sargos, Chief of the Raven Tribe?"

"I will," Althea said, her woman's voice quieting the assembled tribesmen as if a huge hand had been cupped over the hollow.

Sargos heard one voice off to the left, from the ranks of the Longhorns say, "I hear the woman is a witch. It is said she slew twenty of the Grassmen with only her knife!"

Voices erupted from every camp.

"By what right is this woman allowed to speak!" Mordar shouted; his arms and thighs may have withered, but his voice was still big.

But not as big as the presence of Vanar Halgoth. "By the right of *vergelt!* This maiden, my niece, has blood right on her side. Althea lost her entire family to the Grassmen and by her own hand cut five of their throats!"

There was a rumble of amazement and surprise.

With her uncle by her side, Althea strode to the Judgment Table, her long blonde hair following like a banner. As he watched her, Sargos thought to himself, *this is what we are fighting for, the safety and protection of our women and children. They are the future of all the Tymannes.*

She paused to make sure she had everyone's attention before speaking. "My tribe was slain by the Grassmen. They attacked our camp while our men were at the hunt. They did unspeakable things to our women and killed all our boys over the age of six winters."

This brought forward a collective gasp. Most Tymannes had heard the story around the campfire, but the tale became truth to the warriors, when spoken at the Council by a survivor.

"When our men returned, they were ambushed and killed, by those coyotes in human form, the Grassmen. If it were not for Warchief Sargos, our tribesmen's ghosts would still be seeking their vengeance. Warchief Sargos led a surprise night raid upon their camp and all the Grassmen were killed, their women taken prisoner and all their horses taken."

Even though the Raven Tribe's raid had been talked about for days, there was still a moment of silence as the assembled tribesmen thought about the hundreds upon hundreds of horses that had swelled the Raven's herds to unheard of size.

Althea's eyes locked upon Sargos own as she said, "I think there can be only one choice for Warlord of the Tymannes and that man is Warchief Ranjar Sargos!"

The bowl erupted with thunderous applause and shouts of agreement.

"It is unanimous then," the Clan Chief said, despite the frowns on Mordor's face and that of his subchiefs.

Chief Mordor spit on the ground and walked away with all the dignity he could muster.

"The new Warlord of the Tymannes has been chosen. Ranjar Sargos is your Warlord. Come, Ranjar Sargos and speak to your people." The Clan Chief looked as if he were relieved to be able to shift the responsibility for the clan's survival to someone else's shoulder, and at that moment Sargos felt as if he were carrying every clansman—man, woman and child—on his back. The look upon Althea's face as he passed by her somehow made it all worthwhile.

Warlord Sargos stood before the Tymanni warriors. "I make a mighty oath to protect our Clan and our women! I swear this by the Raven Hag of War! Death to all our enemies. Our Clansmen who have died will be avenged!"

The Raven flag was hoisted before Sargos and waved vigorously. The big black bird, with a red morsel in it's beak, appeared to take flight as the flag flapped, and when a flock of crows flew overhead it was called a mighty portent. "The Hag herself rejoices in our Warlord!"

As Sargos watched the big black birds, the scavengers of battlefields, the new Warlord wondered whom they came for? The Tymannes or their enemies? Sargos had a feeling deep in his bones that the answer would not be long in coming.

II

Trader Tortha followed Great King Kalvan into his private audience chamber. He was wearing his formal mink-collared robe and welcomed its protection from the drafty castle halls. He had been impressed at how quickly Kalvan had grasped the idea of secrecy as a weapon; the moment he'd heard from his steward that Tortha was a friend of Trader Verkan's Kalvan had arranged for him to be quickly escorted into a private chamber with a goblet of Ermut's Best—which was good enough that Tortha planned to take some back to First Level with him when he left. He'd have to be careful to watch his consumption, even though he had his alcodote, a First Level alcohol neutralizer, with him. He didn't want to make Kalvan suspicious, since the former Pennsylvania State trooper was noted for missing very little of what went on around him.

Kalvan stretched and eased himself down onto a highback chair. Tortha was pleased to note that his chair was not only the same height, but of the same quality as Kalvan's. Here was a man without obvious insecurities and one who valued his friends' comfort over his own elevation—admirable qualities on any time-line.

After a long sigh, Kalvan picked up the small cask and filled his own goblet with Ermut's Best. "I read over Verkan's post, before I left the audience room. I'm pleased to see that his affairs go so well in Greffa. Let's toast to his success in gaining the friendship of King Theovacar for Hos-Hostigos!"

Alcohol toasts were almost a universal constant on every Level, but an absolute constant throughout Fourth Level. They both clanked goblets.

"Our friend also had good things to say about yourself, Master Tortha."

Tortha shrugged. "I've known Verkan since he was wearing teething gowns! Our Houses have been friends since my grandfather's time. He has grown into a fine man, and a good friend."

Kalvan nodded his agreement. "His letter tells me that your House is based in Xiphlon. Can you tell me of events there; We have gotten very little news since the Mexicotál siege."

"We've suffered these sieges before, even before there were Five Kingdoms, before there was an Iron Trail. The plains are like the sea, they send storms—some are bad, and some are terrible. We have learned to build our walls stout enough that not even the highest sea can breach them. Yet, you have unleashed the formula for fireseed so that now all the tribes and clans to the west and south can make their own. Soon, they will buy better cannon, and even the Great Walls of Xiphlon will be endangered."

Kalvan looked thoughtful. "You don't seem angry?"

"If not you, then someone else—god-sent, or man—would have uncovered Styphon's Mystery. Does one blame the sea for breakers that beat upon the shore? No. It only means that we will have to forge our own guns and make our army more mobile; two things that you have proven to be your providence. I see a great future in trade between our two Kingdoms."

Kalvan smiled. "You have a quick and deep mind—like our friend, Verkan. Were it in my power We would send a great host to Xiphlon to teach these feathered cannibals about our god of war—by Galzar's Mace!"

"I believe you would, King Kalvan. I also believe you would be a good friend for Xiphlon and, if my word has any value in King Rolthoff's ears, I will tell him of your words and the sincerity behind them."

"If your king values good words, as he does good soldiers, your words will be heard. How go events in the upper Middle Kingdoms?"

"King Theovacar's plans for the new lighthouse are quickly coming to fruition. It will be the grandest monument since the days when the Iron Trail was bustling with traffic. Trade has been good during his reign and both our House and Verkan's were flourishing until the Mexicotál fought their way to our City walls. Verkan has helped our Greffa branch grow under his aegis and we, ourselves, may soon be able to trade with Hos-Hostigos."

"Styphon has been generous with his treasure, as he has left Us many empty temples with their gold roofs to add to the Royal Treasury. We would be interested in expanding Our trade to more houses in the Middle Kingdoms. We welcome Our friends from Dorg and Wulfula as well as Xiphlon and Greffa. You have Our permission to tell any of your trader friends that Hostigos is always a good market for quality arms and guns. And that Hos-Hostigos pays with gold and silver of higher purity than any other realm in the Six Kingdoms."

Talking to Kalvan reminded Tortha of trying to get a point across in the Executive Council, where every declarative word could be used against you like a club. Kalvan had very quickly mastered the Zarthani indirect mode of speech, which boded well for his survival among a people who took a man's word as his oath—so it couldn't be given easily, or without qualification. Still, he hoped that someday the two of them would be able to talk freely as friends. Tortha liked Kalvan and wished him the best, even though he knew, with all that was coming Kalvan's way, that was like whistling into a deep cave.

III

Duke Skranga held up the parchment to the oil lamp and reread Prince Bythannes promissory note for eighteen thousand gold crowns. In his hand he held the future of the Princedom of Thaphigos. If this letter were to fall into Lysandros' hands, it could spark a major war between Harphax and Thaphigos. Put into Styphon's House's lap and they might finance a baronial revolt among the Thaphigos nobility.

To Kalvan the note was a guarantee of Thaphigosi opposition to Lysandros' election as Great King of Hos-Harphax. Briefly Skranga wondered how much gold and land Prince Lysandros would reward him with for ownership of the parchment. Then he made a long sigh of resignation. He couldn't betray Kalvan; the only man who'd seen something finer in him than what was shown on the outside. Who else but Kalvan had guessed that he could read and write, an advantage Skranga has used more than once to swindle some uppity noble?

This had to be Lyklos the Trickster's work! After a lifetime of horsetrading and petty thievery, when he finally found "the big one," he'd already given his bond to a man he both trusted and liked.

Kalvan also had been responsible for sending Skranga to Nostor, where he'd been granted a title, a dukedom yet! When the war finally ended Skranga might well find himself a respected nobleman and a landholder in Hos-Hostigos. What had happened to the gangly youth, whom even his father had predicted would finish this life at the end of a rope? These were strange times indeed!

Skranga put down the promissory note and returned to the letter he was writing to Great King Kalvan:

I'm not sure what Lysandros will do when he discovers that Bythannes had paid off his outstanding notes, with gold other than that from Styphon's coffers. I expect he will be livid, but he has to do something decisive to break the Elector deadlock and unify Hos-Harphax before the campaign season starts next spring.

If I were Lysandros, I'd go over the heads of the Electors and the Regency Council, by making one of the friendly Princely Houses, like that of Prince Bosphros of Kelos, the ninth Elector and use him to break the tie. If done quietly and decisively with soldiers to guarantee their presence, the Electors can be cowed into obedience. After all, they too feel the shame of losing a great part of their Kingdom to the new Great Kingdom of Hos-Hostigos.

What else had he wanted to tell Kalvan? Oh yes, that he'd finally met the new Captain-General of the Harphaxi Army.

At a party I attended last night for Baroness Demara, I finally met Captain-General Phidestros, the new commander of the Hos-Harphax Army. He is a natural leader of men, as knowledgeable of military strategy as Harmakros. A worthy adversary—it's sorrowful that Lysandros is such a good judge of manflesh.

I made as many hints as was politic about Your Majesty's "enlightened" policies concerning good commanders and, in the process, learned why he was so suddenly elevated out of obscurity. This Phidestros is the same mercenary captain who looted Sarrask of Sask's baggage train at the Battle of Fyk! Since Sarrask is well known throughout Hos-Hostigos and Hos-Harphax as a Prince who nurses a grudge as well as his ale, Prince Lysandros knows that he can only work for Styphon's House. And that Phidestros is as likely to attempt to pay Sarrask back as Sarrask is likely to accept payment! This is as close to a guarantee of loyalty that Lysandros can expect from any mercenary Captain-General, since few are devout followers of Styphon.

If he were writing this to any other Great King but Kalvan, Skranga would have recommended a discrete accident for Sarrask and a quite generous bribe for Phidestros. Even if they couldn't outright buy his services, they would certainly bribe him to fight less well—a not unknown custom among mercenary captains. Yet, for all his fault's Sarrask had his value as well. For one, besides Ptosphes and Prince Phrames, Sarrask was Kalvan's most loyal Prince—and not a bad soldier either as he'd amply proven at the Battle of Ardros Field.

Of the other Hos-Hostigos Princes, only Prince Pheblon of Nostor was as loyal and that was because he owed his thrown to Kalvan's intervention into Nostori affairs. Prince Balthames would have sold out to Styphon's House long ago were he not encircled by Hostigos, Sask, and Beshta. Prince Armanes didn't have the good sense to be disloyal and it had cost him a nasty gut wound at Phyrax that had left his digestion as sensitive as an Archpriest's of the Inner Circle. Prince Kestophes of Ulthor and Tythanes of Kyblos were as loyal as convenience allowed, since they both resided closer to the sphere of the Upper Middle Kingdoms than to Hos-Harphax and Styphon's House. He doubted that their loyalty could be numbered in more than days were Lysandros to bring the war over the Iron Mountains. Praise be to Dralm and Galzar that Kalvan won every battle he fought, otherwise his allies might melt away like spring snow in the Moon of First Planting.

Certainly there was little to be gained by Hos-Hostigos from the farcical union, which called itself the League of Dralm. To end this war once and for all, Kalvan might well have to conquer Hos-Agrys and Hos-Ktemnos as well as Hos-Harphax. And, despite his bias, Skranga wouldn't have given three white-hocked black horses for Kalvan's chances to accomplish that miracle, Dralm-sent or no!

A knock at the door took him out of his reverie and he learned that his first visitor of the day had arrived. A few moments later, after he'd carefully hidden the letter to Kalvan, his personal servant brought in Master Trader Mynellos into Skranga's chamber.

When Trader Mynellos was comfortably seated with an ice-chilled goblet of winter wine in his hand, Skranga asked, "Now, what is it that I can do for you, Master Mynellos?"

"A precious vintage, Duke Skranga. You are to be complemented. And, I must thank you again for this gracious invitation on such short notice. I do not, however, just represent my own house. I was sent here as a representative of the Mercantile Council of Harphax City."

"This is all very interesting, Trader. But why go to such a bother to make audience with myself? I am but a simple march nobleman who had the foresight to send the greater portion of his wealth to a Harphaxi banking house, when he saw that the Usurper Kalvan might well appear to be more than the bandit chief my late liege lord mistakenly took him for."

"Not quite *so* simple, Your Grace. There were several hundred other noblemen in Nostor and Sask who did not—to their everlasting misfortune—share your foresight."

"I grant there is some truth in your words."

"Nor, were any of these others fortunate enough to escape from Kalvan's dungeons either, Your Grace. No, from this evidence alone, you are a most exceptional man."

Skranga's fingers went under the chair arm to make sure that the clasp holding the hidden dirk was released. "Please, Trader, make your point. I have other petitioners to see this day and a party to prepare for this evening."

"Certainly, I would not wish to delay one of your famous revels, especially one at which I hope to be in attendance." Skranga's fingers slowly began to relax.

"Essentially, what we want is information. Information, concerning the new Great King and his policies, especially as they relate to travel—and trade. Also, I might add, that anything one party can discern can be learned by another."

Skranga nodded, then bent down to pick up his pipe. That meant the Temple guard would be here next. He probably had until tomorrow to make himself scarce in Harphax City. Well, it wasn't unexpected and he would have everything he needed ready before first light. Canceling the party was out of the question, since it would raise more suspicions than his absence. Dralm damn-it, he had only one evening left to get Demara into his chambers.

He lit his pipe, took a deep draw and exhaled. "I understand that King Kalvan is well aware of the importance of inter-kingdom trade and that considerable amounts of it are taking place, especially concerning Hostigi fireseed, despite Styphon's Ban."

"Yes, we are aware of this smuggling. But that is to be expected, with or without his approval. Right now, though, Hos-Harphax is without access to the ports along the Saltless Seas and this is causing great hardship to a number of houses, my own included."

"I see your problem. However, you might as easily blame Lysandros and Styphon's House who have enforced their bans, not King Kalvan who would welcome your wares. Not that I'm an impartial observer, but King Kalvan has made many reforms throughout Hos-Hostigos. He has removed all tolls on bridges, roads, and pastures. Outlawed slavery and involuntary servitude. And has made it illegal for any noble to pay his debts in other than specie."

"These are not the acts of a madman or cutthroat as Styphon's high-priests made Kalvan out to be. This will interest the Council greatly."

"Yes and let it not be forgotten that Kalvan lets artificers, merchants, guild masters and other commoners sit upon his Councils. Now, I pray you go with the gods. I have many preparations to make before nightfall."

Master Trader Mynellos rose to his feet, bowed, and said, "Truly, I understand. It has been a pleasure making your acquaintance and I wish you the gods' own favor in your future travels."

He wasn't sure if that was a warning from a potential ally, or a sugges-tion that he get out of town before someone got the idea of a tar and turkey feather party—or a hanging! Regardless, he would be on his way before tomorrow's sunrise. He would try and contact his agents before he left, but only if he could do so without raising an alarm or risking their covers. Kalvan had told him stories about fifth columns and cells. Skranga would not want to live in a place where such activities were accepted or common-place, but the stories were instructional and he had used a few of their techniques in Harphax City.

EIGHTEEN

The plank table that ran the full length of the upper chamber, or war room, was almost filled with the General Staff of the Royal Army of Hos-Hostigos. As Great King Kalvan looked down the table at his friends and advisors he felt blessed that so many were the same faces that had occupied these seats last year. Despite the years hard campaigning, the only members who were absent was Major Nicomoth, his former aide-de-camp, one of the casualties of the Battle of Phyrax, General Hestophes, who was commanding the Army of Observation along the Harphaxi border, and Prince Phrames, who was up to his knees in beeswax as Prince of the troubled Princedom of Beshta.

Kalvan sat at the head of the table, while to his right sat Queen Rylla and to his left sat Colonel Krynos, his new aide-de-camp—one of Harmakros' top students of military science and a former mercenary captain. To Rylla's right sat Captain-General Harmakros, Duke Mnestros, as a friendly representative of the League of Dralm, Baron Zothnes, former Archpriest of Styphon, General Baldour a former mercenary Grand Captain from Hos-Ktemnos, who knew more about the southern Kingdoms than anyone else in the chamber, and Prince Sarrask of Sask, who'd just arrived to pay respects to his Great King—or as one wag put it, 'to try some more of the new Hostigi brandy at the Blue Halberd Grog Shop.'

At Colonel Krynos' left sat General Alkides, of the Royal Artillery, Captain-General Harmakros, just returned from Royal Army tour of the inspection, Captain Ranthar of the Mounted Rifles, who was sitting in for his superior Colonel Verkan, Prince Pheblon of Nostor, with his hand out for more foodstuffs for his war ravaged Princedom, and Prince Ptosphes. Great Captain-General Chartiphon, nominal commander of the Royal Army and at this moment looking none too happy for it, sat at the foot of the table.

Just as Kalvan was about to start the General Staff Meeting without him, Klestreus came puffing into the room. The Chief of Intelligence was a boar of a man and Kalvan estimated that he, Harmakros and Princess Demia could all fit inside his barrel-sized back-and-breast. "Sorry, I'm late, Your Majesty!" Klestreus wheezed. "But that third flight of steps is a killer."

"Too much sitting in wine shops, Klestreus," Prince Sarrask bellowed, while patting his own flat stomach. It appeared to Kalvan that not only had the Long March from Tenabra built Sarrask's character, but had removed most of the surplus gut as well—which surprisingly had not returned!

"What you need, my friend, is to get back into the saddle. I'm sure our Great King will do his best to see that that can be arranged next spring."

Several council members broke into open laughter and Rylla ended up in tears trying to hold her laughter in. Klestreus's face reddened as he squeezed into the chair between Duke Mnestros and Baron Zothnes. Over a year ago Klestreus' had been Captain-General of Nostor's mercenary army, which had unsuccessfully tried to conquer Hostigos; his ineptitude as a general had played no small part in Prince Gormoth's loss. Klestreus had joined the Hostigos Army, where Kalvan had been careful to keep him out of the field. His long service had made him invaluable as a source of information and gossip on all the major mercenary captains and the various noble houses throughout Hos-Agrys and Hos-Harphax.

Kalvan waited until the laughter had subsided, then lit his pipe and stood up. "First of all, I'd like to have Captain-General Harmakros give a status report on the state of preparedness of the Royal Army."

"Your Majesty," Chartiphon interrupted. "Could I be given leave to say a few words, before General Harmakros begins?"

Kalvan nodded and sat down. Chartiphon was a loyal, old-style soldier and very good as long as he stuck to pre-Kalvan tactics and strategy. Kalvan had promoted him as high as he could, to keep him off the field of battle, but there was going to be no changing his traditional beliefs. Chartiphon and Xentos were becoming Kalvan's greatest obstacles to progress. He was not going to win the war against Styphon's House, if he had to spend as much time trying to outflank his friends as his enemies.

"I know your Majesty's views on these new *bayonets,* but I question their performance on the field of battle. With my forty years of combat experience, first as a mercenary and later as Captain-General of Hostigos, I cannot see these metal twigs stopping a troop of lancers. By Dralm, I pray, I am wrong, but I fear that many of our pikemen will view them likewise."

Kalvan took a long draw on his pipe, then rose to his feet There had been a time in Hostigos—not all that long ago!—when no one would have questioned Kalvan's words, not even if it had been to ride their muskets like flying broomsticks. While Chartiphon's healthy skepticism was an improvement over his attitude of yesteryear, it had come at a particularly bad time.

"I don't believe it is all that big a problem, Chartiphon. I doubt the Styphoni cavalry will be able to make a direct hit on the front ranks of the Hostigi infantry. The wall of lead our lines can hurl will equal or better the Sacred Squares of Hos-Ktemnos. Not even the Zarthani Knights will be able to press home a charge against such a storm of firepower—much less the usual mercenary rabble."

Laurrey, Napoleon's Surgeon General, had checked his hospitals after several major battles and found very few examples of bayonet wounds. Most infantry and cavalry units broke off before contact, with one fleeing and the other pursuing. Ardant du Pica came to the conclusion that the traditional picture of an infantry charge, where the charging column smashes into the defending line, was mythical. At some point in a charge, either the column decided the line was going to hold and stopped, or the line decided the charging column was not going to halt and broke. It was this observation and his mastery of it that had put the "great" in Frederick the Great.

However, Kalvan wasn't just depending upon his infantry. With his mobile artillery he expected to rake the enemy pike and musket blocks before hitting them with massed salvo fire. The tremendous number of casualties would leave them shaken and vulnerable to cavalry or infantry charges. He could do the same to any mass cavalry charges. Most battlefield casualties were taken by broken and fleeing units, if the other side decided to pursue—not by those who stood their ground. Kalvan could not afford too many more battles with the butcher's bill as high as it had been at Fyk, Tenabra or Phyrax.

"Also, Chartiphon—despite all the stories about gallant pike companies fighting to the last man, isn't it true that in more than half the battles the pikemen drop their pikes and run hell-bent-for leather the minute the cavalry reaches the front ranks? In *our* histories there is the story of Great King Maximilian who created the first pike armies in his Kingdom's history. Knowing his pikemens' willingness to drop their pikes at push-of-pike he created double-pay soldiers to man the front and last ranks—those in the last rank to kill any of those who sought to escape by dropping their pike and running. That's why Styphon's Red Hand are as often deployed in the rear ranks, as in the front."

General Baldour nodded in agreement. "It is done that way in Hos-Ktemnos too. The veteran bill and shot troops are paid double to man the first and last rank, which may be why they are among the finest in the Great Kingdoms." The general was an exceptional soldier and proud of his former employers in Hos-Ktemnos. Kalvan expected that the last part of that statement was a sop to Hostigi egos rather than his measured opinion.

"There is no need to double-pay a Hostigi pikemen to get him to do his job," Chartiphon stated bluntly.

Seeing Baldour's face begin to burn, Kalvan quickly interjected, "It's not our place here to judge the quality of either Hostigi pikemen or Ktemnoi billmen. Both are among the finest soldiers I have ever fought with, or against. By the Wargod's Mace, musketeers are infamous for running the minute cavalry or enemy pike approach. The point with the 'New Model' Army is to put out enough firepower that no one will ever reach the Hostigi lines. But if they do, the bayonets will hold them until we can bring in cavalry or artillery support."

Kalvan made a slash with his arm that said the arguing was over, but he noted from the set of Chartiphon's face and Prince Ptosphes furrowed brow that he'd not yet won over the opposition. Ptosphes had refused to retire his own Princely pike even when Kalvan had offered him the muskets and bayonets to do so. It would probably take a field demonstration to change their minds and that he intended to give them more than one such this spring.

He nodded to Harmakros and his top officer began to give a breakdown of the capabilities of Kalvan's 'New Model' Army, with four one hundred and ten man companies per brigade rather than two, which meant a full strength regiment now mustered a thousand men—counting the headquarters units, too. "There are now eight foot regiments, including the new Hostigos Rifles—a line regiment with, four hundred riflemen and six hundred arquebusier. They're not at full strength now—not enough rifles, but they will be come spring. By the winter after the one coming up, they'll all have rifles."

That got their attention, Kalvan was happy to see, and even put a smile on old Chartiphon's face. Price Ptosphes practically beamed, although the name Hostigos Rifles had been Rylla's inspiration rather than his own. "The other three new regiments are the Third and Fourth Regiments of Foot and the Cordoba Regiment of Swords—named after a famous Captain of our Great King's homeland."

Machiavelli had always believed, based on the classic Roman legion versus the Greek phalanx model, that the sword-and-buckler man was the perfect counter to the Swiss and Landsknecht pike armies that had vanquished the Italian armies and brought ruin to the land during the French-Italian Wars. The Spanish sword-and-buckler men—although never in the numbers proposed by Machiavelli—went a long way to proving him right under Gonzalo de Cordoba, the Great Captain. Since Providence had given him a plenitude of sword-and-buckler men, mostly from Ulthor where the sword was favored, Kalvan had decided to test Machiavelli's theory on the field against a pike block or two.

He'd added two companies of musketeers to the Cordoba Regiment as insurance, though. Theories had a disarming way of going awry on the battlefield.

Kalvan had also doubled the size of the cavalry regiments, otherwise there would have been more colonels in the cavalry than captains, still adding eight new cavalry regiments. "The best news," Harmakros finished, "is that we've tripled the size of the Royal Mobile Force. We can now field two thousand dragoons armed with muskets and bayonets, and two full companies of the King's Mounted Rifles."

There was a loud whistle of appreciation from General Baldour who'd learned to respect the Mounted Rifles at the Battle of Phyrax, where he'd been a mercenary under the flag of the now deceased Captain-General Leonestros.

Kalvan next asked General Alkides to report on the Royal Artillery. The former mercenary ran his fingers nervously through his ginger-brown hair, which Kalvan noticed was beginning to gray at the sides. One of the penalties of high command. Rylla reminded him of his first gray hairs every time he complained about Princess Demia's crying in their bed when he was trying to sleep. The words Demia's wet-nurses used to exclaim this barbaric practice of letting an infant sleep with its parents would have made a gathering of infantry sergeants blush—fortunately, for his health and the respectability of wet-nurses, Rylla didn't indulge in this fancy too often. But she demonstrated no shame by referring to his few gray hairs as signs of incipient senility, whenever he did complain.

"By the Grace of Dralm and the the Mace of Galzar," Alkides opened, "we now have fifty four and six-pound demi-cannon or sakers, all mounted on carriages, for a total of five mobile light batteries. The Royal Artillery also has one complete battery of twenty-four and thirty-two pound brass guns for heavier work."

"Like the besieging of Tarr-Harphax and Harphax City, Praise Galzar!" Rylla cried out.

Her voice was echoed by a dozen cries of "Down with Hos-Harphax!"

The cat was out of the bag. Kalvan grinned and said, "This time we're not going to hit and run. We're going to blast Harphax City down to its foundation, if that's what it takes!"

Sarrask of Sask had his sword out and raised it to the sky. "Kill the Harphaxi devils. Burst their tripes! Down Styphon! Hail Great King Kalvan!"

When the hubbub had run its course, Harmakros continued, "We also have one new regiment of Sappers and Engineers to help with that siege work, By Galzar!"

When another round of "Down Hos-Harphax!" a short chorus of "Marching Through Harphax," and "Down Styphon!" had died down, Kalvan—realizing that little more in the way of work was going to be done this day—had Cleon bring in a cask of winter wine and goblets and led a toast "To Victory Over Styphon and All His Minions Wherever They Be." This toast soon led to more and Kalvan found himself in as bright a mood as he'd been in for some time.

And why not? This new crop of mercenaries was every bit as good as their predecessors—and they were the core of the victorious Royal Army—so there was every reason for high spirits. With hot lead and Galzar's help, this time next year they'd be making their rounds of toasts to the new Great King Phrames, King of the Great Kingdom of Hos-Harphax. Then let Styphon's House try and beat the team of Hos-Hostigos and Hos-Harphax!

WINTER

NINETEEN

I

Despite the early winter chill in the air, Grand Master Soton felt his tunic grow wet from the exertion of guiding his pack horse along the series of switch backs that cut through the cliffs of the south bank leading up to Harphax City. The rock-paved road was lined with swarms of beggars and hideously scarred veterans of the war with Hos-Hostigos. The fact that last year's maimed and their poor cousins kept their curses under their breaths showed that the Order's banner—a large white flag bearing a black, broken sun-wheel with curved arms—was still feared in the Great Kingdom of Hos-Harphax, if not always respected.

Not that Soton relaxed the tight grip he maintained on the warhammer that rested against his saddle pommel in plain view. He had reasons to be cautious, the House of Styphon and its military arm, the Holy Order of Zarthani Knights, were held responsible by many in Hos-Harphax for the beating the Harphaxi took at the hands of the Usurper Kalvan at the Battle of Chothros Heights, where the heir to the throne and a quarter of the Harphaxi nobility had been slain.

Not surprisingly, the Harphaxi appeared to have forgotten that Soton himself had lost another equally disastrous battle to this self-proclaimed Great King Kalvan—who had appeared out of nowhere like a demi-god— a moon later at the Battle of Phyrax. Despite the reform movement within

Styphon's House, the Temple's control over its earthly allies was in great
jeopardy. Fortunately, Archpriest Roxthar and his followers had put new
mettle into Styphon's Will on Earth. They had given Soton an unlimited
draft on the Temple's earthly resources; much of which, gold and arms
especially, he was going to need if he were going to turn the broken Harphaxi Royal Army into any semblance of a military power.

Soton halted his party before the next steep grade and peered down onto
Port Harphax, which was busy for this late in the year. Galleys, galleasses,
and wide-bottomed carracks were scooting across the harbor below like
water beetles. The Harphaxi warships were all going into dry dock on the
island naval base. As he kneed his mount into reluctant motion, Soton
cursed the memory of Erasthames the Great, the legendary king who had
conquered the Iroquois Alliance. Four hundred years ago it might have
made sense to put Tarr-Harphax up at the top of these cliffs, when the
native Ruthani were an everyday threat.

Now it was a beastly nuisance, making the provisioning and feeding
Harphax City and the castle, topping an even higher hill, a nightmare.
Since the lower Harph flooded almost every spring, cutting off river transport, the city had to take in enough stores to last a long winter and spring
as well. Food that arrived by sea had to be carted or packed up the Upper
Road, at great expense in time and animals, or pulled up in great iron buck-
ets by the rope tramway.

During a bad year such as this one, when fields had been trampled and
burnt, most of Harphax City's food had to be imported by seagoing merchants, which explained the great number of boats crowding Harphax
Port's limited docking facilities. It was now dangerously late in the season
and soon winter storms would make sea passage impossible. Most of the
captains were less than pleased by chancing the seas this late in the year
and only generous gifts of Styphon's gold kept them at sea at all.

As if this wasn't bad enough, the burnt fields and farms had brought
tens of thousands of refugees into the already bursting-at-the-seams capital. Plus, all the war casualties who were too crippled or maimed to work,
yet had to be housed and fed. Already the strain of short rations and over-
crowding were visible on the lean faces of the city's beggars. Only great
need could force them to take their chances on the steep Upper Road and
the occasional visitor's generosity.

At the top of the cliffs, the city walls showed the abuse of a hundred years of neglect and civil complacency. Here and there teams of workmen were shoring up walls and replacing fallen stones, but as Soton could see—it was clearly a case of too little, too late. He was certain that Kalvan's four and six-pounder mobile field guns would quickly bring down these walls upon the head of the neglectful inhabitants of Harphax City. As for the old castle itself, Tarr-Harphax, Kalvan would have a dozen breaches in a moon-half with a few good siege guns.

Soton shuddered to think of the slaughter Kalvan's veterans would make upon the shattered remnants of the Harphaxi Army. It was a good thing that Prince Lysandros, since his brother King Kaiphranos's death three moons ago, had taken his advice and appointed the mercenary captain, Phidestros, Captain-General of the Royal Harphaxi Army, rather than one of his cronies or aging mercenary captains. Phidestros was young for such an important position, but he was one of the few captains to have fought against the Usurper Kalvan three times and lived to tell about it.

If anyone could turn this whipped rabble into a fighting force again, it was Phidestros. He had more ambition than an Archpriest of Styphon's Inner Circle and as much gall as Kalvan himself. Even so he would need Appalon's luck and Lyklos' cunning to forge this Harphaxi base metal into good fighting steel. Soton would have to watch his pupil did not come to best his master, for someday Phidestros' quest for glory and power might pose a threat to Styphon's House's own plans.

The cobblestone and dirt streets of Harphax City were lined with make-shift tents and temporary housing. The stink alone was enough to bring tears to the eyes of a seasoned soldier. Twice, Soton had been forced to use his warhammer to fend off attempts by thieves to steal the trappings off his horse—right under the noses of his guards. It took several candles for his party to navigate their way through the narrow city streets and up Harphax Trail to Tarr-Harphax, where Captain-General Phidestros had established his headquarters.

Soton was pleased to note the severe appearance of Phidestros private audience room; the only adornments were a pair of crossed muskets, a well-used sword and a large deerskin map of Hos-Harphax, which included the Usurper's "Great Kingdom" of Hos-Hostigos outlined in red ink within Harphax's borders.

"Please take a seat, Grand Master."

"Thank you, Captain-General. My men will bring it in." This time he'd had his own chair brought with him from Tarr-Ceros, by way of Balph, and when he sat down on his elevated chair, he was eye-to-eye with Phidestros. The broad-shouldered Captain-General looked tired and the lines in his face were etched bolder than when he and Soton had met last spring. Soton sighed; at least, it showed that Phidestros was keeping late hours and had no illusions about the near impossible task set before him.

After his chair was positioned, he signaled for Sergeant Sarmoth to step back. After the battle of Yargos Pasture, Sarmoth had become part of his personal retinue. The young Knight displayed obvious leadership potential and Soton needed someone around him, who was not locked in the old ways of war, to help sift through all the changes that had occurred since Kalvan had arrived. He also needed aides he was certain were not in Roxthar's purse.

"You may stay, Sarmoth." Soton wanted to give his aide an opportunity to watch the political side of leadership; a talent the Knights would need if they were to survive both Kalvan and Roxthar's Investigators.

After Phidestros' servant had filled their wine goblets and left, Soton asked, "How does your command look these days?"

Phidestros frowned. "Not good. The Harphaxi Army was not much of a fighting force before Kalvan ground them up. Now they're little better than rabble. I've had more luck with the mercenary companies I've been able to recruit."

"That bad?"

"Many of the units are at half strength, probably more due to desertions and the grippe than Kalvan's lead. Some, like the Royal Lancers, were almost annihilated at Chothros Heights. That might have been a blessing. I would like to disband the entire unit if Lysandros would let me—or his nobles let him! The Lancers are more worried about gaining honor than winning battles, I fear."

Soton nodded. "You might think that Kalvan's artillery would have taught them a thing or two."

"Those iron hats! No such luck. They see Kalvan's style of fighting as unjust and dishonorable. With the Succession Crisis, Prince Lysandros doesn't dare dismiss them. But, with Kalvan's help, I've reduced their number by almost half. I'm now turning them into more of a household guard rather than a line unit. I've also recruited about two thousand more mercenaries and brought the Royal Pistoleers back up to full strength. The Foot Guard is still seriously undermanned."

"How many troops could you muster if Kalvan and his army were at the city walls tomorrow at sunrise?"

"A little more than four thousand Royal troops and another five thousand mercenaries. I'm supposed to have about twelve thousand city militia, but they are next to worthless—even though I've made them spend at least two days a moon-quarter in training. Most of them would take off—as they did at Chothros Heights—at the first sound of cannon fire. At least, I've managed to get them uniforms and handguns that fire.

"You wouldn't believe the ordnance I had to replace—musket locks that were rusted shut, stocks half-rotted away and barrels fouled beyond belief!"

"I believe it," Soton said. "Kaiphranos the Timid was more a tightpurse than a coward. I was aghast when his son asked to meet Kalvan on the field man to man; well, he paid for his stupidity. What you're telling me is that I'd better not depend upon the Harphaxi Royal Army for any duty more pressing than staying behind the city walls."

Phidestros looked crestfallen. "If Kalvan invades Hos-Harphax next spring, only the gods will be able to stop him from taking the entire Kingdom, not just Harphax City! The only bright news is that I don't believe Kalvan has any idea just how bad our situation really is."

"I take it you have told no one else this."

"Only Prince Lysandros. Kalvan has his intelligencers everywhere, even here in Harphax City. We almost caught a big one posing as an exiled Nostori baron a moon-quarter ago. We've made a big show of parading the militia, half of them in Royal Army colors, up and down the city streets in their new uniforms and arms. To anyone other than a grizzled veteran, they look like real soldiers, but those whoresons couldn't be counted upon to stand up before a strong sneeze!"

"What are your plans to revitalize the Army?"

Phidestros took out a highly polished walnut pipe and began to fill it with tobacco. "I'd like to get your opinion on this before I act upon it."

Soton nodded. "Yes."

"One of our big problems is that Styphon's Best is unfit for use in combat, when up against Hostigos fireseed." Phidestros held himself still as though waiting for one of Kalvan's exploding cannon balls to go off.

Soton nodded. "You are right, it's not."

Phidestros smiled and lit his pipe. "I know you are an Archpriest—"

"And you thought I might be angered by the very idea that Kalvan's fireseed is superior to Styphon's Best. Yes, I am—as Grand Master of the Order of Zarthani Knights—an Archpriest of Styphon's House. But I am a soldier, first. And, I do agree. I have already discussed this with several of the Archpriests and they have formulated a new fireseed that is almost the equal of Kalvan's mixture."

"Good! I wasn't sure how my request might go over. I've already appointed a system of Inspector-Generals to evaluate the Harphaxi Army, its armament, supplies and fireseed. My Chief Inspector tells me we should condemn all supplies of Styphon's fireseed and only use it for practice."

Soton shook his head in disbelief. Phidestros was a bold one all right! If some of the more hidebound archpriests had heard these words, they'd of had Phidestros stripped of his rank and burned alive. "I will do my best to see that you obtain sufficient supplies of the new formula fireseed for next spring."

"Thank you," Phidestros said, as if he meant it. He then went on to tell Soton the other reforms that he had undertaken. He wanted a big stockpile of supplies for next year, useful for both a siege or for a campaign. Phidestros had also set up a Retiring Board to prune away the deadwood, starting with former Captain-General Aesthes's cronies, in the Harphaxi Army. Aesthes himself had disappeared shortly after the disastrous Battle of Phyrax and was rumored to have fled to Hos-Zygros, where he had a summer mansion. Meanwhile, Phidestros had begun a program to promote competent officers for when Lysandros started hiring more mercenaries in the spring.

"I have watched with envy," Phidestros continued, "at how the Usurper has been able to integrate mercenary units into the Hostigi Army. I don't have the power to make the kind of land grants that Kalvan does, but I am promoting the better Free Companion captains to grand-captains in the Harphaxi Army."

"How much gold is it costing?" Soton asked.

"I'm only offering a half-pay raise. The captain like the promotions and the raise in pay is good, but what they really like is that as part of the Royal Army of Hos-Harphax they get paid all year round. This is a trick I learned from Kalvan." He looked warily at Soton to see if he would object and when he didn't continued. "After their captains leave, I then put the mercenary companies under the command of Harphaxi Army officers. Also all Free Companions are placed under Harphaxi military justice, with the sole provision that any court-martial panel judging a Free Companion will itself consist of one-half Free Companions and one priest of Galzar Wolfhead."

"You've done well," Soton replied, "now it is up to the gods and I believe they have done well by us. I have come up with a plan that will keep Kalvan busy all next year. And, with Galzar's Grace, it may even cost him his throne."

"By the Wargod's Mace, tell me! What miracle is this?"

"I plan to let the nomads fight the war against Kalvan for us. The Mexicotál in their strike against Xiphlon have driven the fierce southern pony warriors into the Sea of Grass, driving the tribes from their traditional hunting grounds into the Middle Kingdoms, where they have received a harsh reception. Many have been forced to cross the Great Mother River in their desire to find a safe haven. Only fifty hundred thousand have crossed the River so far, but already the entire lower Sastragath is a boil as new tribes move in and others use the disorder to settle old scores or build great clans. The Order has had to fight battles against barbarians trying to move into Hos-Ktemnos and Hos-Bletha.

"Now things are beginning to settle down as the tribes search for shelter and forage for the winter. The Order has seen these migrations from the Plains many times before and events should come to a head next year. The nomads are caught between the anvil of the Middle Kingdoms; and the Ruthani hammer in the south. The only place they have to go is across the Great Mother River and into the Sastragath, or north into Grefftscharr. Next year will see ten times as many tribes crossing the river, which will kick loose all the tribes of the Lower Sastragath and push them either east into our forts or north into the Upper Sastragath and Trygath.

"Instead of fortifying the border and holding our forts, my plan is to move half the Order Lances into the Lower Sastragath and drive the

nomads up the Pathagaros Valley, into the Lydistros Valley and from there
into Kalvan's backyard. With a nomad invasion threatening the Trygath and
Kalvan's own western-most princedoms, Kalvan will be forced to go on the
offensive and have to call a halt to his buildup on the Harphaxi border."

"It's a brilliant plan, Grand Master. But, surely things are not so bad that
we are forced to allow the barbarians to enter the Five Kingdoms through
our own backdoor?"

"In words only for your ears, our situation *is* that desperate. If Kalvan
invades Hos-Harphax, he will conquer it before the end of the first moon
of summer. With Hos-Harphax defeated, Great King Demistophon of
Hos-Agrys will quickly sue for terms; especially after the beating his mercenaries took from Prince Ptosphes last summer. Great King Cleitharses of
Hos-Ktemnos is still in shock over the losses his Sacred Squares took at
the Battle of Phyrax; he won't go to battle again unless ordered to by the
assembled Inner Circle of Styphon's House. Hos-Bletha is too far away to
be of any consequence and Great King Sopharar of Hos-Zygros is flirting
with the League of Dralm. So, without the Great Kingdom of Hos-
Harphax as an anchor, the war against Kalvan is doomed."

Phidestros massaged his temples as if he had the grandfather of all headaches. "Things wouldn't be so bad, Grand Master, if I could hire more
mercenaries. They are nowhere to be found outside of Hostigos. I know it's
winter and that a lot of them died at the battles of Fyk, Tenabra, Chothros
Heights, and Phyrax, but still—where are they?"

"My agents in Beshta have learned that Kalvan has been offering mercenaries bonuses and year-round pay for signing up in his Royal Army of
Hos-Hostigos. I fear that is where many of them have gone."

Phidestros groaned. "Why didn't I think of that?"

"Because it has never been done before—like many of Kalvan's strategies. You have learned enough from our opponent to recruit the best
mercenary captains for the Army, but Lysandros would have never given
you permission to hire Free Companions year-round, with bonuses yet!"

Phidestros nodded, and mumbled something about what he'd do if he
were Prince of Harphax.

"It is said," Soton continued, "that in the border princedoms, the remaining mercenaries have been hired by barons and princes for protection from
the nomads. In all of Hos Ktemnos there are no mercenaries to be hired at

any price; I understand that things are likewise in Hos-Agrys. There has been talk in Balph of recruiting mercenaries from the lands of the Middle Kingdoms."

"Are things that desperate?" Phidestros asked, his pipe out and dangling from his hand.

"Yes, they are. Even if Kalvan destroys the nomads this next spring, he will do more than just give us breathing space."

"How so, Grand Master?"

"He will give us the greatest gift of all—time. Time for you to train the Harphaxi rabble. Empty the prisons and the gaols. Take the strongest and the toughest and forge them into an army."

"By what magic will I turn riffraff into soldiers?"

"By the magic of Styphon's gold, your will and your ideas. You've already made a good start. However, if you can't do it, I will find someone who can."

Phidestros' brow furrowed. "I will do it, if I have to turn their tears into blood."

"Good. I will go to Prince Lysandros and tell him that you will need to build an army twenty thousand men strong. Styphon's House will supply the gold and victuals."

"It can be done—I'll use the Royal Foot Guard as my petty captains. They will train the rabble night and day until they drop. It doesn't take great marksmanship to make an arquebusier or musketeer, but it will take a lot of work . . ."

"Excellent, Captain-General, you are already thinking along the right lines. Kalvan will think twice about invading Hos-Harphax—if he defeats the nomads and learns of a huge army holding Harphax City. Even if it is—for now—an army in name, only."

Phidestros smiled for the first time. "I say a toast to Grand Master Soton and the new Royal Army of Hos Harphax."

Soton downed his goblet in a single gulp. When it was filled again, he made his own toasts, "TO VICTORY! TO THE USURPER KALVAN'S DEATH! TO STYPHON'S HOUSE!"

TWENTY

I

King Theovacar's palace was as old as the mole, at least parts of it. Five or six great waves of building had left its ground plan so complex that it would have taken a First Level Professor of Mathematics to describe it adequately. More practically, it also made the palace impossible to visit without being guided every minute. The guides were King's Companions, wearing their palace-guard outfit of lobster-pot helm, back-and-breast, bell-mouthed musketoon and short sword. They also had oval buffalo-hide shields, heavy enough to turn a small pistol bullet or almost any edged weapon, which Verkan had seen them use for riot control work. Painted on the shields black face were the crossed white thunderbolts of Theovacar's device.

There were never less than two Companions with their eyes on him and Kostran, so Verkan tried not to be too obvious in noting down the route through the palace. First Level mental disciplines would provide him with perfect recall of all the passages. He still couldn't overlook the signs of military activity: an underground passage with a portcullis being re-hung, fresh paint on the carriage of a small saker commanding an open courtyard, several doors freshly loopholed for muskets.

When they reached the antechamber to the audience hall, the Companions left them, if not exactly alone, at least able to whisper privately. Verkan was tempted to use some language other than Zarthani, but that would arouse suspicions that mere whispering would not.

"What enemies are Theovacar worried about?" Verkan asked.

"None that I can think of," Kostran replied. "I've talked to a few of the palace servants over wine, and they say most of this is just the repair of many years of neglect. Theovacar's grandfather wasn't much of a soldier and his father was a real close-purse, so there's a lot of work to be done without needing an enemy to justify it.

"Of course, the palace is the biggest barracks in Greffa, or can be. King Theovacar could be repairing it to hold the men of the northern Greff-tscharrer lands should they have to come south for a war against the nomads."

"Or if they are to sail east to find a war there?"

Kostran's expression said the question was none too safe to ask, let alone answer, but that the answer was a definite maybe. "Theovacar does not know fear, and why should he, in his own palace with two hundred sworn Companions ready at every moment?" Kostran added this last loudly enough for the Companions to hear if any were eavesdropping. That also told Verkan that the garrison of the palace hadn't been strengthened.

Verkan was more relieved than he dared show. King Theovacar's attempts to make himself independent of his over-mighty subjects were the kind of efforts those subjects were sooner or later going to resent and resist. So far, however, it seemed that the resistance hadn't taken any form that caused Theovacar to fear being besieged in his own palace.

Verkan hoped this state of affairs would continue in Grefftscharr until the War of the Great Kings was over in the East. Without passing any judgment on the merits of Theovacar's ambitions or the justice of his nobles' complaints, the fact remained that a king whose nobles wanted to cut his throat was of dubious value as an ally. He could hardly send royal troops, he might not be able to spare mercenaries or silver, and if civil war broke out—That was as far down the list as Verkan had reached before a herald flung open the door at the end of the antechamber and bellowed:

"Enter, all ye who seek audience with Theovacar, fourth of that name, King of Grefftscharr, Protector of Chiefs, Champion of Sharn."

The herald led Verkan and his companions into a short, broad corridor with three more carved wooden doors on the far side. Between the doors were equally lavishly carved wooden benches. On each bench sat three Companions, in full armor, carrying shields and spears that looked perfectly efficient in spite of their silvered heads.

Verkan went through the ritual of disarming, handing his uncocked pistol butt-first to the Companion who stepped forward to take it, then showing his hands empty with fingers outspread. He did not offer up his sword or dagger; no free Grefftscharrer not outlawed could be forced to give up his steel—even in the king's presence.

The ritual lasted long enough for Verkan to survey the entire corridor without any suspicious movement of head or even eye. It was low ceilinged and dark in spite of a lavish display of candles. The granite blocks of the walls were half-hidden behind trophies of weapons, armor, and the heads and hides of buffalo, mountain lions, longhorn bulls, bears and wolves. At the far end of the corridor, Verkan saw that the stonewall had been loop-holed at about the height of a sitting man's musket. The brickwork and mortar around the loopholes were fresh.

It was obvious that Theovacar was well defended against a revolt or palace uprising. Verkan wondered if all these safeguards were prudent fore-sight, or incipient paranoia.

That was all Verkan found time to note before the herald summoned him forward through the left-hand door. Verkan was halfway across the room before he realized, except for five more Companions and the man on the carved wooden chair at the far end of the chamber, he and his friends were alone with the King.

Verkan's spirits rose. A private audience was normally granted only to nobles or to men who'd sworn a blood oath to the king. To grant one to a man who was neither might be a way of taking the sting out of a refusal of his petition, or to apologize for the lengthy time in granting the audience. More likely, it was Theovacar's way of doing honor to the foreign king the man served, and perhaps also of ensuring that no unreliable ears heard what the king and trader said.

With some kings, Verkan had known, the private audience could also have been a way to reduce the number of witnesses to treacherous murder. Theovacar did not have the reputation of that sort of king, and indeed he'd be a Dralm-damned fool to acquire it if he wanted peace with his nobles. They were a proud and touchy lot, but at least had the virtues of those vices; wantonly bloodthirsty rulers in Grefftscharr seldom died in bed and still less of natural causes.

Verkan also noted with approval that Kostran was unobtrusively taking positions where he could watch both Verkan's back and the door to the chamber. If matters did become bloody, the drill would be for Verkan and Kostran to use their disguised sigma-ray needlers.

Verkan saw for himself that Theovacar's reputation, as both a warrior and a trencherman seemed justified. His face was ruddy above its blond beard, his belly strained his knee-length velvet robe and both face and muscle-corded arms showed a fine collection of scars. Apart from the fur-lined robe, Theovacar wore doeskin trousers and boots, a wide gold torc on his left arm and a small cap of state of wolverine fur sewn with gold wire and fresh-water pearls. The effect was barbaric; the man inside those clothes, Verkan knew, was nothing of the kind.

Verkan went down on one knee, his friend on both. "In obedience to Your Grace's summons, the Trader Verkan comes to submit to your judgment."

Theovacar nodded. "The Trader Verkan is welcome." Then signaled the Trader's party to rise. He said nothing more until he'd taken a pipe and tobacco one of the Companions handed him and lit up, but the wide gray eyes never left Verkan.

Finally, Theovacar had his pipe going to his satisfaction, leaned back in his chair and said, "Nothing will come of delaying the news. It is my decision, after taking council with those whose wisdom I trust in matters of trade, to grant your petition for a charter for your trading company, Verkan's Hos-Hostigos Trading Company.

Verkan thought he heard Kostran stifle a sigh of relief and kept his own face straight only with an effort. "Your Grace does us a great honor."

Theovacar clapped his hands and one of the Companions stepped forward, carrying a heavy leather tube on a gilded bronze tray. Another brought a jug of wine and two silver cups.

"You will not find everything in that charter which you asked," Theovacar continued. "Nor do I expect you will find everything that is there pleasing. There were those whose advice was to deny you the charter, for falsely claiming the rights of a subject of Grefftscharr."

If Verkan Vall had been subject to heart failure he would never have lasted in the Paracops. He did shift his feet to an unarmed-combat stance in what he hoped would be taken for a nervous shuffle and tried to look bemused.

Theovacar saved him the trouble of further acting. "Those, who said the sworn witnesses to your Grefftscharr rights were sufficient under the law, had the stronger voice. Yet it could not be denied that you had not served as apprentice or journeyman in any of the lawful Guilds.

"So under the charter you must pay a double tax on what you earn, one share to the Crown and the second to the treasury of the Council of Guilds. The Crown's share may be remitted at my discretion after the first year."

Such discretion to be exercised depending on how much valuable information I bring you and how much influence in King Kalvan's councils I give you, out of gratitude for not being thrown to the wolves of the Council of Guilds. Verkan mentally noted the elimination of one potentially nasty problem: If the judicious use of hypno-truth drugs hadn't produced the required quota of witnesses to cover his identity, he would have probably been denied the charter. Even worse, the rumor that there was no Free Trader from Grefftscharr named Verkan would have surely reached Kalvan's ears, and he was the one man outside First Level who might draw the appropriate conclusions from that.

Verkan knelt again. "Your Grace's reputation for justice and wisdom was not exaggerated. Indeed, the Guilds have a lawful claim and I would hope to number them among my friends and even partners before too many years."

The Companion presented Verkan with the leather tube and a cup of wine; he tucked the charter under his arm and emptied the cup as custom required, without taking it from his lips.

King Theovacar drained his cup without even stopping for breath, and then swallowed half of a second cup before speaking. "You should also know that your petition for the right to hire mercenaries as guards for your trading venture has been denied. This is not for any doubt of your need for good fighting men to protect your goods and ships. It is out of Grefftscharr's great need for all its sons who have good sword arms and keen shooting eyes. The nomads who live on the Sea of Grass are on the march as they have not been in living memory. I would be a poor protector of my people if I left them defenseless against such a horde."

The horde on this side of the Great Mother River was not the tribes who'd been knocked loose from their traditional territory by the northward advance of the Mexicotál against Xiphlon, but the Zarthani and Urgothi nomads who'd been driven from their Great Plains' traditional hunting lands by the fierce southern Ruthani. Many of these tribes were encroaching on Grefftscharrer territory in their desire to find a safe haven, while others were using the disorder to destroy old enemies and build great clans.

To the south it was even worse, although only few tens of thousands of the Great Plains nomads had actually crossed the river. But add in the tribes along the Great Mother River the nomads had knocked loose, and the tribes of the Lower Sastragath and Lydistros Valley they'd knocked loose in turn, and all the people of the Upper Sastragath whose fields were being overrun and eaten bare—'horde' was no exaggeration. A quarter of a million fighting men would be a conservative estimate of their combined numbers. By next spring that number could be doubled or tripled.

Not that Verkan believed Theovacar was telling him the whole story, or that Verkan was particularly disappointed at not being allowed to hire Grefftscharrer mercenaries for Kalvan under the guise of caravan guards. He'd put that clause in his petition to give the naysayers something to keep them happy, and also to give Theovacar a chance to present his views of the military situation. So far Verkan had succeeded in the first and suspected he wasn't going to with the second, but if he gave in without an argument Theovacar might smell something.

"No one could ask you to do otherwise, Your Grace. Yet, it is known that the Zarthani Knights are in the field against the Horde, under Grand Master Soton himself. Will any of the Horde live long enough to need a single charge of Grefftscharrer fireseed?"

Theovacar shrugged. "Perhaps not in the East. But already there have been two great battles outside Wulfula and one in Dorg against the Sea of Grass horde. We ourselves have had to 'encourage' several small clans to look elsewhere for forage and lands. No, Trader Verkan, this year, and certainly next year, all Grefftscharrer fighting men must look to their own walls."

A politer refusal than Verkan had really expected. The real reason for keeping the Grefftscharrer mercenaries at home was one Theovacar could hardly be expected to discuss in public with a near-stranger known to be in the confidence of a foreign ruler. In Greffa mercenaries were mostly drawn from men not sworn to the service of one of the noble houses Theovacar was trying to subdue. They were the king's own best military asset, and it was not in his interest to let them leave home, perhaps never to return, certainly to be unavailable for years.

"I submit to Your Grace's judgment in this matter. Yet I must ask for the right to find some men to guard my trading ventures. Those going overland must fear the nomads' outriders as well as common bandits and barons made lawless by weak princes and kings, as those crossing the Saltless Seas must fear pirates."

King Theovacar scribbled on a small piece of parchment and motioned for one of his Companions to take it to Verkan. "Here, you may hire a company of caravan guards. That should be sufficient. And, if what we hear is true, there are more than pirates to be feared on the Saltless Seas. It is said that Prince Varrack of Thagnor is gathering a war fleet."

Verkan had heard the same; he saw another opportunity to draw King Theovacar into talking freely. He nodded. "It is common rumor in all ports on the Saltless Seas. As to whether it is true or not, I can say very little, for I have seen very little with my own eyes. I would not care to think I was doing Your Grace a disservice by repeating tavern rumors as knowledge."

"You would not be doing me a service, indeed. But it has reached my ears that your ship did put in at Thagnor for one night."

Verkan made a mental note to find out if there was any way to learn who'd talked freely to whom, then nodded. "We put in to take on fresh water, because some of our barrels were leaking, and also to have one of our men tended to by the priests of Lystris at the sailor's hostel in Thagnor City. We were there only during the hours of darkness and anchored out in the river as well, so although we sought the truth of those rumors, we did not find it. Certainly there seemed to be more than the usual number of ships in port, but most of them were at the Salt Wharf.

"We have heard that all three Great Kings with ports on the Saltless Seas are preparing salt provisions in great quantity, so it may well be that Prince Varrack is sending a second Salt Fleet in the spring, with chartered ships."

"Perhaps," King Theovacar said. "Certainly I will say nothing against Varrack's desire to win gold from other's wars. Yet, I have heard also that

Varrack is taking gold from a Prince who has a quarrel with his overlord Great King Demistophon of Hos-Agrys. Whether that gold is buying Prince Varrack's fleet or merely buying his good will, I have not heard, but certainly it is best that we in Grefftscharr know."

Verkan had heard no such rumor, but admitted to himself that he might not have heard everything, with reliable informants thin on the ground. He had heard that Prince Varrack lusted after a throne for himself and only saw himself nominally, at best, a vassal of King Theovacar.

The Prince in discussion, who was supplying Varrack with gold, was undoubtedly Prince Clytoblon of Glarth, whose pro-Kalvan sentiments were known by just about everyone, including his distant overlord Great King Demistophon.

"The tavern gossips would say this Prince is Prince Clytoblon, but I have no proof that there is truth in this idle gossip. Nor does it tell me much about this Prince, to say that he has a quarrel with Demistophon the Wrathful. If there is a Great King or Prince in the north who has not had quarrel with Demistophon since he came to the throne, it is because that man lacks the wit or courage to recognize offense when it is given. One has heard tales of what Demistophon called you on your accession, and how moderate you were to content yourself with fining all the Agrysi merchants in Grefftscharr."

Theovacar smiled back, but the smile didn't reach his eyes. Verkan knew he'd have to give the King better. In any case, Theovacar was really asking the reasonable question: Was Kalvan trying to raise Thagnor in rebellion against his overlord? The Princes of Thagnor normally lived well enough off the profits of their salt mines and shipyards, not to mention whatever they kept back of the tolls charged for passage along the Thag River. Their distant Greffa king ruled them with a light hand, and everyone who sailed the Saltless Seas or needed salt for preserving food was the better for it.

Three times in the last two centuries, however, a Prince of Thagnor had rebelled against Greffa, setting up an independent Kingdom. Three times the Princedom, or Kingdom, had become a nest of pirates, outlaws and rebels, making travel on the Saltless Seas perilous. Once, the pirate Kingdom collapsed after the Prince was murdered in a drunken brawl, but twice it had taken armies and fleets to restore peace. Theovacar had every right to know if Kalvan was willing to risk this happening a fourth time to strike back at King Demistophon for his treachery. The fact that he was also asking the question as a test of Verkan's willingness to betray Kalvan for a price made little difference.

"I am not so much in the confidence of Great King Kalvan that he tells me all his plans, even if I were often enough in Hostigos for him to have the chance to do so," Verkan began. "I do know that Kalvan values his trade with Greffa, and that a war in Thagnor would disrupt that trade and be a setback for his plans to buy victuals and guns from Greffa for his war against Styphon's House." He continued with a long recital of Kalvan's love for peace, while only taking up arms in self-defense and for the honor of the true gods, using phrases cribbed from diplomatic speeches and notes in half a dozen different time-lines.

King Theovacar appeared amused without being impressed. He obviously wanted hard data. Verkan emptied another cup of wine and continued. "Great King Kalvan does wish to have ships and men to balance Styphon's Great Fleet. He may well be hiring both from Varrack and paying a good price for them in Styphon's gold. If Prince Varrack uses that gold to turn pirate, however, Kalvan will be the first to turn against him. The Great King is no friend to pirates; he is no enemy to Greffa or Hos-Zygros or the Sastragath, and he is not even a willing enemy of Great King Demistophon."

"I have heard nothing to suggest you are telling other than the truth," Theovacar said. "Therefore I bid you farewell and will pray for your prosperous voyaging and continued friendship between King Kalvan of Hos-Hostigos and myself."

It was an elegant, even warm dismissal that boded well for future Greffa-Hos-Hostigos relations, but Verkan was glad that etiquette required him to back out of the chamber and not turn his back on either King Theovacar or the armed Companions around him.

II

Duke Skranga was still in his riding cloak when he entered Kalvan's private audience chamber. He noted with satisfaction that Kalvan had already taken the clay stopper out of a small cask of Ermut's Brandy and was well on his way to emptying his own goblet.

"Ahhh, thank you, Your Majesty," he said, after taking the proffered goblet. Underneath the cloak, his clothes were soaked to the bone and only long periods of discomfort in the past made it easy to disregard them.

"Duke," Kalvan opened, "I must say I've been pleased with your reports. You've given good value for the gold we've spent."

Skranga smiled, he couldn't help himself. This praise from Kalvan was more warming than Ermut's Best! "Thank you, Your Majesty. If I could have stayed two more moons I'd have had the Thaphigos Succession lines tied in so many knots it would have taken Lyklos the Trickster to straighten them out!"

Kalvan laughed. "Hostigos could use a regiment of intelligencers with your resourcefulness. Although we may not need them, I plan to run the Royal Army through Hos-Harphax like lime through a goose's gullet."

Skranga laughed. "You've got the men for it. You should see the sorry toss-birds from every gaol and dungeon that Lysandros and Phidestros have parading up and down the streets of Harphax City! I wouldn't use them to clean the Hostigos army barracks' latrines. If they can't find any better soldiers than that the Hostigos Royal Army should clean out all of Hos-Harphax like the flux!"

"Is there any chance Phidestros is hiding the *varsity*—I mean the good troops?"

"Har, har, har!" Skranga sputtered. When his coughing spell was over, he poured himself another goblet of brandy and topped off Kalvan's. "True, there's some good mercenary troops—if they don't all desert before spring! And some good Royal soldiers perhaps survived the Chothros cutting, but even Galzar himself couldn't turn that motley mob into a real army. No, there's not much to fear from Harphax next year—except who to make the new Great King."

"Phrames is my choice."

Skranga nodded. Just like Kalvan to have the answers to questions before he even got around to asking them. Skranga paused to tamp his pipe, and then lit it with his tinderbox. "A good leader, even if a bit womanish—I don't mean on the battlefield or in the cot. But, he's delicate about other matters, like killing prisoners and such like." From the frown that creased

Kalvan's brow, Skranga knew he'd stepped in a cowpie of some kind, but not exactly sure how. He attempted a quick save, "Even a good farmer has to shoot a few old dogs if they don't keep the foxes out of the turkey pens."

"You're right, but Phrames has learned a few things cleaning up Prince Balthar's stables in Beshta. I think he'll be a good king."

"What do you say, a toast to Great King Phrames, long may he reign!"

"It's a bit premature," Kalvan said, "but why not." The two goblets clinked together soundly.

TWENTY-⊕NE

I

It's pretty and bubbly," Rylla said, dropping the cold lump of green glass into Kalvan's open hand, "but I don't believe even Allfather Dralm, could turn this bauble into that far-seeing telescope you talk about."

"The bubbles can be removed by proper heating and air control, but it's the milkiness that bothers me. I think Master Ermut may have too much slaked lime and not enough potash in the mixture. I'll talk to him tonight and help him revise the formula.

"Once we have decent glass all it will take is proper grinding to make a lens. With good lenses we can make telescopes for all our commanders, and maybe even captains. The tactical advantages we will gain will be worth two or three regiments of shot."

"I do not doubt you, my husband, not even Endrath, has shaken the land as much as you have."

There was a distant look of awe on Rylla's face that bothered him until she finished her thought, in typical Rylla fashion. "Of course, I'd be happier if you spent more time shaking our marriage bed than talking to your cronies at the University."

"Those 'cronies,' as you call them, might well be my greatest gift in the long run to the Kingdom's future."

"I beg to disagree, but I believe that Princess Demia is your greatest gift."

Kalvan smiled and nodded his head. Rylla was right; their dandelion-headed little Princess was the greatest accomplishment either one of them had done, alone or together.

"Maybe it is time I spent more time at home."

Rylla looked up at the ceiling as if beseeching the gods. "How many times have I heard those words? And, Kalvan wipe that smile off your face. If you think you're going to keep me locked up for another entire campaign season, you're drunker than Pandros. Sick, pregnant or in chains, I'm going to be on my horse, with a sword in my hand, no matter what you do. Is that understood?"

"Yes, kitten," Kalvan said, resigning himself to the inevitable. "Which reminds me, I have to send Duke Skranga's Harphaxi agent another fifteen thousand gold crowns. Prince Bythannes is so in debt he's having trouble raising his daughter's dowry, and Skranga wants to loan him the money before one of Styphon's agents buys him lock, stock and barrel. Things are not going so well now that Skranga's back in Hostigos and Lysandros has stopped playing general and started wooing the Elector Princes himself."

"Has Skranga learned anymore about Lysandros' replacement, Captain-General Phidestros?"

"The information is sketchy. He's spent most of his career in Hos-Zygros and Hos-Agrys. Klestreus says he's a former Zygrosi mercenary with a reputation for ruthlessness and battle savvy. The rumor mill has it he's the by-blow of some high placed Zygrosi Prince or nobleman, so he's always been able to get his hands on enough gold to run a first class outfit. But Klestreus was as surprised by his sudden elevation as Duke Skranga was. It looks like with Lysandros in charge we're going to be facing real military leaders, rather than the nincompoops King Kaiphranos put in charge of the Harphaxi Army."

"Too bad," Rylla said. "I'd like to teach King Demistophon some manners as well as Lysandros. And I still haven't forgotten Prince Araxes insult."

"Are you still chewing on that?" Rylla nursed a grudge better than anyone he'd ever known, even better than some of the Appalachian hillbillies he'd had to arrest. "We didn't need the Phaxos army anyway and when Araxes sees us the walls of Harphax come down, he'll come running."

In a tone of voice that encompassed years of wifely frustration—even though they'd only been married little over a year, Rylla said, "You don't understand. Prince Araxes, by not heeding Our call to arms, has given the Crown of

Hos-Hostigos a deadly insult. I can hear Soton and the Archpriests laughing now! Balthames is already pleading that he won't be able to muster his forces this spring, because the planting season was delayed by last spring's campaign! Next, we'll be hearing excuses from the Ulthori and Kyblosi princes."

"We will settle Araxes hash when we have less pressing problems on our plate," Kalvan said. "He never actually joined Hos-Hostigos, just opened discussions. I do not want to get the reputation as a Great King who takes umbrage at every minor slight. As Duke Mnestros, pointed out, many of the Agrysi princes are worried that we will usurp their princely rights and we must act with caution."

"Caution! Does Styphon's House worry about what this princeling or that noble thinks of their grand strategy; no, they march where they will and let the loser beware!"

"My point, exactly. By this reckless policy, they have alienated many of the northern princes and barons. We need to exploit this, not follow in Styphon's footsteps. Someday, remind me to tell you about the Marshall Plan, where the Great Kingdom of America sent its enemies food and clothes and all manner of goods to help them regain their former strength as great kingdoms."

There was a hesitant knock at the chamber door.

Rylla, who had been about to fire back a rejoinder, asked, "Who could that be? I told Xykos to bar the door to anyone but Demia's wet-nurse. I'm tired of not being able to talk to my own husband!"

Kalvan snatched a rifled flintlock pistol off his desk.

"Come in," Kalvan said.

The door opened a crack and the Royal Page Aspasthar stuck his head in, like a turtle warily sniffing the world as it came out of its shell. "Brother Mytron to see you. He says it's important."

Kalvan set the pistol back on the table. "Show him in, Aspasthar."

"Brother Mytron entered the room apologetically, "I apologize Your Majesties. But I have made an important decision and I wanted to tell you both as soon as possible."

"What is it?" Kalvan asked, shooting a look to Rylla who looked like she was about to bite the priest's head off.

"Highpriest Xentos has told me that it was my duty to take over as head of the Temple, since he will be leaving for the Great Temple in Hos-Agrys as soon as the roads are passable."

"We expect that," Kalvan said, trying to hurry him along.

"Xentos also wants me to return the University robes and take over as Hos-Hostigos Highpriest of Dralm."

Kalvan mentally cursed Dralm, and Styphon, under his breath. This wasn't unexpected, but Mytron had made a wonderfully capable Rector. He had the ability to see both sides of any argument without taking either side, and still leave both opponents believing that he had taken their position. Now, one more job he didn't need—University recruiter.

"Congratulations, Highpriest Mytron," Rylla said, looking pleased. Mytron had occupied a special place in her heart after the birth of Demia; he had overseen her birthing as if the new baby was his own.

Kalvan joined in the congratulations, while he mentally catalogued all the possible replacements for the position of Hos-Hostigos University Rector. He turned to Cleon, who was standing by the door. "Another cask of Ermut's Best."

II

Verkan and his party were back at the rented estate, which housed both the offices of Verkan's Hos-Hostigos Trading Company and the Kalvan's Time-Line conveyer-head before Verkan felt it was safe to talk. In the scrambler-shielded barn, they sat down on bales of hay while Zinna poured three beers.

"I'd like to find out who talked to Theovacar's spy about your stop at Thagnor City," Kostran Galth began, but Verkan cut him off.

"That's not important even if we could do it safely, and we can't. We'd risk offending the captain of my ship by bothering his men. Offend him badly enough, and he'd take the matter before the Mariners' Guild. Then we'd have Styphon's Own Time getting any shipmaster to sail for the Hos-Hostigos Trading Company. The spy could easily turn out to have been one of Theovacar's agents buying a drink for one our crew."

"We could use the hypno-truth drugs," Zinna said.

"We could, if we didn't have to assume that King Theovacar has enough spies to detect any pattern of interest we show in anybody. I'd rather assume that until Theovacar owes us enough to overlook any little games we play on our own that aren't directed at him. Right now, we're too dependent on his goodwill.

"While on the surface Grefftscharr appears less sophisticated than the civilization of the Six Kingdoms, things run much deeper here. This civilization is a thousand years older than the Eastern Kingdoms and has survived in the midst of a sea of competing barbarian tribes and kingdoms. If poor Great King Kaiphranos had had Theovacar's network of spies and agents, Kalvan might be moldering in a box instead of on the throne of Hos-Hostigos.

"Then, too, there's another category of people I'd rather probe. The Council of Guilds seems to include a few of our enemies. I want to find out who they are, without giving them *or* Theovacar any clues about what we're doing."

Verkan paused to sip his beer. "Our not being able to hire mercenaries may be a stroke of luck. We can post notices that we're hiring experienced caravan guards for duty both on land and shipboard. Our enemies on the Council will take the chance to plant spies among those we hire. Once we're out of Grefftscharrer territory, any spy we detect can be interrogated freely.

"Also disposed of freely, if we find that necessary," Zinna put in. Kostran frowned at this casual ruthlessness, but Verkan wasn't surprised; Zinganna had spent the first twenty years of her life in Old Dhergabar. Anyone who did that, and came out alive and sane, could have few illusions about the virtues of being too nice to your enemies.

"Exactly. It may take a while for the spies to turn up so I'll want you both to prepare a supply of false data we can feed them to pass to their masters on the Council of Guilds. That will also help us trace who those masters are. Who do you recommend for interrogating the spies in the field?"

The discussion of possible candidates for this certainly thankless and probably grisly job lasted nearly half an hour and several more rounds of beer. By the time they had the names of three Paracops, Verkan was sure Kostran and Zinna had completely forgotten that he'd been arguing for a degree of caution in dealing with potential enemies near settled communities that was unusual for Chief Verkan Vall.

He hoped he'd prevented the asking of unanswerable questions—unanswerable not just for security reasons but also because of inadequate data.

Verkan was satisfied that one or more of the University people was a spy for Hadron Tharn. Now that almost all the necessary locals had been hypno-conditioned for establishing believable covers, any widespread use of hypno-mech interrogation, where there'd be Fourth Level witnesses, might now reach the ears of a qualified First Level observer who could understand what was going on. So interrogations that might otherwise pass unnoticed might reach the Opposition Party, to provide them with yet another charge against the Paratime Police.

Then the power pile would begin to overload. It was the next thing to public knowledge that the Opposition was making its peace with some of the trading interests who were unhappy—to put it mildly—over the possible shutdown of Fourth Level Europo-American. Given a solid case of "police abuses," the Opposition might slip the leash. Dalla's renegade brother would be howling loud and clear near the head of the pack.

The two men had never liked each other; even at first sight! He'd always thought Dalla had babied her younger sibling, while Tharn resented Verkan taking up her time and attention from him. But there was more than sibling rivalry and displaced affections going on in the Tharn family; serious mental illness, along with genius, was the family's legacy. Even ex-Chief Tortha had warned him—without getting specific—about involving himself with the Hadron family. But he'd been be-witched by Dalla, and still was; she was the most interesting and vibrant woman he'd ever met. He had lost her once to his career and ambition, and he had promised himself that would not happen again. And he certainly would not risk losing her to her brother's compulsion for revenge.

Twice Dalla had talked him out of filing a complaint with the Bureau of Psych-Hygiene—a Paratime Police Chief's complaint resulted in compulsory testing and treatment of any First Level Citizen. With all his other problems and trying to live a double life, Verkan was beginning to regret giving in and letting her brother—who needed a Mentalist scrub—run free. Not only was Tharn dabbling in First Level politics, but also he was trying to setup the University of Dhergabar as a weapon against Verkan and the Paratime Police.

Verkan doubted that Hadron Tharn had anything to do with the shipboard spy; that thread would probably lead back to the Council of Guilds and some merchant who was in hock up to his eyeballs to Styphon's House.

Or one of King Theovacar's agents who kept a watch on the Saltless Sea shipping. Verkan would have been much less frustrated if there'd been even a little more he could do about the probable spy. Investigate, identify, neutralize or terminate (though not always as thoroughly as Zinna had suggested) that was standard Paratime Police procedure for dealing with intelligence leaks.

With the leak on the University study teams, he couldn't do any of these without offending the University as an institution, instead of just a collection of individual scholars and Opposition sympathizers. He couldn't investigate without somebody noticing the investigation. If he identified the spy without an investigation, he couldn't neutralize them without somebody noticing the re-routing of data or the supplying of false data. And, as for terminating him/her, better to stick his own sigma-ray needler in his ear and fire. It would do the same job with much less time, effort and mess.

What he could do was limited to talking things over with Tortha Karf and Dalla as soon as he could. They always helped, if only by making him feel that he was something more than a fixed and highly visible target. He'd also commend Ranthar Jard for compiling the dossier on the data leaks, tell him to keep it secret from everyone except Verkan personally and have him keep an even closer eye than usual on where the University people went and what they did. It was unlikely that this would turn up the spy; it was possible that it would reduce the risk of one of the University people getting accidentally killed, and that would be one less grievance the University could have to lay at the door of the Paratime Police.

Verkan found that he wanted more beer. He reached for his mug and discovered Zinna had refilled it so quietly he'd never even noticed. She had the knack of knowing when somebody wanted to be alone with a problem and a steady supply of food and liquor. Perhaps not a very heroic virtue, but Verkan had ducked bullets in a civil war caused by poor bar service in a medium-priced whorehouse, and certainly it had kept Kostran Galth married for eight years, which considering how valuable a subordinate Kostran was—

Verkan laughed and swigged more beer. He would have to be careful, not to imitate Tortha Karf's grandfatherly concern for his subordinates personal lives. He was not only the youngest Chief in the history of the Paratime Police; he was barely half the age of some of his chief subordinates. He'd only make himself look ridiculous without doing any good.

TWENTY-TWO ⊕

Archpriest Anaxthenes, First Speaker—who sat at the right hand of Styphon's Voice On Earth, in the Council Hall of Tarr-Ktemnos—put forth the next Dracar sponsored motion. "On the behalf of Prince Lysandros of Hos-Harphax, I move that we send one million ounces of gold to Hos-Harphax to re-equip the Royal Army of Hos-Harphax. All in favor, say Yea."

It was a good motion, he thought, the Royal Army needed rebuilding. Hos-Harphax was the keystone in the Temple's war against the Usurper Kalvan. They were also sending food and stockpiling all they could make of the 'new'—dare he even think it—Kalvan-style fireseed, for shipment by galley to Tarr-Harphax in the spring.

"All opposed, say Nay"

Only Archpriest Cimon was opposed. Styphon's Voice did not bother to vote; he was already asleep snoring loudly enough to keep everyone else awake. One too many of Holy Investigator Roxthar's harangues today.

Archpriest Dracar had become so enamored of Roxthar it was a wonder he wasn't wearing one of the Investigator's white robes. Still the axe had not fallen. What was Roxthar's real game? Surely it was not doing Grand Master Soton's work. What was the Investigator really after at this Council? Would he wait until the last day of the Great Council of Ktemnos and then denounce him before all thirty-six assembled Archpriests of the Inner Circle? Roxthar, without a doubt, had enough evidence to have Anaxthenes' most ardent supporter crying out for his death in hot oil.

Sesklos, his mentor and Styphon's Own Voice was in no position to help. Even awake the old man sat as if frozen to this seat and would not look, much less talk, to his former protégé. As First Speaker, Anaxthenes had read all of Sesklos' opening statements and acted in all other ways as Styphon's Voice in uttering declarations.

Anaxthenes most ardent supporters refused to meet his eyes. They knew he was out-of-favor and likely doomed; most of them had voted with Roxthar and his faction on every issue. Only a few die-hards such as the Archpriest Syclos, Highpriest of Agrys City, and the Peasant Priest Cimon offered opposition to Roxthar. The ash of defeat was bitter in his mouth.

Not that open opposition to Roxthar would have bought much at this late date. The Holy Investigator had used his new powers of Investigation to consolidate his power base in Balph the past few moons. While Roxthar had kept to his bargain and not Investigated any Archpriests of the Inner Circle, he had not held back in Investigating the lesser upper-priests and temple highpriests among the opposition. More than a hundred of Anaxthenes allies and followers had disappeared into the former Temple administration building that Roxthar called his Inquisitory and only five, all maimed and showing evidence of torture, had exited alive.

According to those survivors, the two that would talk to him, the Investigators cut off the first joint of the index finger to show the seriousness of their task, then removed another joint from his other finger, on a rotating basis, every time they found a suspected lie or a reluctance to talk. None of those who had seen the survivors of Roxthar's Full Investigation being wheeled out on carts—limbless, eyeless, and mute like beasts—were unaware of the power he held.

Archpriest Dracar, the man who was Sesklos' heir apparent, stood up to address Styphon's Voice. He looked timorous and not at all triumphant, as he should. It seemed that Dracar had learned that dealing with Roxthar was as difficult as holding Lyklos, God of Lies, to the truth or as dangerous as dealing with Hadron, the Snake God.

"Speak, Archpriest Dracar."

Dracar looked over at Roxthar and, after receiving a nod, began to speak. "First Speaker, I would like to offer the assembled Great Council of Hos-Ktemnos, on the third day of the Moon of Long Nights, the proclamation that henceforth Styphon's Own Guard will act as the martial arm of the Holy Office of Investigation and that each Temple Band shall have its own Investigator Captain for instruction and fidelity to Styphon's Way."

The Great Hall became so quiet that the only sound to be heard was the labored snore of Styphon's Voice. Archpriest Roxthar looked Anaxthenes right in the eye, as if to say get on with it. Anaxthenes felt his heart freeze; Roxthar owned Dracar and the rest of the Inner Circle—the only remaining question was, did he own him too? Anaxthenes looked to the other Archpriests for support but most would not meet his eyes.

Did the fools not realize the implications of Roxthar's latest demand? If Roxthar were granted the power to place his own captains in charge of the Temple Guard, the Holy Inquisitor would from that time forth be immune to any action the Inner Circle might take against him. It would make him Tyrant of Styphon's House and he would rule the Temple as no Archpriest had before him in Styphon's House's history. Already many of the Temple Bands supported Roxthar and his Investigation; if this proclamation passed, they all would.

What should he do? What could he do—even Grand Master Soton had deserted his ranks? It would probably pass even if he made a suicidal gesture and opposed it. The world he had known all his life was changing and he didn't like the form it was assuming. *Maybe most of all, because he no longer had a say in how it changed.*

Ever since Kalvan the Usurper had appeared out of seeming nowhere, turning the backwater Princedom of Hostigos into a Great Kingdom, everything had begun to fall apart—turn sour. And, yet, if any man could alter Kalvan's destiny, Roxthar was that man; the only priest in Styphon's House who could face up to Kalvan and mobilize the full resources of the Temple. Yet, he could also end it with his fierce determination to cleanse the Temple and its followers.

Yet, Roxthar already owned power enough to defeat the Usurper. This time he had gone too far, and it was up to Anaxthenes to try and stop him. Anaxthenes spoke loudly into the farhailer, saying, "No. The martial arm of the Temple has always been under the direct control of the Inner Circle.

There is no evidence of treachery or impropriety within the ranks of Styphon's Own Guard. The Holy Investigators have all the power they need to do their Investigation. The Guard is needed to fight the Daemon Kalvan, not question peasants and farm priests of Dralm.

Anaxthenes noticed the other archpriests were sitting taller in their seats, watching him with interest. Maybe all was not lost. As Thessamona had said, Roxthar could never rule the Temple. Sesklos was only a winter or two away from his last breath. Who else was there to lead the Temple? This was a perfect opportunity to rally his supporters and show the Inner Circle that Roxthar did not yet own Styphon's House.

"I, First Speaker, move that this Proclamation be denied. I will vote nay. Who will join me?"

"Halt!" Roxthar's voice shattered the air. "Styphon's Own Guard only exists to serve Styphon's Will and Styphon's Will is that my Investigators root out all priests guilty of heresy and disbelief in the True and Only God—Styphon, Be Praised!"

Every archpriest in the Great Hall turned and looked away from each other's eyes. In Roxthar's own words they were all guilty. Anaxthenes felt a flutter of hope inside his chest. The Investigator had gone too far this time. Did he not truly realize they were all unbelievers?

"Earlier, did not Archpriest Dracar say, it was Styphon's Will that we gather the Temple's gold and fireseed to defeat the Usurper Kalvan? The Kalvan who stole our Fireseed Mystery and 'gave' it to every bandit and horse thief in the Five Kingdoms! I say Styphon's Will is fighting the Holy War against the Infidel Kalvan and the Rogue Princedom of Hostigos. Not Investigating Styphon's Own priests."

Anaxthenes looked into each and every archpriest's face. They were coming around. Starting to realize that if they gave Roxthar and his faction any more power, someday it would be the Inner Circle that would be Investigated. And, only one archpriest—other than Roxthar—would survive that purge, Cimon the Peasant Priest.

"Again, I, First Speaker, move that this Proclamation be denied. I will vote nay. Who will join me?"

There was a moment of stunned silence, a sudden babble of voices, then dozens of heads slowly nodding affirmation. There were many who voted aye, but enough who voted nay to doom the proclamation. Roxthar himself gave a look to Anaxthenes that would have turned his flesh into stone had Roxthar been a god. This was Roxthar's first defeat since his rise; he hoped that it would not be the last.

"So be it, the Proclamation has been denied. The Council's will has spoken, Praise Styphon!"

The world had just tilted and nothing would ever be the same. Anaxthenes dismissed the Council for the day, and surely and steadily walked past Arch-priest Roxthar. It was a small victory, but a needed one to maintain what little was left of his self-respect and the Temple's independence.

II

Accompanied by Xykos and his aide, Colonel Krynos, Kalvan rode his horse through the mild winter snow to the University. Xykos knocked at the plank door and announced his presence. Ramakros, the big Hostigi Uncle Wolf, with dark brown hair and Indian skin-tone—evidence that Erasthames the Great had not killed all the Indians, or Ruthani as they were called here-and-now, in the northeast—opened the portal. "Come in, Your Majesty."

There was a roaring fire in the big stone hearth and Kalvan greeted it like a long lost lover. It was near freezing outside and an hour horseback ride had left him chilled, despite his silver-fox fur cloak and warm undergarments.

"Your Majesty, I'm sorry, but Rector Mytron is no longer here to greet you. He is in Hostigos Town at the Temple. He left several days ago. He is studying under Patriarch Xentos for his position as Highpriest of the Hos-Hostigos Temple of Dralm."

"I know Ramakros. Bring Master Ermut, unless he's asleep."

"Ermut sleep—that one! No, he says he still has three years of slavery to make up for before he spends more than a few hours a night in his bed. I'll get him. Is it about the glass?"

"No. We have other matters to discuss." It was amazing how scientific and scholarly thought brought out the egalitarian instinct in people who formerly hadn't even known the meaning of the word. The hierarchy of the University was really quite simple; those with knowledge and learning were the aristocrats. And anyone with brains, who aspired to find truth and the mysteries of the universe, could join the faculty and reach their own level of excellence. He wondered when it was that universities back on otherwhen stopped operating on that level, and instead became hotbeds of academic intrigue.

While he was waiting for Ermut, Artillery Captain Waklos came over to the hearth and started talking enthusiastically about his attempts to master and teach Morse Code. "It's not all that difficult, Your Majesty, it's just that it requires a new way of seeing words."

"Yes, it's called substitution. As the runes form written words, the dots and dashes form traveling words."

"Traveling words—I like that, Your Majesty. I will use that with my next class."

"Oh, Thalmoth has you teaching now?" Captain Waklos had been one of Brigadier-General Alkides under officers before he'd surrendered to the army of Hostigos last year—or was it the year before last.

Note: reform the Zarthani calendar.

"Oh yes, Master Thalmoth says his most important job is to be there at the birthing of new guns at the Royal Foundry."

"How does he get along with the Zygrosi foundry workers, Waklos?" Kalvan asked, wondering if Thalmoth was becoming a nuisance. He couldn't afford to alienate his Zygrosi specialists, until he'd trained several more crews; one of the reasons he wanted the Nostor Royal Foundry started right away.

"Quite well. They appear not to enjoy firing the guns and are quite happy to let Master Thalmoth shoot them to his heart's content. I fear he's not as impressed with the Zygrosi workers themselves; he says they argue in their tongue all the time. The women, too, take liberties with the male servants and treat men of lower class as lesser beings. He thinks they all need a good beating! Well, not all of them, he speaks fondly of the red-haired lady—Sirna, I believe she is called. And the other one that rides horses all the time."

"I hope he keeps this to himself, as all those ladies are part of the Royal Household."

"Oh, yes. When they talk loudly to him, Thalmoth pretends not to understand. Now, they treat him as a dumb beast, who has listened to too many guns, which he much prefers to their full attention and bad humor!"

They both laughed. "Thalmoth must have a wife somewhere."

"Oh, yes. He married late, a few years ago. His wife lived in Hostigos Town. She ran off with a cavalry officer during one of his terms of service. Master Thalmoth still says it was the best thing that ever happened to him, saying she only married him for a trip to Agrys City!"

"Fortunately, he does love his guns. I suspect he would court a Sastragathi fire-walker, if she brought him a brass twenty-pounder!"

"Oh yes," Waklos said, laughing. "They would both have much in common!"

"How is the semaphore project coming along?"

"Captain Nathros is still out in Beshta scouting out where to locate the signal towers. He left me in charge, while he's away," Waklos said proudly. "He would love to perform miracles and have the towers built before spring, but the early snowfall has made this impossible. And we will need at least fifteen hands worth of signalmen, and I'm still training the second class. I have two students who are already proficient in the code and I will use them for the next round of classes."

"Good. I knew it would have taken Dralm's Own Miracle to have the semaphore to the Harphaxi border ready before the beginning of campaign season, but we should have at least the branch to Beshta complete by next winter." Kalvan had meant to build the semaphore posts the year before, but didn't have the trained men to oversee the prisoners-of-war building the Great Kings Road, teach the codes and build the semaphore stations.

Waklos looked at the ground as if not having it finished was his fault. "We will have it done, by then. The Sask branch as well."

"That is more than I have any right to ask for. When it is done, we will be able to pass messages from General Hestophes' Army of Observation to Hostigos Town in a matter of a few candles!"

"Truly, a miracle. Praise Dralm." Waklos was about to say more, but was interrupted by the arrival of Master Ermut.

"You Majesty, why aren't you at the palace? Have Styphon's dogs found a way to travel through snow?"

"No. I came to tell you that Rector Mytron has resigned from the University faculty. He will be the new Highpriest at the Hostigos Temple."

Ermut rocked back and forth nervously. "He's been troubled of late, by spiritual matters. With Xentos moving to Agrys City in the spring, he is the senior priest. None of my business; I got more than enough of gods and priests at Styphon's temple farm! I was not aware he was leaving the University—we will miss him."

"We all will," echoed Kalvan. "But, I bring good news as well. It is Our wish that you become the new Rector. This was Mytron's wish as well."

"Please, Your Majesty, you have already honored me enough for one lifetime. Just being able to do this 'work' makes my life complete. Please, I must ask you to find another director. My 'experiments' take up all my time; there are others who can tend schedules and fill slates better than myself."

Kalvan was taken aback. Not many people turned down prestigious appointments, either in otherwhen or here-and-now. He could tell by the set of Ermut's mouth and body that this decision was not subject to further consideration. "I accept your decision, although I am disappointed. You would have made a good Rector, but you would have had little time to experiment—that much is true. Who do you suggest for the post?"

"Highpriest Uncle Wolf Tharses. His hospice is now running itself and he's been spending his nights at the Crossed Halberds with old companions, drinking too much of my Brandy!"

He's not the only one, thought Kalvan pensively.

"Good choice. I will inform him in the morning. I've got some suggestions on how we might improve the glass, but it can wait until later."

"Why wait? I'm getting ready to make a new batch, which was why I was so long in obeying your summons. What do you suggest, Your Majesty?"

Kalvan was secretly pleased; he didn't want to return to the palace right away. The endless talk of war and great kingdom politics was giving him a headache. This great kings' game was awful dirty at times, and the burden resting on his shoulders was getting as heavy as the nearby Bald Eagle Mountains.

Kalvan took out his pipe and refilled the barrel. "It's the lime—we might be using to much. And maybe a touch more potash."

Ermut nodded thoughtfully. "We could try less. Come into my laboratory, and we'll work up several new test batches."

TWENTY-THREE

I

Dhergabar Metropolitan Police Chief Vothan Raldor came into Chief Verkan's office with several spools. He was not only tall, but also thick like a gnarled oak; his iron-gray hair was cut short in a Metro buzz cut. "Verkan, I think you're going to want to see this."

"What is it Raldor?" Chief Vothan Raldor was a good administrator and very good cop. He'd been Metro's best Investigator until he was promoted to fulltime desk job some fifty years back. Vothan had been appointed Metro Chief three years ago and was in the middle of straightening out a mare's nest of corruption and police malfeasance. He'd always had a good working relationship with the Paratime Police and Verkan was pleased to give him any help he needed. These days Verkan was not only running short of allies, but friends, too.

"You know yourself, that Year-End Day has always been a busy time for us. A few times we had to borrow officers from your former boss, Tortha Karf."

"Is this your way of telling me you think you are going to need help tomorrow?"

"Think it. No, I know it. And, yes, thank you very much; I'll take you up on your offer.

Verkan laughed. "What offer? Here's my viewer. Let's see what your problem is. Then we can figure out how many officers I can loan you."

"First, have you heard of The Leader?"

"Yes, the Commissioner was telling me about him. A pocket Hitler, a real third-rater, who won't even identify himself. Other than that I haven't heard anything—but then I haven't spent a lot of time in the City lately."

"You won't hear about The Leader in the places you frequent, Vall. The sleazy dives, ecstasy palaces and tranq bars, those are his levels. We've been having a lot of problems with the young folk—not kids, but young adults. Mostly from families on the dole. I know we like to pretend that all Home Time Liners have good jobs and work hard—and most do. But, the average Citizen doesn't realize there are millions of technologically unfit non-citizens and genetic culls on the streets and in the warrens. Old Dhergabar is full of them. And, despite the prohibitions, they have children—in some cases lots of them. In the past, they managed to either work at servile jobs or just disappear into the woodwork, but this new 'servant' fad that is bringing in tens of millions of Fifth Level Service Sector Proles is upsetting the status quo.

"Our non-citizens are getting their faces rubbed in the fact that they're not working members of First Level. It's gotten worse recently, since many of the second-generation proles are becoming Citizens. They have become the real underclass. Despite, the dole and their aimless lives, they've always felt superior to outtimers. But now, when they see former outtimers getting jobs and doing things they couldn't hope to do—well, it's an open fire in a drought area. Fortunately, no one—until now—has come up with a way to mobilize the growing anger and discord among the non-citizens. The Leader appears to be doing just that."

"Do you have any clues as to his identity?"

"No. We don't have any clues. He's a ghost walker. Take a look at this!" Raldor pushed in one of the spools and immediately the viewer was crowded with hundreds of marching young people shouting, "Hail, to The Leader. Hail, to The Leader." Most were dressed in blue clothing, a few in what appeared to be blue uniforms. The scene had been taken in Old Dhergabar, where there were still ground level streets and crowded buildings; many of them underground so they wouldn't be visible to citizens. Some of the youths were carrying truncheons and bats of some sort. The marchers came to a stop in front of a small grog shop, the One-Eyed Lady. "Death to Proles! Go home wogs!" shouted the voices. Someone tossed a stone against the window, which deformed and then popped back into shape sending the fragment back into the crowd.

The marchers went wild with fury, tearing the doors off their hinges and charging inside. There were screams from the grog shop. Suddenly about seven or eight people, men and women, with ripped clothing and bloody noses, were pushed through the door. The crowd fell upon them with their makeshift weapons. Even Verkan was forced to look away.

"It goes on like this for a while. The crowd scattered when my first squad arrived. All the proles, except one, were dead. Most of them weren't even proles! We got this recording from a neighbor who was out on a walk. We've already picked up two hundred of the rioters. All of them went under narco-hypnosis. None of them know anything. Someone overheard someone else talking about some prole at the One-Eyed Lady forging false ID for proles so they can pass as Citizens—that kind of stuff." Raldor laughed harshly. "As if proles could actually counterfeit First Level documents; it shows how ignorant and uninformed this bunch really is."

"Ignorant they may be, but in the wrong hands they could become a potent weapon."

"That's what I'm afraid of, Chief. This is a black eye for the City and not the kind of outtime nonsense I ever thought I'd see on the streets of Dhergabar."

"Any of them know anything about The Leader?"

"Not a thing. Sometimes people get real messages on their coms from him, but they really don't know who he is."

"This whole operation is very similar to a Fourth Level racket I ran into a few years back. It's called fascism—a state sponsored free-for-all at some minority's expense. Mass murders in the name of racial cleansing, and other aberrations. When the fascists won, we had to make that entire Subsector off-limits." Verkan, thinking back to his talk with the Paratime Commissioner, shook his head in disgust. "Didn't think I'd ever see its like here on Home Time Line. The Commissioner warned me about The Leader, but I didn't take it seriously enough. What does Bur Psych-Hygiene have to say about it?"

"Bureau Secretary Latok rattled some jargon off about it, finishing with, "In summation, our Metro Mentalist claims 'it's an over-reaction syndrome, based on childhood stimulation-deprivation, combined with low self-esteem and xenophobia.' It sounds like they don't understand it either. He did say that involuntary admissions are at an all-time high and that he hopes we can solve the problem because most of their facilities are overflowing!"

"What's supposed to happen tomorrow on Year-End Day?"

"Mass demonstrations all over the capital and in outlying cities, too. There's talk about occupying the prole living sectors and moving them out—by force, if necessary."

"How many officers will you need?"

"Ten thousand if you can get them."

Verkan whistled. "Sorry, not even with a ten-days notice. Most of my troopers are stationed outtime. I can give you a couple hundred, if I cancel all leaves. Tell me where you need them most."

"Thanks Verkan. Maybe we can put the lid on this."

II

Grand Master Soton looked up at the nondescript three story stone building with surprise. This unremarkable building did not look at all like the home of the most powerful and feared Archpriest of the Inner Circle of Styphon's House; no it resembled the dwelling of an underpriest or novice. This feeling was confirmed when he went to the door and it was opened by a proctor. The only thing that was different from any other such dormitory in Balph was the presence of a squad of Styphon's Own Guard in the first floor antechamber and the lack of giggling young harlots— although, he suspected they no longer frequented the dormitories as they had in his youth, considering all the other changes in Balph. The guards appeared bored and were talking among themselves about the chances of being sent to Hos-Harphax, where there was bound to be plenty of fighting and other sports, such as burning villages and plundering wealthy residences.

Soton was dressed as a Brethren of the Zarthani Knights, in a black tunic with Styphon's white sun-wheel device, over his jerkin and trousers— not wanting to attract attention and comment with a large retinue. The guards of Styphon's Own Guard eyed him with challenging glares, as if he were a Hostigi soldier who had suddenly materialized on the streets of Balph. He pointedly ignored their stares. He made his way upstairs and stopped when he came to a room with two more guards, only these guards wore the white robes of the Holy Investigation. Both held wickedly sharp halberds at the ready.

"Grand Master Soton of the Zarthani Knights to meet with Holy Investigator Roxthar."

"Go in, Grand Master—you are expected."

Soton opened the door to a room that most closely resembled a cell. The walls and floors were bare, with only a cot and two hardwood chairs of primitive manufacture. Roxthar sat in one of the chairs, his eyes staring fixedly at the wall.

Soton felt as if he'd walked in on someone at the privy tanks. He started to back up, when Roxthar said, "Sit, Grand Master. I was talking with our Lord God Styphon. He tells me He is pleased with your work in his name. He promises you great glory when the Usurper is vanquished."

Soton felt chills ride up and down the bumps of his spine. He had negotiated with Sastragathi snake-handlers who were saner than this, the most powerful man in Balph. "I will do my best to fulfill his will."

Roxthar smiled in a manner that might have made a she-wolf's milk curdle. "You and I are a lot alike. Both orphans and soldiers in Styphon's war against iniquity. Someday we shall rule the earth in Styphon's Name."

Soton was glad to be included in Roxthar's plans, since not to be included probably meant not to be among the living. Not knowing how to answer, he turned to one of Roxthar's stock replies, "Let Styphon's Will Be Done."

Roxthar nodded as if giving him a benediction, which he probably was. Soton suddenly wished he were somewhere safe—like at the head of a Lance of knights charging into a mass of nomads.

"Your arrival in Balph was propitious. I have been thinking about the war against the Usurper."

Soton who'd been called away from Tarr-Ceros in the midst of winter for this meeting could not think of a reply that would ensure his future health or longevity. So, instead he nodded sagely.

"We need more soldiers; yet, you tell me in your letter that almost every mercenary in the Five Kingdoms is employed."

Soton nodded again. "Kalvan has recruited most of the northern Kingdom mercenaries for his army. Phidestros took his leavings for the Harphaxi Army. With the nomads and clans of the Sastragath stirring, even the Middle Kingdom mercenaries are contracted."

"Then we must look farther afield."

Soton had to bite his tongue to keep from blurting something he might well regret. He didn't give priests instructions on their devotions, so why should they bedevil him with strategies and bad advice. Still, it had to be admitted that Roxthar and himself were the only two men in Styphon's House with any strategic vision. "What are your suggestions, Holy Investigator?"

"I need your advice, since you will be leading the crusade against the Usurper next year. What about the Ros-Zarthani across the Iron Trail? They are fierce warriors and their kings are eternally in need of gold. Archpriest Prysos, who has been advancing Styphon's word in the Middle Kingdoms, tells me that they are renowned for their war prowess."

Soton almost had to bite his tongue to keep from laughing out loud. By Styphon's Privy Parts, what new madness had Roxthar conjured up in his febrile brain! Or was it another of this Prysos' schemes. He had never heard of this Archpriest until recently, then as an agent of Speaker Anaxthenes. Now he was Roxthar's man, as well; it certainly could be said that Archpriest Prysos followed the Balph political winds like a weather vane. "If the stories are true, the Ros-Zarthani still fight with darts and bows! How long would they stand against Kalvan's cannon?"

Roxthar nodded. "This is true, but they are fierce warriors. In the past, we have proscribed trading fireseed with them because their kings are so ambitious and their warriors are so spirited. Now that Styphon's Mystery has been revealed by the Daemon Kalvan, it might be a good time to ally ourselves with them, so that we can introduce them to the One-God."

"It is true that we dearly need more soldiers, even if they are only bodies to throw before the Usurper's guns. In this manner, they would be most useful. I don't know how many mercenaries they will sell us, but we could use at least five thousand. Ten thousand would be even better."

"Good. My thinking, too, Grand Master. I will send Archpriest Prysos at the head of a diplomatic mission to speak to their Tyrant. He will arrange for the recruitment of ten thousand solders to be paid for in gold and

fireseed. In the past, Prysos was the intermediary used by Sesklos and
Archpriest Anaxthenes to trade fireseed to the Mexicotál for gold. This has
been stopped since their attack upon Xiphlon. Upon his return to Balph
Prysos was coerced—or so he claims—by Anaxthenes to attempt to enlist
you in their revolt. As a 'self-proclaimed' true believer, he came to me after
being approached by the First Speaker. I am wary of his loyalties, which
seem to be mostly to himself, so I suggested that he head this mission to
test his loyalty. If he returns, he will gain a place in the Inner Circle; if not,
one less empty yellow robe."

Soton suspected that Prysos had jumped out of the pot and into the fire.
He did not envy the Archpriest both his travel and dealings with the mercurial Ros-Zarthani. It was said their kings were absolute rulers and
dabbled in unclean arts. However, Soton did need more disciplined troops
and the Ros Zarthani could be the answer. "It could work. If nothing else,
maybe they will die well for Styphon."

Roxthar grinned and brayed his hacking laugh. "I thought as well myself.
At best, we have additional soldiers; at worst, another traitor has died."

Roxthar went back to staring at the wall and Soton decided this meant
he was excused. Well, he'd rather have the Investigator staring at the wall
than at his back. Roxthar's opponents did not fare well; although, he suspected the treacherous Prysos deserved whatever hand he was dealt.

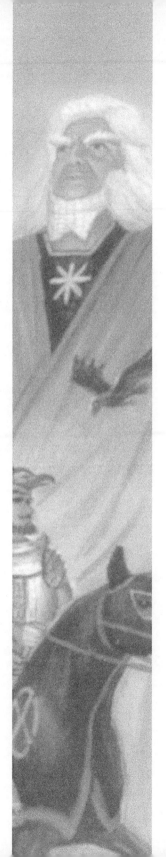

SPRING

TWENTY-FOUR

I

Ranjar Sargos leaped out of the tree, flapped his wings and caught an updraft, which propelled him high into the sky. It was dawn and the sun was rising above the distant horizon, bathing the world in red flames. Sargos looked up and there were black ravens circling above him. Looking down he saw a great herd of stampeding beasts flooding the Pythagaros Valley.

As he glided closer to the earth, he was able to discern the true nature of the teaming animals—only they weren't animals, but thousands upon thousands of men, the two-legged beast. They were painted in war colors and carrying bows, spears, axes and all the weapons of war.

Sargos glided above their heads and they looked up at him. Suddenly they began to beat their weapons against their shields. It was as if he was the sign they had been waiting for and it came to him that it was his destiny to lead this sea of warriors.

At the other end of the valley there was a rumble like thunder; he flew closer to see another great clan of men wearing the metal skins of the dirtmen. They were pointing their firesticks and pulling huge guns behind teams of horses.

He shrieked a warning to his followers and raised his talons. The roar of war cries smashed against his ears like clubs—

"Ranjar, wake up! Wake up!"

Ranjar Sargos, Warlord of the Tymannes, removed his hands from his ears and slowly rose up off the thin mat he had been sleeping on. *Where am I?* The open door let in enough moonlight that he could see that he was inside the Chief's hut, where he had been sleeping since becoming Warlord of the Clan.

"What is it?" Ranjar asked.

"Ikkos has returned."

"Where are the others?" By the others, of course, he meant his eldest son, Bargoth, who against his private council had ridden off with the scouting party.

"I do not know, Chief," the sentry, said drawing back as if he thought Ranjar might hold him responsible for the bad news. "Only Ikkos has returned and he was on foot with many wounds."

Sargos brushed the sleep out of his eyes. "Take me to him."

"Follow me."

Sargos tucked his pistol into his belt and followed the sentry into the night. The Clan's longhouses and sweathuts filled most of the small upper valley and he could just make out another score of men gathered near the palisade's gateway. *If none of the sentries have stayed at their posts, there will be blood spilled this night!*

Tymannes from all over the Sastragath had come to this Clan Gathering, not as in the past to settle tribal boundaries or exchange furs and trade goods before the coming cold, but to talk about the great movement of peoples that was taking place in the lowland valleys and along the Great Mother River. Never in living memory had so many tribes and clans been uprooted from their traditional lands.

Interrogation of the prisoners had told them little, only that many tribes and bands were being forced to flee their homes by the invading Grassmen and the Black Knights. Sargos had once fought against the Knights as a mercenary, and he had no desire to cross swords with the Order again. While the clans and tribesmen of the Sastragath had fought the Black Knights many times in the past, the Knights had not burned villages and slain whole tribes without provocation. Thus had the Gathering of all the Tymannes continued from winter into the time when the tribesmen should be setting traps, hunting and fishing.

I wonder if this upheaval has anything to do with my vision? Before he could mull this over, they had arrived at the circle of men surrounding Ikkos. A few held torches and he could see that Ikkos was bruised and shirtless. Several subchiefs were trying to question him all at the same time, while the Clan healers were cleaning his wounds. Sargos stilled their voices with a clap of his hands.

"Where is Bargoth?"

Ikkos shook his head as if dazed. "I left him with all the others when we were ambushed. He may be coming behind me. I don't know. The last I saw him, he was shooting his bow and telling me to escape."

Sargos mentally steeled himself for the worst. Bargoth had never been one to turn away from a fight, no matter what the odds. He was big for eighteen winters and could run, chase and fight as good as any warrior in the tribe; yet, Sargos had often wondered if he had the cunning necessary to make a good chief, or to lead his people. Tomorrow, at first light, he would send a party to find out what had happened and to see if anyone else in the scouting party had survived.

"Did you recognize the tribe that set the ambush?"

"No, Chief Sargos. But one of them wore the blue tattoos of the Great Mother River tribes—" Ikkos broke off and began to shake with fatigue and cold. Someone passed him a blanket and he curled up into a ball.

"We will get little more out of him tonight," Sargos told the gathered clansmen. "Let him sleep so that he can talk to the Headmen tomorrow. You others, get back to your posts before our foes walk in through the gate!" The men trotted off as if stung by wasps. When everyone had left, Sargos squatted down in the grass and clenched his hands over his chest as hard as he could until tears streamed out of his eyes.

As he walked back to his hut, Sargos felt the presence of someone walking beside him. He turned to see the lovely face of Althea framed by moonlight.

He tried to speak, but no words would come.

Her fingers brushed his cheek like feathers. "You don't have to speak. I heard about Ikkos coming back alone."

He couldn't hold back the tear that slipped from his right eye. Althea's fingers brushed it away.

Her silence was more comforting than any words. Sargos knew in his heart that Bargoth would not be returning: the knowledge pierced him inside like a knife blade. Without Althea's support he doubted he would have been able to find his own hut.

He stopped at the doorway and told her, "Stay. I cannot be responsible for what will happen if you enter."

"Tonight you need a woman's arms, my Chief," Althea answered.

"But you're a maiden. I have lived many winters—"

Her hand came up and covered his mouth. "The maiden I was, I am no longer. If I am old enough to take a man's life, I am old enough to share your mat."

II

Kalvan got up to greet the Xiphlon trader as he entered the private audience chamber. "Have a seat, Trader Tortha."

"Thank you, Your Majesty." The full-bodied older man sat down, with a grace that belied both his size and age. His mustache had grown much fuller, but he was still beardless—in the style of the Middle Kingdoms. Over the winter, Kalvan had grown to enjoy Tortha's visits and found it welcome to talk to someone who was not beholden to him, or appeared to believe he was semi-divine.

Kalvan paused to light his pipe, before asking, "How was your hunting trip?"

"I got two bucks and a doe. Colonel Ranthar brought back four! We got a bear, too—Ranthar again. He's a dead straight shot with those *rifles* of yours."

Kalvan laughed. "He got lots of practice last spring shooting at Styphon's soldiers." His smile disappeared. "I wanted to talk to you about the Sastragathi tribesmen, since you're the only person, besides Captain General Harmakros and General Baldour—and he's from Hos-Ktemnos, not the Sastragath—who has any knowledge of them."

Tortha's face grew grim. "There are almost as many tribes and clans as there are different kinds of trees in your woods. Xiphlon has been fighting them since the first wooden wall was put up, about one day after we arrived at the mouth of the Great Mother River! I do know this; the Sastragathi tribesman can fight like cornered wolverines, but—fortunately for us—they fight as individuals not as an army. They have very little discipline and their leadership goes from inspired to hide-bound, depending on each clans' warlord. Fortunately, for Hostigos, they rarely leave the Upper Sastragath."

"They have now. We got word after you left: the first tribes have already entered the Trygath. The rumors tell us that they are being burned out of their hunting grounds and huts by the Order of Zarthani Knights."

"Phew!" Tortha mocked wiping his forehead. "For the last several hundred years the Order has been all that's come between the teeming clans and the Five Kingdoms. I don't know what you did to provoke, Grand Master Soton, Your Majesty, but he's after your hide!"

"We pretty much ground up four or five of his Lances last spring."

"That'll do it. Soton's not much of an infantryman, but he's the best cavalry officer this side of the Great Mother River. If he's aiming to drive the nomads into the Northern Kingdoms—and, by what you've just told me, I'd say that's exactly what he's doing—you're going to have an invasion the likes of which the Northern Kingdoms have never known!"

"That's what I was afraid of, Tortha. Here's my problem." Kalvan liked the way Trader Tortha leaned forward, giving him his full and undivided attention. He used to be able to talk like this with Verkan and Prince Ptosphes, before the Prince took a licking at Tenabra. He'd missed it, too. It was nice to have someone to bounce military strategy off of, besides Rylla, again. He didn't always like telling her his plans, because she wanted to take charge, with an emphasis on charge! "We've got a once-in-a-lifetime opportunity to conquer Hos-Harphax and put her under our rule. The new Captain-General, a former mercenary, is rebuilding the Royal Army, pretty much from scratch. If we hit them now, we can go straight to Harphax City and blow the walls down—which I hear could barely stand a good sneeze—and be out in a moon-half. Then we could take the individual princedoms—those that didn't surrender—in detail.

"My question is: Can we afford a two front war, with the nomads in back and the Royal Army of Hos-Harphax at the front?"

Trader Tortha grimaced and said, "You might find yourself with a third front, with the Knights attacking from Hos-Ktemnos again."

"No. The Knights are busy driving the nomads and Great King Cleithar-ses is still licking his wounds. It'll be a two front war—this spring. I just want to know if you think we might be stretching our forces too thin?"

Tortha paused to drain his goblet of winter wine and pulled out his pipe. As he was loading it with tobacco from his red suede pouch, with the insignia of a golden fish, he said, "I am honored that the Great King seeks my council. And, I fear, I may be giving him advice he would rather not hear. Shall I continue?"

Kalvan nodded; he had been afraid of this.

"If the nomads and Sastragathi clans are both being driven into your backyard, you are going to have a big problem. You could be invaded by anywhere between a quarter of a million to a million human locusts who will eat, steal and destroy everything they touch! Now, King Nestros of the Trygath has his city walls—mostly patterned after Xiphlon's own, but much smaller—which have kept the nomads at bay for the last hundred years. Rathon City will hold, but most of the smaller towns and villages will be destroyed. When he opens his gates, it will be to a desert. His barons will turn on him like a pack of wolves.

"The most likely situation is that the nomads will stay there and use the Trygath as a base of operations to make raids on the border princedoms of Hos-Hostigos and Hos-Agrys. This means your border princes will be howling to the gods like coyotes—a small wolf which lives in the Sea of Grass. You will be forced to send a dozen armies to chase light cavalrymen who will disappear before their eyes. If Nestor comes out from behind his walls, you will have to guard his back and your back, as well. It's a job that would keep an army twice the size of the Hostigos Royal Army busy day and night.

"If this happens, the clansmen will gather in force and sow terror and destruction upon your kingdom like no one has seen for two hundred years! Every farmer, every trapper, every hunter, every trader will have to stay behind your walls or risk death—and their families, too. The best strategy would be to raise the largest army, with as many of your liegemen as you can gather, then rise up and strike the nomads before they have established themselves within the Trygath, or worse—within your own borders!"

"Now, what's the good news?"

"There isn't any. You have to destroy this horde before it cleans you out of Hos-Hostigos like a wave of wolves!" Tortha leaned back and puffed on his pipe. "Maybe you can send them back to Soton with a Name Day ribbon on them. That's what I'd be thinking about doing."

"I have read of such nomad armies in the chronicles. Tortha, you have given me much to think about. It's time to call another Council of War, but I fear it won't be about just the war we were planning to fight."

TWENTY-FIVE

I

orand Rarth pushed his chair back, to ease his bulging belly, and listened with pleasure to the jingle and clang of the slot machines in the front room. The slots were a recent *import* from Fourth Level, Europo-American Sector and they were proving to be—as had so many other Europo-American imports—a great hit. He estimated the average take was up fifteen percent at all three of his Dhergabar clubs since their introduction. He was going to have to *import* more and send them to his other clubs outside the capital before one of the other Bosses got the same idea.

While the Bureau of Psychological Hygiene saw gambling and playing games of chance as evidence of an anti-social character, gambling itself was not strictly illegal. To a society that liked to see itself as free of pre-literate and pseudo-scientific superstition, it was a social embarrassment—a continuing reminder of the irrationality of human nature. As such, Psych-Hygiene agents liked to keep records on those who frequented gambling dens.

In an ongoing attempt to protect customer anonymity, the gambling syndicates carefully guarded the location of their clubs, moved them around at irregular intervals and paid large sums of hush money to certain captains in the Dhergabar Metropolitan Police Department.

Jorand needed to talk to his contacts at Tharmax Trading right away about acquiring more slot machines. It didn't help that they were quasi-illegal on most Europo-American Subsectors, either. If Paratime Police Chief Verkan Vall hadn't been monitoring that Sector so vigilantly, Jorand would have solved his problem very simply. He would have run a big con-veyer into one of the Fourth Level slot machine factories, taken all the trained mechanics and setup men, blown a gas main under the old factory and then sent them across time to an uninhabited Fifth Level time-line where he would have set up his own slot machine business.

Making them was clearly not as easy as hijacking them, but then slot machines were not as easy to obtain outtime as Fourth Level jukeboxes or Second Level subliminal hormone exciters. Plus, by using slave labor, the syndicate could save a lot of credits as well as create a dependable supply base—one not dependent upon outtime politics and Paratime Police good will to operate. Wars and revolutions had a nasty way of mucking up supply and delivery, especially when they splashed over whole subsectors, contain-ing hundreds of millions of time-lines.

Jorand's door sensor beeped and Metropolitan Police Captain Sirgoth Zyarr entered the room. Jorand quickly rose to his feet. Sirgoth had never physically come into one of his clubs in more than twenty years of 'work-ing' together. He wondered if he were about to be raided. Raids were ritualized; with both sides warned long in advance so each could play out their part to perfection.

Something big was coming down. "What is it, Cap—"?

"No names."

It suddenly hit him that Sirgoth was not wearing his regulation blues, but a gray street toga and cape.

"One of my men flagged your name in a data pool we share with the Paratime Police. They've tagged you for pickup. Don't know when or where, but if I were you I wouldn't waste any time finding a hole to crawl into."

"Why the warning?" Everyone knew about the ages old antagonism between the Metropolitan Police and the Paratime Police; the Metros—along with almost everyone else—thought the Paracops acted like a second government—with more authority than the Metropolitan Police and the Executive Council combined. Maybe they needed their autonomy to guard the secret of Paratime Transposition, but that didn't mean everyone else had to like it. Or that the Paratime Police had to be so self-righteous in carrying out the duties of their job.

"I'll give you one reason. Then I'm getting out of here and as far as you are concerned you've never heard of me and I've never heard of you. Make any attempt to re-establish contact with me, and I will see you are terminated."

Jorand gulped.

"Ever since Chief Verkan and his Paratime squads saved our butts on Year-End Day, by helping us put down the riots, we've been given orders to assist them with all on-going investigations and to share our data pool. It's a new game under Chief Raldor and all the old rules are changing. If the Paratime Police get their hands on you, the first thing they'll do is pump narco-hypnotics into your system until you squeal like a frightened little girl. Then you're going to throw out everything you know. My name is going to appear in that mess you regurgitate. If I were smart, I would have wired your aircar and cleansed the whole operation in one blast. But there are problems with that approach too. Be thankful that in the past you've always been on time with the slush, and that you haven't splashed any dirt on me."

With that said, Captain Sirgoth spun around and left the small room.

Jorand felt his heart pound like a trip-hammer. *I could have a heart attack right this moment, race to the nearest hospice and wake up with a new heart and a Paratime Policeman at my side.*

He willed his heart to slow down and quickly began to draw up a mental list of what he had to take with him and what he had to destroy.

II

All the chiefs of the Tymannes sat in the clan's Council Hut. Old Daron had his son with him, a middle-aged man with too much belly and watery eyes. *Why, if the gods had to take a son, couldn't they have taken one such as this?* Sargos shook his head to help clear his thoughts; then he rose to make the opening prayers so the gods might bless the Folk in this year of great trial.

When the rituals were finished, Sargos had Ikkos called into the hut.

"We traveled five days until we reached the banks of the Great Mother River. Many times we had to hide from strange tribes and war parties. Many of the camps we passed were burned out or deserted. At the camp of the Lyssos we discovered only the dead; the entire tribe had been massacred, even the women and children."

There was a collective shriek at this news. The Lyssos had long been allies of the Tymannes and all had lost friends and kin in their unclean passing. To kill unarmed women and children was against the will of the gods.

"At the banks of the Great Mother River we saw many Grassmen crossing on rafts, some so large they could hold the entire clan! We saw little fighting there, but the river was clogged with the bodies of the dead. Whether from some earlier battle, or one upstream, we never did learn.

"Downstream we came upon a great battle. The Black Knights were attacking a large village, ten times the size of our own camp. They burned the palisades and used great fire tubes to knock them down. When the walls collapsed they stormed the village, killing everyone who did not flee and burnt everything left behind. We too ran for fear they might attack us as well!

"Later we talked to some of the villagers who escaped and they told us the Knights were burning and destroying every village and camp in the Sastragath. They claimed the end of the world was coming. They left us to flee north where they hoped to join up with others of their people. After that we left to return to the valley, when three days later we were ambushed by the Grassmen." Ikkos went on to detail the ambush and their fight against overwhelming odds.

Hearing about the ambush brought the emptiness back again, but Sargos brushed it aside. Little new was told during the questioning so Sargos pondered over the death of his son and the vision he had been gifted with three nights ago. *Was his son the gods' price for leadership over all the clans, or was it some jest?*

Before he could make sense of all this, his other son, Larkander entered the hut. The boy's eyes were red and Sargos felt his stomach drop like a stone. Sometimes Larkander resembled his mother so much it took him back over sixteen winters ago when he had brought the Zarthani maiden, the daughter of a Trygathi merchant, back with him to the Tribe. She had named Larkander after her favorite uncle.

"Father more riders have returned . . . They brought Bargoth's body back with them. They say he died with honor, surrounded by the bodies of the slain. Why, Father, why?"

Before this son embarrassed them both, he ordered, "Sit. The time has come for you to prepare for your place in the tribe."

Larkander took control of his emotions and sat down with all the dignity his fourteen winters—no fifteen winters, now!—could muster. Not for the first time, Sargos was proud of his young boy—no, almost a man now. His voice had already broken and he was halfway through his last growth. The time had come for him to take on a man's duty and responsibility.

Sargos rose to speak to the clan Headmen. "Where there is one army of Black Knights, there are more. Either they or the Grassmen will soon come to drive us from our lands. We have two choices: we can stay and fight—and die, since our foes are in number like the summer grass. Or we can join the other tribes and clans and move up the Pythagaros Valley. How do you vote?"

There was little discussion. The clan leaders agreed to move north as their Warchief had suggested. The women and children would go into the hills with the warriors of Old Daron's tribe to protect them.

As they left the Clan Hut, Larkander moved close to Ranjar and asked, "Father, may I come along with the rest of the warriors?"

Ranjar Sargos looked down at this youngest son, now his only son. *Was this to be the price of his visions? Both sons' dead?* He shook his head.

"But Father, I can ride a horse and shoot a bow as good as any man in this camp."

Sargos knew this was no idle boast. "Larkander, you are my only son now. I need you safe. Someone has to watch the womenfolk."

"Not all the clanswomen. I heard you tell Althea she could come!"

Sargos bit down so hard that he cut his tongue and tasted the salty tang of his own blood. "Son, you still haven't passed your manhood rites."

"Will it be safe in the hills with the women and children? If it is my time, I can die anywhere. After all, I am only a few moons from my manhood rites. It is time I learned how to lead our people, and where better than at my father's side?"

Sargos clenched his hands. "If it is your wish, you can go. But it is up to you to tell your sister."

Larkander let out a loud whoop and took off at a run. At another time it might have lightened Sargos' spirits, but at the moment all he could see in his mind were the countless dead bodies drifting down the Great Mother River. The gods were capricious: sometimes they gave a man great gifts, but, in payment, they often took much more in return. If the god who had favored him, was—as the witch woman said—the Raven Hag of War, the price would be high indeed—both for him and his Clan.

III

As soon as Colonel Kronos nodded, signifying that everyone was seated, Kalvan banged his pistol butt on the table for silence. "We don't have much time. So, princes, lords, and generals, please keep the questions to a minimum. General Baldour, would you bring us up-to-date on the nomad invasions.

General Baldour was more familiar with the western territories than any of the other Hostigi generals. Baldour walked over to the deerskin map of the northern Great Kingdoms, east of the Great Mother River (Mississippi), and pointed to a spot just north of the Middle Kingdom city of Kythar (Louisville, Kentucky) with his sword point. "We just had a merchant return from Kyblos; the word there is that the northernmost horde is just outside of Kythar Town. Typically they would have avoided Kythar like the plague, since it's also the site of Tarr-Ceros—the chief fortress of the Zarthani Knights. But Grand Master Soton's army, which is less than a day's ride away, is driving them in that direction.

"Remember, Your Majesty, this information was a quarter moon old when it reached Kyblos City and it took another half moon to reach us. We can expect the nomads to follow the trade routes along the Lydistros River so by now they could be into the Trygath."

There was a collective gasp from around the table.

Rylla pointed at General Baldour. "Do you think the tribesmen will move into Kyblos or go east into Hos-Ktemnos?"

"If they weren't being chased by the Knights, there's no doubt they would go straight into Hos-Ktemnos because the way is easier and the pickings there are so much better. But if they travel east they're going to run right into Tarr-Lydra, where they'd be caught between Grand Master Soton's army and the Order's fortress garrison—which would be suicidal.

"Prince Kestophes of Ulthor has every right to believe the nomads will soon be on Ulthori lands and thereby a legitimate claim to his overlord's protection. There is no way to avoid supporting Kestophes with a substantial force without Your Majesty acquiring the name of a King who advances himself at his Princes expense."

"That was my own analysis," Kalvan said. Rylla nodded her agreement.

Chancellor Chartiphon rose to speak. He'd been given the promotion after Xentos returned his chain-of-office and left for Hos-Agrys. "It looks as if we are going to have to delay the invasion of Hos-Harphax until the nomad problem has been settled."

Which was exactly what the Styphoni wanted, thought Kalvan to himself, cursing Soton and his progenitors in four languages. Trader Tortha's analysis had been right on the money. *Did he dare split the army into two smaller forces as he had done to such disastrous results last spring?* It would be interesting to see what his General Staff thought.

"Harmakros, what do you think of splitting the army in two corps, sending half to go after the nomads in the west and the other corps to invade Hos-Harphax?"

"Your Majesty. We have reports that the nomad clans and tribes number anywhere from one hundred thousand men to just over a million, and that depends upon whether you're talking about the advance horde, the main horde and all the divisions. To say nothing of breaking down the number of fighting men in proportion to old men, women and children. We just don't have enough information to judge what's waiting for us. If we don't take at least thirty thousand soldiers we may be overwhelmed by sheer weight of numbers. I, for one, do not believe we can risk a two front war again."

"On the other hand," Prince Ptosphes added, "we can be certain that the Army of Hos-Harphax is going to stay within its borders and not be on campaign unless we attack first. If we do that now, we may find ourselves fighting the Harphaxi in the east, the Ktemnoi in the south and the nomads everywhere else. As our Great King has told us repeatedly, the only thing worse than fighting a two front war is fighting one on three or four fronts. And that's just what we may have here if we invade Hos-Harphax!"

Kalvan sighed deeply. He was going to have to be more careful about throwing out military maxims in front of his General Staff. Although in this instance, his own advice struck him as frightfully sound. Here he was not only caught on the horns of a dilemma, but on the prongs and antlers as well!

"I agree with Harmakros and Ptosphes. We must abandon our plans for the invasion of Hos-Harphax and draw up new ones for the defense of Kyblos."

All the assembled Princes and generals nodded in agreement. Prince Sarrask of Sask rose up and said, "A cheer for Great King Kalvan, who has brought us several good seasons of fighting and now promises us more!" There was a collective cheer and a chorus of "Down Styphon!" Then Sarrask added, "Aye, and when we've finished giving the barbarians a good arse kickin,' let's come back and finish the job we started last year in Hos-Harphax!"

There were more cheers and Sarrask sat back down.

"Thank you, for the vote of confidence," Kalvan said. "Now let us get down and work out the details of how we're going to get there and which troops we're going to take. First, General Hestophes is going to need reinforcements for his Army of Observation at Tarr Beshta." Kalvan had decided that he wanted his best general, Harmakros, with him in the field, so he had left Hestophes where he was in charge of the border force. "We don't want to give Captain-General Phidestros any fancy ideas while we're gone. How does Hestophes' force look right now, Harmakros?"

"He has four regiments of Royal horse and one of infantry, plus about another two thousand Beshtan cavalry." Harmakros nodded to Prince Phrames, who was sitting at the other end of the table next to Sarrask.

"That's less than five thousand men," Kalvan said, "let's send him the Second Musketeers and the King's Heavy Horse and the Heavy Cavalry—they won't be of much use where we're going." Since so many of his cavalrymen, even the former mercenaries, were titled or younger sons of nobility, Kalvan had been forced to create three regiments of old-style fully armored cavalry. He had considered them worthless until they'd dented Grand Master Soton's flying wedge of Zarthani Knights at the Battle of Phyrax.

The heavy cavalry's value now was in the east where they could help shore up his defenses against the Harphaxi. They would be a real liability in the broken terrain of the Trygath up against the much lighter nomad horse. Regardless, he would still be stuck with his Lifeguard, the heavies of all Hos-Hostigos heavy cavalry.

"That gives General Hestophes seven thousand good troops. Prince Phrames, can you spare anymore men?"

"Some, Your Majesty. I can send a thousand musketeers and pikemen. But no cavalry, since I need every single man jack of them to train my recruits. I don't have to tell Your Majesties the shape I found the Beshtan Army in after the invasion."

Prince Sarrask hooted. "Half-dead, half-starved and half-naked. Old Balthar was a chokepurse, he was."

No one bothered to mention that Kalvan had taken the cream of the mercenaries into the Royal Army, leaving only those free companions too infirm or too old to fight for Prince Phrames and the other Princes. Still, all in all, Phrames had done wonders with the remnants of the old Army of Beshta and had managed to re-take a border castle that had renounced fealty during the war with Beshta in the dead of winter.

"Thank you, Prince Phrames. We'll leave Queen Rylla"—Kalvan ignored Rylla's grimace as she realized she wasn't going to be invited to this party— "four infantry regiments, including the Hostigos Rifles." That got a smile out of Rylla. "And two regiment of horse. The rest will form the nucleus of the Army of the Trygath."

"That will give us better than eleven thousand men, not counting the Royal Artillery," Harmakros said. "Are we going to take any of the field guns?"

"A battery, two at most," Kalvan answered, "the guns will only slow us down. We'll be covering everything from mountains to swamps. Mobility is going to be crucial in our war against the clansmen; if I could, I'd mount every infantryman in the army. We will mount as many as we can.

I want to take the entire Royal Mobile Force, which will give us another five thousand men."

"You're not leaving me with much of anything," Rylla said.

"Right. That's because you are not going to need anything more than glorified garrison troops while I'm gone. I want you to stay right here in Hostigos. Unless Prince Lysandros is crazier than a rat in a drainpipe, he's going to be sitting firm in Tarr-Harphax. Grand Master Soton is busy in the Trygath and Great King Cleitharses of Hos-Ktemnos is back to counting the scrolls in the Royal Library, so I don't think you have anything to worry about from the south. You're staying here to keep everyone else honest. If it makes you feel any better, I'll leave you the Army of Hostigos and the Army of Sask under the command of Prince Sarrask."

Sarrask rose to his feet sputtering, dropping half a cup of dark wine down his robes. "But Your Majesty, I'm not one to set watch over the Royal Nursery—excuse me, Queen Rylla, no offense meant. But I'm a man of plain words."

Rylla was up and fumbling for her dagger as if she meant to beard Sarrask or cut off his tongue.

"Order, please!" shouted Kalvan. "Prince Sarrask, you are a valiant warrior and one of my best commanders. I would prefer to have you at my side fighting the nomads, but I need someone here I can trust to guard my home and household. I can think of no one better able to protect my throne in my absence." Actually Kalvan could think of half a dozen in a second, but all of those he needed by his side and those he didn't, like Prince Ptosphes, would take it as a personal insult if he left them home.

Sarrask swelled up like a peacock on display and made a courtly bow in Kalvan's direction. Rylla, who sat at Kalvan's right, turned so that no one else could see and made a horrible grimace at her husband. "I will ask Prince Pheblon of Nostor to support us with three thousand of his troops, Prince Balthames of Shasta with another two thousand, three thousand from Nyklos, and I'm sure we can count on Ulthor and Kyblos to provide even more men, since they will be defending their own lands and can call out their lordly levies. Duke Mnestros has already 'offered' us the use of his troops." Younger sons and adventurers from all over Hos-Agrys had swelled Mnestros' cavalry force to better than a thousand mounted troopers.

Harmakros grinned. "That should give us thirty thousand or more for the Army of the Trygath. Enough teeth to grind their bones into dust."

Everyone smiled at that thought and there was another chorus of "Down Styphon!" followed by an equally loud one of "Death to all Barbarians."

"Harmakros and Chartiphon I want you two to get together with General Baldour and decide which passage we take, the northern Nyklos Road or the Akyros Trail through Sask. Besides the trail itself I want you to go over foraging areas, possible ambush sites and where to set depots in case we have to make a hasty retreat. Also consider that we might want to link up with some of the more civilized kings and princes once we reach the Trygath. Duke Skranga and General Klestreus I want you to make a list of every major Trygath king, prince, and baron and everything we know about them, from their fighting ability to whether they're known Styphoni sympathizers. I'd like it by tomorrow morning at the latest."

Skranga nodded and smiled as if he'd just been given a tasty morsel. His other intelligence officer, General Klestreus, looked like a fish that had just snagged a hook.

"Now, one last thing before I dismiss the council. The Pony Express route we've set up between Hostigos Town and the Army of Observation at Tarr-Locra has given us a four-day jump in our border communications. Unfortunately, the semaphore system I wanted for this spring won't be up and running until after next winter. I'd like to run another Pony Express route into Ulthor, and possibly Kyblos, so we can get some adequate intelligence rather than depending upon itinerant peddlers and vagabonds. Colonel Krynos I'd like for you to attend to that. Don't hesitate to pull as many of the experienced riders you need off the Great King's Highway route.

"That's it for now, gentlemen. This meeting is dismissed." Actually Kalvan would have preferred a working semaphore system to the pony express, but he'd decided that building the Great Kings Highway was more important. He didn't have enough trained manpower to do both. By Father Dralm's White Beard, he didn't have a tenth the trained manpower to do any of the things he wanted done, but give the University a few years ... Then would he not only have good interior communications and roads, but then he could start working on some reliable vehicles, like a Butterworth stagecoach. Anything would be an improvement over the Conestoga-style wagons the Zarthani used for everything from overland transportation to mobile homes.

Note: After road is finished start stagecoach line. With leaf springs, too!

TWENTY-SIX

I

Verkan Vall gazed at the mass of info wafers, message balls and data cubes that covered his desk and sighed. He was cooped up with beeping computers and chirping data writers while outside it was a beautiful spring day. At times like this Verkan wondered why he had allowed Tortha Karf to talk him into becoming his successor.

Being the best-trained man for the job did not make him the best man for the job, nor did it make that job any easier—especially when that job was being the final arbiter over a near-infinity of worlds. They all had to be policed. Maybe it was too much job for one man—Tortha Karf had been saying that for years. But committees do not like to make decisions, and when they did, their decisions were too often compromises. So, until the Executive Council legalized cloning, it looked as if Verkan was stuck with the job.

Verkan had spent the winter, shuttling back and forth between Home Time Line and Greffa, establishing his cover as Trader Verkan. It would not do to have Kalvan bumping into another Grefftscharrer who had never heard of Trader Verkan. The consequence was he had neglected his work here at Paratime Police headquarters and would have to spend the next two or three ten-days catching up. The squawk of his intercom interrupted his thoughts. He touched the com button with his toe and said, "What is it, Orthlan?"

"Vlasthor Arph to see you, Chief. Code Red."

"Send him right in."

Vlasthor Arph was a short stocky man with a quick step and bright gray eyes; if Dalla was his right hand, Arph was his left.

"Hate to bother you, Chief, but this could be important."

Verkan nodded for him to continue.

"We turned up some interesting irregularities on that list of Opposition heavy contributors you had me check out with the Metro Records Division. Our prime suspect is one Jorand Rarth—have you heard of him?"

"No. Who is he?"

"He's an outtime importer with possible connections to the Novilan syndicate, mostly gambling and prole prostitution."

"Those two Wizard Trader suspects who allegedly committed suicide last year both had connections to the Novilan syndicate."

Arph smiled, showing his teeth.

"This sounds like the link between the Wizard Traders and the syndicates we've been searching for," Verkan said. The Wizard Traders had been a large band of First Level slavers posing as outtime sorcerers. Unauthorized, they had infiltrated dozens of time-lines, using First Level technology as magic to take advantage of ignorant and superstitious outtimers. The Organization, as its members called it, had captured migrants and other disposable locals on isolated time-lines as slaves to be sold for gold and fissionables on other time-lines. The Paratime Police had closed the operation down eight or nine years ago, and were still trying to penetrate the upper layers of the Wizard Trader Organization.

"Where is Jorand now?"

"That's the bad news, Chief. We've had his quarters under close surveillance for the past four hours. Less than fifteen minutes ago, we picked up the landing beam from his aircar. Before we could move in, he fled. We lost his aircar in the city lanes."

"I take it his locator was off?"

"Yes, first thing we checked. Nothing registered for his car on the traffic monitors, either."

Verkan sighed. "Where do you think he may have gone, Arph?"

"A syndicate hideout—for now, would be my guess, Chief. Then he'll hop the first outtime conveyer. There's no place on Home Time Line to hide for more than a few days. I'll put a search warning out on him to all the registered outtime firms."

Verkan moved his head in agreement. "I want an ID and picture of Jorand Rarth distributed to every Transtemporal terminal on the First Level. I also want his face on every news broadcast in this city by this evening. Arrange a pickup for all known associates. This is one fish I don't want to see slip away."

"Yes, sir."

"Rarth may be the key we've been looking for. So far, we've been looking everywhere but in the right places."

"I've got a few suggestions. Take a couple of the Opposition Party bigwigs and put them under narco-hypnosis; we'll get some answers, all right."

"You may be right, but it's prohibited to question any Party elected official unless he's actually caught in violation of the Paratime Police or Transtemporal Codes. Our hands are tied."

It was one of the many reasons Verkan preferred to spend his off time on Kalvan's Time-Line; there you could cut through the regulation knots with the nearest sword.

II

After boarding their horses at the Red Hound stable, Danar Sirna and Baltrov Eldra walked down the main street of Hostigos Town to the Silver Stag tavern where they were to meet a Dazour grain merchant named Tynos. As they walked down the wooden-plank sidewalk, Sirna asked, "Eldra, how are things back at the University?"

"It was nice to go back, if only for the showers. It wasn't much fun, though, having my brains picked twenty hours a day for two ten-days, I'll tell you."

"I didn't think there'd be that much interest in Kalvan's Time-Line.

"Thanks to the Danthor Dras publicity machine, Great King Kalvan is grist for every Dhergabar talk show and tavern in the city. Dras updated and rewrote his **A Study of Techno-Theocracy in Action** and re-titled it **Fireseed Fanatics** and it's selling faster than Voltor Lyra's latest outtime cookbook. There's even talk about sending in a First Level strike team to aid Kalvan in his war against the nasty priesthood of Styphon's House."

"That violates every precept of the Transtemporal Code! I'll wager Chief Verkan is not too happy about that."

"If Verkan Vall had his way, he'd quarantine Kalvan's Time-Line and make it his own personal playpen."

"You sound bitter, Eldra. Do I detect a bit of jealousy over Kalvan."

"I'd like to make him my personal plaything all right!" Eldra smiled in a way that reminded Sirna of a cat she once shared quarters with and how it grinned after tasting fresh prey rather than prepared food. It also reminded her that, despite her young appearance, Eldra was centuries older than herself and much wiser in the ways of the world. Eldra was a renowned historian, while Sirna was a lowly graduate student; Eldra was also considered one of the experts on Europo-American, Hispano-Columbian Subsector which was how she wrangled her way on to the Kalvan Study-Team.

"I hope that Tynos doesn't stand us up." Sirna had never ridden a horse in her life until last year and she still found them an unpredictable and uncomfortable means of transportation.

Eldra laughed. Sirna's dislike for horses was the camp joke, whereas Eldra was an excellent rider and horsewoman. "If his message boy says he'll be there, Tynos will be there. He loves wine second only to gold."

The Silver Stag tavern was a two-story plank and plaster building with an inn and house of ill repute on the second story and a tavern at street level. Inside the sides of the walls were lined with rough-hewn plank benches, which were filled beyond jostling capacity. At the center was a bar, made up of planks resting upon large ale barrels. Set around the rest of the tavern were small wine barrels acting as tables for men sitting on three-legged stools. Eldra pointed to an unoccupied 'table' in the corner.

Unescorted females were no novelty to the Silver Stag patrons, and before they were a quarter of the way to their table Eldra was jostled by a drunken muleskinner or trapper—so Sirna judged by the stench he gave off. From her previous visit to a Hostigi tavern, it appeared that *any* unescorted woman in a drinking establishment was fair game. One of his hands rudely groped for Eldra's chest, but before he could touch her,

Eldra's poniard was pressed tightly up against his not insubstantial stomach.

"Presume on my person and I'll open you up from groin to sternum!"

The drunk's eyes turned mean and Eldra made as if to press her blade home when a loud stentorian voice boomed through the tavern. "That is Royal teat you're trying to grasp, Eyllos! Release the lady's person and put your hands on a fresh tankard at my expense."

The drunk frowned and then let go. A fresh tankard arrived almost as quickly. "To your health, Prince Sarrask!" Eyllos bowed, chug-a-lugged the tankard, and then promptly passed out.

The room greeted this spectacle with uproarious laughter and Sirna figured the trapper wasn't the first drunk to find himself so disposed—good crowd control technique on Prince Sarrask's part.

When they passed by Sarrask's table, Eldra bent over—giving the Prince an eyeful of her bosom—and whispered something in the big man's ear. As Eldra pulled away, Sarrask roared with laughter. "My fair lady, some day I may hold you to that promise."

When they reached their stools, Sirna asked, "You like him?"

"Sarrask's type can be a lot of fun, if you like your men hale and hearty. I've had worse. But I'm after much bigger game than a mere Prince.

Sirna shook her head. "You had better be careful before your head winds up on a pole decorating the outer walls of Tarr-Hostigos. Rylla strikes me as the type who doesn't like competition, especially regarding her husband's affections."

"They are not always going to be together . . ."

Sirna thought Eldra was being stubborn, but there wasn't anything to be gained by upsetting her only female ally on the study-team, so she changed the subject. "Where is Tynos? We need to leave for Nostor Town in less than a moon."

"I thought he'd already be here finishing last night's dregs. Maybe he's more sober when it comes to business. Or maybe he's hoping we'll be in our cups."

"Why do we need him anyway? If we are going to establish a second Royal Foundry at Nostor Town, we will have to put in a transtemporal conveyer-head sooner or later. Why not sooner and save all this bother?"

"Chief Verkan is only building a foundry in Nostor Town at Kalvan's insistence. It's nice to have an unlimited pipeline of goods, but you don't want to get the locals curious as to where it all comes from."

Their conversation was interrupted by Tynos' arrival. After being introduced to Sirna and giving orders to his bodyguard, Tynos said, "You are a clever trader, Lady Eldra, to bring so lovely a vision to becloud my mind from business."

Tynos was a swarthy black-haired man with the deceptively soft look of a fighter gone to fat. Sirna suspected that underneath that layer of fat was a lot of healthy muscle and she wasn't about to get into a verbal, or any other kind of, wrestling match with him.

"My good trader," Eldra said, "I suspect Styphon's next miracle will occur before any woman clouds your mind regarding matters of business."

Tynos started to laugh, then looked around furtively.

"No, Tynos, you'll find no priests of Styphon's House or their agents in this hot-bed of heresy."

"You may be right, my Lady, but Styphon's agents multiply faster than bedbugs in the cots upstairs. In Hos-Harphax a man learns to grow ears at the back of his head if he wishes to keep it on his shoulders. But enough of this unpleasantness, how can I be of further service to you Ladies?"

"Let me remind you, Tynos, you were to search out sources of lead ingots for us."

"Oh, yes."

"We make many molds for our casting masters and have a great need for lead. Like yourself, we too are foreigners here, come to make money. We see little to be gained by involving ourselves in local matters in these uncertain times, unless—of course—there is a profit to be made."

"By Tranth's Teeth, you speak truly. Since the selling of war materials to any Hostigi is under Ban of Styphon we will have to break up your ingots into three or four shipments—this of course will be more costly."

"Of course."

"Since you are a citizen of Grefftscharr, you are not directly subject to the Ban. But as you are residing and working in Old Hostigos, the agents of Styphon's House may see it otherwise, so there will be bribes to be paid and additional men-at-arms to be hired. Does this meet with your approval?

"Yes, as long as you understand that this is lead we are talking about and not silver or gold."

"Speaking of silver and gold, Lady Eldra, I must make it clear that our return will be even more dangerous than our coming and we will wish to travel light."

"Plain speaking, you wish to be paid in gold."

"Now you are speaking my tongue, Lady Eldra!"

Eldra brought up her purse and dropped a dozen gold Hostigos Crowns onto the table. The trader's eyes shined as brightly as the golden coins.

"Truly, by all the True Gods, you read my inner-most thoughts. Yet," he added, pointing to the coins with the crossed halberds on the obverse and Ptosphes' image on the face, "with all your skills at casting might it not serve us both better if these coins were transformed into some image—well, less offensive—in the eyes of Styphon's priestly agents. Men of commerce love gold in all its myriad forms, but priests are different that way."

"Yes, that is agreeable, Trader. Now as to price. In the past, we have paid one piece of silver and ten coppers for each ingot—"

"Impossible, my Ladies. With all this fighting, lead is becoming as scarce as your most precious of metals. Why in Harphax City I saw a lead ingot sell for ten pieces of silver. To cart it all the way here over mountains and past Styphon's plague of agents, well, I think two golden Rakmars for each ingot is only fair."

"Two Rakmars—highway robbery!" Eldra shouted. "At those prices we could use silver to cast our molds and save money. We two are not Sastra-gathi bumpkins who have never seen a city before, Trader. We are Ladies of birth and breeding from a city of such antiquity that your forefathers were herding cattle in the Cold Lands while ours were trading iron for gold with the Ros-Zarthani in the far west."

"Forgive me, if I inadvertently insulted a Lady of breeding, but my wife and four children would never forgive me were I to be picked up by Roxthar's Investigators—mistakenly, of course—and burned in boiling pitch for trading in Hos-Hostigos. Were I, however, to end this life, leaving behind a substantial sum, I could acquit myself in Dralm's Hall with honor. What do you say to one gold Rakmar and twelve pieces of silver?"

"If I were to return to the Royal Foundry after making a deal such as this, my own father would strip me of my robes and cast me out into the streets, and, by Tranth's eyes, my own mother would not find fault with him."

The haggling continued on in this vein for almost ten minutes until Tynos and Eldra had agreed upon a price of twelve silver pieces per lead ingot. Sirna herself was reeling from too much drink and mental fatigue. Eldra and Tynos, on the other hand, were covered with sweat, but other than that, could have continued this match for another hour or two. She almost welcomed the sounding of horns and the clatter of horses' hooves outside on the cobble stone streets.

The tavern emptied, other than those few too far into their cups to rise. Sirna, Eldra and Tynos quickly followed the crowd out the door.

On Old Tigos Road, a squadron of Kalvan's Royal Lifeguard crowded its way down the narrow cobblestone street. It was identifiable as the Royal Bodyguard by Kalvan's Royal Standard, a maroon keystone on a dark green field, as well as the maroon sashes and helmet plumes.

"Where are they going?" Eldra asked a soldier, with a brown beard and a lead-splashed burgonet helmet.

"To Hostigos Town Square where Great King Kalvan is addressing the townspeople, my Lady. Would you like an escort?"

Eldra gave the soldier such a dazzling smile in return he blushed down to his boot-tops. "Yes, we could use a proper escort. Tynos, will you come along, our business is not yet concluded."

"Yes, my Lady." There was sweat beading on his forehead and she wondered if Tynos believed the stories spread by Styphon's agents that Kalvan was a demon in human form.

After the squadron had passed, the soldier led the way using his halberd to force a comfortable passage.

"As we discussed earlier, Tynos, we are planning to build a new Royal Foundry in Nostor Town where, despite the Great King's largess with food stuffs and victuals, there are still food shortages and some lingering starvation. We would like to contract with you to supply our party, some thirty persons in all, with proper fresh victuals from Dazour."

"This should offer no great problems, my Lady. I have a friend who has established trade for victuals between several of the noble families of Nostor and himself. He should be able to satisfy all your wants and for a reasonable price."

"Good. You can introduce us."

"My pleasure, Your Ladyship." Tynos smile suggested he was contemplating a possible kickback.

"We've almost reached the Square." Sirna said. "Look at all the people!"

Hostigos Town Square was close to bursting with soldiers, towns' folk, visitors, and traders. Great King Kalvan himself was standing on the stairs of Prince Ptosphes' palace, addressing the assembled crowd. Kalvan, Sirna thought, had star presence; he held his audience in thrall. As they drew closer, Sirna began to make out his words.

"The false-god Styphon's agents have stirred the tribesman with lust for Hostigi blood and treasure. But if the nomads think to grow fat and old in Hos-Hostigos, they had better learn to breathe fire rather than air. When the smoke clears, it'll be their bodies covering the ground."

A great roar greeted these words and most of the assembled men looked as if they were ready to pick up arquebus and sword and march boldly with the King's Army into the Trygath right then and here.

"Don't you just love that man," Eldra whispered into Sirna's ear.

"For the moment," Sirna answered. "Just don't let Rylla catch you casting moon-struck eyes his way. I wouldn't put it past her to pluck them out with her own fingers! Or blame her, either!"

"You're no fun."

Kalvan continued with a speech that reminded Sirna of movies she had seen of outtime religious leaders as he damned the false god Styphon and praised the hosts of Father Dralm. Old Xentos would be in trouble if Kalvan ever decided to take up the religious game, she thought as she watched him work the crowd.

The speech ended with chants of "Down Styphon!" and a chorus of "Death to the invaders!" When Kalvan walked down the stairs and mounted his horse, leaving with his bodyguard, the crowd quickly dispersed heading to the local taverns to quench thirsts and raise the rafters with hot air. It was obvious that this outtimer from Europo-America had made many new friends here and accurately felt the pulse of the land. This was going to be a tour of duty Sirna would remember all her life.

TWENTY-SEVEN

I

Ranjar Sargos heard the pounding of hooves coming from behind as he and his band of followers led the oath-brothers toward the divide. After a moon and a half of being chased and driven by the Black Knights, Sargos had decided it was time to turn the table on their attackers. It was one thing for a man only concerned with survival to flee like a woman, but another for a Warchief whose destiny was to lead clans and nations. Ranjar's horse, a big paint, was breathing so hard he could feel the lungs labor through his cloth saddle. "Soon," he whispered.

Up ahead, his clansmen had built an abattis, in a deep valley, behind which was a wall of stones and tree trunks. If his party could lead the pursuers into the valley, the abattis would be released and the Black Knights and their oath-brothers would be buried alive.

The trick was to get the oath-brothers and the Knights angry enough that they did not see the trap. Sargos had heard stories of the Knights and their oath-brothers, who were brought together and made as one in an initiation ceremony. It was a rude jest among the tribesmen that part of that ceremony was oath-brother and knight lying together as man and woman. Sargos did not believe that story, for it was very much what he wanted to hear and he'd learned to distrust easy answers. However, they

did go through long years of training and fighting together so the bond
between oath-brother and knight was often as strong as that of man and
wife. He hoped this was true, because when the Knights saw their oath-
brothers dishonored it would be an insult impossible for them to leave
without vengeance.

Sargos watched with his heart in his mouth, as his youngest son, turned
in his saddle, drew his horn bow and released an arrow. The boy moved
with the grace of a panther bringing down a buffalo. Sargos' eyes followed
the arrow's flight, which ended in the throat of one of the bare-chested
oath-brothers. The Ruthani warrior gasped, grabbed the shaft with both
hands and pulled the arrow out, releasing a torrent of red blood. He toppled off his saddle and the oath-brother following behind in anger shot
one of his pistols. Sargos' heart jumped, but the shot went wide and Larkander dug his heels into his mount, jumping ahead.

Sargos was beginning to regret not only this mornings hastily arranged
surprise, but bringing his only son along on what might well prove to be
the last trail for father, son and tribe. They were almost to the ravine now,
cut by the heavy spring rains. The Black Knights were visible and now
came the most difficult part of the trap. He had to bring the oath-brothers,
who were the Knights' scouts and advance war party, past the abattis, and
let them lead the armored Knight into the death trap.

At the peak of the valley were the rest of his clansmen, some seven
hundred warriors; they would dispatch the Ruthani oath-brothers while
the boulder and tree limbs took care of the Knights. Of course, it would all
be for naught if they balked and did not enter the valley. He had to give
them an offering they could not refuse—a score of his clansmen dressed
in captured armor and wearing the King Kalvan's colors! The false soldiers
of Hostigos were a sight he did not believe the Black Knights could resist.
Every tribesman in the Sastragath had heard of Kalvan's great victories
over the Black Knights and the soldiers of the false god, Styphon. As
Sargos had hovered over the ravine, in his dream vision, he had watched as
the tree trunks and giant stones had crushed the ironmen, like crayfish
fresh from the pot and about to be devoured.

To make the false soldiers of Hostigos even more convincing, Sargos
had given them his own pistol and every firestick the Tymannes had

collected in the past fifty winters. If this ruse failed and the clansmen lost their precious firesticks, he wouldn't have long to worry about asking the gods why they had misled him—his clansmen would see to that, if the Knights didn't dispatch him first!

Except for a few suicidal changes, most of the tribesmen and clans had allowed themselves to be driven father and farther north by the armies of the Black Knights. Those who had resisted or fought to avenge their burnt homes had been ruthlessly destroyed. Unless the clans banded together and united, Sargos knew the heavier armor and fire tubes of the Knights would give them a great victory. Sargos knew it was his destiny to lead this great host, but first he would have to distinguish himself from the scores of competing headmen, chiefs, sachems and warchiefs. Last night he had prayed to the Raven Hag for their guidance this dream had been the result. The false soldiers of King Kalvan had been his own idea; it had better work.

The valley was up ahead, around a copse of willow trees. Sargos' horse was starting to falter and he raised his voice in a war cry to embolden the stallion's heart. Suddenly he was in the valley, a huge gash torn from the earth by torrential rains. He was near the end of the war party, bait for the following oath-brothers. It was time to speed up before he got caught in his own trap.

He heard the shouts from the oath-brothers as they saw the false troop of Kalvan's soldiers at the head of the valley. "Kill the Daemon!" they cried.

Into the valley they thundered. His old friend and tribesman, Kagdar, who rode behind him, cried out as an oath-brothers tomahawk was thrown into his back. Sargos made a quick prayer and promised Kagdar's spirit he would come back and release it to Wind. He smacked his horses' haunches with his calloused palms. He could hear the false soldiers cry, "Down Styphon!" The oath-brothers behind him were riding like water over a cliff, if he weren't careful, they'd ride him into the ground in their haste to reach the Hostigi soldiers.

He passed the abattis and jumped off his horse to land hard on the embankment. Hard hands grabbed him and raised him to his feet. The oath-brothers ran by, oblivious to anything, but the insult of the red and blue colors of Hostigos. From the distance, the blue axhead on the red field looked real even to Sargos. Then he heard the rumble of the Black Knights as their iron-shod chargers entered the valley in pursuit. Up ahead, the false Hostigi were firing into the massed oath-brothers. The Knights began to shout, "Kill the Daemon! Kill the Daemon!" There was an even louder roar when the rest of the Tymannes rose from behind the crest, as if they were supporting Kalvan's soldiers.

The Black Knights rushed into the valley heedless of any dangers. Sargos raised his right arm, made a fist and pumped it twice. Swords cut the leather and twine ropes holding the abattis and all of a sudden there was a rumble that sounded like thunder. The Black Knights looked to their side in dismay. Moments later they were buried in an avalanche of tree trunks, boulders and dirt. The oath-brothers turned their horses, too late, and were set upon by the false Hostigi and the clansmen. With surprise and numbers on their side, the Tymannes made quick work of the oath-brothers, who were trapped by the sudden wall from behind and the clansmen's spears and swords from the front.

Sargos led his party to the still quaking death mound, searching for any Knights who might have survived. He came upon a full-helmed Knight who was buried up to his waist and bleeding profusely from his visor. A quick sharp jab with his poniard through the visor slit stilled the thrashing arms and he took the Knight's pistol, still cached in his white sash, to replace the one he had given away. He could hear the screams of dying men and horses all around. Sargos lifted the pistol and fired into the sky—today's slaughter was another sign of favor from the gods.

While the force he, Sargos, had destroyed today wasn't a Lance; there were enough dead Knights for three points—not counting oath-brothers, almost two hundred of the Black Brethren gone to Wind. The Tymannes would gain many pistols and much armor from this battle. For the rest of the day, his clansmen would be moving boulders and tree limbs until they had picked up every pistol, cask of fireseed, weapon and piece of useful armor this great victory had won them. Then they would cut the heads off of all the Knights and their oath-brothers, pluck out their eyes, cut off their noses and mount the heads on a forest of poles for the Order to find. For once, let the Black Knights choke back *their* tears!

II

Jorand Rarth felt weight return as the wheels of the air-car struck the landing stage and shut down the pseudo-grav. His driver opened the rear door and asked, "What should I do with the car, boss?"

Jorand looked around as though expecting a blue Metro or green Para-cop police car to materialize on the landing stage. Yesterday afternoon he had been forced to flee his own tower just minutes before a squad of Para-time Police raided the place. Now there was a warrant for his arrest and the cover he had so elaborately devised a century ago was gone.

"The police should be able to ID it before long, so drop it off at a public tower and meet me at Constellation House in two hours. We can steal a new air-car out of the parking lot if we need one."

The driver nodded and took off. Jorand stepped into the lifthead of Hadron Tharn's penthouse; he keyed in his password and pressed his thumb on the thumbblock. The lift door rose behind him to cut off the view of Dhergabar City under a winter sky as bright and blue, and as coldly unsympathetic, as Paratime Police Chief Verkan Vall's eyes.

One level down, the lift door dropped again, letting Jorand out into the maroon-carpeted entry hall of Hadron Tharn's private quarters. A robot rolled forward to take Jorand's coat. Behind it rolled another robot, hold-ing a tray with hot spiked simmer root in a silver cup. Jorand took the cup triggering the robot's vocal circuits.

"Citizen Hadron Tharn is waiting to see you in the lounge."

Jorand mumbled an automatic thank you in return, which told more about his prole origins than he liked known. He had spent decades setting up his First Level Citizen identity and had lived it for close to a century. Maybe he'd gotten too fat and lazy. Jorand would need all his old skills and moxie to survive this fracas.

A century ago he had been the head of an underground gambling syndi-cate in Novilan City. While all the First Level Citizens' children become Citizens, proles had to qualify by passing an intelligence and general psych test. Proles could be adopted and made Citizens, but even so they must pass the tests. The problem was that few Proles received a First Level education.

Jorand had tried with tutors, but hadn't liked the hard work. Instead he had searched for a decade to find a compulsive gambler within the Bureau of Identification. It hadn't been easy because the Bureau of Psychological Hygiene made periodic sweeps of the Records Division of the Bureau of Identification to keep fraud to a minimum.

When Jorand had his mark hooked and gaffed, the 'disappearance' of a respectable Citizen and the substitution of Jorand's DNA record for his had been effected. No one had been the wiser for ninety-eight years—until yesterday.

Jorand didn't have the time, or the patience, to set up another false ID, so he had no other choice but to go outtime. With his usual contacts under suspicion, he would have to use his influence in the Opposition Party. Influence he had spent decades building with heavy Party donations and conscientious attendance at boring political meetings.

Jorand had also been a boss in the Organization, a criminal syndicate that had kidnapped outtime peoples and sold them at high profits on other time-lines. Since most of these outtimers had been victims of wars or famines, he'd been pleased to arrange their sale to those who could make good use of their labors. After all, the outtimers gained their lives while he gained a fair return on his investment.

Besides, none of those outtimers would face anything Jorand hadn't faced himself during his childhood on Fifth Level Industrial Sector, where his own father had sold him to a slum overlord for drug money. Jorand had been raised by a man who had bought him as a slave and raised him to second-in-command of his own theft syndicate.

Now as a member of the Organization's second level, Jorand knew just how 'involved' in the Organization many of the top politicos of the Opposition Party had become. Unfortunately, the Paratime Police had put his branch of the Organization out of business—and his boss had been detained and never heard of again. There were tales that he'd committed suicide while under Paratime Police interrogation. Recently, Jorand had heard a new rumor that the Organization was back in business, but no one had contacted him, or he wouldn't be here trying to cash in on that information—regardless of Citizen Tharn's feelings on the subject.

Fortunately, as a member of Tharn's Opposition Action Team, he hadn't even had to twist Tharn's arm for a private audience. Jorand had almost been looking forward to the day when the Action Team discovered they had a prole among their membership. Despite all their egalitarian cant, he had heard enough prole jokes to know their true sympathies. It had been his private joke, one that kept him awake through their interminable meetings. Too bad he would not be there when they learned the truth about him.

Jorand gulped the last of his simmer root as he entered the Blue Lounge. He thought of ordering another, then decided to wait since he would need a clear head for today's meeting.

"Welcome, Citizen Jorand," Hadron Tharn said, stepping lightly toward him. "I trust you had a good journey." Unfortunately, the warm greeting didn't extend to Tharn's chilly eyes.

"Except for the stratospheric winds, yes. That's why I'm late."

"It hardly matters. Would you care for another drink?"

Jorand shook his head and sat down in his usual red-leather chair. The only other person in the room was Warntha Swam, Tharn's bodyguard and who-knew-what-else. Warntha was in his usual stance, hands clasped behind his back and eyes roaming the room, and in his usual position guarding Hadron Tharn's back.

Citizen Tharn gave one of his famous grins, but the blue eyes were as icy as an arctic gale. "What can I do for you Citizen?"

Jorand didn't bother to return the smile. "I'm in trouble and I need your help."

"I'm sorry to hear that, Citizen, but why me?"

"Call it a return on a three million credit investment. I need to go outtime."

Warntha visibly tensed. "The only reason I'm not having you thrown out of here," Tharn said, "is that you've been extremely helpful in the past. I don't know what your problem is, but I suggest you go elsewhere for its solution."

"My rooms have just been sealed by the Paratime Police and by now I suspect I must be high up on their most-wanted list."

"You have my sympathies, of course." Tharn held both hands out to express his helplessness. "However, my brother-in-law, Verkan Vall and I have an unspoken accord; he doesn't ask me for favors and I don't ask him for any."

"Citizen Tharn, let us get to the heart of the problem. I have been one of the heads of the Organization, or Wizard Traders as the Paracops call it,

for about thirty years. Don't look so shocked; I can name a dozen prominent Opposition Party members who are equally involved."

Hadron Tharn nodded, his face expressionless.

"If the Paratime Police pick me up, the lid will be blown off what's left of
the Organization and the Opposition Party. Really it is in both our interests
to see me disappear from Home Time Line." Jorand saw a stealthy look slip
between Warntha and his master and added, "My driver has a message ball
he's to take to Verkan Vall if I don't leave this tower according to schedule."

"Where do you get these ideas?"

"Because, like you, I've found that the simplest solution to most problems is often the most elegant—in this case, my disappearance. Therefore,
I've taken certain precautions, just as you would have done."

Hadron Tharn leaned back in his chair, his forehead furrowed in what
appeared to be concentrated thought. He remained frozen for some time
until he sat up abruptly. "I don't have as much access to Paratemporal
Transposition as you seem to think, but we do have one operation where
you might fit in."

During the height of the Wizard Trader's operation, Jorand would have
had his choice of thousands of time-lines to hide on, but now he was forced
to take whatever crumb Tharn threw his way. At best it was a vast improvement over psycho-rehabilitation, a year of unremitting physical and mental
agony, the ignominy of having his private thoughts probed and twisted by
Mentalists and finally the horror of emerging as someone who would not
be Jorand Rarth.

"What is it?" he asked.

"You've heard of Kalvan's Time-Line?"

"Who hasn't? We've talked this time-line to death at the Action Meetings. What about it?"

"Kalvan's Time-Line has become Verkan's major political vulnerability,
one the Opposition Party intends to exploit. One way we can force Verkan's
hand is by making life difficult for his outtime friend, Great King Kalvan.
If things get sticky enough for Kalvan, Verkan might commit a breach of
the Paratime Code—and then we will have him."

Right, thought Jorand, a scandal big enough to break Management
Party's stranglehold on the Executive Council. Sweeping reforms inside
the Paratime Police would help many of the commercial houses who felt

constrained in their theft of outtime resources. It was enough to make an honest thief wonder who the real crooks were.

"So where do I fit into all of this?"

Hadron Tharn leaned forward, locking eyes. "Rarth, I could use a trusted agent I can send to Kalvan's Time-Line to oversee a very important operation. Last year was a very good one for King Kalvan. He defeated probably the largest army in his time-line's history. Now he's built up his army to the point where only the most concerted effort will root him out of his so-called Great Kingdom of Hos-Hostigos.

"Fortunately for us, the opposition has some good leaders, Archpriest Roxthar, Prince Lysandros of Hos-Harphax, and Grand Master Soton of the Zarthani Knights. They are planning a major counter-attack, but need help. Kalvan has either killed or recruited most of the available mercenaries in the Five Kingdoms and the national armies aren't that strong yet on this time-line.

"But the picture isn't all bad. On the west coast there are a number of city-states who have built up formidable armies after a millennium of constant warfare. Now, for the first time in centuries, they have a great leader in one of the city-states, Antiphon. A leader who has become strong enough to conquer most of the others. The problem is that he is unstable and unpredictable, more a Hitler than an Alexander. Like Hitler, this leader—Dyzar—suffered from an untreated case of syphilis, which has left him with delusions of grandeur, a homicidal temper, and massive mood swings—"

Jorand stifled a grin as he realized that this description might equally cover Hadron Tharn himself, who on occasion had been known to scream and berate his cohorts for hours. "What do you mean, suffered?"

"A month ago my agents used a neuro-prophylactic on Dyzar and were able to stabilize his condition. Due to the primitive conditions, the advanced stage of the disease, and the lack of a fully trained medico, they were not able to restore normal emotional functions. In the end they were forced to use the rejuvenation treatment to insure he survived the treatment. Dyzar should live a long and painful life."

"You used rejuvenation formula on an outtimer! Next to the Paratime Secret that's the most heavily guarded invention we have. We could all be brain wiped for this—"

Hadron Tharn smiled a most unpleasant smile. "That is why we need an agent of utmost discretion for this job. One who will not be particular about a lengthy and somewhat primitive assignment."

And someone very expendable, thought Jorand to himself. Unfortunately, for him, there were no other choices. "What is it you want me to do?"

"First, we will put you under narco-hypnosis and give you a pseudo-memory overlay as a Dorg merchant—they're not well known in the Five Kingdoms. Then we will put you in charge of the contact team that is to meet and lead the Ros-Zarthani army. We want you to prepare the Ros-Zarthani for their role in the war against King Kalvan."

"Why not," Jorand answered. It wasn't as if he had any place else to go.

TWENTY-EIGHT

I

Knight Sergeant Sarmoth, wearing his black tunic with Styphon's broken sun-wheel over his breast, stood outside Grand Master Soton's large tent, which held the Grand Master's maps and impressive personal armory. He was waiting for the wounded oath-brother, who had stumbled into camp two candles ago, to be brought back from the infirmary tent for questioning.

Soton was inside eating his dinner. Usually he ate with the Brethren, unlike many of his fellow commanders in the Order, Soton didn't require a special kitchen or household staff, but tonight he was eating alone. It was said that soldiers under Grand Master's personal command always had the best mess of the Order. In his six moons with the Grand Master, Sarmoth would have to agree. He knew it was not at the Grand Master command, but because the cooks wanted to make a good impression upon their commanding officer. Having watched Soton eat, he was convinced it was wasted effort—the Grand Master had no taste for anything but strategy and war.

At last, the wounded oath-brother, his head swaddled in white wrappings and supported by two soldiers, was brought to the tent.

Sarmoth led the small party inside, where Soton was seated at a desk going over maps by candlelight and smoking his pipe. His plate, still full, sat neglected by a brace of pistols. Soton's expression was grim; the northernmost expeditionary party was still a half moon overdue and a lone oath-brother from the party had just stumbled into camp, suffering from a serious head wound and dehydration.

The oath-brother was still winded, but he was able to croak out slowly. "We found the Daemon Kalvan . . ." He coughed, spitting blood on the hard-packed earth floor. "His army is here!"

Soton's face blanched. Sarmoth was unable to believe his ears; the latest reports had Kalvan's army still inside the border of Hostigos—outside Kyblos City. Of course, that report was more than two evenings old, not considering the moon-quarter it took for the scouts to come and go. Still, the Daemon Kalvan would have had to have grown wings and taken flight to reach the Sastragath so quickly.

"Are you sure it was Kalvan?"

"We were chasing a band of Sastragathi warriors . . ." The oath-brother paused to catch his breath. "When we entered a valley—" He paused to cough and went into a series of wrenching spasms. When his chest stopped heaving, he spoke again, "Kalvan and his troops fell upon us. They had the Hostigos flag and were wearing red and blue colors. Who else could it be, Grand Master?" The oath-brother shook his head wearily.

Soton looked closely at the wounded Ruthani oath-brother. "You're Red Knife—Knight Tydocles' oath-brother."

The Ruthani, clearly exhausted from speaking, nodded his head.

Soton turned to Sarmoth, saying, "Tydocles fought at my side at the Battle of Phyrax with the Eighth Lance. So Red Knife is familiar with Kalvan's banners and colors."

"What happened?"

"It was a trap. Kalvan is in league with the clans."

Soton grunted. "Are you certain?"

Red Knife said, "As certain as I can be without laying eyes on the Daemon himself. They set a trap. A wall of stones and trees fell upon the Knights. We were at the front, so I escaped the trap, but was shot out of my saddle by one of Kalvan's soldiers." He pointed to his head, where the bandage was thickest. "That is where I was hit. I was knocked out for a long time—I don't know how long. When I awoke, I was half-buried under my horse and some brush. My horse had dragged me out of the valley of death, or I would be there yet." He mumbled a prayer. "What nomad leader could have conceived such a trap?"

"Where is the rest of the party?"

"Grand Master, they are all dead—if none have returned. Kalvan and his nomads buried them with an avalanche of stones and then dug them up, cut off their heads and mounted them on poles!"

Sarmoth heard a loud crack, as Soton's teeth bit through his pipe stem. The barrel dropped to the ground.

"This cannot be Kalvan's work—he does not desecrate the dead, he takes prisoners. It has to have been a ruse by one of the warchiefs. We shall send a party to attend our dead and then we shall seek revenge upon the dogs that desecrated the Order—I so order!"

Sarmoth wondered how they were to search a single band among the hundreds of fleeing tribes and clans. Most of the tribesmen had chosen to flee rather than fight and this was the first serious loss the Knights had sustained in the campaign to drive the clans into Hos-Hostigos.

"I will attend this killing field, in person. Sergeant Sarmoth, tell Knight Commander Aristocles to gather his Lance and arrange a burial detail. If it is truly Kalvan's work, I will sow the fields of Hostigos with the blood of its women and children."

II

The moment Jorand Rarth left, Hadron Tharn turned to Warntha and asked, "What do you think of that one? Can we trust him?"

"For about two heartbeats after the Paratime Police pick him up. I tossed a sticky locator on his tunic when he walked by. Do you want me to follow and dispose of him and his driver? I don't believe his story about any papers to go to the Paratime Police."

"He was flying by the seat of his pants! Still, we could use another agent on Kalvan Prime—Prysos has been useful, but in his last communiqué he asked for more help. I think he's getting tired of traveling across the continent by horseback."

They both laughed.

Hadron Tharn continued. "We have to be very careful on Kalvan Prime; there are more Paracops there than at the Dhergabar Paratime Terminal. Verkan has been pressuring the Executive Council to put a Paracop on every outtime conveyer. Not even Management will go for it, because there are thousands of firms with outtime licenses and they'd have to curtail business or increase the police by several orders of magnitude. Unfortunately, some of our late friends in the Organization got sloppy and gave Verkan valuable ammunition. If Verkan caught an unauthorized Paratime conveyer on Kalvan Prime—all bets are off! Still, it's too good an opportunity to give that sanctimonious bastard a black eye. This Jorand is perfect; no one will miss him and he no longer has any ties to the Organization. When his job is done—"

Warntha smiled. "I get to pull his plug."

"Prysos, too. No witnesses, no crime."

III

Sirna was on the last Foundry wagon, trying to get the brambles out of her stockings, when she heard the sound of gunfire coming out of a small copse of trees. There were more shots and a growing cloud of gray and black smoke. She spotted several ambushers in morion helmets, with back-and-breasts and calivers. Their colors were black and green and she saw a green banner with a black boar; it looked familiar, but she was unable to place it.

The Foundry wagon train was three days outside of the Hostigos border and well inside Nostor; only a few days from Nostor Town. Sirna wished that Aranth was here, but Aranth had gotten into a fight with Talgran Garth and decided to stay in Hostigos. They had a small squad of Hostigi Royal troopers and five Foundry guards.

Sirna dropped to the bottom of the wagon, trying to find a pistol in the half-light of the canvas covered wagon. There was a loud bang and the driver let out a scream and slumped over. She and Eldra were the only ones left in the supply wagon and Eldra was already taking the reins.

"Who is it?"

"Bandits, I think," Eldra shouted through clenched teeth.

"I don't think so, they're wearing green sashes and armor. I saw their banner, too."

"What did it display?" Eldra asked, as she pushed the dead driver off of the bench and out the wagon.

"A black boar on a green field—I know I've seen it before."

"You have. It's the flag of the princedom of Phaxos—remember, Prince Araxes, who seceded from Hos-Hostigos when the Harphaxi Army came calling."

"Is it a revolt? They must know most of the army is either in Beshta or out of Hostigos with Kalvan."

"I don't know. But I hope I'm not the one who has to tell Rylla what happened!"

There were more shots, some coming from the wagon train, and screams of pain. She saw one Hostigos trooper fall out of his saddle. Suddenly the wagon began to turn. "Where are you going?"

"Getting out of here!" Eldra shouted.

Sirna made her way forward to the front of the wagon, asking, "Why?"

"You're a woman, I'll give you two guesses!"

"You think they'll capture the wagons."

The wagon tipped precariously, as Eldra maneuvered her way past two huge trees, with trunks the width of air-cars. "I'm not going to stick around to find out. If they capture us, they're going to have to kill me." Eldra pulled out a wicked looking horse pistol. "This is no First Level park. If the bandits don't shoot us on sight, after a week you'll wish they had. Life in a Zarthani brothel would be nasty, brutal and forever!"

Sirna had never thought of a long life as anything but a benefit; suddenly she could see there were two sides to every coin. "Not if they have to shoot me first!" Then she started to laugh as the wagon sped up, rocking back and forth.

"What are you laughing about? Eldra asked. "This is no time to get hysterical."

"I was just thinking of Varnath Lala being drug into a Nostori brothel—giving one of her lectures on male-paternalism and it's deleterious effects on woman's rights to the madam!"

Eldra laughed. "Better yet, envision her, with her bony shanks and flat chest, in one of the shifts the harlots at the Silver Stag were wearing!"

"Now, that's a vision!" Sirna said, trying to keep from falling out of her seat. There was an explosion and she turned to see what was happening with the rest of the wagon train—all she could see was a cloud of smoke.

"One of the kegs of fireseed must have gone up!" Eldra cried.

Two of the wagons were on fire and there was the distant pop of firearms. For the moment, they appeared to have gotten clean away as there was no one in pursuit. Sirna said a quick prayer to Dralm for the rest of the Team.

IV

Arch-Stratego Zarphu, who had fought in thirty battles in as many years without giving in to fear, noticed a tremble in his legs as he entered the Lord Tyrant's audience chamber. Dyzar, the Tyrant of Antiphon, was truly one of the greatest rulers in Antiphon's history, but that was not enough to make him a great man in Zarphu's eyes. Neither was the sparse beard that grew upon Dyzar's cheeks.

Dyzar did not view other people as living, feeling beings like himself; instead they were pieces to be moved or removed from life's game board. His outbursts of temper were as notorious as his women's quarters, which were filled with young slave girls and other young ladies 'lost' on the city streets after catching Dyzar's eye.

These days there was more silver than bronze in Zarphu's hair, and despite the recent victory over the Army of Leuctramnos, Dyzar might finally have decided that it was time for a younger man to command the city's army. Maybe one more malleable to his will. He was certain he had not done anything recently to make Dyzar doubt his loyalty and good service. Yet, since when had the Lord Tyrant ever needed proof of anything beyond his own whims and suspicions?

The two palace guards, both Eternals, wearing gilded chain mail and sporting red horsehair crests in their helmets, stood as if cast in metal. Zarphu wondered how they endured the constant inactivity; perhaps they were secretly amused by the parade of visitors into—and sometimes—out of Dyzar's chambers.

The door swung open and the Chamberlain bade him enter.

The Lord Tyrant Dyzar wore a rose and black velvet robe and his scruffy beard was intricately braided with gold wire. The Tyrant was reclining on a long red divan trimmed with gold mesh. He indicated that Zarphu was to sit on the other end of the divan.

After kneeling and touching the floor three times with forehead, Zarphu rose. "Your Magnificence, I am your slave to command—"

"Arch-Stratego, We will dispense with the usual formalities for We have an urgent matter to discuss with you. Are you familiar with the former refugees from Our lands who have settled beyond the Iron Trail?"

"No, Your Magnificence."

"Certainly you have heard the fables from the Time of Troubles about those who chose to flee to the lands beyond the Sea of Grass?"

"Yes, Your Magnificence. But I did not know there was truth behind those tales."

The Lord Tyrant nodded his head. "They are mentioned in the Lost Chronicles of Domitios. These I'm sure you have heard whispered words about."

Discourse with the Lord Tyrant was like sword fighting against a skilled blademaster; any feigns or missteps could be instantly fatal. "Yes, Your Magnificence, I have heard about them although I did not believe they still existed."

The Lord Tyrant grinned. "The Chronicles are part of my secret library. Of course, any mention of what has passed between us in this chamber will cost you and your family dearly. Is that understood?"

Zarphu nodded.

"Good. As you know the Time of Troubles began with the Echini War against the Echanistra Confederation and lasted for almost a thousand years. Near the end of the war, Echanistra's fleet was nearly destroyed; so many of the northerners decided to flee their homelands. Invited by King Chaldorec of Grefftscharr, many of them followed the Iron Trail and beyond to new lands, where in the winter snow is as common as the sand on our beaches. There they conquered the Ruthani, as our ancestors did three thousand years ago, and took the land as their own.

"We know few details about their conquest, but in time five major king-doms were established—each dominated by a great city-state, much like our own rule. For many years they have grown and prospered, all without tribute or tithes to the lords they fled. Now a new kingdom has formed and they have asked for our help. Maybe the time has arrived for us to re-establish our dominion over these strayed children."

There was an intense inner light in the Lord Tyrant's eyes that worried Zarphu. The Tyrant Laertru, Dyzar's father, had built the greatest army in the history of Antiphon. His son had used this army to subdue and con-quer his neighbors, a feat no one had accomplished since the Time of Troubles. Now the Lord Tyrant's power extended from Amcylyestros in the south to Tyrantor in the north. Apparently, not even the domination of the Great Cities was enough to appease Dyzar's appetite for power. Were the rumors that the Lord Tyrant wanted to forge an empire from Great Sea to Great Sea actually true?

"We have been approached by agents of Styphon's House—the Temple of an Eastern god—with a request to hire part of our army. The terms are generous and we have accepted their offer. Now that we have wrested peace from Amcylyestros, and have so soundly defeated Leuctramnos that they too seek a settlement—all due to your brilliant generalship—we have an unparalleled opportunity to learn about the land and their peoples."

"Who is this Styphon, Your Magnificence?"

"Some false god of war they worship." Dyzar continued. "He cannot be a very good god or they would not need our help. According to their emis-sary, they are embroiled in a war with a demi-god named Kalvan and desire our help to defeat him. Demi-god indeed! I care not one whit for their petty struggles, but there can be much to gain by going to their aid. We need to know more about these barbarians if we are to exploit their troubles to our advantage."

"How much of our army do they wish to hire?"

"Four stratgi of horse and fourteen of foot, including two stratgi of plumbati."

"Your Magnificence, that is almost a quarter of our entire army. Can we afford the loss of so many valuable men?"

"Yes. With Leuctramnos suing for peace there is no other city-state left to oppose us but Sybariphon in the north, and they are still at war with

Echanistra. We may never have a better opportunity to search out the Easterners' weaknesses."

Zarphu felt weak in the knees, as if he had been ordered to run his army into the ocean to fight the waves. What madness was this? He would have to cross the Sea of Grass, fight the warriors of Greffa and defeat the barbarian kingdoms, who—if stories were to be believed—fought with fire and metal, shot by sticks farther than the fleetest arrow.

"I need you to lead them, Arch-Stratego. Only you will be trusted with the true secret of our mission."

Yanked out of his reverie by this pronouncement, Zarphu knew chances were small he would ever return and see his beloved city again. Maybe, as his friends had warned, his own success on the battlefield had made him too dangerous to be left alive. Certainly an honorable death on the battlefield, no matter how far from home, was to be preferred to the assassin's dart.

"How long will we remain in the barbarian's employ?" Zarphu asked.

"Until next winter, or this Kalvan—be he man or demi-god—is dead."

Seeing the boy—for boy he still was, to Zarphu, for all his arrogance and lofty ambitions—seated there looking so completely alone, an upsurge of that wretched emotion called loyalty stirred in Zarphu's heart. Without thinking he knelt before his sovereign with the ridiculous gold-threaded scruffy beard, took his hand and placed it atop his head in the older gesture of fealty among the Ros-Zarthani and quietly said, "I will serve Your Magnificence, until I bear Kalvan's skull as a drinking cup or my shield is hung in Hadron's Hall."

"I knew my trust was well founded," Dyzar purred. "I want maps drawn of the entire journey, a list of all cities and fortifications you encounter, samples of all new armor and weapons, notes on how an army can be supplied on each part of the journey and any documents of military importance you can obtain. I will send scribes and mapmakers to aid you with these chores. In addition, I will entrust you with a bodyguard drawn from my Eternals; they will guard you with their lives."

The Eternals were the Lord Tyrants own personal bodyguard, as well as his eyes and ears, and occasionally his assassins. Zarphu was being both honored and kept safe. Why couldn't he shake the feeling that he was caught in an invisible undertow?

"Do not worry about your affairs in the city, Zarphu." Dyzar paused to stroke his beard. "Should you not return to us in two years time, We will gift your heirs Our weight in gold."

The Lord Tyrant was notoriously tightfisted; Zarphu couldn't help but wonder why the sudden benevolence. While a few of his friends had whispered their complaints about the Lord Tyrant's growing capriciousness, he had never in any way encouraged this kind of talk. He had also heard from one of his confidants that there were actual factions opposed to the Lord Tyrant's rule, so perhaps Dyzar had some justification for his worries about his security and the loyalty of his stratagi.

His own loyalty was incorruptible. "I thank you for your generosity, Your Magnificence. I shall return before the passing of two winters so your generosity will not be wasted." Zarphu prostrated himself before the crown again and kissed the Lord Tyrant's feet. He then rose, pausing only as he was about to cross the threshold to ask one last question. "When do we leave?"

"In a moon quarter, Arch-Stratego. We are having the fleet fitted and provisioned to take you and your command as far as Mythrene. There you will disembark, buy additional provisions and wagons and take leave for Olythrio. The Styphoni will have additional guides there to help you with your travels. Now We will give you leave to muster your men and prepare for the coming journey."

TWENTY-NINE

Thunder roared and shook the rooftree of Ranjar Sargos' temporary longhouse. For a few moments it drowned out the squeal of horses and the babble of more tongues than he had heard in all his days. Not since the time of his grandfather twice removed had such a great wave of humanity flooded over the Great Mother River and spilled its way into the Sastragath. Like flotsam tossed by the River, Sargos and his tribe had been picked up and pushed up into the Lydistros Valley.

Yet, as a flood replenishes the land it destroys, there was good which came with this river of humanity. Since few of the chiefs knew these lands, the Plainsmen had been forced to rely upon the knowledge of those who did. Ranjar Sargos, having spent four years of his youth as a mercenary in the Army of Gyroth, knew more about the Trygath than all but a few headmen in the great war band. This, along with Sargos' renown as a warrior, had placed him at the forefront of this human tidal wave.

Now only the constant pressure of the Black Knights gave the wave its form and kept it from dispersing into hundreds of separate war bands. Once that push was gone the horde would break up and lose its cohesion, whereupon they would all be destroyed piecemeal by the Trygathi iron hats and their allies. The time had arrived for a great warlord to guide the horde and Ranjar Sargos knew that there lay his own destiny—for had not his own dream vision foretold of such triumphs? So it had and much more!

Sargos took several deep breaths, held them, and waited until Thanor's banging upon his great anvil in the sky had ceased, then he spoke again to the assembled Plains headmen and Sastragathi chiefs. "The gods have allowed the Black Knights to take the field. They have allowed the demigod Kalvan of Hostigos to enter the Trygath—"

"Demi-god or daemon, this Kalvan is no friend to the Trygathi, less so to the Black Knights," Chief Alfgar interrupted. "Let all three of them fight one another, I say. *This* is what the gods intend. Then let us pick the bones of the survivors!"

"Or Nestros and Kalvan swear brotherhood and pick *our* bones," Sargos snapped, his voice growing in volume. He had never been even-tempered and knew it. He also knew that since the Tymannes had left their ancestral hunting grounds he had grown even sharper of tongue.

"By Thanor's Hammer, that is as the gods will—" Chief Alfgar began.

A wordless muttering interrupted him, as Headman Jardar Hyphos once more tried to form words with a mouth and jaw yet unhealed from the blow of a Knight's mace. His son held his ear against Hyphos' mouth for a moment, and then nodded.

"My father says he doubts the gods have willed it that we come so far only to fall to our pride as well as our enemies."

"You yapping puppy!" Chief Alfgar roared. "Your father is a man. You are—"

"Silence," Sargos bellowed. He did not know what this would do, except perhaps make all the chiefs angry at him rather than at one another. That could be a gain, if he were able to do something with their attention.

"To be proud is the mark of a warrior, as all are here," Sargos began. "To let everything yield to that pride is the mark of a fool. More than four hands worth of tribes in this great warband have set aside their pride and sworn to follow me. The gods have not punished them. Why should you fare otherwise?"

"Witlings and women," Alfgar muttered just loud enough that Sargos alone could hear. Sargos decided for the moment to ignore him and willed his blood to slow its pounding beat.

"How many of those tribes are now north of the Lydistros, fighting as they please?" Chief Rostino asked. Of all those present, he seemed to have the most Ruthani blood as well as the most dignity.

Sargos chose an equally dignified answer. "I am not a Great King, with a host of armed slaves to punish disobedient warriors as if they were children. I am Warchief over the Tymannes. Those who swear to follow me as Warlord do so by choice."

"Well, then," Chief Alfgar said. "It is my choice not to swear any oaths to Ranjar Sargos, nor any other sachem or chieftain. We of the Sea of Grass have held that each chief was his own master since the Great Mountains rose from the earth. Maybe the dirt scrapers and log builders of the Sastragath are more accustomed to following at the heels of their masters like curs!" Alfgar punctuated his words by slamming his hands against his bone vest, making a sound like that of a shot being fired.

The hands of about half of the two score of chieftains inside the longhouse streaked for their knives, the only weapons allowed inside during the parlay. Sargos was glad that Althea had obeyed his request to stay in their hut. He hadn't had to explain to Althea that her presence would a strike against his leadership by the more hide-bound Grassmen and clansmen. He also knew that she would not only have drawn her knife, after Chief Alfgar's insult, but used it as well!

Sargos signaled for attention. "This is not the time to hurl baseless insults nor fight among ourselves. There is great treasure to be won and much glory to be gained in fighting our real enemies, not each other."

Most of the chiefs sat back down and nodded their agreement to this sage advice.

But Hyphos' son held his ground. "You have not fought Kalvan, Alfgar. We have fought others like him many times in the Trygath and we have learned that to win we must stand as one—like wolves, not curs."

"You, a milksop not long from you mother's teat, dare instruct me!" Alfgar replied, with his face twisted into an ugly leer. "What has Sargos given you, that you take his word about the Daemon Kalvan, whom he has never seen?"

Hyphos' son would have drawn his knife if his father's arm had not been sounder than his jaw—the bronzed arm gripped the young man's wrist and twisted. He gasped and dropped his knife.

"See! How the Sastragathi lick their master's hand. When Sargos nods his head, the old rein in the young. This is not the way of the Plains!"

Rage flowed into Sargos, lifting him like a giant's hands—or perhaps the hands of the gods. Certainly he had never felt their presence more strongly, even in the sweathouse of his manhood rites.

"Let us submit this matter to the judgment of the gods." Sargos drew from the hides of his chieftain's chair the sacred axe of the chiefs of the Tymannes. "With this axe and no other weapon I will fight Chief Alfgar, this day, in this place. He may use any weapon his honor allows him."

"No!" Chief Ulldar exclaimed. Next to Sargos, Ulldar Zodan was the wisest man in the room in the new ways of warfare. Two of his sons had served Chief Harmakros in Kalvan's wars and told him much. They had also brought him a tooled and engraved horsepistol that was the envy of every chief in the longhouse. "The gods have taken away Chief Alfgar's wits. What if they have taken away his honor as well?"

Several of Alfgar's fellow chiefs had to restrain him from trying to kill Ulldar with his bare hands. When the uproar had subsided, Alfgar had found his voice again. "I will fight with the handspear against your axe, you godless son of a she-bitch who weaned you on stinkcat piss!"

"Let it be done, then," Sargos pronounced. His rage was already fading, and in its place were doubts that he was really in the hands of the gods after all. If he fell—and Alfgar promised to be a formidable foe—neither he nor his son would ever see the Tymannes great longhouse again.

Why not be hopeful? he thought. *If I win, it will prove the gods' favor and my own prowess as well. Then all the chiefs and clan headmen assembled here will proclaim me Warlord, and those lesser chiefs who are not here will quickly follow. Cast the bones and let the gods see to where they fall—by Thanor's Hammer!*

Sargos led the chiefs and headmen out to the square in the middle of the longhouses. The rain was still falling and what had already fallen made the square a sea of foul-smelling mud. Sargos judged this would be to his advantage: Alfgar, a plainsman, could seldom have fought on foot, on a slope and in mud up to his ankles.

Sargos' hopes quickly faded, as Chief Alfgar lost not a moment in charging—his spear point passing only a few fingers from Sargos' thigh. Mud splashed high, but Alfgar seemed as fleet as a boy. Again, Sargos avoided the Alfgar's jabbing spear thrusts, While Alfgar danced away from his return strokes with the axe.

So it went for a half-score of passes. Sargos quickly realized that he had one advantage. Alfgar was so confident of his greater youth and strength that he was careless of what fighting in mud would do to them. If the time ever came when Alfgar could not move away in time—

As if to warn Sargos against hopefulness, on the next exchange Alfgar drew first blood. It was barely more than a thorn prick and on Sargos' left arm, but it held an arrogant message: *I can do this at will. The next time, who knows where it will be?*

Both warriors' friends had been shouting threats and promises. If Alfgar won, there would be a permanent broach between the Grassmen' and Sastragathi chiefs. At this first blood, all fell silent and remained so. Althea watched with a stubborn set to her jaw and one hand on her knife's handle. At that moment he knew that even if Alfgar killed him, his rival as Warlord would not be far behind in going to Wind.

Sargos said nothing at all. He had better uses for his breath.

In time the rain stopped. Both men now bled in five or six places, though nowhere seriously. Sargos began to wonder if he would have breath for any use at all before long. Beyond any doubt Chief Alfgar was spending his strength freely. Alfgar's feet began to slip, and Sargos used this opportunity to bring his axehead down to Alfgar's torso. The plainsman used his spear butt to ward off the blow, but at the cost of two of his fingers—taken off at the second joint.

Alfgar's hand was bleeding and his energy was slowing, but he'd had rather more than Sargos to begin with. The mud, it seemed, might not be the gods' way of saving Ranjar Sargos. Nor could he trust to his luck in avoiding a crippling wound much longer. Alfgar made a thrust that would have disemboweled him had he not jumped in time, slipping in the mud. Sargos had to use all his arts in war while he still had the strength and speed to use them.

Silently he prayed to the gods, Aram One-Eye, Thanor, Fryga, Yirtta, Tyron, Myrr: *Guard my folk and my son. Send them wisdom and courage, if there is justice in you. And, if you sent Kalvan to be as a wolf to the flocks, you are not the true gods and my spirit will tell my sons to worship something else!*

"Pray for an honorable home for your spirit, old man," Alfgar sneered. "It will soon need one."

Then he sprang forward so fast that if Sargos had not been prepared, both in mind and body, for the final grapple he would have been doomed. As it was, he had already begun to turn when Alfgar closed, presenting his left thigh to the thrusting spear.

Offered a target, Alfgar thrust hard, forgetting that his target was mostly bone. As his spear point grated on that bone, Sargos' long arms whirled His left gripped the spear, jerking it from Alfgar's hand. In the blink of an eye, Alfgar slipped his knife out of its sheath.

Sargos' right arm brought the axe down hard on Alfgar's knife hand, as it leaped toward Sargos' groin. For an instant the gods might have turned both men into stone. Then the knife splashed into the mud.

The spear whirled in Sargos' hand and struck Alfgar's belly, which instantly sprouted a curious red bloom. The knowledge of what had just happened was just dawning in his eyes when Sargos' axe came down upon his head, crushing his left cheek and jawbone.

"The gods have spoken," Sargos gasped. He hoped if more needed to be said, the gods would say it themselves. Neither his wits nor his wind seemed to be fit for the task, and, as for his legs, he prayed they would not tumble him into the mud beside his foe.

Ranjar, son of Cedrak, you are too old for this and so you will learn the next time not to confuse the voice of the gods with the memories of your own youth.

Egthrad and Old Daron, chiefs of his own Clan, ran forward to aid him, but were pushed aside by Althea. "Stop treating me as though this was my first wound!" he growled. "It's more like my tenth, and one of the least." In truth, it would need some care, and he would be riding more than walking for the next moon quarter. But only the flesh hurt.

In his ear, Althea whispered, "You own them now. It was a magnificent victory."

Meanwhile the crowd around him had grown and was beginning to chant, "Sargos! Sargos! Warlord Sargos!" He wasn't sure if his own Clansmen had started the chant or if it was a spontaneous outburst; regardless, he knew how to grasp the moment and squeeze it with both hands. He stepped back and raised his arms.

Together, Headman Jardar Hyphos and his son stepped forward and lifted Alfgar's motionless body.

Behind them came Chief Rostino. He knelt before Sargos and pressed his forehead against Sargos' hands. "The gods have truly spoken. What do they wish, Warlord Sargos? That we swear to you?"

Had it been a Sastragathi chieftain making this pronouncement rather than a Plainsman, there might have been jeers and catcalls—as it was there was naught but silence.

"The gods ask little," Sargos panted. He took several deep breaths until he found that he could hope to speak instead of gasp. *At least I will ask little. The gods will not help a man who asks for more than those who follow him are willing to give.*

"Little indeed," Sargos repeated. "Only that you follow me in war and peace, save when I ask for war against blood-brothers or peace with blood-enemies. And that you yourselves are bound by this oath until I release you or Wind take you."

"I swear—" Chief Rostino began, but Sargos stopped him, extending his hand to help him to his feet.

"Rise. I will have no brave warriors swearing anything to me on their knees. That is more pride than the gods allow."

There was a boisterous round of oath-taking as many of the assembled chiefs, who had not already done so, swore their allegiance to Ranjar Sargos as Warlord.

After all the oaths had been given, Sargos said, "Let us take a visit to the bathhouse, while the women heat us some beer. Or there is wine if any of you wish it."

Sargos could not tell what drew more enthusiasm, the gods' judgment, the baths or the prospect of a good drinking party.

THIRTY

P resent—aaarrrmmmmsss!"

Fifty bayoneted muskets snapped into position across fifty Hostigi breastplates. A hundred sabers leaped to the vertical. Even in the watery spring sunlight, the reflection from all the steel made Kalvan blink.

The herald of Nestros, King of Rathon and self-proclaimed High King of the Trygath, rode forward. His mounted escort rode forward on either side of him, fifty big men on beer-wagon sized-destriers. By the customs of the Trygath, heralds went guarded until they were actually in the presence of the men they were sent to parlay with. Also by custom, the horsemen rode with their visors up and their swords held upright by the blades, as proof of peaceful intent.

Kalvan studied the guards as they rode up the slope toward him. They reminded him more than a little of the Royal Lancers of Hos-Harphax, swathed from head to foot in armor about as useful as cheesecloth in keeping out a musket bullet or a chunk of case shot.

Except that this was the Trygath, where in nine years out of ten the only fireseed available was what neighboring Eastern Princes were willing to sell illegally, risking both shortages and Styphon's Ban. Against other armored knights or lightly armored nomads, riding around looking like a black-smith's version of a lobster made a certain amount of sense.

This had already started to change, with the emerging trade of Hostigos Unconsecrated (plus a little Styphon's Best on the side) for horses, mead, and furs. It was about to change more, but not quickly or easily. Military technology was generally about as slow to change as priestly ritual. So for now, the Trygathi fully armored men-at-arms had a few more days in the sun.

The herald signaled; the Rathoni guardsmen reined in, leaving him to mount the slope alone. At a nod from Captain-General Harmakros, Aspasthar rode out, his first sword reversed in his hand and the sun shining on his first suit of armor, emblazoned with the Great King's keystone.

"Who comes to the host of Great King Kalvan of Hos-Hostigos?" Aspasthar's voice was high-pitched but steady.

"Baron Thestros of Rathon, herald and envoy of High King Nestros." The herald took another look at the Royal Page. "Does the Great King lack men, that he has me greeted by a beardless boy?"

"Had he thought you saw wisdom in a beard, my lord, the Great King would have sent you a he-goat!"

In the ensuing silence, Kalvan and Harmakros exchanged eloquent looks. Kalvan's said, *If the boy's tongue has run away with him and we have a fight, he is going to get the flat of my saber across his backside.*

Harmakros' reply was, *Don't worry. The boy knows what he is doing.*

The herald was the first to break the silence, with a roar of laughter. Seeing themselves given permission, the Rathoni Royal Guard also broke into laughter. Then everyone was hooting and guffawing, and Harmakros was riding forward to clap Aspasthar on the shoulder so hard the boy nearly fell out of his saddle.

At last silence returned, except for a distant rumble of thunder. Baron Thestros wiped his face with a yellow-gloved hand.

"Well-spoken, lad. You do honor to your sire, your king and your realm. But I think there must be a person of more rank than you, in a host as large as this. Might I seek the honor of speech with he who holds the most rank among you? Captain-General Harmakros, I believe?"

Harmakros nodded. "At your service. But I am not highest among those present." He turned in the saddle. "Your Majesty?"

Kalvan urged his horse forward, letting his cloak flow back from his shoulders. Baron Thestros did a good imitation of a man whose eyes are about to pop from his head. Then he swung himself swiftly if not grace-fully from the saddle and went down on one knee.

"Your Majesty! In the name of High King Nestros, greetings!"

"Surely you have more than greetings to bring, since you have four thou-sand cavalry at your summons. Your King has a name for wisdom, and would not send such a host with a message a beardless boy could bring."

The imitation of eye-popping was even better this time; Kalvan let it go on until he was sure the herald needed reassurance.

"No. I have no demonic arts, only good scouts. They saw your men yes-terday and rode swiftly to bring word to me. I came up, that there might be no misunderstandings about why the men of Hos-Hostigos and its allies have come to the Trygath."

"I believe Your Majesty. But then, pray tell what *is* the reason for such a host being upon the domain of King Nestros? He wishes peace with all who wish it with him, but those who wish peace seldom come with twenty thousand armed retainers!"

"Your scouts are not inferior to mine," Kalvan said with a grin. That was a remarkable accurate count of the Hostigi who'd crossed into the Trygath. Another ten to twelve thousand were strung out all the way across Kyblos, ready to either join the main body or cover its withdrawal. Kalvan had hoped for a greater feudal levy from Kyblos, but many of the southern barons had not responded to Prince Tythanes' request for men—and probably wouldn't at anything less than sword point. He understood their hearts—along with their soldiers—were with their homes, but at some point Kalvan would have to find a fit punishment for their willful neglect of feudal duty and custom. Or risk wholesale desertion by his barons' levy every time the Styphoni armies threatened, which would be disastrous.

"I thank Your Majesty. But—forgive me for being inopportune, but I have only the cause of peace at heart. I ask once more, why are you in my King's realm?"

That was a bit of exaggeration, thought Kalvan, since Nestros' sover-eignty was only recognized by four of the Trygath's nine 'legitimate' kings and princes and, in fact, two of them, Ragnar and Thul, were subjects of King Theovacar of Greffscharr. Diplomacy, however, was the order of the day. "We do not come in search of peace."

Kalvan could have sworn he heard the thud of the baron's jaw hitting the ground. Quickly he added, "We come to wage war on the horde from the Sastragath and the Great Plains, enemies common to all of us."

The herald shook his head. "King Nestros has taken counsel with his princes and lords, and he has devised ways of meeting the nomad host. It insults him to think that he must wait upon Eastern realms for defense of his own."

"I am sure that the true gods fight for King Nestros, and his Princes and people likewise," Kalvan said. "Yet is it not true that the nomad horde counts more fighting men than the Trygath and Hos-Hostigos combined?" Three times, Kalvan thought, if the estimate of a hundred and fifty thousand on the way northeast was correct.

"Is it not also true, that during the last moon, riders of the horde reached the Lower Saltless Sea, sowing death with every step their horses took? They did not return, but would it not have been better that they not even start?"

Kalvan wanted to meet the local magnate who'd caught the raiders on their way back from the shores of Lake Erie.

King Crython of Ragnar had outthought as well as outfought the raiders, by all reports; that kind of man would make almost as good an ally as King Nestros. But first, King Nestros would have to refuse the alliance before Kalvan could safely seek allies among his princes and nobles.

"Indeed," the herald said, "and no such raids will come again this season."

"Is this certain? Certainly they will cease after the valiant men-at-arms and footmen of King Nestros have broken the strength of the horde. But Nestros will do this only if he gathers all his strength under his own hand. Who will be left to defend the lands of those who march against the horde, against handfuls of raiders and outlaws?"

Kalvan had pitched his voice loud enough to be heard by the Royal Guardsmen. All of them would be nobles or sons of nobles; all must share the fear of what would happen to their lands at the hands of nomad outriders and bandits.

"Your Majesty, do you swear you can prevent this if King Nestros and you become friends?"

"We are not enemies even now, nor shall we be. What you mean is, if we become allies. I only say this. If we become allies, there will be twenty-five thousand Hostigi, perhaps more, to strengthen your King."

"And if there is no alliance, will there be twenty-five thousand fewer?"

"The host of the Great King will fight the horde wherever we find it," Kalvan answered. "But is it not better that we fight it together? Sticks separated are easily broken. Tied into a bundle, they defy the strength of a giant."

"Your Majesty speaks eloquently. I think, perhaps, it would be wiser if you spoke thus to King Nestros."

"Nothing would give me more pleasure, if I knew where to find your High King?"

"Let Your Majesty ride to Rathon City, and I believe you will find no obstacles in your path."

Rathon City was the here-and-now equivalent of Columbus, Ohio: about fifty miles away—three days easy marching.

"The High King will see me in Rathon City before the horde can wreak any more harm upon his realm. Now, I see that the sky promises rain. Would you and your guard commander care to accept the hospitality of my tent, which I think is closer than your own?"

Baron Thestros and his guard commander exchanged looks; then the herald nodded. "We are honored by Your Majesty's hospitality."

"Call it the first repayment of the hospitality we have received from King Nestros' subjects," Kalvan said. Baron Thestros frowned, and still looked puzzled as he led his guards off behind Aspasthar.

When the Trygathi commanders were safely on their way, Harmakros rode his horse beside to Kalvan. "Your Majesty, far be it from me to tell you how to guide the realm—"

"If you ever stop telling me, Harmakros, I'll find another Captain-General. Out with it. I don't want to get caught in the rain if I can help it. A fine spectacle for our allies, me leading a charge with sword in one hand and handkerchief in the other."

Harmakros quickly ordered the First Royal Horse Guard into a wide circle, and then put them in movement toward the tent. Riding practically boot to boot with Kalvan, he grinned.

"Your Majesty is as silver tongued as any bard, but is this the time to be so truthful about what we want?"

"It is the best time. Any earlier would have given the Union of Styphon's Friends or the League of Dralm time to make noises. Not to mention, letting the Zarthani Knights send scouts on to our line of march, and maybe more than scouts. Ten thousand Trygathi could give us enough trouble. Think about ten thousand Knights."

"I'd rather think about more pleasant things."

"Like that blonde at Mnebros Town?"

Harmakros flushed. "I didn't know Your Majesty noticed."

"Just because *I* slept alone doesn't mean I don't know the officers who didn't." They were silent for a moment, guiding their horses over a rough patch of ground.

"It's Mnebros Town that made me think the time was ripe to tell the truth," Kalvan went on. "Those people were so Dralm-damned *glad* to see us, it was pathetic. We could have had anything we asked for, not just wine, women and banquets. They were truly frightened of that horde.

"What the Styphon! A horde that size scares me! But our lands are farther than they're likely to reach. Around here, nobody knows if they'll have a roof over their heads and all their family alive come winter."

Kalvan stopped speaking while his horse trotted around a bush that separated the two men. "Nestros will do his best, but if that isn't going to be good enough . . ."

"If that isn't good enough," Harmakros replied, "his Princes and barons will start looking around for someone whose best might be good enough?"

"Exactly." The gray sky was overhead now, and to the northwest was turning black. The royal pavilion was in sight ahead; the herald's party was just turning in to it. "The Trygathi nobles have always had more independence than the ones in the East, at least since fireseed came along. Things aren't as settled here and a good castle gives you more bargaining power when the only way to take it is starving it out. King Nestros will be down to lord mayor of Rathon City if he lets too many of his nobles' lands be overrun."

Harmakros shook his head. "And you learned all this from those old parchments?"

Kalvan nodded. He knew that Harmakros had risen from a commoner's family and had never learned to read or write, which was typical of here-and-now, where—for the most part—only the nobility, and priesthood, had any education. "An alliance with us is really a gift from the Gods; now, all we have to do is convince Nestros of that. All the second-line troops he probably couldn't feed anyway can go back and defend their homes. We will put our men into line with his, and he'll have twice as big an army as he would otherwise. And a better one to boot! He'll keep the loyalty of his barons, defeat the horde and have his title recognized all at once. How could any man resist—?"

At the word "resist," the skies split apart in a thunderclap that made the horses jump. As the thunder rumbled into silence, the hiss of rain took its place. A few drops spattered across Kalvan's hands, a few more across his face, then the deluge struck.

He reined his horse to a walk and sneezed as drops found their way up his nose—so much for royal dignity.

THIRTY-⊕NE

I

Knight Commander Aristocles took a moment to light his pipe. "I talked to the messenger myself, Soton. The Usurper's troops have already reached the Trygath. Soon we shall cross swords with our true enemy, not these miserable curs that we have been driving into Kalvan's lands."

Grand Master Soton drank deep from his tankard. "We must not only harass Kalvan, but defeat him as well if we are to keep his armies from the gates of Harphax City."

"Better yet, let the nomads bleed him dry. Every day their forces grow and so does their battle prowess. This new Warlord of theirs may prove to be our problem someday. For now, let him be Kalvan's thorn."

"Well said, old friend. Although it sickens me to despoil any Zarthani lands with the nomads we are sworn to keep at bay."

"This Trygathi gaggle of pretend princedoms and petty kings are only a few generations removed from their cowhide wagons and tents! They are not true Zarthani, but mostly decadent tribes, remnants of the Urgothi migrations. I will shed no more tears over their passing than I would that of a herd of buffalo."

"That may be true of the Sastragathi peoples, Aristocles, but some of these Trygathi princedoms go back a century or two. You forget my own village was on the Trygath/Ktemnos border. True, their ways are crude, but their hearts are strong and they do know how to fight. I'm glad it's Kalvan and the nomads who will be ground against their spears and swords."

Knight Commander Aristocles reached over and poured another cup of the bitter chocolate into his tankard. At Tarr-Ceros he preferred his chocolate laced with honey to sweeten the taste, but the Grand Master kept his table as spare as those of his lowliest troopers. He raised his tankard up and toasted, "To the mighty walls of Xiphlon and long may they keep the Mexicotál at bay."

"A good toast, Aristocles." The Grand Master took a long draught from his own silver tankard. "It would be a tragedy if those flesh-eaters brought down the walls of the noblest city of our age."

In a lightning-swift change of mood, Soton slammed his tankard down on the table, spilling the dark brown fluid over the deerskin maps and parchment letters. "We should be marching toward the Mexicotál's rear instead of herding nomads!"

Aristolces shook his head. "The spiders of Balph would never allow us to march to the aid of a Middle Kingdom city. They would rather have us guarding turkey pens from foxes instead!"

"Baaaah!," Soton muttered, glaring down at the brown stains on the tapestry covered floor of his tent.

"What's wrong, old friend?" Aristocles asked. "You haven't been yourself since you last returned from Balph. You refuse to talk about your audience, but even the dimmest of the Brethren sense your dark mood."

"I should keep my own counsel, but this concerns your fate as well as mine. You have saved my life in battle many times, and I have felt sick at heart with all that I have had to keep to myself."

"I have only saved your life, as you have saved my own."

"True, we have known each other far too long to hold secrets. Besides, you will need to know these things—if only to protect yourself. I will not live forever, or even tomorrow, if some barbarian's arrow pierces my armor. Investigator Roxthar holds the entire city of Balph in his thrall—"

"So I've heard. What does that have to do with the Order?"

Soton grimaced. "Everything. What you don't know is that Roxthar now pulls the strings of the Inner Circle."

"Archpriest Anaxthenes would never allow—"

"Anaxthenes, like many others, has no choice but to submit to the Investigator. Those who oppose Roxthar vanish into the bowels of the Investigation, never to return. Roxthar has cooked up some deal with Sesklos where Roxthar cannot Investigate the Inner Circle, but that has not stayed his hands from their allies and minions. With Sesklos and Dracar's support, Investigator Roxthar has overcome most of the opposition. Only Anaxthenes dares oppose him—for now. Those who don't fear Roxthar, fear Styphon's Own Guard who have become the Investigation's other hand."

"Truly. Is it that bad?"

Soton looked up, his eyes hard. "Nay, it is worse."

"How could it be?"

"Roxthar has records on many of the Order's commanders and leaders; records that could prove blasphemy to Styphon—at least, in his hands. You know, words spoken out of turn or in the heat of battle. He even has your own criticism of the Inner Circle. Taken out of context," Soton paused to make washing movements with his hands, "they could lead to a charge of treason."

"What? I've devoted my life to Styphon's work. More than any temple rat—"

"See! Such words are but fireseed for Roxthar's guns. He could use them to have you thrown out of the Order, purged of your priestly rank and even Investigated. Such were his words to me . . ."

"So, you bent your knees to that madman because of me! Why don't we turn this army around and march on Balph. We have the Order with us; they will willingly follow you anywhere, Grand Master. We can purge the Temple of this wharf-rat Roxthar, and fumigate the Inner Circle as well!"

"You scare me as much as Roxthar, with your loose tongue, old friend! You have lost sight of the forest. What will Kalvan and his minions do while we kill priests at Balph? And, do you think Styphon's Own Guard will sit idly by as we kill the Investigators and corrupt priests—or those we think corrupt? The Temple Bands will die to the last man before they see us sack Balph. And what about the Sacred Squares of Hos-Ktemnos?"

Aristocles felt his mouth twist into a smile. "But what a war. We could sow the fields of Hos-Ktemnos with the bones of Styphon's Red Hand, as well as Roxthar's Holy Investigators. We could arrive before they would have time to muster the Sacred Squares."

"Many are true-believers. I could not in good conscience kill those who fight for Styphon's House. What would the Temple have to say about such foul infamy from its Own Holy Order, dedicated to protect its lands? Sometimes I think this Kalvan has infected more than Hostigos with his new ways and constant questioning of everything we hold true and dear."

"I'm sorry," Aristocles said. To himself he added, *but your heart is too soft, old friend, and you do not have the friends in Balph you like to think you do. Sometimes I fear you take this Styphon worship as serious as some ignorant village lower priest; it may turn out to be your downfall.* Aristocles had spent two years at Balph and had learned first hand that the only true believers of Styphon were those who did not live in that foul cesspool of a city, ripe with priestly intrigue and corruption. Unlike Soton, he was from Ktemnos City and his father was a baron, who had chosen the Order as a good place for a younger son. At the time, he had been thankful his father hadn't decided that he needed a priest in the family! No one he knew had believed in Styphon, especially the priests. Soton's devotion to the Temple had always been hard to accept in a man so practical in all other things. Soton had not been as blessed by the Temple as he thought; the Grand Master had forged his own destiny with his iron will and by the strength of his mace.

"The more they feed Roxthar, the bigger he will grow."

Soton nodded wearily. "This is what I fear. Where will his Investigation wander next—into our own ranks?" He slammed the table, buckling it with a hand as hard as horn from decades of sword practice.

Sergeant Sarmoth stuck his white face into the tent. "Is all well, Grand Master?"

"Yes, this is none of your concern. Go back to your cot!"

Sarmoth looked stricken, but quickly closed the flap.

"See, I take it out on everyone. My sworn duty as an Archpriest of the Temple is to protect Styphon's House. It is not my job to cleanse the Temple."

Aristocles wisely kept his mouth shut. *If someone inside the Temple doesn't do it, then an interloper such as Kalvan would! Roxthar was going too far with his 'purges' and his personal crusade to remove all non-believers. Where would it end? When Styphon's House was as full of mealy-mouthed priests, as the Temple of Dralm?* He spat on the floor.

II

None of the forts and towns Kalvan had encountered in the Trygath had prepared him for the sight of Rathon City. Unlike the wooden stockades and palisades surrounding most Trygathi towns, Rathon City was encircled by immense stonewalls—about the size of the Great Wall of China— which dwarfed the outbuildings and storehouses that had sprung up at their base. Not even the Eastern Kingdom capitals had such massive stone bulwarks, but then they were not subjected to periodic nomad invasions and large-scale migrations.

The Great Gate was large too, wide enough so that four of the Conestoga-style wagons could pass abreast. Most of the city's two and three-story buildings were the usual beam and plaster construction. At the city's center were a score of large public buildings constructed of stone, half of which appeared to have been built within the past decade.

Kalvan figured the city's population at about seventy-five thousand: smaller than a comparable Eastern Kingdom capital, but impressive for a so-called 'barbarian' capital city. Most of the people he saw in the streets wore homespun trousers and shirts, although there was a goodly number of hunters and trappers in furs and buckskins. There was a small sprinkling of nobles and merchant princes, resplendent in fur-lined velvet or corduroy robes and rich brocades. The men, with few exceptions, wore full beards, rather than the trimmed beards and goatees worn in the East.

Kalvan suspected that being in Rathon City was like visiting one of the Great Kingdom capitals two or three hundred years ago.

At the center of the city was a great plaza, at least two-city blocks square. At the center, surrounded by a magnificent garden, towered King Nestros' palace; a magnificent building that made Kalvan's own 'palace' (actually Prince Ptosphes' summer palace) look like a poor relation's summer home. When this Great Murthering War with Styphon's House was over, Kalvan was going to build himself a palace more suitable to his station—maybe something along the lines of Louis XIV's Palace of Versailles—or he was going to have problems maintaining the respect of despots like Nestros.

Half a dozen richly dressed ambassadors came to meet the Hostigi party at the garden gates. Kalvan noticed that all of Nestros' retainers had their beards cut and trimmed in the Eastern fashion. To either side of the road leading to his palace stood the King's Guard, infantry men all over six foot, with finely engraved ceremonial halberds and black and gold armor. Two dozen of the Guard formed an honor guard at the head of a big procession, which led the visitors through the center of Rathon City to the palace.

Inside the palace Nestros himself looked every inch the warrior king, from his broad shoulders to his big calloused hands. Nestros had the ruddy complexion of an outdoorsman and a face that was dignified if not handsome. He and Kalvan locked eyes and neither turned away until they both did in unspoken unison. Kalvan could see right from the beginning that Nestros was going to be a hard horse to ride.

"Welcome, Great King Kalvan, to our humble abode. Can I get you some refreshment? Ale or winter wine, perhaps?"

"Winter wine will be fine, High King Nestros." It took two goblets of wine to complete the usual diplomatic niceties. Before starting on his third, Kalvan stated, "As I told your herald, we have come as allies. I have brought my army to aid you in your war against the nomads."

"If this be true, then fine. Yet, I have to wonder what real errand brings a distant King to our land. Truly, in all our history, we have found that the Eastern Kingdoms care little about our wars and struggles. Why should this suddenly change now?"

"There are great changes afoot in these perilous times."

"Change may be new to you in the Eastern Kingdoms, but here it is a constant like the seasons."

"Not these changes! Since when have the Zarthani Knights driven the nomads into your lands, instead of sending them back across the Great Mother River?"

Nestros' forehead furrowed. "We have pondered this question. It appears that the Knights are using the nomads as a threat against Hos-Hostigos."

Kalvan was impressed with Nestros instinctive grasp of *Realpolitik*. "Yes, that is exactly what Grand Master Soton intends to accomplish. And because your lands are between Hos-Hostigos and the nomads, they are going to take the brunt of the blood letting."

Kalvan could hear a harsh rasp as Nestros ground his teeth.

"The Grand Master may think we are but tools to be used, but we have prepared ourselves well for this invasion. I need neither his Knights, nor your help to keep my lands."

"How do you plan to keep the nomads at bay? They are now within days of your City gates. While your men-at-arms are renowned, the nomads are as numerous as the trees in the forest we just passed through."

"We are well provisioned and these great walls will keep out ten times the nomads number. All farms and gardens within a day's march of the City have been burned to the ground. We have four tons of fireseed for Tarr-Rathon's guns. All villagers and peasants within Rathon have been ensconced within the nearest walled town or city. There are royal store-houses in every large town and city in Rathon, Mybranos, Cyros and Lythax. We shall feed our own while the nomads starve like wolves in the midst of winter famine. When they have grown hungry and weak, our men-at-arms will slake the soil with their blood."

"That may have been a good plan for past times, but not now. Your armies have never fought a horde of this size. There is not a town or city in all Rathon, except for this City, which can hold back the nomad flood. But, say that you are right, and the walls of your towns and cities keep the nomads at bay. What then? In their anger, the invaders will poison your wells, burn your villages and sow your fields with salt in retribution. What will your people have to return to then? And what will your nobles say about a High King who saves lives by hiding behind walls so they can starve when the wolves have fled?"

Nestros' face burned bright red and for a moment Kalvan feared he had gone too far.

"Your words are foul, but as bad as they taste there is truth in them. From all reports, the nomads are as numerous as the great herds of bison upon the Sea of Grass, whose numbers stretch from horizon to horizon. It is enough to make one believe the old legends and their tales of endless waves of invaders. What help do you offer, Great King Kalvan?"

"My plan is simple. I say we join our armies and drive the nomads back south as the Knights have driven them north. Let them find *our* steel even less to their liking than that of the Zarthani Knights!"

Nestros' eyes brightened at the idea of a direct attack. Obviously, hiding behind Tarr-Rathon's walls was not his idea of protecting his lands. "Will we have enough swords, even together, to drive such a great horde?"

Not if we were facing the Huns or Mongols of otherwhen, thought Kalvan. *These nomads have horse archers, but fight more in the manner of Caesar's Gauls or Hadrian's Picts. And they lack a great khan like Attila or Genghis.*

"Their great numbers will give us the advantage, King Nestros. With so many warriors at their command, the nomads are forced to fight together like heavy infantry. Yet, they wear little armor and make massed targets for our muskets and arquebuses. Also, they have many leaders instead of one great chief."

"No longer, King Kalvan. We have just learned that the nomads have elected a Warlord, a Sastragathi chief named Ranjar Sargos. He is a former mercenary, who served in the Trygath, and knows our ways of warfare."

"A Warlord!" Kalvan paused to ponder the implications. "He may know Trygathi strategy, but I doubt he's seen service in the East and faced a Royal Regiment of Musketeers. Also, as a new leader his hold will be uncertain, and it is up to us to exploit that by moving quickly. How soon can you muster your troops?"

"Most of my Army is within a few day's ride of Rathon City, where there is enough victuals to feed them. But, before we lock arms on this alliance, I have a request to make of you."

Suddenly Kalvan feared for his presentation sword and richly-chased silver breastplate. In a past incarnation, Nestros must have been a horse trader like Duke Skranga. "How can I help you?"

"I would like to take the title of Great King and claim my lands as a Great Kingdom, as you have done with Hos-Hostigos. Have I not suzerainty over more square rods of land than Hos-Agrys? I do. Have I not more subjects than Hos-Bletha? I do. Have I not more men-at-arms than Hos-Zygros? I do. All I ask is that you recognize my claim as Great King and give me your support. Do I have your blessing?"

This sounds too easy! There has to be a catch in here somewhere. If he recognized Nestros as Great King of the Trygath, it might legitimize him in the eyes of his people, but it wouldn't mean twiddle-dum to the Five Great Kingdoms, none of whom even recognized Hos-Hostigos. Furthermore, Nestros claimed sovereignty over several princedoms that were traditionally within Grefftscharrer borders. He certainly didn't need a war in the west with King Theovacar because he needed to placate Nestros now.

However, if Kalvan worked this right, he could bind Nestros to Hos-Hostigos and possibly recruit him as an ally in the war against Styphon's House. Neither Grand Master Soton, nor the Inner Circle at Balph, would be pleased to find a new Great Kingdom with ties to Hos-Hostigos upon their own western borders. With the Council of Dralm refusing to support his title and claims, Kalvan needed all the allies he could muster.

"King Nestros, in return for your support and allegiance in Our war against the nomads and the Zarthani Knights, I will recognize you as Great King of all those Trygathi kingdoms, princedoms, dukedoms and baronies who agree to be part of your new Great Kingdom and who are not already under the sovereignty of King Theovacar."

Kalvan went on to make the usual terms and conditions binding upon two states who barely knew one another and yet whose kingdoms were joined as allies. It took several hours of tough negotiating between himself and his councilors and King Nestros and his council to come to final terms. He had General Klestreus draw up the proper binding documents. Trader Tortha was certain they would receive a warm reception in the Middle Kingdoms, except in Grefftscharr. But, Tortha agreed, there was nothing in the agreement to openly affront King Theovacar.

From the furrowed brow on Nestros' face, Kalvan knew he had safely navigated one minefield, but if he judged Nestros correctly this would not be the last, or the most dangerous.

"I welcome Your Majesty's support of the new Great Kingdom of Hos-Rathon. I only pray that you will be equally swift in helping us to modernize our army."

This request was going to be easy to fill for Kalvan, since he still had warehouses filled to the bursting with half the ordnance of Hos-Harphax captured during last year's war—most of the firearms dropped without a shot being fired! Not that he would let Nestros know that. He frowned and stared at the murals of old battles on the high ceiling.

"It will be done. We will send the orders to Hostigos Town tonight by fast messenger. Two thousand arquebuses and five hundred muskets will be delivered to Hos-Rathon to cement the alliance between Our two Kingdoms. We will also send five tons of Hostigos' fireseed, and will train two score of your selected apprentices in its manufacture at Our new University of Hos-Hostigos."

This must have struck Nestros as more than satisfactory; he jumped out of his throne to give Kalvan an un-kingly bear hug that all but crushed Kalvan's ribcage.

"Truly, Great King Kalvan, you are as generous as you are wise and master of the art of war. But enough of this, we will have plenty of time to celebrate when the nomads have been vanquished. Now we must plan our campaign. I have ten thousand troops billeted in and around Rathon City and two times ten thousand within a two days' ride. And another ten thousand within five days' ride."

"Excellent," Kalvan said. "Send riders out to all those within a two days' march. Meanwhile, we can gather provisions and prepare our soldiers for the battles ahead."

Nestros rubbed his huge hands together. "You speak my tongue, Great King Kalvan. The time has come to teach the nomads that it is safer in the Caverns of the Dead than it is in Hos-Rathon."

THIRTY-TWO ⊕

I

Danar Sirna watched as Queen Rylla, flanked by Chancellor Chartiphon and Xykos, Captain of the Queen's Own Bodyguard, sailed
into the Great Hall followed by a dozen ladies-in-waiting and six of the
Queen's Own Bodyguard. Rylla's bodyguard wore a red and black livery
trimmed in gold and had taken the name of the Queen's Beefeaters, after a
story Kalvan was supposed to have told Rylla about some famous Europo-
American Queen. Today Sirna noticed they were wearing the thick white
neck ruffs, which Kalvan called 'St. John's Platters.'

The moment Rylla took her chair of state, Outtime Studies Director
Talgran Dreth, Lathor Karv, and Varnath Lala poured forth a cacophony
of complaints, which sounded more like the gaggle of geese than educated
discourse from Home Time Line scholars. Listening to them it was hard
to believe, but Sirna had heard these same over-educated dunderheads
complaining about the barbarity of the 'local' Hostigi customs and their
crude discourse.

"Silence!" cried Queen Rylla, in a tone-of-voice that could carry over the
roar of a battlefield. In the Great Hall where she was holding audience, it
rang from the stone walls.

Sirna jumped like a stung horse. No pleasant simile that, either. Sirna,
with her abominable horse riding skills, had ruined most of her riding

outfits. It hadn't helped that the remainder of her clothes had been in one of
the wagons captured by the Phaxosi bandits. Sirna swore by every god she
had ever heard of that she would *not* specialize in any Sector that depended
upon horses for transportation in any future Paratime assignment!

Her mind settled on that point, Sirna turned her attention back to the
Great Queen.

Rylla had been out riding when the University foundry party had
returned with its story of an attack by "bandits." Queen Rylla hadn't bothered to change before seeing the Foundry team, merely girding on her
dress sword and pulling on the Great Queen's crown over hastily brushed
hair.

"I thank you for your attention," Rylla said. "Now, I wish to hear a tale.
Not the gobbling of a farmyard full of turkeys! Captain Ranthar, you speak
first. I judge you to be the most seasoned soldier among those present."

Both Lathor Karv and Varnath Lala looked ready to protest, the first at
his seniority being ignored and the second at a man being given prefer-
ence. A look passed between Sirna and Aranth Saln, to say that if their
colleagues made a spectacle of themselves before Queen Rylla they would
soon wish they hadn't. Assuming, of course, there was anything left of the
two after Rylla got through with them . . .

Ranthar Jard delivered the account of how the University's wagon train
had been attacked by "bandits" while crossing Mythonos Ford. They had
lost six wagons, five horses, twelve oxen and two men killed, seven more
wounded. The bandits had surely suffered losses, but they had taken great
care to remove all of them. They had even tried to take away all their fallen
weapons and horses.

"By the favor of the gods, we stopped them from removing everything.
The horses we gave to some peasants, who looked in need of meat. The
weapons and tack, we brought with us."

"Good sir," Rylla said. "You sound doubtful that these were bandits."

"I was doubtful then," the Captain said. I am more so now. They were
too well mounted and too disciplined. They were also trying for the
foundry supplies. Bandits mostly try for food, horses or weapons. The
foundry supplies would be hard to move, but they would do the most harm
to Hostigos."

Rylla's expression hardened, "Indeed! And the captured gear?" She seemed on the verge of licking her lips. Sirna was reminded of a cat that has just sighted a tasty morsel of unprotected meat.

"Every piece that had a mark of origin on it, was either Harphaxi Armory or Phaxosi."

Before Sirna's eyes, Rylla appeared to turn into another and far more formidable feline—an Indian tiger ready to spring. She recalled a film she'd seen, of a hunt in some Sino-Indian Subsector and a pair of the creatures at bay.

"Prince Araxes, you have gone too far this time!" Rylla pronounced. She might have been praying. "We are going to return what you've been handing out to bandits. We will lay it at your very feet, in your very palace. Of course, you may not be in a condition to appreciate our gift by the time you receive it."

Sirna could almost see the bared fangs.

Rylla sat back down and regal dignity seemed to settle on her like a cloak. "To repay you for the dangers you have been through on Our behalf, the Foundry deserves some suitable gift, to show the Throne's gratitude."

"If Your Majesty would care to entertain a suggestion—" Aranth began. Rylla nodded. "The best gift, would be to let me take a band of the Foundry men with you, when you invade Phaxos. The debt we want to pay isn't as big or as old as the Great Throne's, but it is enough."

The only person on the University Team who didn't conceal his or her surprise was Sirna. She merely raised an eyebrow.

"With pleasure. We will let you decide who goes and who stays. Meanwhile, We would ask of you one more service to the Throne. Seek out Prince Sarrask at the Silver Stag and say that his Queen requires his presence."

Sarrask was Acting Captain-General of Hos-Hostigos while Harmakros was campaigning with Kalvan. In spite of the time he spent at the Silver Stag or one of his other favorite haunts for emptying wine jugs and bedding available women, he was doing a fairly good job.

"I will go," Ranthar said. "My horse is fresher than Captain Aranth's." He bowed, then rose at a nod of dismissal from Rylla.

The University party filed out between the guards. The Queen's Own Bodyguard still bore halberds and two-handed swords, Sirna noticed, but since her last visit to Tarr-Hostigos they had sprouted pistols as well. The guards at the Tarr doorway had two apiece.

Ranthar Jard was long gone by the time they rode under the portcullis and downhill across the switchbacks to Hostigos Town. As soon as she could, Sirna dropped back to ride abreast of Aranth Saln.

"Aranth, you can't be volunteering for military service."

"Afraid you can't handle Lala without me?"

"Oh, you know what I mean! Rylla's been itching for Prince Araxes' giblets on toast for a year. Now she's finally got an excuse to take them."

"I can't un-volunteer, Sirna," Aranth said with a grin. "Not now, and not with Rylla and Sarrask running the show. I don't know whether I'd be accused of treason or mutiny, but it would be something capital. Don't worry, I won't take anybody with a family or who doesn't have some soldiering experience. Let the rest of them spend the next moon arguing over replacing damaged materials and how or when they're going to return to Nostor. I'm past being bored and this looks to be the most entertainment I've had since I left Home Time Line."

Sirna opened her mouth to reply indignantly, when she saw two of the Foundry guards trying not to smile. They probably thought she was Aranth's mistress, worried about his riding off to war!

Her silence let Aranth go on in a whisper. "Look, Sirna. This campaign in Phaxos is going to make trouble no matter what. It will make less if both the University and Paracops have a credible observer on hand. I'm credible to both. Ranthar isn't available or credible to the University. Or, at least not to Danthor Dras, and right now that's the same thing."

"May Styphon's demons piss on Danthor Dras!" Sirna muttered. She felt wholly unrepentant at such a thought about one of the University's most distinguished Scholars. Danthor might be the dean of Aryan-Transpacific scholars, but right now his century-long feud with the Paratime Police was *not* an asset to the people actually on the spot and getting shot at!

The hill became steeper, and Sirna had to give all her attention to controlling her horse. Her mind found room for only one memory; how that film of the two tigers had ended. They had attacked the hunters around them, dying in the end of spear and arrow wounds, but killing between them no less than eight men.

Prince Araxes had signed his death warrant by cornering Rylla. What price would the Great Queen pay?

II

Prince Sarrask of Sask, splendidly attired in green and gold velvet, entered Rylla's chambers with a flourish. Under his silvered and plumed high-combed helmet, Sarrask's face was flushed, from either exertion or drink. While his features were more fleshed out than at the end of last year's long campaign, it was apparent that Sarrask had not regained all the weight he had lost. On many occasions, Rylla had seen the Prince out in the inner courtyard early in the morning practicing arms.

"I heard about the ambush of the Royal Foundry team, Your Majesty. A terrible travesty! Prince Araxes has gone too far, by Dralm's Beard—excuse me, Your Grace!"

"You are excused, you old rascal." It was bad enough that Prince Araxes had bolted from Hos-Hostigos during the middle of last year's war against Styphon's Holy Host; now he added insult upon injury. Kalvan, with his soft ways, didn't understand how the insubordination of princes could spread like an epidemic. Maybe things were easier in the Princedom of Pennsylvania, but here compassion was seen as weakness.

And this dangerous and subversive idea that underlings could do as they pleased had spread!

Their former Chancellor, Xentos, had slapped her in the face with his refusal to bring the Council of Dralm to heel. What good was his being Primate, if all he did was fill parchments with dead words? Hostigos needed deeds, gold and weapons from her friends, not empty words and promises! She refused to even think about the Leak of Dralm—*But to business,* she told herself. "What should be our reply to such a egregious violation of our border, Prince Sarrask?"

"I say we go into Phaxos Town and hang Araxes from his own battlements! That should teach him, once and for all, the price of insolence to his betters.

"Good. Your view matches my own. I grow weary of this upstart's insults to the Great Throne of Hos-Hostigos." Rylla motioned Demia's nursemaid, who had followed Rylla into the audience chamber, to bring her over to Rylla.

"Demia, say hello to your Uncle Sarrask!"

Demia goo-gooed and squealed with joy. The nursemaid, after looking at Rylla for approval, set her in the bear-sized Sarrask's lap.

Sarrask caught Demia and lifted her up to his face where he proceeded to make a series of most un-Princely noises. "Little Demia you have your mother's eyes and nose, your father's forehead, and Prince Ptosphes' smile. What a fireseed shell you're going to make! If you were a little older, why I'd think about making you Princess of Sask."

Seeing Rylla's up-turned eyebrows, Sarrask reddened in embarrassment—a sight Rylla had not expected to see in her lifetime, or any other!

"No—I didn't mean that as it sounded, Your *Majesty,* I mean no disrespect to you or your daughter!"

"None taken, Sarrask. I pray to Yirtta Allmother that when Demia grows up that she has many retainers as faithful and loyal as yourself."

Sarrask smiled and brought Demia closer for a chaste buss on the cheek.

Rylla found her stomach beginning to turn. What had come over her? Not long ago she had hated this man above all others, except maybe for Gormoth of Nostor. Had she changed that much in little more than a year—or had they both changed? Kalvan must have bewitched them both. Yet, if he had, it was a good spell, for Sarrask of Sask made a much better friend than enemy.

The nursemaid removed Demia from Sarrask's lap and she began to cry. Rylla signaled it was time for the little princess's nap.

Now for the true test. "Prince Sarrask, what would you say, if I told you I wanted you to act as joint commander of a punitive expedition to go into Phaxos and teach those Styphoni-lovers a lesson in fireseed diplomacy?"

Sarrask smiled as if he had just been given the first of three wishes. "How soon can we leave?"

"That's exactly what I wanted to hear, Prince! Soon. Very soon. I want you to draw up a list of all the troops we can muster divided into those we should leave here to garrison the town and Tarr-Hostigos, and those for the Army of Retribution. Then I want you to help me draft letters to General Hestophes and Prince Phrames."

"What about your husband?"

"I will write to Kalvan when we have finished our work in Phaxos. We would not want to divert his attention from his great purpose in the Trygath, would we?"

Sarrask smiled again, only this smile was more predatory then friendly; Rylla was sure it mirrored the one creasing her own face. Unfortunately, her husband did not understand that a Great King could not let petty Princes, like Araxes, walk unmolested on their betters' toes. Because, if you let them get away with that, the next thing you knew someone bigger and even nastier would be turning over the throne.

It wasn't Kalvan's fault he didn't understand these things, as he liked to remind her things were different in the City of Brotherly Love. However, it would be a long, long time before even Princes and Great Kings treated each other as equals in the Six Kingdoms. That was just the way things were. And no amount of wishing, praying or hoping was going to change this; at least, not until Styphon's House was vanquished once and for all. That reminded her, she needed to talk with Baron Zothnes and find out how many of Styphon's temples were housed in Phaxos; the treasury could use more gold and silver coin. After the war in the Trygath was over they would need to invade Hos-Harphax; well, that was, if Kalvan returned before the fall rains. If not, maybe she could cook up a surprise of her own, assuming that Phaxos was justly served.

III

Verkan Vall was reviewing the last of the message balls on his horseshoe desk when his secretary buzzed. He looked out the big window and saw Ranthar Jard, still in his Aryan-Transpacific breastplate and morion helmet. *I hope nothing bad happened to the Foundry party on their way to Nostor,* Verkan thought. Even two years AK, After Kalvan, there were parts of Nostor where bandits and robber barons held sway, in anybody's book, a dangerous place for a party of academics. And, today of all days, Verkan did not need a dust-up with the University crowd. He was cleaning off his desk in preparation for a trip to Greffa, with Dalla along this time. It was as close to a holiday as they'd had since he'd taken over as Paratime Chief.

Lately, former Chief Tortha Karf, as Trader Tortha, was spending more time on Kalvan's Time-Line than he was. And that struck him as awfully unfair.

Ranthar practically ran into the room, shaking his head.

"What's up?"

"Chief, we've got problems. A group of Phaxosi soldiers hit the Nostor Foundry party—"

So much for this vacation. Any foul-up involving the Kalvan Study Team was a possible public relations disaster. "How are the Study Team members? Any losses or serious injuries?"

"No, Chief. A few cuts and abrasions, but there were no serious injuries, except some hurt pride. And we know who they're going to take that out on, don't we?"

Verkan expelled his breath. "Well, that's good news. I guess."

Ranthar laughed. "I wouldn't have lost any sleep over it, if Talgran Dreth or Varnath Lala had taken a lead pill!"

"I would have, think of all the forms we'd of had to fill out."

Ranthar slapped his head. "Forgot about that. Sorry, but that's all the good news. The bad news is that Rylla is going to use this as an excuse to declare war on Prince Araxes of Phaxos!"

"While Kalvan's away, fighting the nomads." Verkan paused to whistle. "Rylla could blow the lid off Hostigos' relations with both Hos-Agrys and Hos-Zygros; to say nothing of all the other princes and barons who will see this as evidence of Kalvan's empire building. On top of that, there's no real precedent for women generals on Aryan-Transpacific; if Rylla fails in her attack, she makes Hostigos—and by extension—Kalvan a laughing stock. If she wins, it could be good publicity; plenty humiliating for the Styphoni, but there's more to lose than to gain here. Or else prove that Kalvan can't maintain control in both the bedroom and the battlefield. He loses either way. Does Kalvan know?"

"No. And, thanks to some of Ermut's Best, at the Silver Stag I learned that she's not about to tell him. Of course, Rylla has good old Sarrask of Sask, as he told me with great pride, firmly in her corner."

"Ouch. He's a good fighter, but not much of a thinker. Can we get word to Kalvan of her plans?"

"Not without disrupting his work in the Trygath, where he's most needed. You got my message ball about Kalvan recognizing Nestros as Great King of Hos-Rathon?"

"Yes, I wondered about the advisability of that move," Verkan said.

"It seems that was Nestros' price for joining forces with Kalvan against the nomads."

"Cheeky bastard, isn't he! I think Nestros is letting the short term benefits outweigh the long-term liabilities. Wait until Styphon's House learns they have a 'new' *Great* Kingdom along their western border. Maybe it will work to Kalvan's benefit; certainly, he's found a reliable ally—at last. Now, if only Nestros can fight!"

"He's done a good job with the kingdom of Rathon, which was about half its present size at the death of his father. That expansion proves he can fight. And these nomad invasions are almost a yearly phenomenon in the Trygathi hinterlands. We'll know before long, Chief.

"Just before I left, I got a radio message from Dalon Sath that Kalvan and Nestros have taken to the field. A lot of Kalvan's strays have caught up, thanks to the delay. It looks like between the Army of the Trygath and the Hos-Rathon Army they have fielded over sixty thousand soldiers."

"But will that be enough? Latest visual confirmation and computer projection of the nomad army estimates the main nomad horde to contain close to two hundred and fifty thousand fighting men."

"I hadn't heard those figures. If Kalvan's not careful, he could end up in hot water all the way up to his chin. Is there anything we can do to help?"

Verkan shook his head. "My hands are tied. We've already come close enough to Transtemporal Contamination on Kalvan Prime, so a few well-placed lightning strikes—or Thanor's bolts, as the Urgothi clansmen call them—are out of the picture. Kalvan's on his own this time.

IV

Ranjar Sargos shook his head in frustration, as the gaily-decorated warwagon jerked its way up the hillside. The brightly painted warwagon was a flatbed wagon pulled by four sacred white horses; there was a mast with a crossbeam from which hung a white banner with a black raven—the Raven Tribe's banner. A number of his Tribesmen, led by Warchief Vanar Halgoth, had formed a Raven Cult to worship the Raven Hag of War. At the top of the mast was a jawless cow skull, with both horns sheathed in hammered gold. At both sides of the front of the wagon were red poles, topped with impaled human skulls, the domes festooned with red, blue and yellow colored streamers.

How could Sargos mount an attack with more than a quarter of his force two to four days away, foraging for food for this marching belly of an army? An army, which, when it wasn't bickering among itself, was belching in hunger. His advance scouts had just reported that Kalvan's Army was less than a day's ride away! Already, entire tribes were breaking off so that they could have the 'honor' of being first in battle. Next it would be clans leaving, if he did not call the War Council soon.

Sargos turned to his second-in-command, Warchief Ulldar Zodan. "How do we proceed against the dirtmen?"

Ulldar's beaked-nose face was covered with war paint in runic designs. Upon his head sat a horned helmet, his long gray hair hanging behind in a braided queue. "The Easterners will try to pick the battleground. It is their way. They wish to concentrate their firepower, since they are out-numbered. The Daemon Kalvan, unlike most of the Eastern Lords, has horses to drag his large guns with him—they are the most dangerous, as they are packed with chains and metal scrap. One shot can empty two-score of saddles."

"Then we must bring Kalvan to us, not go to him."

"Warlord, that is easier to say than to do. While our army is great in number, they are poor in what the Easterner's call 'discipline.'"

Sargos nodded. "There is much truth in your words, Warchief Ulldar. Maybe we can use our hotheads to cover our movements. Allow those without patience to blunt Kalvan's swords."

"There is much wisdom in this path." Warchief Ulldar, grabbed hold of the side of the wagon for support, as it traversed an especially bumpy stretch of terrain. "The Daemon Kalvan is a master of the arts of war. It will be most difficult to draw him into an ambush. Instead, let us pick a spot where our superior numbers will take the day. Men die just as easily from arrows and darts as they do from 'bullets.' Kalvan may have the gods' favor, but his soldiers are men like any other."

"Kalvan is not the only one who is touched by the gods," Sargos cried, thumping his chest.

Once again, the war wagon lurched from side to side and Sargos held tightly to keep his balance.

"We all pray, Warlord, that your medicine is stronger than the Daemon Kalvan's." Like many chiefs, Ulldar was also a wizard and healer.

"You speak the truth. But, unlike Kalvan, we do not have the gift of time. Our warriors grow more unruly every day. Entire clans threaten to desert us. But many remain who are willing to sacrifice their lives in their lust for glory and loot. It is up to us to spend them wisely."

Warchief Ulldar made a barking laugh. "Spend them we will. And when they have bloodied the Daemon's army we shall set loose our wolves of war."

THIRTY-THREE

I

Great King Kalvan placed his chapped and freezing fingers as close to the cook fire as he dared. All around them were snores of sleeping soldiers, the clanking of armor and the whinnying of horses. Great King Nestros, Captain-General Harmakros, Prince Ptosphes, Duke Mnestros, the Rathoni Captain-General, General Alkides and half a dozen other members of Kalvan's general staff huddled around the small fire, framed by the rising sun. Kalvan, who had called this impromptu war council, began, "I have received word from our 'agents' among the horde. Today they will attack in force."

"But why?" Nestros asked. "We have not budged from this mountaintop for a moon quarter. Why should today be any different than any other day?"

"Because we have won the waiting game; almost a third of the horde has dispersed, deserted or just plain vanished. Warlord Sargos knows this and realizes that if he doesn't commit his troops soon he will be the warlord of all the digits on his hands and toes and not much else. Even if we had wanted to bring the war to Sargos, we couldn't have since his forces have far greater mobility and speed. Sargos has been gambling that we would make the first move; now the waiting game is over and it's his turn in the barrel. The plain truth is the horde is running out of food, out of grazing land and forage and just plain patience. Now, they will come to us on our killing field."

"At last!" Captain-General Harmakros said. "Now we can finish off these interlopers once and for all. Kill most of them and disperse the rest; they'll starve soon enough returning over the blasted lands they left behind. Maybe then we'll have time to invade Hos-Harphax before the fall rains make the roads impassable."

"No. That's not what I have in mind." Everyone drew closer to see what new rabbit Kalvan was about to draw out of his hat. "First, we are too far west to be able to return to Hostigos, raise up another force and attack Hos-Harphax with any certainty before the fall rains come. To do so, we would have to stretch our lines too thin and fight with an army that's been in the field for seven moons or better." Kalvan went on to explain the physical demands that would be placed upon the Army of the Trygath to defeat and expel the nomads, for if they retired to soon, it would hearten the nomads and they would return in force, since there were more tribes still migrating into the Upper Sastragath and Trygath territories. To then turn around and march back to Hos-Hostigos and then, without any rest, invade Hos-Harphax—would be inviting disaster, especially if the weather turned severe or Prince Lysandros managed to raise a credible force to oppose them.

"However, if we can drive the nomads against Tarr-Ceros, the Archpriests will be shaking in their robes. They will be sending their gold and victuals to the Order, rather than to Hos-Harphax. The Inner Circle of Styphon's House knows all too well the nomads would love to pillage Hos-Ktemnos. And what is the plumpest prize in all Hos-Ktemnos: the Unholy City of Balph—right?"

There were murmurs of agreement from the assembled generals.

"Are we not agreed that the real enemy here is not these nomads and clansmen? Kalvan asked. "The clansmen are just pawns? No, our real enemy is Grand Master Soton and the Order of Zarthani Knights. It was Soton's plan to send the horde into the Trygath, to delay our attack upon Harphax City: Are we all agreed on this?"

"Your words ring with the truth," Harmakros replied. The others nodded their heads.

"Therefore, the tribesmen are not responsible for the lands they have ravaged. In truth, it is the Order—Styphon's hammer—which is responsible for their pillage and rapine."

Again, all heads nodded agreement.

"Then what could be better revenge than bringing these nomads into our camp and turning them upon the very Knights who sent them into King Nestor's realm?"

His question was greeted with a big savage grin on Harmakros' face, while Nestros displayed a lupine and toothy smile. "I like the way you think, King Kalvan," the latter said.

Kalvan grinned. "It's not going to be easy. We're going to have to defeat this bunch—and don't forget they out-number us two to one—without destroying their military effectiveness. All without taking too many casualties ourselves. Of course, we'll keep this plan to ourselves, no need in confusing the rank and file. One of our priorities will be to isolate Warlord Sargos and his top command, splitting them off from their warriors and capturing them alive—if at all possible. Without Sargos and his headmen, we will not be able to control the horde ourselves. So top priority is capturing Warlord Sargos."

"What if something happens to Sargos?" Nestros asked.

"Then forget all about turning the horde upon the Knights. Kill them all and pray to Galzar Wolfhead we don't run out of ammunition first!"

II

Kalvan dismounted at the top of Grax Hill. While his dignity might require meeting King Nestros on horseback, his horse required a rest. The retreat of the Hostigi Royal party from the left flank had been more speedy than dignified, over rough, muddy ground. A few of the Royal Horse Guard were still fishing themselves out from under bushes and rounding up their horses.

From the hilltop, Kalvan had his first good view of the battle in more than an hour. The nomad horde was large, maybe seventy-five to a hundred thousand warriors, a flood of men, as hard for Ranjar Sargos to direct as for Kalvan to stop. Not much had changed, and of that little for the better. The enemy's right and center, under Sargos, still overlapped the allied left. They had even advanced all the way to the redoubt on the banks of the Lydistros, now stopped among the caltrops and pitfalls, under the fire of the one four-pounder Kalvan could spare for fixed defenses.

As Kalvan watched, a large force of what appeared to be medieval cavalry out of the Thirteenth Century on otherwhen—wearing chainmail hauberks and kettle helmets—broke off from the enemy center, riding their horses into the caltrops. The screams of the falling and injured horses ripped through the air and beat on his ears. The impromptu caltrops had been welded together out of broken swords, spear points and plow blades. Before the dust settled, two regiments of mixed musketeers and arquebusier were pouring volley after volley into the stalled cavalrymen, blunting the horde's attack. Still, the horsemen drove on, over fallen comrades and horses. Already, the Hostigi musketeers were falling back to the next prepared position.

Kalvan turned to one of his messengers, pointing at the retreating musketeers. "Request Prince Ptosphes to send two companies of Mobile Force rifleman to shore up that position."

"Yes, Your Majesty!" The officer jumped onto his mount and rode off.

On the allied right, masses of horsemen, light infantry wearing boiled leather armor and chainmail, a few score fully armored knights Sargos had picked up Styphon knows where and an occasional chariot surged back and forth. Each chief was giving his own orders to his followers and taking none from anyone else, including Sargos. They were the less dangerous but more numerous part of the enemy army; roughly seventy thousand against Sargos' forty thousand, give or take a few thousand.

They faced mostly Nestros' Trygathi, eight to nine thousand heavy horse, with twice that number of supporting infantry, spearmen, swordsmen, and missile troops—crossbowmen, archers, some arquebusiers and even a few slingers. The Trygathi were stiffened by three Ulthori pike regiments, two regiments of Royal Musketeers, a brigade of riflemen and two four-pounders. Not that the Trygathi needed much stiffening; they were fighting with the knowledge that they had a chance of victory and that meanwhile their homes were safe. The alliance with Hos-Hostigos had let Nestros leave a third of his army home to make raiders a poor insurance risk. The twenty-five thousand he had on the field were his best.

"General Alkides!" Kalvan called downhill. "Is the flying battery ready to move?"

"With Galzar's favor, yes," the smoke-blackened artillery general replied. "I wish the guns really did have wings. This cursed mud's going to butcher the horses!"

"Not half as fast as those guns will butcher Sargos' warriors," Kalvan called back. The gun crews cheered their Great King's words. That started a chant of 'Down Styphon!' mixed in with 'Down Sargos!'

There were only eight guns for the Flying Battery; three more were in emplacements and one had been lost in a swamp on the Nyklos Trail. As much as he wished for another battery or two, with maybe some six or eight-pounders, the Flying Battery was a far cry from the half a dozen catapults the enemy was using.

Kalvan walked over to General Alkides and asked quietly. "How is Great Captain Mylissos doing?" Nestros' chief of artillery had started the day a bit peevish over the council of war. It had been agreed that his ancient bombards would remain with the reserves, and not try to advance with the major attacks. Kalvan could even sympathize with him; after all, it was the first time in memory that Mylissos actually had enough fireseed to fire his massive hooped-iron pipes more than once or twice without exhausting his powder magazines.

"A sight happier than he was, now that he's got targets and fireseed to burn on them. I think he shifted a couple of those twenty-pound bombards without orders, but I'm not complaining. A twenty-pounder loaded with rocks and old nails isn't something I would care to face!"

Kalvan would have liked to have said more, mostly to Aspasthar. The boy was fighting his first battle away from his father, riding with Alkides as one of his messengers. But the boy looked as if he would take the encouragement as an insult, and by Dralm, there was Nestros and his guards in their red and white colors coming up the other side of the hill!

By abandoning royal dignity and running back to his horse, Kalvan was mounted by the time Nestros reined in and hailed him.

"Greetings, friend and ally! We are smiting the horde as if the gods themselves fought for us!"

So we are. Maybe too hard. Corpses can't fight the Zarthani Knights. Thank somebody for Ranjar Sargos. He made the horde more dangerous, but if we had to take the surrender of every petty chief one at a time we'd be here until winter!

A Hostigi messenger rode up and saluted both kings. "The lookouts in the Willow Spirit Grove report that Warlord Sargos is advancing on the Grove. They spotted his banner, the black raven on a white field."

"Tell them to wait as long as they can, and imitate a strong force meanwhile," Nestros said. "Then they can withdraw. Meanwhile, Sargos will be drawn forward, perhaps we can meet him hand-to-hand!"

Kalvan and Captain-General Harmakros exchanged amused looks. Nestros was no fool; he was familiar with feints and deceptions. At heart, though, he was also an old-style Trygathi warrior, whose highest ambition had to be meeting the opposing leader hand-to-hand and defeating him.

"As the gods will it," Harmakros said. Kalvan decided to let his Captain-General speak, even if protocol said he should be talking King-to-King. Even four-star generals needed something to take their minds off their sons' winning their spurs—or their shrouds.

"The gods willed that Sargos should be a fool," Nestros said cheerfully. "They also willed that Kalvan should come and bring his fireseed and strength to join ours. I think they will give us this one more small favor."

Kalvan doubted the accuracy of Nestros' description of his opponent. The Warlord had pulled his chariots back the moment he realized the ground was too muddy to let them get up speed. He still had his in reserve, while the other chiefs had mostly lost chariots, riders and teams together.

"Let the gods will that all our men hold their fire until they have a clear target, and that they be an enemy," Kalvan said. "We have more fireseed than any army ever seen in the Trygath, but not yet enough to waste!"

"My men are not children," Nestros said with offended dignity.

"Then let the heralds sound for the advance," Kalvan said. Both kings looked at Harmakros; he signaled the trumpeter. The brazen voice sounded, was picked up and relayed, triggering the launching of two signal rockets.

When the green rockets rose into the sky over Grax Hill, six thousand reserve cavalry would be launched at the heart of Sargos' army.

III

Sargos flung a javelin high into the willow branches. A scream rewarded him; an enemy lookout toppled from his perch and lay writhing until an archer dispatched him with a knife.

The heavy thud of many horses on the move reached the Warlord over the noise of his warriors clearing the willow grove of enemies. Sargos jerked his horse around and drew his last javelin from its leather bucket next to his right stirrup. His household guards followed suit, and the whole band streamed at a canter around the left side of the grove. He had left the war-wagons behind with the reserve, three thousand heavy lancers—mostly hillmen, and six hundred chariots that were as useful on these muddy fields as udders on an ox. Warchief Vanar Halgoth and his Raven Cult berserkers were beating upon their shields and screaming taunts into the air. Althea and Headman Jardar Hyphos were on the move with twelve thousand light archers, most armed with horn bows and leather armor. Sargos didn't hold them in high regard, since they were as wheat before Kalvan's steel scythe of iron hats and cannon, or fire tubes as the tribesmen called them.

Ah, would that I had men to be my eyes and ears on parts of the field I cannot reach myself! Such is Kalvan's way, or so the prisoners have told us. Yet how could they reach me, in the midst of my foes, to bear their messages? To remain in the rear, merely so that I may know more—that is a coward's way and no warrior would follow me.

A contrary voice in Sargos' mind muttered, *Kalvan leads that way, as often as not, and who says that those who follow him are not warriors? Enough of your warriors are with Wind after meeting them!*

Clear of the willows, Sargos reined in and stared in disbelief. Riding down the hill in the enemy's center moved two mighty bands of armored horsemen, like vast steel-scaled serpents. Toward the head of each band floated banners, the red and white colors of King Nestros and the maroon and green of King Kalvan.

So Kalvan will take his chance of joining the spirits today? Well and good.

As Sargos prepared to charge, he saw Althea riding up to him shouting, "There you are!"

Sargos smiled and lifted his arms. "To victory, or to death!"

"If you don't wait until my archers arrive, it will be death from my bow!"

Sargos gave Althea a smile that forced her to sit back in her saddle. "Now, you will have your chance to proof your archers, my dear. They will test their mettle on Kalvan's armor."

Althea put her hand up holding a short arrow with a wedge point. "These barbs have been tested against the Black Knights! Now let Kalvan choke upon them."

Sargos laughed! "If I should die today, we will meet again in the Hall of Heroes!"

Althea leaned over and bussed him on the cheek, saying, "Together, my hero. If you fall, I will die avenging you!"

Before Sargos could reply, Headman Hyphos rode up at the head of a small army of mounted archers. He waved his spear. Sargos called Hyphos over, "The Kings are coming. Let us join them. If Kalvan falls, his army will die!" Sargos knew that statement was true with a certainty that told him it had been delivered by the gods.

Ranjar Sargos stood tall in his stirrups. "Hyphos, send the archers to the flank. Sting them good! Halgoth tell your berserks to follow me. Ikkos and Trancyles, ride like the wind and bring in all the warriors Chiefs Ruflos and Egthrad can spare! Tell Warchief Ulldar it's time to use the reserve."

"The chariots, too?"

"Yes. Let Kalvan's iron hats break their teeth upon them."

The two were young men on fresh horses; they vanished in a spray of mud clods. Sargos drew his sword and adjusted his throat guard, his one piece of armor that was metal all through instead of metal over leather. Althea waved as she rode off with her small army of archers. Headman Hyphos was just there for those hardheads who could not accept having to take orders from a woman—already, as Althea proved her prowess with the bow and as a commander, they grew fewer and fewer in number until now it was truly her command.

Sargos' sword hummed over his head as he whirled it. The day was too overcast for sunlight to shine on it, but those close by saw it and heard it humming. Their shouts told others what was happening, and the war cries rose until they seemed a solid wall across the front of the advancing foe.

Then Sargos made a quick prayer to the Raven Hag, lowered his sword and spurred his horse through the thicket. Behind him came the thunder of thousands of charging horses. A moment later he broke through the hedge and onto a rise, where he surprised a troop of Rathoni iron hats. One lifted a poleax and before he could strike, Sargos' sword buried itself in his armpit, where the chainmail armor was most vulnerable. The axeman lost his balance, bleeding profusely, and dropped both poleax and reins. Sargos slashed his sword at the horses' neck, opening a long scarlet wound; the horse bucked off its rider and knocked into two more horses. The iron hat was lost in the churning hooves.

Moments later the archer vanguard was by his side, sowing death and confusion among the Rathoni iron hats. At this close range, their arrows went through the Rathoni chainmail armor like cheesecloth. "Red!" he cried. One-Eyed Red, splattered with blood, but uninjured, rushed to his side.

"Warlord?"

"I've got a message for Althea. Tell her to ride right up to our foes before they fire. If they'll hold their formation and fire at twenty rods, they can cripple Kalvan's flank!"

One-Eyed Red nodded, pumped his arm, turned his mount and rode away.

IV

Only one of the green rockets flew high enough to be seen. That was enough. The cheers from both armies drowned out the trumpeters and captains like a hurricane drowning out a mouse's squeak.

King Nestros was pointing frantically downhill. "There! Behind that hedge! Sargos forms his battle line! We must reach it before he brings up reinforcements."

Nestros couldn't have been in more of a hurry if he'd read Napoleon's maxim, "Ask me for anything but time." Once again he was doing the tactically sound thing, out of a desire to cross swords with an enemy chief.

On his head be it, thought Kalvan.

No, wait a minute. If Nestros gets too far ahead of you, the Trygathi will say their Great King was braver than the Great King of Hos-Hostigos.

"Harmakros!" What would have been a shout under other circumstances was about as audible as a whisper.

The Captain-General reined in beside Kalvan. "Yes, Your Majesty?"

"You stay back here with the mobile command post. I have to charge with Nestros."

"That Dralm Bl—" began Harmakros, who thought better of using his trooper's vocabulary about an allied king, instead he mock-saluted. "As Your Majesty wishes."

Kalvan started to count off guards to ride with him, then saw Nestros and his heavy cavalry digging in their own spurs. This time Kalvan had to restrain *his* curses. Instead he signaled his own bannerbearer and dug in his spurs. It was a good thing Rylla wasn't here; she'd never let him forget this charge!

The bannerbearer took the reins in his teeth and drew his sword. Bearing the Great King's banner had been a much safer job than fighting in the front ranks—at least, until today!

V

Sargos jumped his horse over a ditch and turned it, meanwhile drawing his sword. To retreat was cowardly more often than not, but to stand with the men he had would not even slow the enemy. Like the Great Mother River flooding, the enemy horse flowed on as if only the gods could stop them.

Crossbowmen were running up, but the range was still long. At this distance against armored men they would most likely waste their bolts. Against the enemy's horses, perhaps—"Hold your fire! Wait until they're closer and aim for their horses."

"Look, my chief!" Warchief Halgoth was pointing. He had just arrived with a hundred and fifty of his Raven Clan, some of them panting and foaming at the mouth, not six deep breaths ago. "Warlord, the kings offer themselves to the gods!"

It was true. The two royal banners were forging steadily toward the head of the enemy horsemen. Under those banners, Sargos could now see tight bands of splendidly armored cavalry. Their polished and silvered armor glistened under the lances of sunlight than poked out of the dark clouds above. *Is this a warning or blessing from the god?*

"They offer themselves to us!" Sargos snapped, since the gods refused to give their answer. He tried to quiet his own doubts. *Have the kings had an omen, that the gods will give victory if they offer themselves as a sacrifice?*

"Then let us take what is offered," Warchief Vanar Halgoth cried.

Sargos patted his horse's neck and looked about him. The warriors he'd summoned were streaming toward him from all sides. Already the first of the chariots was in sight. Not all would be with him before he had to face the Kings, but the rest would know enough to fling themselves on the foe.

"Hoaaa! Tonight we offer two Kings' heads, to the gods of our land and the spirits of our dead!"

THIRTY - F⊕UR

I

Captain-General Harmakros paced back and forth, puffing on his pipe, as he watched the two kings race down the hillside with their armies trailing behind. He was sweating so much, that he took off his burgonet helmet and wiped his forehead. This was the kind of stunt he expected from Rylla, not Great King Kalvan, for Dralm's sake! If anything happened to Kalvan, this army of the Great Kings would fall apart like a rock-gutted ocean galley.

Even worse, Harmakros truly enjoyed being in the thick of the action, as Kalvan called it, rather than watching the battle like a spectator. His hand, of its own volition, found his sword hilt and he had to forcibly restrain himself from drawing steel. Down the hill, he saw the Warlord's men leaving the Spirit Grove to support their center. There was a colorful wagon that had to be Ranjar Sargos war wagon, with the Warlords Raven banner —a black raven on a white field.

Then Harmakros saw a sight that almost took his breath away; a large force of light archers coming out of a copse of trees. The archers were angling toward the Army of the Trygath's right flank, where the Rathoni Army was thickest. Harmakros had fought with the Sastragathi archers and knew first hand how much damage their compound bone and sinew bows could wreak—even on good plate armor.

343

Harmakros turned to one of his colonels and ordered, "Tell the Mounted Rifles to mount up and protect the right flank. There's about fifteen to twenty thousand light archers about to hit Nestros' Army. If they have a commander who's worth his pay, they'll turn the Rathon flank and Dralm knows what damage they'll do!"

The Colonel looked at his Captain-General as if he'd taken a sharp rap to the head without his helmet on. "Archers!"

One of the problem with the new crop of officers, since Kalvan had arrived in Hostigos, was they tended to think only in terms of rifles, guns and rate of fire. They had never watched a Sastragathi mounted archer shoot a pigeon—the kind Kalvan called Passenger Pigeons—out of a tall tree, or fire three arrows in the space of time it took to say the words.

"Yes, tell Colonel Democriphon that an army of archers are about to join the right flank. He'll know what to do." Democriphon was a good soldier, even if he was a bit of a dandy. Kalvan was thinking about raising his rank to general, with the general rank inflation that occurred when an army doubled its size every winter, it was well deserved.

Already Colonel Democriphon and the Mounted Rifles were advancing downhill. The archers were harrying the Rathoni flank and Harmakros could see the formation begin to fray. Meanwhile, Sargos substantial reserves had come out of the woods, joining the large host of tribesmen and nomads at the bottom of the hill, waiting for the allied army. He saw the colorful great six and eight-man chariots, he'd only heard about before in tales around the campfire, strengthening the nomad center.

The flying battery, was limping—rather than flying—its way down the hillside. One of the larger guns, probably an eight-pounder, had hit a pothole and was tipped over on its side. Engineers and artillerymen scrambled over the disabled cannon like a horse-kicked termite's nest. While the rest of the battery was continuing down hill, Sargos great host was forming up to meet Kalvan and Nestros head on!

II

The advance of the two kings was turning into a race. Nestros reached the horde first. Kalvan swerved without slowing, nearly colliding with his bannerbearer, holding Kalvan's personal flag—a maroon keystone on a green field. The trooper's sword pricked Kalvan's horse, which protested by nearly bucking his rider into a ditch.

By the time Kalvan had sorted himself out, Nestros was crossing swords with everyone in reach. Nestros had won the race but not by enough to dishonor his ally.

In fact, his ally was going to have a busy time in about two minutes, keeping this from being Nestros' first and last battle as Great-King-Elect. On both right and left, warriors were streaming toward the battle of kings.

"Stands the standard of Great King Kalvan!" the bannerbearer shouted. He thrust the butt-end of the staff into the muddy ground and drew a pistol. The bannerbearer pistoled the first warrior to come within lance-range, but the nomad stayed in the saddle. Kalvan shot him with his horse pistol, then drew his own sword and cut a second opponent across the face, a third in the arm.

Few of the nomads here had real armor and Kalvan's old-style heavy horse cut through the first ranks of light cavalrymen like a sword through a wedge of cheese. Kalvan took a few sword blows, but gave five times what he received. His heavy armor easily absorbing the blows, although his muscles ached and a sword point had left a cut on his cheek. The nearest he came to being hurt was when his horse was shot in the chest, but the heavily gilded horse armor that Nestros had given Kalvan as a gift, did its job and his horse was just shaken up rather than mortally wounded.

After that, Kalvan lost count of his opponents and all track of what he was doing to them. Somewhere in the next five minutes he managed one coherent thought that was not concerned with his own survival. *If I was fighting armored opponents, I'd be dead by now.*

Then, about five minutes after that, it struck him that armor might not make all that much difference. These nomads were damned hard to kill, like the Moro *juramentados* he had heard an Old Army veteran describe. *Come on, Alkides! Are you the Flying Battery or the Flighty Battery?* Kalvan moved his head down, just in time to avoid decapitation by a double-headed axe wielded by a warrior wearing a buffalo-head hat with horns and all.

Suddenly the mass of tribesmen and light cavalry moved aside as scores of huge chariots drove forward straight towards Kalvan's center, which was already stalled by the attacking clansmen and the thousands of dead littering the battlefield. Kalvan pulled out his last loaded pistol and fired a shot at the lead chariot, and by some miracle—since it was better than a hundred feet away—the ball hit the driver full on in the abdomen. The driver was pitched out of the chariot, while the horses panicked, tossing the chariot into a band of heavy lancers, knocking riders and horses every which way.

Then the chariots slammed into the charging Hostigi cavalry and it was a real donnybrook! Kalvan saw Nestros, surrounded by his heavily armored bodyguard, attacking one of the chariots. Kalvan's own Lifeguard was trying to push him back, while simultaneously moving into the thick of the nomad lines.

A moment later, Alkides' octet of four-pounders signaled their arrival with a blast of case shot that tore into the ranks of friend and foe with awful impartiality. A chunk of iron snapped the banner staff; the banner-bearer dove to keep it from hitting the ground and sprawled with his nose digging up the mud. He held the banner clear of the ground, though.

Kalvan leaned down to pick up the banner, and then found his horse sagging to one side. As the animal toppled, Kalvan leaped clear, the weight of his armor driving him to his knees. The horse fell on his side, crushing its armor, blew blood from his nostrils and died.

Kalvan waved his sword at the enemy and cursed Alkides' gunners, both emotionally satisfying if not very useful. At least the scattered dead men and horses around him included more enemies than friends. *If this were a hurricane,* he thought, *it would definitely be the eye.*

Let's hope to Galzar we didn't wing Nestros!

More cavalry were riding up, a second troop of Nestros' Bodyguard. Their captain reined in, shouting a request for orders.

"Look to your King!" Kalvan shouted back. "He's beyond that hedge. If you get no orders from him, advance cautiously five hundred rods."

"As Your Majesty commands," the captain called. "Will you be here?"

"Here or in Hadron's Realm!" was Kalvan's parting shot. The regiment cheered as their colonel maneuvered his horse through the hedge. More shouts of 'Down Sargos!' and they disappeared into the woods.

Kalvan mentally crossed his fingers, hoping he had not sent away men he would need for his own protection. But no live enemies were within lance range that he could see, and Alkides' guns were now firing steadily. That meant Harmakros and the reserves had to be closer than any organized enemies.

He was safe enough, from his enemies. He wished he could say the same about Rylla's tongue.

When my lovely wife hears that I raced a Trygathi king into the enemy lines, the first thing she'll do is laugh herself silly. The second is remind me never to complain about her leading a charge from in front again as long as I live!

III

For the first time in her life, Althea knew what it was like to be a man—as bullets whizzed by like metal bees and the screams of wounded horses rent the air. It made her both sick and exhilarated. Her archers were within spitting distance of the Rathoni cavalry and the armor-piercing arrows were taking a terrible toll on the surprised and now disorganized Trygathi. The air was so filled with arrows that it was as if a veil had been put between her and the sun. If she could put enough fear into these dirtmen, they would break: it had always been this way. Then her warriors could turn upon the rear of the Hostigi soldiers and grind Kalvan's warriors between the teeth of her archers and her man's great army.

Althea saw one captain try to organize a counter-attack and put an arrow through the eyehole of his helm, knocking him backwards off his horse. The dirtmen were beginning to stall and the constant deluge of arrows was thinning the enemy ranks. She saw one light cavalryman with a leather jerkin, who had so many arrows sticking off of him he looked like a porcupine as he fell out of his saddle. Arrows pierced many of the armored men and some of them had five or six wounds, leaking blood. She smiled fiercely as Headman Hyphos faced down a charging iron hat and grabbed his lance with his hand, upending the horseman.

Then she heard a sound like that of thunder, but different from that of the firesticks. Hundreds of her archers were knocked down or pitched out of their saddles. She pushed her way though the milling men, hitting them with her bow. "Keep shooting!"

There was another thunder clap and hundreds more dropped. Now the iron hats were reforming. Althea had to see what was happening to her army. Something sharp parted her hair and for a moment she was blind as blood filled her eyes. Ignoring the pain, she used her sleeve to wipe her eyes. Her archers were completely disorganized now. Many had turned their mounts and were fleeing back to safety. Others milled around like sheep caught in the open and surrounded by a wolf pack.

Althea looked up the hill and saw several hundred dismounted cavalry-men with the firesticks that Sargos called arquebuses. But these weren't the usual firesticks that had to be right next to a target to hit it. She doubted that her strongest archers could match the range of these 'new' terrible firesticks.

As another thunderclap sounded and cleared saddles by the score, Althea gave the order to sound retreat! It was time to disengage from the enemy and find Sargos to tell him about these new firesticks before they surprised him, too.

IV

Warlord Sargos had just sliced the arm off a Hostigi soldier with his bat-tleaxe, when he saw Althea—her face bloody—riding toward him. His heart almost stopped beating until he realized that it was dried blood, not fresh. "What news do you bring?"

Althea looked down to avoid his eyes.

"What happened to your archers?" He knew in his heart the news was bad because she would have never left them otherwise.

She looked up. "Kalvan's men hit us with far firesticks. They shot my army apart, far beyond even our arrows range. I had the horns blown rather than see our archers die like puppies in a bag tossed into the river."

Sargos said, "You have done all anyone could. We are losing ground here, too. Kalvan's big fire tubes are butchering our warriors. Right before Sargos' eyes, one of the chariots took a direct hit from a cannon ball, snowing the clansmen with splinters.

He saw a big chunk heading their way and shoved Althea out of her saddle. Then something hard hit Sargos' head and before he could react the world turned pitch black.

V

Captain-General Harmakros hastily pulled on his high-combed helmet. The battle of the two kings had changed dramatically in the last half candle. The Mounted Rifles had taken a terrible toll on the archer cavalry and after half a dozen volleys the archers had left the field. That allowed their heavily battered Rathoni allies to reform and re-join the main battle downhill, which had already changed momentum following the arrival of Alkides Flying Batteries. Using case shot, the guns had scythed through the horde, killing thousands and putting even more to flight. He had watched in amazement as entire troops disappeared and war chariots were blown into kindling.

Harmakros gave marching orders for the rest of the reserve and then mounted his horse and left to join the waiting Mounted Rifles. He noticed that his pipe was still clenched between his teeth, and when he removed it from his mouth he saw that the he'd almost bitten through the stem.

Harmakros spurred his horse on. He might have missed the battle's main course, but he was determined to get his share of the table scraps!

VI

Kalvan knew the tide of battle had turned for good when he saw there were no nomads within pistol shot. Already the nomad army was breaking up and scattering to the wind. His soldiers and Nestros' were gearing up for the chase and slaughter to follow; soon it would be time to give the order to the horn blowers to sound a halt.

As Kalvan and his Lifeguard were maneuvering between the dead horses and piles of bodies, he spotted two soldiers, one a clansman the other a Rathoni soldier, pinned together in an eternal embrace by crossbow bolts. The battle was still in force, although on this part of the battlefield it had evolved into a hundred small desperate actions—each one a life and death struggle to the participants, even though the main battle of the horde had broken. The Urgothi were similar to the early Germanic tribesman, who faced the Roman legions; they often chose an honorable death over capture and possible imprisonment—or slavery. Having seen more than his share of Styphon's Temple farm slave pens, Kalvan didn't blame them.

One figure drew Kalvan's eye. In the midst of a mound of dead bodies five or six high and surrounded by Nestros' men-at-arms, stood the largest soldier Kalvan had ever seen here-and-now—bigger even than Rylla's big bodyguard Xykos. Kalvan had thought Duke Mnestros was big—if this giant wasn't seven feet tall, he was six foot, eleven inches. The giant Urgothi, with his winged conical helmet and a blond walrus mustache, looked as if he'd just stepped out of a Viking dragonship.

The giant, and eight or nine other warriors wearing the same winged helmets, were grouped around a Raven Banner that Kalvan identified as belonging to Warlord Sargos. These winged warriors must be part of Sargos' personal bodyguard, thought Kalvan. He had heard that Sargos was 'blessed' with visions from the Raven Goddess. If Kalvan remembered correctly, the Viking berserkers often made sacrifices to their Crow Goddess. He motioned to his Lifeguard to follow behind and made his way carefully over the littered battlefield on his borrowed horse.

At almost the same moment, a company of Mounted Rifles led by Colonel Democriphon, rode up to the battling warriors. The tableau froze, friend and foe alike, when the Mounted Riflemen aimed their rifles at the battling Urgothi.

Everyone on the battlefield has seen those rifles in action and knew that death was in the air. The fighting stopped and Nestros' heavy infantry began to pull back. The giant Viking laughed and held up his huge sword and began to twirl it in circles above his head in preparation for the berserker death charge.

"HALT!" Kalvan shouted.

Everyone paused, including the giant berserker. "The battle is over."

One of the riflemen started to aim his rifle, but the flat of Democriphon's sword blade knocked it aside. "Don't try that again, or it'll be your head. That was your Great King!"

The giant looked back and forth, between the two men, his lungs laboring like bellows. Then he lowered his sword and sunk the point into the muddy loan. "If I am to surrender, let it be to a real King." He nodded to Kalvan.

Kalvan rode over, his Lifeguard crowding him like mother hens. The other winged warriors had set down their axes and swords.

When Kalvan rode up within arms distance, the giant bowed his head and said, "I will surrender, but first I must know the name of the man who saved my life."

"I am Great King Kalvan of Hos-Hostigos."

"Your fame has traveled far, Great King Kalvan. I offer you my sword." Even before his Lifeguard could draw a breath, the giant had reached over, drawn his sword blade out of the ground and, in a magician-like maneuver, flipped it in the air so that the sword hilt, not the blade, landed in Kalvan's hands. The sound of breaths being drawn in and then suddenly released in relief sounded all around him.

Kalvan's hand felt as if it had just been hit with a bat, but he didn't blink.

The giant watched and then smiled. In a thick Trygathi accent, he said, "Yes, this King is worthy of respect. I am Vanar Halgoth. Someday I will fight at your side."

Kalvan nodded his head. "Vanar Halgoth, I would be honored to count you among my warriors and as a friend. If you give your word, not to try and escape or harm my soldiers, I will grant you parole."

"You have my word as a man and my honor as a disciple of the Raven Hag of War."

Kalvan turned to Colonel Democriphon, "Give parole to any one of Sargos' Bodyguard that give their oath. These are honorable men."

Halgoth turned to his warriors and rattled off a speech in Urgothi. After each one held his hand over his chest, the giant turned and said, "They give their word."

Kalvan nodded. "Follow this man, Colonel Democriphon. He will take you where you can get your wounds treated and find food."

Kalvan looked back at the battlefield and turned to Colonel Krynos, saying, "It's time to end this slaughter. Sound the horns!"

Krynos raised his saber, the prearranged signal, and the great Zarthani horns sounded a loud melancholy bellow. The Royal Army's advance came to a quick halt. Nestros' men, on the other hand, acted as if they hadn't heard the horns and started after the tribesmen. Kalvan had prepared for this eventuality and gave Colonel Krynos an order for General Alkides.

Meanwhile, Kalvan worked his way over to his King Nestros, who was still fighting a body of nomads. His bodyguards had to wield pistol butts and the flat side of their swords to get their Rathoni allies out of their Great King's way.

Although Kalvan knew the best advice on the battlefield was to prepare for the unexpected, the sight of his Royal Page mounted on a huge black destrier—that would have done King Nestros proud—and pushing his way through Nestros soldiers with his sword raised—was one that caused him to rein his horse to a dead stop. Aspasthar's face broke into a smile as he spotted his king and rode determinedly to his Great King's side.

"Prince Ptosphes sent me, Your Majesty!" the page said quickly.

Kalvan bit back a sarcastic reply and said, "What news do you bring, Aspasthar?"

"They've captured the Warlord! He has a bad head wound. I think he's going to die!"

"Take me to him."

Moments later the air was split by the sound of half a dozen cannons simultaneously firing round shot over the heads of the Rathoni Army. In the moment of absolute silence that followed this unexpected display, the horns bellowed again. This time the Rathoni Army came to an abrupt halt.

VII

Ranjar Sargos awoke with the sense that a blacksmith was driving a chisel into the side of his head. He stifled a groan and tried to reach for the pain.

It was then Sargos discovered his hands were bound.

Before he could voice his outrage, he heard Althea's voice cry out, "Is this honor—to treat a warrior like a rebellious slave?"

He tried to agree with her words. From the blank looks on the faces around him, he suspected he had croaked like a frog.

Althea shouted and cradled his head in her lap. He noticed a blood-stained bandage on her head and remembered the wound she had taken at her hairline.

A face Sargos remembered thrust itself forward, and the others gave way to either side. It was the last face he had seen before the chariot had been hit, when what seemed a thunderbolt crashed into the side of his head and flung him from the saddle.

"Ranjar Sargos! I am King Nestros. Who has bound you?"

"No one, Your Grace," a gray bearded man said.

"Captain-General Mylissos, he did not bind his own hands!" snarled the man, who must be King Nestros. Nestros drew a fine, if somewhat mud-specked dagger, from his riding boots, knelt and cut Sargos' bonds with his own hands.

"I trust your honor as I would my own or Great King Kalvan's," Nestros said. "You led your men most valiantly to the end, but the gods' favor was not with you. Yet if you are willing, you may win more in defeat than you could have gained by victory."

Althea said, "Only the gods could turn our defeat into a victory, and I see none on this field."

Sargos shook his head; it seemed to Sargos that King Nestros was talking in riddles. Beyond him a tall man in fine armor stood, smoking a pipe and nodding slowly. *What victory could come out of such a loss as this?* His mouth felt as though it were full of ashes and his head banged like a drum-head being beaten upon by one of Tymannes medicine men.

"Kalvan?" Sargos asked, pointing toward the man smoking a pipe. Nestros nodded.

So they have both come to gloat. No, that is not true. Nestros was truly angry with those who dishonored me.

"I have fallen and doubtless those around me," Sargos said. "That does not mean victory for you or defeat for me."

Althea, who stood tall and proud as ever, nodded her agreement with his words.

"Your men from here to the redoubt are trapped against the Lydistros River," Kalvan said. "The rest are fleeing. We have let them go in peace. We still could pursue them, as wolves pursue rabbits."

Sargos turned his head slowly to Althea. "Is this true?"

She nodded. "The horde has broken. Kalvan shot his cannon at his own troops to stop their advance! I would not have believed it if I hadn't seen it with my own eyes. He is a man of his word."

King Kalvan moved closer, saying, "Warlord Sargos, if you will sit down with us and discuss peace, We shall continue to hold our pursuit and spare your warriors. Otherwise, the Sastragath and the Sea of Grass alike will be lands of widows and orphans."

If he lies, he does so well. Althea can be trusted, but she may be hostage to my life. She would lie to save me. If Kalvan is telling the truth, he can be trusted . . . But I must see for myself.

Sargos tried to rise. He not only failed, but also would have fallen if Nestros and Kalvan both had not aided him.

To take healing from one's enemies is a sign of submission. Yet if submitting will save those who swore to follow me . . . ?

"Can you summon a healer and a horse? If I see with my own eyes what you have told me, we shall talk." Althea came to him offering her shoulder as a crutch.

The two kings nodded as if their heads were on a single neck.

VIII

Kalvan stepped out of the royal tent and nearly stumbled over Aspasthar. The boy woke up with a squeak of panic.

"Your Majesty!"

"Aspasthar, sleeping on watch is still a serious offense. Even after doing so well in your first battle."

"Your Majesty, I beg forgiveness. But my father came by and said he would watch in my place. He—" A rumbling snore interrupted the page.

Kalvan looked into the shadows on the other side of the tent door and saw Harmakros curled up under a blanket, even more soundly asleep than his son. Making sure that the armed sentries were all in place, Kalvan ducked back into his tent, burrowed into his piled baggage, and came out with a jug of Ermut's Best.

By the time he came out his unofficial 'sentries' were awake. "Thanks for coming, both of you," Kalvan said. "I feel like celebrating, but I didn't want to drink alone."

"What about our friend and ally, Great King Nestros?" Harmakros asked.

"Please," Kalvan said. "Remember when I said it was all over but the shouting? I didn't know what I was saying. A discreet whisper for both Nestros and Sargos is what you would use for drilling a whole regiment! I'd be as deaf as a gunner if we had any more private sessions. But, Dralm be blessed, this was the last one!"

"Then we have an alliance?"

"Signed, sealed and about to be delivered to Grand Master Soton. Ranjar Sargos is no fool. The Zarthani Knights are the hereditary enemies of the Sastragathi. He'll fight them rather than anyone else if he has half a chance of victory. We are giving him much more than that."

"And the nomads?"

"Those sworn to Warlord Ranjar Sargos will follow us. The rest have a moon half to either join us or leave the Great Kingdom of Hos-Rathon. Nestros would like to make it a moon quarter, but he'll swallow hard and accept."

"I imagine most men would swallow a lot more, to be a Great King."

"Likely enough." *Being a Great King must be the dream of everyone who doesn't know what a headache it is!* Not to mention aches in other places. Kalvan couldn't recall having been out of the saddle for more than twenty minutes at a time from dawn until dusk. He could recall the fields three-deep in dead men and horses, and worse, those who weren't yet dead. He didn't want to recall them, but they had glued themselves to his memory.

Kalvan uncorked the jug and passed it to Harmakros. As the brandy gurgled, Kalvan added, "Even with what we have in hand now, we'll be leading a hundred thousand men south. That should be a real headache for our friend Soton, and no aspirin for it either!"

"Aspirin?"

"An alchemy potion from my homeland. Willowbark tea has the same effect, but it's not as strong. Good for the headaches we'll surely have if we finish this jug."

"I'll gladly take the burden on myself, Your—"

"Hand that jug over, Harmakros, that is, if you don't want to be charged with treason.

THIRTY-FIVE

I

Great Queen Rylla was going over the requisition forms for the Royal Granary, when she heard a knock at the study door. Her lady-in-waiting Lady Eutare entered with a curtsy, "Your Majesty, Prince Phrames requests an audience. I know it's late, but he has just arrived from Tarr-Beshta!"

Rylla welcomed the interruption from the endless order writing that her husband had set in motion with his invention of paper. She longed for the days when her father gave orders and they were simply carried out, or not, and a courtier informed them of the problem.

She was definitely curious as to what had brought Phrames all the way from Beshta. Had Captain-General Phidestros finally begun to take the Royal Harphaxi Army—a polite term for the half-ragged gaggle of Harphaxi misfits and youngest sons, who had survived the Battle Chothros Heights—outside the gates of Harphax City?

Before her gods-sent-husband, had arrived to save the small princedom of Hostigos from its enemies, Prince Phrames had been her betrothed. Their marriage had been arranged at childhood; it had not been a bad match. They had always been good friends; although, admittedly, Rylla had never felt the magnetic attraction to Phrames she had felt instantly toward her husband. Somehow—and she was sure it was due to Phrames' good heart—they'd remained friends, even after her marriage. On several occasions she had introduced him to good marital prospects, but he never seemed interested. Until he met Lady Eutare—she wondered if his real reason for traveling to Hostigos was an assignation.

"My Queen," Prince Phrames said, after bowing. Rylla was displeased to see the hard fatigue lines that clawed his long face. His clothes were still travel stained, and it appeared he had not even bothered to shake the dust from his cloak.

From his appearance alone, Rylla knew that this trip had nothing to do with the Lady Eutare. "Phrames, what's wrong? Have the Harphaxi threatened Our borders?"

The Prince shook his head no.

"Let me get you something to drink. She picked up a flask of Ermut's Best and filled a silver goblet.

Prince Phrames took a small sip of the brandy. "Thank you, My Queen."

Rylla waited while he sat down in a high-back chair. Phrames looked as uncomfortable as he appeared exhausted. She decided to wait him out; he would speak in his own time.

"How is Princess Demia?"

"Very well, although she is trying to stand. Walking will be next. There will be no peace in Tarr-Hostigos once the Princess has learned to walk. She does miss her father."

"Of that, I am certain. How does our Great King fare in his war against the nomads?"

"His last letter is over a moon half old, but at that time Kalvan formed an alliance with Nestros to join forces against the nomad horde. The price of that alliance was high; Nestros requested as his boon his recognition as Great King of Rathon. Kalvan believes this is a good thing, as it will both bind himself to Our interests and make him an immediate enemy of Styphon's House. I do not know if they have yet fought the nomad horde."

Prince Phrames nodded, as if distracted.

Rylla rubbed her hands briskly. "Phrames, please get to the point. You did not ride for a day and a half to discuss the state of the Royal nursery!"

"No, Your Majesty, as usual you are right. I came as soon as I learned by courier of your decision to start a war against Phaxos. I believe you are making a grave error."

Rylla felt her blood begin to boil and took into consideration both Phrames' fatigue and their long-standing friendship before she answered. "I am not starting a war, but answering an *insult* made to the Throne of Hos-Hostigos by Prince Araxes, when that son-of-a-she-wolf reneged on his pledge to join the Great Kingdom of Hos-Hostigos. And, then added insult to injury, by attacking the Royal Foundry wagon train in Nostor territory almost a moon half ago!"

"Yes, that was truly a despicable act, by a man who knows no honor. However, your attack upon Araxes is not just an attack upon the Princedom of Phaxos, but an attack on the sovereign territory of Hos-Harphax." Phrames voice raised in volume, "This act of war against Phaxos could lead to a declaration of war by Prince Lysandros and open warfare between our two Kingdoms; an event that your husband went to great lengths to ensure would not happen."

For the first time in their long association, Rylla felt the sting of Phrames' temper. She did not like it. What had happened to her old friends and 'uncles?' First, her father had become lost in grief after his terrible beating at Grand Master Soton's hands on the battlefield at Tenabra. Prince Ptosphes was almost a stranger to her now; she had to take care with her every word or watch as he suffered from the demons set loose by that battle. Next it was 'Uncle' Xentos who had renounced his homeland to gain influence and leadership with the Council of Dralm. Now, her oldest girlhood friend was lecturing her like her husband did when he disapproved of her actions.

"Phrames, I am not the young girl you used to scold when she entered the tilt yard. I am Great Queen and it is my decision—in my husband's absence—to punish the transgression of Prince Araxes. And punish them I will, with or without your blessing."

She could see Phrames forcibly restrain his tongue. "Queen Rylla, you are entering deeper waters than you know. And I mean no disrespect! However, if you continue with these plans to invade Phaxos you will be doing Styphon's work—"

"How dare you! Prince Sarrask has given me his undivided support. I had certainly expected more, if not the same, from my oldest friend."

"Please, stay calm. This is not an issue of friendship, but statesmanship."

"Ahhh. It's because I am a woman—"

"No. You misjudge me. This is an event that is beyond you and me, and even the Great Kingdom of Hos-Hostigos. It affects all Six Kingdoms and the balance between overlord and subject. Hos-Hostigos is under great scrutiny for many reasons. Still, many nobles in Hos-Agrys, Hos-Zygros and even Hos-Harphax support our position; they do not want to become subject states—even by proxy—of Styphon's House. However, neither do they want to become pawns or chattel of Hos-Hostigos. They want things to continue on as they always have. In this, they are sorely mistaken; for, sooner or later, all will either have to choose between Styphon or Dralm and suffer the consequences. But it will not help our cause to make them decide now. Let Styphon's House grow more bold or desperate and the lords will form lines to become allies of Hos-Hostigos."

"You sound like my husband! You are both too soft. All honorable rulers will understand why I punish Araxes. I want them to learn that when they offer alliance to our Kingdom it is not a decision that can be lightly turned away from, as circumstances dictate. We are not Styphon's House, to offer false idols and temple slave farms. They know this and if they do not join in Our cause they will suffer the error of their ways. Araxes has humiliated Us and he will pay for his folly!"

"You might consider that there are few honorable rulers in the Great Kingdoms."

"Then let them fear Us! Are you with me, or against me, Prince Phrames?"

Phrames stepped aback. "With you, of course, My Queen. I was only offering you the benefits of knowledge I gained from my close association to the border princedoms of Hos-Harphax. I am in no position to dictate Royal policy."

"Good. Now, tell me how many men you can spare from your border castles. Sarrask and I have already raised eight thousand men, but we can use more in case Phidestros takes exception to our campaign."

Phrames face paled. "Since Beshta is far closer to Harphax City than Phaxos, it would be more useful to have the Beshtan Army waiting in reserve should any punitive force be led out of Tarr-Harphax."

"There is wisdom in your words. After the false-prince Araxes has been punished, maybe we will meet you outside the walls of Harphax City, Prince Phrames." Rylla pretended not to notice the shudder than ran down Phrames body. *Why are the men I care most about so afraid of getting their hands dirty?* Rylla wondered. This time, however, she had the upper hand. Kalvan, old Chartiphon and her father were hundreds of miles away, and Xentos was no longer Chancellor of Hostigos. She would get her way, and when the dust settled they would see how she had done the right thing— regardless of cost.

II

Warntha Swarn placed his palm over the portal plate and the door to the warehouse slid open. Inside the room was a large silver-mesh dome about fifty feet in diameter, large enough to hold the two score of level runners and smugglers moving around the storeroom. Most of them were dressed in homespun wool, leather and buckskin garments appropriate to Kalvan's Time-Line.

Warntha wore the full-length, hooded orange robe of a Styphon's House highpriest. He couldn't help but notice how even the smugglers quickly moved out of his path, as though the trappings of a Styphoni priest had a sinister aura. Upon reflection, the big man decided it wasn't much different than the usual way Citizens usually acted around him—just more pronounced.

As a counter-military specialist, Warntha had spent over a century on the Industrial Sector, Fifth Level worlds, where he had infiltrated and helped to neutralize prole resistance groups. Warntha had liked this work and had been very good at it. Unfortunately, he had single-handedly killed the top two leaders of a Prole Independence Movement cell unaware that there had been another active agent in the cell. Command had judged him as 'over-zealous' and given him the choice of Psycho-Rehab or retirement at half-pay. He had taken the latter. Had Hadron Tharn not seen some value in his services, he would be living on Home Time Line at about the economic level of the proles he had once spied upon.

In the farthest corner of the warehouse, all by himself, Warntha spotted Jorand Rarth, wearing a battered back-and-breast—that hid most of his potbelly—a large floppy black hat and buckskin trousers with fringe. He approached Jorand from his blind side to gain the maximum advantage of surprise. Warntha hoped this fool proved as useful as Hadron Tharn antici-pated. If not, his existence would come to an abrupt and permanent end.

"By Dralm's white beard!" Jorand cried upon seeing Warntha in his Sty-phoni robes. He quickly reverted to First Level language when he recognized Warntha as Hadron Tharn's bodyguard. "What are you doing here?"

"Councilor Tharn decided I should accompany you on this mission as a Highpriest of Styphon's House. I'm responsible for overseeing the narco-hypnosis memory overlays for the trading team's cover. Then we will stay at Mythrene, the seaport where we're meeting Arch-Stratego Zarphu and his army, until the expedition leaves for the Sea of Grass."

"I thought my cover had already been prepared."

"It's getting more difficult to make unscheduled drops. There will be no stop at Balph, which is why I'm joining the party as an archpriest. The Paratime Police are paying more attention to the University's use of Tran-stemporal conveyers. The University doesn't like it and neither do we. But, it's the way things are now."

Jorand nodded wryly, as though he understood, but didn't like it much. Warntha suspected Jorand enjoyed his company about as much as he enjoyed spending time with the former Dhergabar crime boss.

"I've got some additional instructions for you as well. Instead of guiding the Arch-Stratego to the Marias River, and going by keelboat to Dorg and disembarking there like a 'normal' trading mission; we're going to lead the Ros-Zarthani over the Old Iron Trail into Grefftscharr."

"But why?" Jorand asked. "It'll not only add at least a full moon to the trip, but it might draw us into a fight with the Grefftscharrer. They're not going to look kindly at what they could easily perceive as a nomad invasion."

Maybe Jorand wasn't so stupid after all. "That's what the Councilor wants. The Ros-Zarthani haven't fought against gunpowder weapons before. It's important they have the opportunity to test their mettle before fighting Kalvan. If they break, then we abort the mission—"

The fat man turned pale. "Yeah, but where does that leave me? In Greffa as a prisoner of war or a galley slave on the Great Seas?"

"Then I guess it's important to see they don't break, Jorand—since it is our necks that are on the block." Warntha wasn't the least bit worried, either he'd get killed—in which case all his problems were over, or he'd find a 'job'—probably as a bodyguard, since they were always in fashion—in Greffa. "If the Ros-Zarthani prove their worth, maybe King Kalvan will have a big surprise next year."

"I guess it wouldn't help Chief Verkan's position in Greffa either, if his patron, King Theovacar, loses a major battle to a bunch of barbarian spear chuckers. Nor would he be in a position, the following year, to help Kalvan with men and supplies."

"Very good. You're beginning to pick up the lay of the land. Just look at these kings as syndicate bosses and you'll get along just fine."

"When can I come home?"

"After we get the army safely into Dorg City, or when it has ceased being an effective fighting force; then our job is over. We'll make our way to Balph where Highpriest Prysos will take us to the Balph conveyer-head and back home again. That should give our friends all the time they need to establish a new cover and you'll be able to go back to leading a civilized life on First Level."

Jorand appeared so pleased by this news that Warntha had to choke back a laugh. If Jorand really believed that anyone on Home Time Line would go to that much expense and trouble for a drone like himself, then he deserved his fate. The fat, smarmy prole. Warntha stroked the hilt of the dirk hidden in his gold and leather girdle and repeated to himself, *Your time will come, my fat little friend. Yes, it will come—I promise that.*

III

"How many men does Kalvan now lead?" Grand Master Soton asked. He knew his voice was as high-pitched as the squeak of a newly hatched quail chick. He did not care. The number he thought he had heard could not be what Knight Commander Aristocles had actually said.

"More than a hundred thousand men," Aristocles replied. He sounded like a messenger bringing news so bad that he hardly cared if he was punished for bringing it.

Any gods worthy of the name know that the news is that bad. There is no fault in Aristocles for being unmanned by it. Forgive me old friend.

"A hundred thousand," Soton repeated meditatively. "Is that the grand sum, or only those bound by oath to one of the three supreme leaders?"

"The second, Grand Master. The number of those who will march against us without being oath-bound is not small. It may exceed thirty-five thousand."

"That is very nearly all the rest of the great horde," Soton said. "Also, if the subjects of"—he could not shape his tongue to Nestros' presumptuous new title—"the Pretender Nestros need not fear the nomads, all their garrisons will march south, so add another fifteen thousand men. Everyone will wish to be in at the death of the Zarthani Knights."

"In that, they shall be disappointed, Grand Master. The audience may gather, but the players in the pageant are going to slip out the backdoor."

"Leaving all their tavern bills unpaid, of course," Soton added. "Are you thinking as I am?"

"What else makes any sense? At best, we face odds of perhaps five to one, two of those five are civilized soldiers under captains not to be despised, with more guns than have been seen west of the Pyromannes since fireseed was sent by Styphon! Half our strength are light troops, or half-trained or both."

This bald statement of the truth made it neither less nor more endurable. In the end, that did not matter, if one was the Grand Master and sworn to bear any burden in the name of the Order.

Soton mentally ran over his mental army table of organization: fifteen Lances, comprised of nine thousand Order Brethren and two thousand auxiliaries; seven thousand levy, mostly Sastragathi mounted archers and lancers; and three to four thousand unreliable nomad light cavalry—who in a pinch might change sides or run off the battlefield.

To stand and fight the great horde would be suicide. Yet, it still seemed to Soton that his own death by Kalvan's hand would be easier to face than the orders he knew he would have to give before this campaign was done. Nor could he hope to find peace by seeking that or any other death.

To do that would be to cast the Order into the hands of Roxthar, who in the name of Styphon would surely finish the work Kalvan had begun.

"We must be across the Lydistros within five days. Organize messengers and escorts, to ride with word to Tarr-Ceros. The bridge of boats is to be ready within a moon quarter, or I will decorate the battlements of Tarr-Ceros with the heads of those who have delayed it."

"At once, Grand Master," Aristocles said. No one hearing him could have imagined this was one friend carrying out the wishes of another. He called for his oath-brother, "Ho, Heron! Summon Knight Commander Cyblon to the Grand Master's tent, at once."

When he had heard the order repeated by his messenger, Aristocles turned back to Soton, hand on his sword hilt. Soton wondered if the tales of wizardry in Aristocles' sword had any truth to them. Certainly the sword was the better part of two centuries old. By grasping it in times of trouble Aristocles seemed to soothe himself and sharpen his wits. Also, he had never suffered a sword wound on the battlefield. A half-score of other weapons had left scars, but never a sword . . .

"Grand Master, what about sending some of our boats up the Lydistros to strike at Kalvan's barges?"

"With the river running as it must, after this rain? They would never be able to reach Kalvan's fleet and return in time."

Aristocles wished shameful and wasting diseases upon those who had sent the rains, finishing with some choice comments on the uselessness of Styphon's Archpriests and priests in general.

Soton shook his head. "Again, old friend, guard your tongue, for even I cannot save you from Archpriest Roxthar."

"Roxthar—" Aristocles began, in the same tone he would have used to speak of a pile of dung on his tent floor. Then he took a deep breath. "Roxthar serves Styphon with holy zeal. Doubtless he has done all that mortal man could do even with Styphon's favor.

"Yet I could still wish the rains had not come."

"The gods give with one hand, and take away with the other," Soton replied, grateful for the opportunity to change the subject from priestly politics to other less dangerous topics—such as war. "The wet ground and flooding will slow pursuit.

"Also, we know the Lydistros. Kalvan does not. It will take much luck and more boats than he is likely to have to even cross the river. While he is trying to cross, we can attack his fleet."

"If we are lucky," Soton replied. "Warlord Ranjar Sargos has more knowledge than we would like."

Conversation died for a moment while the messengers rode up to receive their orders. Soton's servants took the opportunity to light the lamps in the tent, sweep the latest coat of dried mud from the floor and ask the Grand Master what he wished for dinner.

"Kalvan's heart," Soton said sharply. "If you cannot produce that, whatever is ready at hand."

The servants departed; Aristocles poured the last wine from a jug into the two least dirty cups in the tent.

"Another message, I think," Soton said, after the first swallow. "To the Commander of Tarr-Ceros, to prepare it in all respects for a siege."

"Holding our whole host?"

"Hardly. We will send within the walls as many Knights as Knight Commander Demelles thinks he can feed for a moon or two. The rest will fall back on Tarr-Lydra and Tarr-Tyros.

"Then we can pray that Kalvan will cross the Lydistros. Once his men have dug themselves into the hills around Tarr-Ceros, they will be like bears tethered in a pit. We will be the dogs, free to move where we will and strike when we think wise. Oh, the bear will take a lot of killing, but we will have him in the end."

It was an improbable vision, unless Kalvan lost his wits, but for a moment it warmed Soton more than the wine. Then he sobered.

"At all costs, we must keep well ahead of Kalvan. That means lightening ourselves as much as possible. All the artillery—after the guns have been destroyed, all the spare armor, all the horse barding—"

"That makes Kalvan a free gift, Soton."

"But a lesser gift than the entire Order! Besides, the gold of Balph can buy blacksmiths to make new armor, saddlers to fit our horses, and brass to recast the cannon. It cannot buy men. If we save our Knights, nothing else matters. Nothing!"

THIRTY - SIX

I

A rch-Stratego Zarphu made room on the cluttered table for a freshly scraped deerskin parchment. He dipped his quill into the inkpot, making a notation that two hundred barrels of salt fish would be arriving from Hellos within the moon half. Zarphu knew that most soldiers considered provisioning and buying victuals scribes' work, but he knew that an army marched on its belly, as well as on its feet; and woe to any Stratego who forgot that fact.

The sea journey from Antiphon to Mythrene had taken over a moon quarter, as the ships had been forced to go against the current and prevailing winds. Even with rowers it was a long, arduous trip and, praise to the weather god, they had only lost one ship to foul winds and none to pirates. Best of all, his stomach was once again his own and not leaping at every lurch of the ship.

Their greeting from the Lord Tyrant of Mythrene had been gracious, befitting an ally who came at the head of an army. The Lord Tyrant had offered him rooms at the palace, but Zarphu had refused. As long as he was in Mythrene, the local Tyrant's spies would be weighing their every move. Still there was no gain in making their job an easy one. Instead Zarphu had hired the Black Horn Tavern as his headquarters.

The army was garrisoned outside the city wall, although keeping them outside the city was a major headache. It would not be wise to have half of them mugged by cutpurses and the other half given the pox by local tarts before they left the coast. In truth, Zarphu could hardly wait until they were on their way. He was going to have to wait for another moon—at the earliest—before he could gather up enough foodstuffs for the initial leg of their journey. If the stories about great herds of bison and cattle moving across the Sea of Grass, like schools of tuna and albacore, were true there would be no end of food. In case it was the stuff of legend, he intended to send several large pack trains out ahead of the army to set up depots, since there was no conceivable way they could take enough victuals along with them over the entire passage.

A hearty knock at the plank door told him his Eastern visitors had arrived. "Enter."

A big priest, with a shaved head and hard eyes, wearing a yellow robe— raiment of the god the barbarians called Styphon—was the first to enter. After him came another priest in yellow robes and several lesser priests in black robes. Next came the merchants, led by a portly man with a solid-metal breastplate that Zarphu would have traded his favorite horse for. The portly man had a wine seller's smile pasted on his face. Zarphu wondered which, if any, of these foreigners he could trust.

The big priest, whom he'd met before and called himself Highpriest Arkemanes, was the first to speak. "My fellow priests, except for two, will return on your galleys to Antiphon as agreed by your Lord Tyrant. I will accompany your army to the Five Kingdoms as advisor and priest to those who need me."

Arkemanes spoke to him as if he were a lesser form of animal; the high-priest reminded him of Dyzar's Bodyguards. Zarphu didn't trust him the width of a lady's dagger. He would like to know more about the 'fireseed' that the priest had shown him the day before. Still, the priest had already crossed the Sea of Grass and, along with the portly merchant and the other priests, had survived the journey, so he might prove helpful in their passage.

"Who will we be fighting when we reach the Five Kingdoms?" Zarphu asked.

"An Usurper and blasphemer who goes by the name of Kalvan," the smaller priest said. He was the priest who had convinced the Tyrant Dyzar to sell the Army to the Temple of Styphon. "I have been sent to aid you in bringing your army to join the Holy Host. You will have your part in what will be a great victory."

Zarphu could tell by his tone that the priest didn't think much of that part or his mission. Good, the priests of Styphon's House underestimated him. That would make his job easier. He was sure that once they arrived in the Five Kingdoms an opportunity would arise where he could return this fool's disdain. He wasn't so sure about the big priest; he didn't look like any priest Zarphu had ever known. The Zarthani, as they now called themselves, might have better weapons, but he was certain they didn't have any better soldiers than his own—even this so-called Usurper Kalvan. If they did, they wouldn't be riding the width of the continent for troops to buy.

One thing that he was certain of, not much good would come of an alliance with these priests of the false god Styphon. What Zarphu really wanted to know was why the other priests were returning to Antiphon. Just what kind of deal had the Styphon worshippers struck with Lord Tyrant Dyzar?

II

The door to Captain-General Phidestros' headquarters flew open and hit the wall so hard it almost sprung its hinges. "What!" he cried, as he pulled out a fully loaded horsepistol from his drawer.

Phidestros quickly slipped the pistol back into the drawer when he recognized Prince Lysandros, who was yelling, "Have you heard! The traitorous Hostigi have invaded Hos-Harphax! The Army of Hostigos has already advanced into Phaxos—or so Prince Araxes' messenger just informed me!"

Phidestros was stunned. "Our last message reported the Usurper was off in the Trygath, chasing after Grand Master Soton. Is Kalvan truly a demon such that he can be in two places at once?"

"Of course, not. He has other commanders, who can act in his stead— Prince Phrames, perhaps?"

"My agents in Beshta reported only yesterday that Prince Phrames is still holed up at Tarr-Beshta, after his surprise trip to Hostigos. Captain-General Hestophes is camped in Beshta as well. Besides, why would

Phrames march all the way to Phaxos, when he could be outside Tarr-Harphax in a few days. Our agent in Hostigos Town hasn't reported in over two moons—I fear for his health. His last report stated that only Sarrask of Sask, of Kalvan's military commanders, was barracked at Tarr-Hostigos, and Kalvan—if he's as wise as evidence provides—would sooner make him Captain-General of privies than have Sarrask lead the Royal forces of Hostigos in an attack upon Hos-Harphax."

Prince Lysandros, his brow furrowed in thought, said, "Maybe Kalvan has come up with another of his great strategic plans; first, lull us into a false sense of security and then pick off our princedoms one at a time, while we're afraid to leave the city walls. Under his tutelage Hostigos has sprouted capable captains like mushrooms in manure. Who knows which one might be leading the invasion."

"It may be a feint, Prince, to draw our forces out of Harphax City and into Phaxos so that Prince Phrames can invest the City while we are busy pulling traitorous Araxes beans out of the coals. You do remember he was one of the first Harphaxi princes to 'offer' fealty to Hostigos last campaign season."

"I have not forgotten," Lysandros said, his lips pursed tightly, "nor how quickly he returned to Us after Grand Master Soton's victory at the Battle of Tenabra. Nor, has Kalvan, I daresay from the message I have received from Araxes, the First Prince of Fencesitters. Once the Usurper has been driven from our lands I have a most appropriate 'reward' for Prince Araxes—should he survive this invasion."

"Is his messenger's report true?"

First Prince Lysandros smiled as though at some private joke. "A Styphon's House underpriest arrived from Phaxos Temple only six candles later and told the same tale. Since Araxes so generously re-swore his *everlasting* fealty to the Iron Throne, I have mistrusted him in all things large and small. Still, I doubt two such messengers are wrong."

Phidestros knew he was in dangerous waters. After six moons of training, and in many cases re-training, the Harphaxi Army was still not ready for a major clash with the Army of Hos-Hostigos. "The question now is: what do *we* do, Prince Lysandros?"

"Captain-General, how many troops can you form up in good order and put into the field by sunrise tomorrow?"

Phidestros mentally squirmed as he tried to come up with a number that both might approximate the truth and not mortally offend his employer. "You know that I did not have a lot to work with when you appointed me Captain-General—"

"I don't want to hear excuses. I want an answer I can count upon."

Phidestros took the plunge. "We will have to leave a large garrison so that Prince Phrames won't be tempted to besiege Harphax City while we're gone. Hmmm. I'd say about two thousand 'reliable' horse and three or four thousand foot."

"By Styphon's Own Purse! Is this all! Kalvan brings twice that number across our borders, if Araxes can be believed, and most of his army is fighting around the Great Mother River! To say nothing of the armies he has based in Beshta. So what am I paying you for?"

"To overcome thirty years of Great King Kaiphranos' neglect and last year's disastrous losses on the field. To even put that many men in the field, will cost us heavily in our re-building efforts."

Phidestros could actually hear the putative ruler of Hos-Harphax gnash his teeth as he chewed over those words.

"You're right, my late brother was not only a chokepurse, but a fool—a blind fool. Not even Kalvan himself could make an army appear out of thin air—although, it appears he has done so. We must frame some response; otherwise, as soon as Phaxos has been subdued, the Hostigi Army will turn to rend other tempting targets, like the Princedoms of Dazour or Thaphigos. If We stand by and let the Kingdom be devoured piecemeal, the army We are building inside these walls will matter little. Furthermore, it will give aid and comfort to those of Our enemies who reside outside of Hos-Harphax, such as that Hadron-spawned League of Dralm being nurtured inside Agrys City. That is, unless you believe that Phaxos will not fall to Kalvan's forces."

"I'd sooner believe that Allfather Dralm himself has come to pay us a visit! Phaxos will fall, but not easily because its Prince has much to fear at the hands of Kalvan. Maybe it is time we conjure up some Kalvan-style magic."

"Good. You have an idea, Captain-General?"

"The first glimmerings. Already we have a mock Royal Army on display in Harphax City. Well, how about we take this mock army on maneuvers, close to Phaxos? Surely, not even Kalvan's captains can expect to subdue the Royal Army of Hos-Harphax with this expeditionary force they've taken into Phaxos."

"Keep coming up with these kinds of ideas and you may finish your career as a Duke of Hos-Harphax."

Phidestros stood up and made a mock bow. "Thank you, Prince. There are some difficulties ahead; after all, if the Hostigi did decide to attack, well, half the Royal Army might desert upon contact! Still, it will be up to me to ensure that the armies do *not* achieve physical penetration."

"It's a strange military strategy, but these are unusual times. So you are saying that all we need do is make a show of our presence, and that should be sufficient to halt the Hostigi advance."

"Let's look at the overall strategic picture, Prince Lysandros. If Kalvan truly meant to attack Hos-Harphax, he would base his operations from Beshta. He already has Prince Phrames Beshtan Army, as well as Kalvan's own Army of Observation under Captain-General Hestophes, who by all reports is an able military leader. Besides, Beshta is the closest Hostigi staging grounds to Hos-Harphax, and he already has built a road that runs from Hostigos Town to Tarr Beshta for his supply lines."

Once again he could hear Lysandros grinding teeth; he had forbidden mention of Kalvan's Great King's Highway, as he considered neither Kalvan a Great King or his goat's path a highway. Phidestros disagreed on both points, but was smart enough to keep such 'traitorous' thoughts to himself.

"Therefore, despite how it may appear," Phidestros continued, "the Hostigi Army attacking Phaxos was not sent to conquer Hos-Harphax. If I were Kalvan, I would send out the Army of Observation and have them move into the Princedom of Arklos, which would act as a feint and keep the Royal Army from reinforcing far off Phaxos. Since he has not done this, we might assume that his intention is to draw out the Royal Army and wait until they have reached Phaxos before swinging down with the Army of Observation and either catching the Royal Army in a pincers movement—allowing him to encircle and destroy it—or have the Army of Observation strike Harphax City. Since the Princely Army of Arklos was mostly destroyed last year at Chothros Heights, he would not be remiss in believing that there would be minimal opposition all the way to Harphax City."

"Thus, you are telling me, we are in a position to do nothing, either to aid our subjects or harass our enemy?" Prince Lysandros asked, in a voice that intimated that his Captain-General had better find a way out of that box he had just put Harphax into.

Also reminding Phidestros that Captain-Generals could be fired as fast as they were made. "There is a way out. We take most of the Royal Army—every worthless one of them—and march them into Balkron, which is close enough to Beshta that Phrames will have to give serious thought to any movement that brings the Royal Army behind him. The army's presence will also protect the princedoms of Dazour, Balkron, Thaphigos and Argros from the invading Hostigi Army."

"What about Phaxos?"

"We have no choice there, all we can do is wash our hands of this faithless dog Araxes. If we take the Army into Phaxos, we take the very good risk of showing the world our sham of a Royal Army, or giving Prince Phrames a free run to the gates of Harphax City. Let us say, as our official position, that Araxes has bought this trouble by swearing an oath to our enemy and that we can see of no more fitting punishment than having his suzerainty abolished by his Hostigi friends."

Lysandros rubbed his hands gleefully. "That might well work. I'll draft a document to that effect. Do remember, I will be watching to see how well the Army of Hos-Harphax takes to the field."

I bet you will, Phidestros thought; so would everyone else who saw him as a puffed-up mercenary captain with more luck than brains. They would learn—assuming he could actually get those whoresons of his into at least *appearing* to be a credible military force! *Royal Army of Hos-Harphax, indeed!*

THIRTY-SEVEN

I

Ahead the smoke of the burning Phaxosi village grew thicker. Behind Xykos the sound of musketry grew louder. Now it was almost loud enough to drown out Prince Sarrask's voice shouting orders. On his right side, the banner of Queen Rylla's Mounted Lifeguard, a white horse under a gold crown on a blue field, flapped in the wind.

Great Queen Rylla sat upon her horse with as much patience as the gods had given her, which wasn't very much. Xykos was glad the gods had sent to the queen a man who could endure her tongue and temper. Himself, he would have thrashed such a woman, and no doubt been shortly repaid with a dagger in the ribs.

In spite of her fidgeting, the Queen had gone quietly enough when Sarrask suggested she might want to observe the right flank. Was she really willing to do her old enemy's bidding, to make him respected in the eyes of the Army of Hos-Hostigos? Xykos had learned enough about war in the past year to know that such things were possible. He had also learned more about the Great Queen, enough to doubt she would move a finger at Sarrask's request unless she had reasons of her own. From the expression on her face, Xykos judged he was about to learn what those reasons might be.

The Hostigos Army had spent the last moon quarter taking border tarrs and maneuvering for position against the out-numbered Army of Phaxos.

Today was the first time that both armies had met on the field. The Phaxosi fighting from dug in positions and on familiar ground had had the advantage, at least all morning long.

"Xykos!"

"Your Majesty?"

"Can you see the First Royal Carabineers?"

Xykos had dismounted to spare his horse; mounts that could carry his weight were none too common. A good stout oak tree was ready to hand, to let him see even farther. He scrambled up, then down.

"They're still behind that little stream, the Ox Bath they call it, Your Majesty."

Rylla tapped her teeth with a gauntleted finger. "Damn Sarrask! No, that's not fair. Few have learned as much about my husband's way of fighting as the Prince of Sask. No great harm that he has forgotten to send the Royal Carabineers here. But the work must still be done. Xykos, how many men can the Queen's Bodyguard spare?"

Xykos grinned. "Your Majesty will stay."

"You dare to bargain with your Great Queen?"

"Nobody else around to do it, Your Majesty. And it's my head too if you lose yours."

"I could take yours first, you know."

"Yes, but you wouldn't. Not for trying to save our Great King from having to sleep alone the rest of his days."

Rylla had the grace to blush, then laugh. "Very well. I will stay out of the village until you say it is safe. How many men, then?"

The bargain they struck gave Xykos thirty of the Bodyguards to lead into the village. That was only half of the Beefeaters in Phaxos, a third of the total strength. The growing strength of Rylla's personal bodyguard had already won Xykos promotion to Captain. Of course, to properly shield Queen Rylla from all the dangers she faced in battle would require a bodyguard so big a Captain-General could command it! As it was, she would have thirty Beefeaters and four squadrons of her Lifeguard to protect her while he was away.

Xykos slung Boarsbane, his big two-handed sword, across his back before he led his small command into the village. He took his horse's reins and it followed behind. The big sword was really too heavy to carry just as

a luck token, but Xykos always felt better with it slung over his back, ready
to hand. He also had two pistols and a musketoon double-charged with
smallshot, at the ready.

The village straggled along the hilltop like an ill-tended flock of sheep.
Since most of it was burning, the smoke veiled the whole right wing of the
Hostigi from Phaxosi eyes. As he passed the first farmhouse, Xykos realized that this might also be shielding the enemy from Hostigi eyes. So that
was why the Queen has asked for a regiment! She wanted to not only find
out what the Phaxosi might be up to, but also to stop them if it was
dangerous.

With thirty Beefeaters, all Xykos could do was learn the lay of the land
and hope he'd live long enough to tell the Queen. Smoke swirled up from a
burning pigsty, hiding two of his men. A shot exploded from the pigsty,
and one of the two staggered back into sight, holding his stomach. Another
shot, a scream from the sty, and the sound of running feet. Two men in the
black and green colors of Phaxos dashed out of the sty, heading for the far
side of the village.

Half a dozen pistols cracked; one Phaxosi threw up his hands and fell.
The other seemed to bear a charmed life, until Xykos leveled his musketoon. The small shot made the man leap and stumble. Before he could get
back on his feet Xykos was on top of him, wrestling him into submission as
if he were a child.

"What do you hear, man?" Xykos shouted.

"Oath of Galzar—" began the man.

"You're no mercenary! You'll guest at Regwarn without your manhood, if
you don't speak up!" Xykos motioned to one of his men, who drew a
poniard.

"We're picketing the village, to warn of any Hostigi movement around
the flank," the man gasped.

"And the rest of your army?"

"I can't say—"

"Tythos, just a small cut." Tythos sliced the soldier's breeches from groin
to waist; then smiled like a man who enjoys his work.

"No! Mercy—I'll talk. We're shifting round, to hit you in the flank when
the rear comes up."

"Hoho."

That made sense, from what the Queen had said. She'd wondered aloud why the Phaxosi had let Sarrask drive in their scouts and fight their vanguard in a simple old-fashioned headbutting kind of battle. Prince Araxes or one of his captains had guessed one of the Great King's tricks—be one place to draw your enemy in, and then be strong somewhere else to attack him.

Well, they would soon learn that Great Queens as well as Great Kings knew the new way of fighting.

"Tythos, take this fool back to the Queen, privy parts and all. Let him tell her what he's told us, then take his Oath to Galzar. Take a couple of—"

Xykos broke off, as the gap between two burning houses appeared to sprout Phaxosi. The pickets' friends had arrived, probably called by the shooting. They were waving swords and running straight toward his small command.

"Run, Tythos! Forget the prisoner! Bodyguards, cold steel!" Xykos had seen that none of the Phaxosi had drawn their pistols, but all had drawn their swords and daggers.

By Galzar's grace, both friend and foe had left Xykos room to draw Boarsbane. The great sword rasped from its scabbard and leaped through the smoky air. It cut under one man's helmet and took his head from his shoulders before he knew an enemy was in striking distance. Another man lost an arm, a third the use of a leg.

"It's one of Kalvan's demons!" a Phaxosi screamed.

This threw the whole band into confusion, then into retreat. Xykos shifted Boarsbane to his left hand and brought down one of the fugitives with a pistol shot.

"Fire!" he shouted. If the men got away, they would give far more warning to the Phaxosi commanders than the sound of shooting.

Xykos emptied his other pistol, saw that some of the Phaxosi were going to get away, and broke into a run after them. Suddenly hoof beats swelled behind him, and he was shouldered aside by one of the mounted Lifeguard. He reeled against a smoldering wall, jumped back as an ember seared his cheek, and turned to see Queen Rylla leading her Mounted Lifeguard out the other side of the village.

So much for Great Queen's promises!

To do her justice, Rylla was back, bloody saber resting across the pommel of her saddle, in hardly more than a few breaths. Without even looking at

Xykos, she ordered two mounted men to ride back and bring up the First
Royal Carbineers.

Then she seemed to notice Xykos for the first time. "Well done, Captain, and for the twentieth time."

"Boarsbane seems to bring me luck, Your Majesty."

"And you hope some of it rubs off on me?"

"Well . . ."

"Never mind. The Phaxosi are moving up on the right, but they haven't
joined up their flankers to their main body. We push both regiments into
the gap, and we can catch the flankers before they deploy."

"Two regiments?"

"Kalvan taught me that even one regiment in time can do more than ten
regiments an hour late. If Sarrask can just hold the Phaxosi by the nose
while I kick them in the pants, we've won the battle."

Xykos nodded and began searching one of the dead Phaxosi for something to wipe Boarsbane. When the blade was clean, he started to sprint
towards his horse, which had wandered away from the fighting. He knew
that the Great Queen was a fine captain. Now he prayed that she was also
a good prophet.

II

Half of Phaxos Town had already looked as if the Hostigi had already
sacked the town and stripped it of loot, but Prince Araxes royal chambers
looked as if he were set to receive a friendly visit from some distant overlord. Captain-General Oroblon followed the Palace seneschal to the
Prince's throne. One of Styphon's yellow-robed Highpriests was chattering
in Araxes' ear. Probably trying to arrange a guard company so they could
take the Temple gold out of the town before Kalvan's demons arrived, not
that Oroblon could blame him. The Styphoni had spent enough rearming
the Prince's army and shoring up Tarr-Phaxos' walls to send the local economy soaring—but not for long.

"What are you doing here, Captain-General? And where is my army?"
Araxes' voice came out more as a screech than the usual modulated voice of
command.

"We've lost two battles in twice as many days. The army is in full retreat to Tarr-Phaxos."

"You brought the army here! Oroblon, I'm paying you and them to keep the Hostigi out of here!"

"We have no other place to go. If we have the gods favor, we'll be able to hold them outside the town walls until the Royal Army arrives."

Prince Araxes shook his head as though he'd just learned his favorite concubine had died. "The Royal Army of Hos-Harphax is not coming. I just received a letter from Prince Lysandros."

Captain-General Oroblon felt as if he'd just been gut-shot. "What? Why?"

Prince Araxes stretched out his hands imploringly. "Lysandros blames me for all this!"

The Highpriest rose up and said sanctimoniously, "You should have never made overtures to the Usurper!"

"SHUT UP! And forget any bodyguards from me, you son-of-a-motherless sow. I hear Kalvan shoots your kind out of cannons."

The Highpriest turned white and fled the room. One of the Prince's bodyguards started off after him, but Araxes motioned him to halt. "He won't go far. Already the townspeople are taking Styphon's priests hostage, thinking they can use them to barter for their freedom when the walls fall. Sometimes the Styphoni forget just how far from Balph they are."

"I'll put my men to shoring up the town walls. I suggest you take your valuables to the keep in Tarr-Phaxos."

"Will the town walls hold, Captain-General?"

"For a few days. The Hostigi carry their own guns and when they go to work these old walls won't last long. Tarr-Phaxos will be a tougher nut to crack."

"Best we sue for peace, then?"

"I don't think it will do any good. If it were King Kalvan, maybe. But that wife of his has blood in her eye."

"You mean you were defeated by a woman?"

Oroblon tried to keep his racing blood in check. If he had any brains, he'd take his pistol out of his sash and drop Araxes where he sat. Then take what remained of his army and join up with Captain-General Phide-stros. However, Araxes still held his oath; Galzar had no patience with oath-breakers. Furthermore, it was difficult to turn his back on the man who'd made him Captain-General of his army—even if he was a back-stabbing dog. "I was defeated by Prince Sarrask, and Great Queen Rylla of Hos-Hostigos, who is the equal of any man I've ever met and then some. From what I've heard, she has even less patience with oath-breakers than the priests of the Wargod."

Prince Araxes slumped down in his throne like a man forsaken by his own self and all others. As far as Oroblon could tell, that was pretty close to the truth. He might even have been tempted to feel sorry for the Prince had he himself not been caught in the web that Araxes had tried to spin.

III

Queen Rylla unconsciously banged her fists on the saddles pommel. She wanted to be at the walls of Tarr-Phaxos, but she was not 'allowed' to be in the vanguard by all her many protectors—sometimes it felt as if the entire Army of Hostigos was in league with Kalvan to keep her 'safe,'—from Prince Sarrask to her bodyguard, Xykos. However, of one thing she was sure: they would all be busy elsewhere when her husband returned from the Sastragath! Kalvan's most recent dispatch told of the combined Hostigos and Rathon defeat of the nomads and the alliance with the Warlord Ranjar Sargos, which had followed. Now the newly formed allies were joined together against Great Master Soton. She wondered how many more moons this campaign would encompass.

Rylla heard the familiar bellow of Prince Sarrask as he forced his way through the tightly packed horses. She called a halt and waited for him to come forward.

"Queen Rylla, I just received word from one of our intelligencers that the Styphoni butt-kissing Harphaxi Army has left Harphax City and is moving toward Phaxos. The Prince of Thaphigos has already called out his Army, about two thousand horse and half as many foot. The Thaphigosi will wait for the Royal Army, but we'll be out of Phaxos before they reach the border—the cowardly swine."

"Just as I predicted," Rylla said, trying to keep the I-told-you-so tone out of her voice. "Captain-General Phidestros doesn't want to risk another beating by the Army of Hos-Hostigos. Besides, he has a hundred and fifty miles of bad roads and more ridges to pass over than Xentos has wrinkles. I suspect he'll take his time, as well. Phidestros is only bringing out the Royal Army to prove to his Prince's already shaken vassals that they are alive and possibly useful in a fight. He almost has to after the humiliation of Chothros Heights."

Sarrask licked his lips, "Har, that were some arse-kicking! Almost as much fun as we've had with this sorry bunch of Phaxosi halfwits."

"If Phidestros had twice as many troops, I might take his army seriously. I've half a mind to go into Thaphigos, after we finish with Araxes and give Phidestros a good thrashing, too."

"Please! Your Majesty," Sarrask cried out. "There'll be enough explaining to do when Great King Kalvan returns. Let's not present him with an all out war with Hos-Harphax!"

"If I had Phrames support, there wouldn't be another war by the time my husband returned, but a conquest! I know that if Phrames marched into Thaphigos we could catch the Royal Harphaxi army flat-footed, encircle it and crush the Harphaxi completely. Then our combined forces could march straight into Harphax City with nothing to stop us but Phidestros' camp followers!"

Sarrask shook his head wearily, as if he'd heard this argument one too many times. "You have my support, Queen Rylla. But without Phrames help we are facing an uphill run. It will take us at least another moon half to besiege Tarr-Phaxos and the countryside. While we're busy fighting here, everyday more troops flock to the Harphaxi Army. Not enough to embolden Phidestros to march into Phaxos, since then Phrames would have to come to our aid. No, what we have here is a stalemate. But be content; we have won two glorious battles with minimal casualties. Even Kalvan will be impressed."

"I hope so," Rylla said, as much to convince herself as Prince Sarrask. "I, however, am convinced we are making a terrible mistake by not conquering Hos-Harphax before they have a chance to recover from the beating they took last fall. Phrames, I could wring his neck—"

"Your Majesty! Phrames is one of the throne's most loyal paladins. He is faithfully following his Great King's orders. It's unfortunate that they disagree with yours, but he is not being disloyal. Too cautious, aye, but not disloyal."

Rylla had to keep from breaking out in a grin. The idea of Sarrask defending Prince Phrames' caution was like hearing a Styphon's House highpriest praise Dralm. A miracle brought about by her husband, so wise in many ways and so thickheaded in others.

"I do have some good news. They've brought up one of the mobile batteries so we should be able to fire the first shots into Tarr-Phaxos."

Rylla smiled happily. With the Wargod's blessing, they should have Tarr-Phaxos invested and broken within a quarter moon. Then her retribution against Prince Araxes and his family could begin. After the example she set here, no mere prince would ever dare embarrass the throne of Hos-Hostigos again, by Galzar's teeth!

IV

Captain-General Phidestros stalked around the perimeter of the camp. He couldn't sit still, not knowing that the Hostigos Army was so close—yet so far away. It was his duty to repel and punish invaders within Hos-Harphax and, yet, here he stood with his shell-army all around him unable to do anything but fume. And worst of all; he was being bearded by a woman! True, not any woman, but Great Queen Rylla of Hos-Hostigos. A battling beauty he'd like to tame himself. Still, she was a woman who commanded an army that demanded respect, but was giving him disrespect.

Phidestros heard some rustling and turned to see Archpriest Grythos, the Styphon's House observer sent to report to the Temple about the Hostigi invasion. Grythos, a former Knight Commander with the Zarthani Knights, was a surprisingly good choice. He understood military realities and why Phidestros was forced to sit and wring his hands, while Phaxos Town burned. As a Knight Commander he served in the Temple as a Styphon's House Archpriest—so he was aware of Balph politics. He was even apologetic about his role as official spy.

Phidestros on more than one occasion had found himself confiding in Grythos and even once or twice asking his advice. Grythos was a tall, bald-headed man with a mustache and no beard. His hair was mostly silver and he walked with a pronounced limp.

In the distance, Phidestros could see an orange halo that marked the burning town. "I can't tell you how much it vexes me to stay here and watch Phaxos Town burn!"

"It has been sacked for a moon quarter, I'm surprised the Hostigi found anything left to burn. When you return to Harphax City, many voices will say you should have attacked the Usurper's army. If they were here and saw the rank and file, there would be no questions."

Phidestros nodded. He was not anxious to return to Harphax City to tell First Prince Lysandros about the Hostigi Army's successful siege of Phaxos Town, only three days of shelling and the walls came tumbling down! It appeared that Tarr-Phaxos, which had been besieged for over a moon quarter, would fall soon, thanks to those mobile batteries of Kalvan's. He needed lots of them for his own army. Maybe it was time for another talk with Kyblannos.

"Captain Geblon, find Grand-Captain Kyblannos for me and bring him here. Some scouts captured some Hostigi gunners today and I know he'll be somewhere nearby." One of the Hostigi mobile guns had lost a wheel and some of the gunners had stayed behind to fix it. When the Harphaxi scouts found them, shots were fired. Three of the gunners had died protecting their gun; two of the gunners were badly wounded and wouldn't finish the night. The remaining artilleryman had been temporarily knocked out and was under heavy guard.

"Aye, Captain-General." Geblon, Captain of Phidestros' former Iron Company, of course, passed Phidestros' order on to a petty captain.

"Who is Grand-Captain Kyblannos?" the Archpriest asked. "I thought I'd met all your officers."

"Captain Kyblannos is a different kind of officer. He's not at all ambitious and would rather spend his time with the wainwrights and artillerymen

than his fellow officers. But he's the best captain I've ever worked with and
the soldier who is working on giving the Royal Army its own mobile
batteries."

Archpriest Grythos shook his head. "What does a soldier know about
wagons and mobile batteries?

"Kyblannos is no ordinary soldier. He'll tell you he's a wainwright, not a
soldier, but actually he is both. He was a former wainwright, who was
apprenticed to his widowed father's wagon-building shop in a crossroads
village in Hos-Agrys. After a revolt against the local prince, an army came
through and burned their village down. Kyblannos and his father ended up
tagging along with the army as camp followers—a couple of wainwrights
are always welcome in any army. The infantry may march on their feet, but
their food marches in wagons.

"His father died on the campaign, but Kyblannos stayed on. When the
war was over he found that his village hadn't been rebuilt and all his friends
were dead or scattered. With nothing better to do, Kyblannos stayed with
the soldiers. He drifted from one army to another as a career camp follower. Yes, even trollops need wagons fixed."

The Archpriest grinned, a most un-Archpriestly smile.

"Over the years, Kyblannos tried his hand at a variety of military things.
He was a gunner in several armies, a quartermaster, a paymaster once,
marched with the infantry, rode with the cavalry, became a petty captain of
cavalry at least twice. One of those times, the company commander was
wounded and Kyblannos took over as captain. Then, when the real captain
recovered, Kyblannos to everyone's surprise turned the company back over
to him. He just didn't want to go into business for himself as a mercenary
captain."

Phidestros laughed. "I can sympathize. Still, over the next moon half the
company deserted. It seems Kyblannos was a much better commander than
the captain he substituted for."

"Many the times . . ." the Archpriest said, nodding his head.

"Eventually Kyblannos ended up with the Sask army at the Battle of
Fyk. After the battle, while the Iron Company was sacking the Saski baggage camp, Geblon and half a dozen troopers found him sitting on the seat
of an army wagon, doing some repairs to the reins. One of the troopers
grabbed a chest that turned out to be Kyblannos' toolbox."

"I remember that," Captain Geblon said. "Kyblannos looked the trooper right in the eye and said, 'You can't do that.'

"I tell him, 'We're taking it with us,' and then I made the mistake of adding, 'unless, of course, you want to go along with it.'

"Kyblannos replies, 'In that case I'll need a horse.' I don't remember the rest."

A loud laugh began deep in Phidestros' belly. "I've heard the boys tell the tale often enough so that I can finish."

Captain Geblon looked sheepishly away.

"Kyblannos, before Geblon knows what's happening, pulls a carpenter's awl and has it at his throat, saying, 'your horse will do.'

"While the troopers are frozen with surprise, Kyblannos pulls Geblon off his horse and is climbing on to it himself! One trooper gets his pistol out and is about to shoot Kyblannos, when Geblon—to his credit—still on the ground, tells him to stop.

"'We could use men like you.' he tells Kyblannos. 'Whatever your name is, you're now in the Iron Company.'"

Captain Geblon turned bright red. "That's not exactly the way it happened—"

The Archpriest slapped Geblon hard on the back. "Captain, it's no fluke that your Captain-General has you in charge of the Iron Company! If you ever decide to retire from the mercenary life, I know a couple of Knight Commanders who could use a man with your resourcefulness."

"Thank you, Archpriest. I'm quite happy where I am."

Both Archpriest Grythos and Phidestros laughed heartily, before continuing the story. "And Kyblannos replies, 'And with a horse!'"

"Poor Geblon," Phidestros continued, "ends up having to steal a mount for himself!"

"Kyblannos proved useful right away. Before we had left the camp, he had talked ten of his buddies into joining up, and not at gunpoint either. We left for Harphax with a cobbler, a saddler, a knapper, a fuller, a fletcher, two coopers, two farriers and even that artisan that every cavalry company could use—a horse breeder.

"We also picked up thirty mercenaries from other companies, and Kyblannos seemed to know most of them by name, so I formed them into a squadron and put him in charge as a petty captain.

"Then I acquired the Blue Company from former Captain Lamochares and what do you know? Kyblannos used to be a petty captain in the Blue Company. So I put him in charge of Lamochares men, which made him for all intents and purposes my second-in-command.

"So when I got promoted to Grand-Captain before Phyrax, there was little question but that Kyblannos should take over the Iron Band as my second. After Phyrax and Hos-Harphaxi Succession Crisis, when the Iron Band was quartered in Harphax City, Kyblannos took advantage of my prestige and pressured the Wainwrights Guild to examine him for Master Wainwright, even though he technically wasn't eligible since he'd never finished his apprenticeship. His master piece was a Kalvan-style field carriage for an eighteen-pounder cannon captured at Tenabra. Without too much argument, the Guild had presented him with the rank of Master."

"That's some tale," Grythos commented. "Now, some highpriests claim that all of Kalvan's work is tainted by demons, but I'm not one of their numbers."

"If they be demons, we could use a few!" Geblon replied, until he realized to whom it was he was talking to, and then gulped.

Grythos slapped him comradely like on the shoulder again. "If Styphon's House is to defeat Kalvan, we need to know all his tools. And from what I've seen they are no more demonic than Grand Master Soton's warhammer!"

Captain Geblon relaxed. "We could use more Archpriests like you, sir."

Now that's a fact, thought Phidestros to himself.

"Captain General, did you perchance bring along that eighteen pounder?"

"Two more just like it and two more batteries of smaller guns."

"I take it that you didn't just bring them along to road test your artillery?"

Phidestros smiled wickedly. "No, I've got a surprise of my own in mind for the Hostigi. There's a fortress, Tarr-Veblos, on the border between Harphax and Beshta. I'm going to invest it after this Phaxos debacle is done and over. The last thing the Hostigi will expect from the Harphaxi joke of an army is for us to besiege one of their tarrs. I'm hoping that we can breach the walls before Phrames can bring his own army out of Arklos, where he's waiting to see if we come after Queen Rylla. Instead, we send most of the infantry back to Harphax City, while the mobile diversionary force, supported by our artillery batteries, attacks Tarr-Veblos."

Grythos looked thoughtful. "With surprise and enough guns, maybe you can do it. Styphon knows it will help re-build Royal Army morale to have a victory under their belts—to say nothing of Prince Lysandros' Election to Great King. Even if you fail to take the tarr, you'll have field tested the Army and proven to the people of Hos-Harphax that they do indeed have an army, more than just in name."

A moment later Grand Captain Kyblannos rode up. "Captain-General, I see you've been watching the burning of Phaxos Town."

"Yes, and gnawing my teeth down to the gums because I can't do one Dralm damned thing about it! That's what I wanted to talk with you about. What would it take for you to put together a real artillery force, not just two or three batteries?"

"It'll take lots of gold and silver."

"Styphon's House has many chests of both," Archpriest Grythos put in. "I don't have any demonic arts at my disposal so I can't rustle you up some foundry casters out of thin air. But I can bring you enough gold and silver ingots to tempt even sober-minded Zygrosi from their villages."

Kyblannos said, "They've got some real good brass casters and founders up in Hos-Zygros, and with the Captain-General's help maybe we can get us a crew or two."

"Done!" Phidestros said. It was time to cash in some of his markers. He was no longer a ne'r-do-well byblow of the Royal family, but a man of substance. Commander-and-chief of the biggest standing Royal Army outside of Hos-Hostigos.

"Also, I'm not going to have time to run the Iron Band anymore and do all this training. I've already got my replacement all broken in," he smiled openly. "Right Geblon."

"We'll promote Geblon to Grand-Captain of the Iron Band, if that's what you want."

Geblon looked as if he'd just been given his pick of the loot in King Kalvan's treasury. "Thank you, Captain-General. And you, too Kyblannos!"

"Kyblannos, as of today you are now Grand-Captain of the Royal Artillery Regiment of Hos-Harphax. All mercenary artillery units will also be brought under your command, including all guns, rammers, wagons, tools and powder magazines. You can recruit any of the gunners worth their salt. We'll use the gold Archpriest Grythos so generously offered to pay off their captains."

The Archpriest nodded sagely.

Kyblannos rubbed his hands together. "Thank you, as well, Archpriest!"

"In return I only want one thing." Phidestros paused to point to the growing orange glow off to the north. "Next year I want that to be Hostigos Town!"

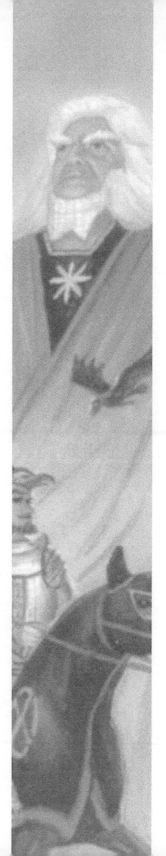

SUMMER

THIRTY-EIGHT

I

Summer heat had come as the allied armies moved south toward the Lydistros River. The rain had not stopped completely, but it had diminished. So had the depth of the streams and the mud. While saddling up that morning, Kalvan had received a message from General Alkides, who had ridden ahead to the banks of the Lydistros to meet the boats coming downriver from Kyblos.

Chancellor Chartiphon, who had a talent for stating the obvious, said, "The high water has left no shallows and few rapids. It has also left less dry ground than one could wish. However, we may thank the gods for this, too. Prisoners say that the Zarthani Knights have withdrawn most of their river galleys and other vessels to Tarr-Ceros."

Thank the gods indeed, thought Kalvan. Counting bottoms, the Zarthani Knights had the second-largest navy here-and-now. Few of their ships could navigate beyond the mouths of the Great Mother River, but they didn't need to. The rivers of the Sastragath, the Dellos (Tennessee) and Ellystros (Alabama) systems, were their domains.

Captain-General Harmakros was less grateful for what he saw as dubious favors. "His Grand Craftiness Soton may just be planning to lure us across the river. Then he can strike us bogged down before the fortress of Tarr-Ceros with the river at our backs."

Harmakros' son, Aspasthar, was seated next to Kalvan, but his eyes were on his father.

Prince Ptosphes, who was lighting his pipe, added, "You have to watch that one. He'd love to get us caught between Tarr-Ceros and his ships."

"We'll play that one by ear when we reach the Lydistros," Kalvan said. "Meanwhile, I won't have to answer to the Kyblosi for wrecked boats and drowned subjects."

Harmakros cleared his throat to get everyone's attention. "Your Majesty, with all due respect, I suggest we decide beforehand. Right now the Sastragathi see us as a gift from the gods. We give them hope of final vengeance on their ancient foes. If we don't cross the Lydistros and besiege Tarr-Ceros, the alliance may wash away down the river with the snags and dead pigs."

"We shall see," Kalvan replied. Now he wished he'd delayed his meeting to question Harmakros more closely. He should have remembered that Harmakros had commanded Sastragathi irregulars in the original Army of Observation, during the Year of the Wolf. The Captain-General knew more about handling them than his Great King, who was so damned tired he forgot to listen to advice even when he had it ready to hand.

Suddenly sheet lightning played along the darkening western sky. At the foot of the hill torches flared, drawing sparks of light from the mountain of armor, weapons and equipment left by the fleeing Knights. The big guns were destroyed and most of the swords blunted, but there was enough left to equip an army, and that fact hadn't escaped the nomad warriors. They were swarming over the piles like ants on a heap of honey.

Shouts of anger joined the shouts of triumph. Kalvan recognized Trygathi accents. He signaled to Colonel Krynos, his aide-de-camp. "Take a troop of Horse Guard and find out what's happening down there!"

Krynos took sixty men, leaving the rest around Kalvan. The Great King dismounted to spare his horse. If the united host didn't end its campaign with everybody walking and half of them barefoot, it would be Tranth's own miracle.

Kronos and the Royal Horse Guard rode up as the shouts reached a climax, then faded. Minutes later the shouting began anew.

A messenger breasted the hill, flinging himself out of his saddle as he reached Kalvan. "Your Majesty. The Sastragathi wish to claim all the

Knights' gear, against your orders. They said they're under orders from Warlord Sargos, and you had promised them first choice."

"Dralm damn-it!" Kalvan growled. "First choice" was a fair offer to the unarmored, sometimes unclothed nomads. It wasn't the same as "everything," but try to tell that to an inflamed Sastragathi warrior! It was like telling a hungry wolf to take only one bite.

Captain-General Harmakros was carefully avoiding looking at his Great King. Then he turned in the saddle, and Kalvan saw his I-told-you-so expression, quickly replaced by surprise. A moment later Kalvan knew he must be matching expressions with Harmakros.

Sargos himself was riding up the hill. The Warlord rode at the head of a gaggle of his guards and subchiefs. Maybe they thought they were keeping a precise formation, but Kalvan couldn't tell which was the main body and which were the stragglers.

"Great King Kalvan! Is this the way you keep your promise to the clans? Your men have laid hands on mine, to keep them from there due. A great treasure lies down there! Will you have us put it to use, or have blood-feud with the tribes and clans?"

"I might ask you the same question," Kalvan replied, more patiently than he felt. Not all of the impatience was with Sargos either. "If blood has been shed, it was without my orders or consent and against my will. Those who shed the blood of tribesmen will be punished (tough luck, Krynos, but you were sent to find out what the trouble was, not to make it worse) and a blood-price will be paid."

"Will blood money guard the backs of men from the Black Knights' swords?" someone cried in a high-pitched voice. Kalvan saw that Sargos' teenage son Larkander was riding with his father tonight.

"No," Kalvan said, raising his voice to keep the argument from turning into a mob scene. There was too much steel and firepower to make this safe; one hothead could blow the alliance sky-high.

"No," he repeated. When Kalvan saw that the nomads were giving him at least half the attention a Great King deserved, he continued, "Yet not all the bare backs are tribesmen. Will not men of the Trygath fight better against our common foe with armor and weapons from the pile down there."

"We of the tribes have fought the Black Knights longer," one of the chief's said.

"This is well known. Yet if the Zarthani Knights are cast down from their castles and the land cleansed of Styphon's minions, who loses? If they survive to fight us again, who wins? Let us all join together and fight as one army."

Kalvan rested his hand on the butt of his pistol; the gold and silver chasing sparkled with each lightning burst. It was a presentation weapon from the Hostigos Gunsmiths' Guild, an unsuccessful effort to prove that they could produce elegant weapons quickly.

"Let us divide the loot into two piles, one for the clansmen and one for those of the Trygath. Then let each chief judge those most in need and give them their pick." This would cost them more than a day's travel, (he could almost hear Soton's chuckle) but if it would keep his so-called allies from each other's throats it would be worth the delay.

"I will begin the first pile with this pistol of mine. Whoever carries it, Trygathi or tribesman, he will carry it with my blessing. So speaks—"

"He seeks our Warlord's life!" somebody shouted. Kalvan's hand completed the drawing of the pistol before his ears could signal his mind to stop the motion. Then the sky seemed to fall upon him, a sky consisting of armored bodies.

Two shots crashed overhead, followed by a scream, a babble of curses and war cries, and Harmakros roaring above everything, "Take the bastard alive!"

The weight lifted from Kalvan, enough to let him draw breath for cursing. There was an audible sigh of relief from his Horse Guard. He spat out mud and grass, and then rose to his knees. A Sastragathi subchief was lying on his back, with Aspasthar kneeling on one arm and several hefty Sastragathi warriors holding other portions of the chief's anatomy—none too gently.

"What the Styphon—!"

Ranjar Sargos answered. "This fool thought you sought to take my life. He drew a pistol. Your war leader's son seized his arm so that his shot went wide of you. It struck my son in the arm. Yet with his other hand he joined—Aspasthar—in dragging the fool from his saddle."

"There is more, father," Larkander said. "Aspasthar shed blood too in the fight, and it mingled with mine."

"You are blood-brothers?" Both fathers seemed to speak at once, then stared at each other. Kalvan swallowed a laugh; he knew just enough about the Sastragathi to know that blood-brotherhood was a deadly serious business among them.

"It is an omen," cried one of the chiefs.

"This seems to be so," Larkander said, as he held his arm against his side. His father's face was as white as if he'd seen a premonition of his own death—or that of his line.

Aspasthar stood up proudly, holding his hand over a shoulder wound.

Since nobody else seemed to have the wits to do so, it fell on Kalvan to call a medic. Uncle Wolf Ramakros dismounted and limped over to the boys, bent down and began to bandage Larkander, who had the more serious wound, first. The question of dividing the loot dropped from everyone's mind until both Larkander's arm and Aspasthar's wound were tightly bound.

"Question him rigorously," Sargos said. "It must be known, whether he was only a witling, or a tool of Styphon's House. Has anyone seen this man before today?"

Everyone within hearing distance shook his heads. Which was not a definitive answer, since there were so many tribes and clans that no one man of the horde knew even half of them. Still, Kalvan relaxed. If Sargos was ready to torture one of his own captains to help the alliance, the worst danger of the split was already past. *Note: Have to give Aspasthar something really impressive as reward—consulting with his father and blood-brother first, of course.*

As the subchief was carried off, Sargos dismounted. He almost stumbled as he touched the ground. Kalvan realized that the Sastragathi Warlord had driven himself to the edge of exhaustion.

"I don't think our dignity will suffer if we sit down and share some wine," Kalvan said. He wanted to wash the grit and grass out from between his teeth. Sargos looked ready to lie down and sleep for a week.

Well, the man's in his forties. He'd probably be just as happy if being Warlord of the Sastragathi was a headquarters job, in a headquarters equipped with cool ale and warm women. By Hadron's flames, that sounds good to me, too!

That brought to Kalvan's mind a picture of his own warm woman. He wondered what Rylla was doing. Her last letter had promised to take no drastic action against the Harphaxi unless provoked, but to patrol the borders heavily and keep the Army of Hostigos ready to move swiftly.

Knowing Rylla, Kalvan knew far too well how "border patrols" could be turned into scouts, then into the vanguard of an invasion. And 'provoked'—in Rylla's mind—was a sufficiently ambiguous term as to leave the gate wide open. Good thing Dalla, Colonel Verkan's wife, was in Greffa with her husband, when Dalla and Rylla got together trouble was never far away. From this distance, however, he couldn't do much but hope and consider praying to Dralm.

II

From the grim cast of Knight Commander Aristocles' face, Soton knew he was the bearer of more bad news. The Grand Master's first thought was that it was too early in the morning to hear anymore.

When he had heard Aristocles out, Soton knew that there was no time of the day or night fit for the hearing of such a tale. Kalvan was driving his host on as though he truly had demons at his command to put them in fear. The vanguard was already past Xenos, two whole days before Soton had expected them. The Usurper and his allies had not been delayed as much by the piles of discarded weapons and armor as he had hoped.

"That means they will be up with us in their full strength before we reach Tryphlon, which is a day's hard ride from Tarr-Ceros."

Aristocles nodded. "Unless they can be delayed."

"By whom?"

The two men looked at each other. They both knew the answer. The rearmost four Lances would have to stand, fight and most probably die to the last man, like the three Lances had at Chothros Heights. "Who is senior Commander among the rearward?"

"Drakmos, of the Sixteenth Lance," Aristocles answered.

"May Kalvan's brother demons flay him alive!" Aristocles looked startled. Soton knew that some of the agony he felt must have shown in his voice.

"No, it is just that I am growing weary of sending friends and faithful Knights to their death just to buy time."

"We could send another—"

"That would take time, which we do not have. His learning the land where he must stand would take more time. Besides, Lance Commander Drakmos would never abandon the Sixteenth."

You are doomed, old friend. All I can do is let you die with honor, as you have lived.

Soton looked at Aristocles, his best friend. The Knight Commander was a trusty right arm, a fine captain and more often than not a wise counselor. Yet he had not been among the company of youths to whose ranks had come one day a peasant boy, small of stature but with an ambition to be a Knight burning bright enough for six giants.

Some of the boys had bullied Soton in the practice bouts, with wooden weapons or unarmed. Others had held back, out of pity for so small an opponent with such a large and clearly foredoomed ambition. Only Drakmos had done neither, giving Soton his best and taking Soton's best in return. Since Drakmos had been the best fighter among the youths, Soton learned more from the bouts with him than from all the others put together. It would not be too much to say that Soton's own prowess on the battlefield, which had saved his life a dozen times over, was in large measure Drakmos' gift.

And now Soton was repaying the gift of a noble life with one of death. An honorable death, to be sure, but there was something to be said for an honorable life.

"Summon a messenger," Soton growled, to hide his urge to scream curses at Kalvan, the gods and anyone else who had brought this about. "Drakmos is to attack Kalvan's main body and keep on attacking until he has drawn that main body on to himself. We need not fear barbarians or light-cavalry scouts sent on ahead."

It hardly needed saying that the barbarians and scouts in advance of Kalvan's great host would cut off what little chance of retreat Drakmos and his Lances had. To balance the odds, Soton added, "We will leave a thousand of our Auxiliary light horse and all our Sastragathi irregulars."

The Sastragathi would probably all desert before Kalvan was within a day's ride, but the Auxiliaries would keep Drakmos from being stung to death by the light nomad cavalry. It was the least he could do.

"More orders," Soton snapped. "All the baggage, everything except a man's weapons and what he wears on his back is to be left for Drakmos."

Aristocles asked, "Everything?"

Soton shrugged. "Drakmos will need what supplies we have left. For the rest of us, it is as true as when I said it before and left most of our supplies. The gold of Balph can buy new armor, new tents, new fireseed, before the snow falls. If we lose the seasoned Knights, not all the gold of Balph will be able to rebuild the Order before Kalvan has crushed and cast down Styphon's House on Earth. If we do not think to the future, there will be none."

But there will be a large debt to pay, Kalvan Servant of Demons. A very large debt indeed.

THIRTY-NINE

I

For once the incessant rains had halted and it was a beautiful summer day. As far as King Kalvan could tell, the host was still in Ohio. Kentucky and the famed Zarthani Knight's castle, Tarr-Ceros, were within a three or four days ride. His men had been on the move for over two and a half months, their rust splotched armor was testament to the hard trail and constant fighting. Without his own personal batman, Kalvan wouldn't have his armor polished and sparkling in the sunlight. Jaklon was a former bootmaker and member of the Hostigi militia who had refused to retire after taking a bad wound in the chest at the Battle of Chothros Heights. Still, marching attendance upon the Great King wasn't the safest job in the Royal Army, Kalvan's last orderly had taken a sword blow to the head that had left him with a crooked jaw and a slash from the corner of his mouth to his throat. Kalvan had stopped counting the number of bannerbearers who'd fallen in action two battles ago.

Great King Nestros was riding along his right side, asking about how Kalvan had arrived in Hostigos. Kalvan had kept him off the subject, with a series of anecdotes about the mercenary who kept showing up in the oddest places and was now Captain-General of Hos-Harphax. Nestros was a good and staunch ally, but as a conversationalist, he was a complete bore.

Up ahead of the pathway, through some trees, Kalvan heard shouting. It didn't sound like an attack, or there would have been a rising cloud of black and gray smoke and the crack of gunpowder. Captain-General Harmakros rode from the front of the main body toward the two kings, his red and blue plumes bouncing at the top of his high-combed morion helmet. "What's going on?" Kalvan asked as he drew within earshot.

"Maybe an ambush. There were some shots up ahead, about half a mile up the road."

The lightly armored nomads made up most of the van and Kalvan, not for the first time, wished he didn't have to play courtier to his fellow Great King and could join Warlord Sargos at the front—if Harmakros allowed! Prince Ptosphes, who had been riding behind and talking to Duke Mnestros and Chartiphon, asked, "What's all the commotion?"

Half a dozen nomads with brightly colored war paint came galloping through the trees. Kalvan recognized one of them as Sargos' son, Larkander. As the pair drew closer, he realized it was his page, wearing the same style buckskins as Larkander, riding beside him. The only thing stopping Aspasthar from looking like a true Sastragathi was the missing war paint—give him another few days! Both boys were wearing cast-off Order helms—of the medieval sort—with the visors up and the black plumes plucked. If these two hellions didn't know what the hubbub was, it was certain no one else did, either.

"King Kalvan!" Aspasthar shouted, his voice breaking. "We bring greetings and news from Warlord Sargos. He has made contact with either the rearguard of the Zarthani Knights, or the van of their army. He thinks they're planning a counter-attack!"

"What's all this about an ambush?" Kalvan asked.

"The Black Knights attacked our van, Great King," Larkander replied, proving that both boys were learning new concepts as well as means of dress. "The first clansmen were halfway through the pass when the hills sprouted Knights and oath-brothers alike!"

"How bad were the losses?"

The young nomad grimaced. "Several hundred clansmen went to Wind."

"Then the Knights must have left a sizeable force behind," Kalvan said. He signaled for King Nestros, Ptosphes, Chartiphon, Mnestros and the rest of the royal party to follow behind. To the boys, Kalvan said, "Lead the way to the ambush site."

When they reached the head of the column, Warlord Sargos was there with his subchiefs. He motioned Kalvan over. "See those hills?"

Kalvan nodded. Ahead was a series of big hills—not quite mountains—covered at the bottom with trees and grass. Up higher there was a series of rock faces, almost quarry-like, with tunnel mouths and switchback trails. "What is this?"

"King Kalvan, this is Pythar." Sargos pointed to a tall, stringy Sastra-gathi with almost white blonde hair, a tanned leather face, a beaked nose and a feather headdress, illustrating the mixed up gene pool of the area. "His clan lives over there beyond these hills."

Pythar nodded. "In my grandfather's time, the men of Hos-Ktemnos used to work the Drynos Mines on this range for iron. The local clansmen still get their ore here. Those mountains are honeycombed with tunnels and pits. The Black Knights are scattered all through them."

Sargos dismissing Pythar with a nod, "Our scouts were allowed through, but as soon as the front of the vanguard was halfway through that pass, the Knights came down from their positions, firing pistols and arrows."

The nomads were still warily removing bodies from the pass, many pin cushioned with arrows, probably from the Knights' oath-brothers and Sas-tragathi allies. Occasionally, when a clansman would get too close to the hills, shots would ring out. After such a fusillade, a band or tribe of nomads would ride out from the main horde—bottled up in the valley before the hills—shooting arrows, darts, crossbow bolts and the occasional firearm into the hills with the predictable and lamentable negative result. The nomads seemed to enjoy the game and he was sure that somewhere Soton was smoking his pipe with a big smirk on his face.

The big question was: How many of the Knights were holed up in these hills? Kalvan couldn't imagine that Grand Master Soton would be any-where within fifty miles of this death trap.

The problem was convincing his allies, neither of them sophisticated in the art of war, that this was a ploy to salvage the larger part of Soton's army. Somehow Kalvan suspected that was not going to be easy. "This ambush is Soton's way of bottling up our armies."

Sargos looked at Kalvan as though he were speaking English. Nestros, too, looked as though he'd rather be off in those hills searching out Knights, rather than discussing strategy.

"Soton has left behind several of his Lances to halt our advance. There must be many passes through these hills. Our best move is to leave these Knights behind, with a suitable force to keep them pinned down, and continue to chase Soton. We must be close or he would not consider sacrificing his precious Knights."

Sargos choked. "Retreat. We cannot allow them to escape their deaths; it is our sworn duty to kill every Black Knight in those hills. How do we know that the Grand Master himself is not hidden in those mines?

Nestros shook his head in agreement. "My men would think it cowardly to leave such a large force at our back."

Kalvan could have chewed the frizzen off his flintlock pistol! "We could leave behind more men than are in Soton's entire army to hold this position and still have ten times Soton's number when we catch up with him." This seemed to go over both their heads.

"We are the superior force so we call the shots, not Soton. If we stay here to chase down these Knights, we will allow the larger part of Soton's army to reach Tarr-Ceros where we will never be able to root him out."

The Warlord was beyond reason. "My warriors are here to fight the Knights. They will not leave until the Knights are all dead."

Nestros nodded in agreement. "If I tried to leave without engaging the Knights, my own men would call me a coward. Many would break away and return home. I would have open rebellion upon my homecoming."

Kalvan shook his head in frustration. "What if I sent an armed force to chase Soton while we are engaged in this battle? Would that be honorable?" His sarcasm was lost on the two leaders, who both gave his words serious consideration.

"As long as it is not perceived that the larger part of the army is leaving, my warriors would not complain," Sargos said.

"Nor mine," added Nestros.

Kalvan turned to Harmakros. "Take the Mobile Force and two regiments of Royal Carbineers and give chase to Soton. You probably won't be able to engage him, but harass him and do as much damage as you can."

Harmakros nodded happily, eager to get away from this botched allied operation. Kalvan couldn't blame him. "Warlord, can you supply a few hundred skirmishers for the Mobile Force?"

"Yes, Your Majesty."

Realizing that the best way to teach his allies military tactics might be letting them learn through the errors of their way, Kalvan suggested that the Warlord demonstrate the most effective way to join the Knights upon the hill in battle. Sargos visibly swelled at the honor. "I will send a thousand infantry to draw them out."

It took the rest of the morning for Sargos to gather the necessary troops and give them orders; his biggest problem was turning down volunteers who felt dishonored that they were not chosen for the attack. His warriors roamed the hillsides poking into holes and pits for almost an hour, finding only one oath-brother, who was instantly turned into a porcupine by hundreds of arrows. Just when they were starting to despair of ever finding the enemy, hundreds of fully armored Knights popped out of the hillside, like apparitions. With sword and pistols they tore into the nomads with fury. Bodies were hacked and dismembered before their eyes, while the nomads swords and spears were turned away or broken on the Knight's armor. It was a slaughter.

"Send reinforcements!" Kalvan cried, but before the first cavalry were less than a quarter up the hill most of the force was dead or wounded, while the knights vanished almost as quickly as they had appeared. Sargos looked shaken and the nomads were spooked.

King Nestros had a smug look upon his face.

"What?" Kalvan asked.

"If those had been Rathoni soldiers, the Black Knights would have never left their holes. Let me take a force up and we will show the nomads how this work is done."

Kalvan threw up his hands. "Do your best." Sargos was blank faced, but unable to keep his left eye from twitching.

Nestros' much larger party of several thousand soldiers moved warily up the hillside, considerably sobered by the slaughter of their allies. Each party contained spearmen who used their spears to poke into anything suspicious. Occasionally a Knight or one of his oath-brothers would be flushed out and emerge fighting, only to be quickly cut down in a flurry of slashing swords and pistol shots. It was a good thing Kalvan still had five wagons loaded with Hostigos fireseed with all this shooting. Meanwhile, the rest of the host stood around making comments and calling out advice. Already their camp followers had caught up with the main body, and there were brightly dressed women, wearing flowing dresses and colorful scarves, with small children running in between horses' legs.

Meanwhile, Kalvan beat his brains against his skull trying to come up with a strategy, which would allow them to root the Knights out of the hills. He didn't have much faith in Nestros' plan. The obvious solution was to starve the Knight out of the hills, but he had no idea of how much food they had, but suspected it was the greater share of Soton's fleeing army. It could take a moon or more before hunger brought them down. As he stood there, a young nomad boy ran up to Kalvan, touched his breastplate for luck and ran away again. *I feel like I'm at the circus, not a battlefield!*

Kalvan watched with interest as several parties of armored men entered the tunnels. All was quiet for a few minutes, and then a battered and bloody Rathoni soldier ran out of a tunnel no one had entered. By the outcry his words raised, Kalvan didn't hold out much hope for his comrades. The soldiers continued poking around for another hour or two, but the results were pitiful—five captured tame Sastragathi and two dead Knights, who took several men with them to Regwarn.

Finally, King Nestros gave up and recalled his soldiers. He shrugged at Kalvan and gave him a 'what now?' look. Shadows were already growing long, so Kalvan sat with Sargos and Nestros, devising a picket of the five hills the Knights held. The scouts had found no evidence of any other nearby party.

By the time equal numbers of Sastragathi and Trygathi soldiers had been dispatched for picket duty, it was time for dinner. Kalvan invited both leaders to the farmhouse that had become his temporary (he hoped!) quarters. For the evening meal they had mystery-meat stew and succotash. When the plates were cleared, Kalvan broke out a jug of Ermut's Best and served both allies' generous cups. Nestros and Sargos got into an argument over the advantages and disadvantages of mounted archers and Kalvan listened to this experienced discourse with a grin on his face. A transcript of this conversation would have served as a doctoral dissertation at any major university with a good history department back in otherwhen. He also smiled because a few years from now, both men might well be making the same arguments in regards to mounted and dismounted arquebusiers. Many drinks later Kalvan excused himself and fell into bed. He was beginning to get used to straw ticks, especially after a few months of sleeping on the ground.

II

Kalvan was awakened by a loud banging noise that at first he feared was coming from inside his head until Jaklon opened the door and told him he had a visitor. He dressed quickly in the same jerkin and slops as yesterday and exited his sleeping quarters. It was Warlord Sargos looking disgustingly wide awake for a man—if Kalvan's memory served him right—who had drank the lion's share of three jugs of Ermut's brandy. "What?" Kalvan asked.

"Great King, I had a vision last night!"

Kalvan stifled a groan. *What demons had the brandy conjured forth in Sargos' drunken wits? And why was he so determined to share this hallucination with him?* "Yes!"

"I dreamt that I was flying again, in the guise of a raven."

Ahh, the spirit of Edgar Allen Poe returns, Kalvan mused. He kept his thoughts to himself, knowing how superstitious the tribesmen were about visions, omens and portents.

"As I flew closer to the earth, I saw this, our own encampment, with the hills that lay before us. Only the hills were on fire, belching clouds of smoke and ash. As I flew closer, I saw that the hills were alive with soldiers running out of the tunnels and pits, like termites fleeing a burning mound. Then I woke up!" Sargos looked expectantly at Kalvan as though he expected him to give him a Freudian dream analysis of this nightmare.

Kalvan shrugged his shoulders, experiencing another round of pounding headache. He felt as though the Hostigi drum corps had taken permanent residence in his head. "Go on."

"Then I thought back to my youth, when my mother used to bake whole boars for the First Day Feast. She would wrap the whole pig in leaves and then bury it in a clay mound beneath hot rocks. When we dug it up that evening, the cooked flesh would fall from the bones." Sargos smacked his lips, as if reliving the memory.

"We called that a *luau*, where I came from," Kalvan said, suddenly remembering that Sargos wouldn't have the faintest idea of what he was talking about. "Beyond the Cold Lands a *luau* is a great feast of welcome in the Kingdom of Hawaii. Oh, I see what you're getting at. Why don't we roast the Knights out of those tunnels?"

Kalvan jumped up, his headache forgotten, and wrapped his arms around the Warlord. "Yes, yes, this is a vision from the gods."

Ranjar Sargos tried to jump up and down, found he couldn't, and began grinning so hard Kalvan was surprised his cheeks didn't split. Suddenly Kalvan was very aware that neither man had bathed in a month of Sundays. It was astounding what a man's sense of smell could grow accustomed to!

Kalvan disengaged from the nomad's embrace and said, "Let us have something to eat and then we will call a Council of War! Jaklon is my breakfast ready?"

"Yes, Your Majesty. Should I heat up the last of the chocolate?"

"Capital idea. Sargos your idea is absolutely inspired. It'll take time to get the wood we need, but nothing compared to what it would take to starve these stubborn iron heads out of those mines!"

FØRTY

I

D alla closed the collapsed-nickel door behind her and took a pack of cigarettes off the shelf. "Ahhh. I miss these when I'm playing Dalla, proper Greffan wifey of Trader Verkan. She lit up and smoke swirled around her head. Then she reached over and gave Verkan a big hug. "That doesn't mean I'm not glad to see you!"

Verkan followed with a smile of husbandly contentment. "We've got two ten-days away from Dhergabar and Paratime HQ to look forward to. I could get used to this."

The three-story mansion's in the heart of Greffa's—merchant district— was his official Grefftscharrer residence. The collapsed-nickel lined basement was Verkan's home headquarters—a piece of Home Time Line on Fourth Level, Aryan Transpacific. The basement was large enough to accommodate, including sleeping quarters, a Paratime Police team of twenty men. The basement even had its own Paratemporal Conveyer—a small ten footer suitable for only six persons, except in an emergency when a whole team could squeeze inside for an evacuation. Not that that could ever happen here; the collapsed-nickel shielded basement was strong enough to ward off anything but a direct hit by a nuclear warhead.

The office was almost a double for Verkan's office on First Level, down to the horseshoe desk and large picture window. He even had a see-through case for his Kalvan's Time-Line souvenirs.

"It's time to see how Kalvan is doing." Verkan hit a button in the sitting room and what appeared to be a solid wall turned into a blank viewscreen. "The sky-eye we put up over Tarr-Ceros ought to pick up Kalvan pretty quickly."

The screen filled with a high earth shot of the Lydistros Valley, with Tarr-Ceros dominating the highest ridge. From this distance the great Order of Zarthani Knights castle looked like a toy model. "Dalon Salth is riding undercover as one of the Mounted Rifles so all I have to do is key-in his locater number and we should find Kalvan and the Army of the Trygath fairly quickly." The picture on the screen changed to a green hilly area with an enormous army bivouacked down below. "They're still there!"

"Why has Kalvan set fire to those hills?" Dalla asked.

Verkan peered closer. Smoke was pouring out of tunnels and pits at the peaks of the five hills. "You're right someone has lit them on fire! From what Dalon told me over the radio, Soton left four Lances behind him to hold Kalvan up—"

"How could a few thousand men hold up an army that big?" she pointed to the sprawling army below.

"It's a case of pre-industrial military honor. Kalvan's allies cannot honorably leave a large force behind them without losing face among their own troops. Since a large part of the cohesive force behind such a horde is based on oath-bonding and personal honor, Kalvan is forced to honor Warlord Sargos' and King Nestros' obligations. So he has to halt the army and finish off this detachment before following the Knights. To press forward would mean dishonoring his allies and as such they would lose not only prestige and manna, but many, if not most, of their retainers."

Dalla pursed her lips and blew out a series of smoke rings. "That means that Soton will escape to his hideyhole. That's going to mean more problems for Kalvan next year."

"Exactly. Of course, when Soton finds out that Kalvan has roasted his men in this stone crockpot of his, Soton's not going to be very happy. Nor will he be pleased if Harmakros and the Mobile Force reach him before he gains Tarr-Ceros."

"You mean it's all right for Harmakros to hare off after Soton, but not okay if Kalvan does it."

"To the nomads, Harmakros is a sub-chief and only doing his Warlords' bidding. Since Harmakros only has a few thousand men—almost a scouting party in relation to the nomad host—honor is preserved."

Dalla took another puff on her cigarette. "Men, I'll never understand them."

"Women—ahhh! Wait until you see the mess that Rylla has gotten Kalvan into. I wanted to tell you about it earlier, but with the welcome back party upstairs and all."

"What's my friend done now?"

Verkan picked up the controller, switched to Hos-Harphax sky-eye and keyed-in the locater number for Ranthar Jard. This time the viewscreen showed a burning town, with what looked to be a fireworks display near Tarr-Phaxos.

Dalla blew out a cloud of smoke. "This is Rylla's handiwork!"

"Oh, yes. And in direct violation of her husband's orders."

"Then I don't blame her. Europo-American is still too patriarchic-centric for my taste."

"Seriously, Rylla went too far even in terms of the mores and customs of Aryan-Transpacific. You remember me telling you how Prince Araxes had ambushed our foundry team on its way to Nostor."

"Isn't that the same Araxes who renounced his allegiance to Hos-Hostigos last year, when it appeared that Kalvan was in trouble?"

"Same Prince."

"Then Rylla has local custom on her side."

"No, a woman does not lead an army on Aryan-Transpacific, but that's still the least of her transgressions and might well be forgiven since she is winning. The real public relations disaster is her actions have given the Hostigos the 'appearance' of being the aggressor. Remember, Aryan-Transpacific is not a place where you find monolithic kings and rulers; each kingdom is made up of princes and barons who owe their fealty and military support to their direct overlord or king. But, that support exists only so long as the lesser rulers are not afraid that their overlords' orders will infringe upon their feudal and historical rights. Until Rylla moved the army into Phaxos, most princes sympathized with Kalvan and Hos-Hostigos in the war against Styphon's House. Many of them suspected Kalvan of being tough on barons and princes who displeased him, but they weren't sure.

Now, with Rylla's invasion of Phaxos, they have proof—and that's a Hos of another color.

"Let's take a closer look."

The lens now zoomed in on the town walls, at least, those that were still standing. "Is that what I think it is on that pole?" Dalla asked.

Verkan instructed the lens to zoom in for a closer shot. On the screen was a head, with its mouth stilled permanently in mid-scream, impaled on the pole. Next to that pole was a woman's head missing an ear and most of her hair.

"Pull back! I've seen enough. Rylla—this time maybe you have gone too far."

Verkan whistled. "Kalvan is not going to be happy about this. Let me see if I can reach Ranthar."

After a short wait, Ranthar's voice came alive. "Verkan, we've got problems here."

"We saw the poles with the heads."

"Those are Prince Araxes' close relations, with assorted war criminals and Styphoni priests. Rylla in her zeal has depopulated about half the noble houses of Phaxos, which includes any of them with ties to either Hos-Harphax or Styphon's House. I don't think this is going to play well in Hos-Agrys."

"Or at home in Hostigos Town when Kalvan returns!"

"She's having a good time, though. So is Prince Sarrask, who—believe it or not—has become the voice of moderation in the Hostigi councils of war. Most of the Hostigi have got caught up in the bloodlust of conquest and sacking a major town. I guess they've been on the receiving end so long that it's a pressure release to be giving it out for a change. There's a party atmosphere here; you know, while the Great King's away—"

"What's holding them back now?"

"Tarr-Phaxos. It's been under constant bombardment for over a moon quarter. Rylla just got a new shipment of shells in from Beshta so I don't think it will hold out much longer. Prince Araxes must be quaking in his boots!"

"If he isn't, he soon will be. I'm sure Rylla's picked out an appropriate punishment for him. Thanks Ranthar. I'll be in touch."

"Over and out, Chief!"

"How serious is this, Verkan?"

"Very. Rylla might have single-handedly changed the course of Kalvan's Time-Line. The one thing Kalvan doesn't need is more enemies. And Rylla's just given him a barrel full."

II

Kalvan sat on his horse and watched as here-and-now's biggest bonfire, at the bottom of the hills, was torched by screaming clansmen. Tree trunks, limbs and branches tumbled like matchsticks a third of the way up the hills. After four days of sunshine to dry them out—there was going to be quite a barbecue. Already, small clouds of smoke were pouring out of the old abandoned mines and iron pits. It had taken a week of hauling and a small forest of trees to fill every crevice and hole, and all that was accomplished between counter-attacks by the Knights. The counter-attacks had been the futile last gasp of the doomed; after all, what could a few thousand men do against a fifty times their number.

It hadn't take the Knights long to figure out the Warlords' diabolical plan, but—even after a short parlay—Knight Commander Drakmos refused categorically to surrender. *He's buying time for the Order*, thought Kalvan, *but at what price!*

The fire, set by a hundred torches, went racing up the hills. The heat was already so intense that the clansmen were drawing back from the hills. Many of the nomads darted back and forth to the flames, like children, daring them to do their worst. A score of black armored Zarthani Knights and their oath-brothers ran out of a hidden tunnel, searching for a bolthole. Moments later smoke came billowing out behind them. The men looked down at the racing fire and then back at the hole, which was now belching smoke like a locomotive. Kalvan aimed his rifle, pushed down the striker and fired. One of the armored men toppled. *A lucky one*, Kalvan thought.

The other riflemen in the King's Lifeguard followed his example and in two breaths, all the Knights were down. Then the fire leaped over their bodies and all that could be seen were flames and swirling smoke. The fire raged up and down the hills all day and through most of the night.

In the morning, the hillsides were covered by blackened trunks and tree limbs. Here and there in the mine entrances were blackened armors and an occasional skeleton. Kalvan sent out search teams to find any survivors. It took most of the morning, but none of the tunnels contained anything living, animal or human. The Hostigi soldiers who returned came back with blackened faces and desolate eyes.

Captain Simodes, a red-haired cavalryman whose hair was now charcoal-colored, told Kalvan, "It's like Regwarn in those tunnels, Your Majesty! I know the Knights are the enemy and all, but I wouldn't wish a death like that on a clutch of Styphon's House Archpriests! We found one point of sixty Knights all glued to one another. Their armor had melted together and we couldn't separate the bodies. It sickens a man to see brave men die like crayfish in a pot. The smell was so bad we had to soak pieces of our sashes in water and tie them around our noses, and still half the men puked their guts out. I don't think I'll ever eat pork again!"

Kalvan dismissed Simodes and called an impromptu council of war. "Warlord, you are to be commended for the battle plan."

Ranjar Sargos looked sick. "I had not imagined the screams and stench that would assault us! I can't imagine a more terrible kind of war."

Warchief Vanar Halgoth nodded in agreement. "The Raven Hag of War cares not how men die in battle, just that they go to Wind. It was truly bad medicine, but, if we could, I would say let us do it all over again at Tarr-Ceros."

The others nodded. Kalvan remembered the mustard gas of World War I and the atomic flames of Hiroshima and Nagasaki and wondered, for about the hundredth time, if he was leading these folk—now *his* people—down the same road.

"This was bad," Kalvan said. "In my land this type of warfare was called 'total war.'"

King Nestros drew back away from Kalvan. "I don't like the sound of that."

"It's neither honorable, nor fair. But it's the future."

Ranjar Sargos made a series of complex hand motions that Kalvan assumed were to ward of demons and evil spirits. "I pray to the gods you are wrong, King Kalvan. Did the gods speak to you, too?"

"Yes, in a manner of speaking." Kalvan had seen the future of warfare first hand, first in World War II newsreels, and then in person on the frozen battlefields of Korea fighting the Chinese. "I will do my best to see that it doesn't happen here." *It sounds like whistling in the wind to me, but maybe one man can make a difference.*

"May the gods give you the strength." The Warlord looked up at the sun. "We have almost a full day ahead of us. Let's find our fat rattlesnake before he hides in his den!"

III

"Toss oars!"

The cry floated up from the boat on the muddy Lydistros River, to the low-lying hill where Kalvan stood gazing at Tarr-Ceros. The great fortress of the Holy Order of the Zarthani Knights marched across nearly a mile of hills on the far side of the river. Some of those hills had clearly been flattened; others carved into the fortress's outworks. Kalvan counted three concentric layers of trenches and wooden palisades, each furnished with artillery positions and covered ways to let ammunition and reinforcements come up. There was a much smaller, older fort and several batteries of guns—bombards he was certain—on the opposite shore of the wide river.

The stonewalls only began beyond the trenches, rising like seats in a theatre up the central hill to the massive keep in the middle. Two, maybe three concentric circles of walls, each with its own moat and array of towers. Light glinted from the towers and the walls alike, evidence of armor and big guns.

In the center, the keep rose up a good thirty feet above the highest tower. And were Kalvan's eyes playing tricks on him, or was the keep faced with something shiny—marble? There were marble quarries up near the head of the Tennessee River in his own world: why not here? Certainly water transportation for the marble wouldn't have given the Knights any problem, not with their river fleet.

Marble was not the stone Kalvan would have chosen for a fortress. Under artillery fire, it would splinter and the splinters scatter like shell fragments.

But then, Tarr-Ceros had been built when the Zarthani Knights had no enemies who could bring artillery against their citadel. Until recently, neither the tribes nor the Trygathi had much to bring against Tarr-Ceros except numbers, archery, crossbows, a few arquebuses and the occasional wrought-iron four-pounder.

Kalvan signaled to the horseholders, who led Harmakros' mount and those of his aides down to the bank. So far, the Tarr-Ceros garrison had paid their visitors less attention than cockroaches. If they changed their mind, some of the guns in the outer fortifications could certainly reach down river.

Harmakros held his horse to a walk as he led his party up the muddy hillside, then reined in and saluted his Great King. The Captain-General's face was grimmer than ever, far more than could be blamed on fatigue and the strain of long campaign.

"Your Majesty, that floating barrier of spiked logs is no tale. There's no way through to the quay until the logs are removed."

"How long would that take?"

"With a few tarred barrels of fireseed and no enemy fire, an hour of any night. But they've got tarpots and what looks like bundles of arrows all laid out in the trenches right behind the quay. They could light up the engineers and pick them off like rats in a privy corner. Even if the barrier went, the trenches would be manned and ready for the landing party."

"So going for the quay would be a waste, even as a feint?"

"The Knights would get a good laugh and we would get a bloody nose," Harmakros said morosely. He did not put into words that which his tone added, *and there was no need to send anyone up under the guns of the fortress to learn this. Once Your Majesty decided it had to be done, it became my duty. But, if I don't have any more such duties for a while, it won't break my heart.*

"Harmakros, for at least the hundredth time—well done. If we find ourselves with a vacant princedom, would you consider taking it?"

"Once Your Majesty doesn't need my services in the field, I won't say no. But I have a nasty feeling that it's going to take a long time to finish this war with Styphon's House. We've driven the badger into his lair."

"Do we have any way of getting him out and taking his hide home?"

Again, tone spoke volumes. "Galzar Wolfhead might knock down those walls with his mace, Your Majesty, but nothing we have will even come close. As for a siege, unless you've figured out a way to feed an army on air, forget it."

Harmakros was right. Kalvan had known as much the moment he laid eyes on Tarr-Ceros. It reminded him of one of the great Crusader castles in the Holy Land—but an aerial picture of a ruin didn't give the same impact. You had to see one of those stone monsters armed and garrisoned in its prime, looming over you, ready to defy the worst you could do. And when that worst wasn't enough to do more than give the garrison a few sleepless weeks . . .

There wasn't a gun in the whole Hostigi artillery that could both be moved here and make an impression on the walls. There wasn't enough food to keep a third of the allied host alive long enough to make the Knights tighten their belts. A simple attempt to storm the place would kill half the attackers and demoralize the rest.

Summon Soton to negotiate? That at least would waste only breath, not blood. Grand Master Soton knew the strength of his walls and the men who manned them. Probably less than half his garrison were seasoned fighters, but behind those walls children with croquet mallets could be deadly foes.

"Well, then there it is," Kalvan said, "we can't do much at their front door. "Let's wait until the scouts to the east and south return with their reports. If it's good cavalry country, maybe we can do something at the back door."

That something was likely to be expensive in time, treasure, fireseed, horses and blood, but it had to be at least discussed.

The rest of the allies had very little notion of what a hollow victory they had won. They only knew that they'd seen the Knights in retreat for the better part of a moon. The Battle at Drynos Mines—if it even qualified for such a lofty designation—against the four Lances of the rearguard had given them a taste for the Knights' blood; they wanted more.

Kalvan remembered Napoleon's dictum about the advantages of making war against allies. Soton could wield his Knights as a single weapon, like his famous warhammer. Kalvan had to be chairman of a committee as much as commander-and-chief.

Maybe the Great Barbecuc had given the Sastragathi the view that the Knights' blood came cheap; if so, they were badly mistaken. The four

Lances and their allies had numbered perhaps four thousand men at the outset and out of that army less than fifty badly burned prisoners had finally emerged from the tunnels. Kalvan doubted that a dozen were still alive, and they faced a terrible future here-and-now with no 'real' medical help. The allies lost less than a thousand men, but then that was hardly a battle—more of a turkey roast.

At least Alkides had all the horse artillery ready to move. Where cavalry could go, the guns could follow. Something might be made of this—not much, but enough to keep the alliance from falling apart because the Great King of Hos-Hostigos abandoned his allies!

Something else that might help, even more than artillery, at least right now—"Harmakros! Do we have anymore of that wine we picked up with the first batch of loot?"

"Yes, I had the barrels loaded on pack mules under a trusted captain. I reckoned we might have a use for it. When I left the Battle at Drynos Mines, you, Sargos and Nestros were finishing off the last of Ermut's Best."

"Another well done. It's time to call a Council of War. Just a small one, so I think one barrel should be enough to keep even Sargos happy."

At least until he finds out that he's still going to have the Knights on his borders, almost as strong as ever and out for vengeance.

FORTY-ONE

I

No one questioned Danar Sirna's bringing up the rear of Danthor Dras's entourage, as he led the party toward the Assembly Hall of Kalvan Subsector's Fifth-Level Depot. Sirna was the junior member of the party, at the Depot only for an inventory of replacement supplies scheduled for the 'new' Royal Foundry in Nostor. In spite of their egalitarian pretensions, University people were as devoted to hierarchy as Styphon's House.

So there was no one at Sirna's back, something she had been in a knife-and-dagger world long enough to appreciate. There was also no one able to pay attention to her grim frown or the set of her jaw—or ask awkward questions about them.

As the Scholar reached the axial corridor, he held up his hand. Two light haulers whispered past, both loaded with Styphon's House Subsector barrels. Danthor signaled his followers into movement again, and then stopped so abruptly that Sirna bumped into the man ahead of her. He was a professor of engineering history, slightly taller than her and half again as broad. She had to step out from behind him to see what had halted Danthor.

Verkan Vall was striding out of the Assembly Hall. The Paratime Chief lacked his usual bodyguards, but his physical presence was enough of an escort. The stares he exchanged with Scholar Danthor were exquisitely measured on both sides. Each man knew exactly where he stood with the other; both were determined to let no one else know.

"Putting telltales in our Assembly hall?" Danthor wore a wholly deceptive grin on his face.

"No, I just wanted to see if the Assembly Hall could be converted back into a storeroom in an emergency."

"What kind of emergency?"

"Needing to supply our Kalvan Subsector people with bulk supplies again."

"Our 'people' includes the University Study Team, of course?"

"Of course, Scholar. The Paracops can live off the land or even go underground if necessary. I wouldn't say the same for most of your people. The best University orientation still isn't the Paratime Police Academy and five years of outtime experience."

Hostility rippled through the University people, like static electricity through a cat's fur. For once, Sirna was thankful for her divided loyalties. They let her find this confrontation darkly humorous rather than threatening.

"I think more highly of University training than you do, Chief Verkan. I also wonder why you need more storage space, particularly at our expense. Surely any bulk purchases can be stored either at the point of purchase or in the Kalvan Subsector."

"Have you ever tried hiding a hundred-foot conveyer loaded with barley, brass ingots and wrought iron? Sorry, I know you have. Just remember that our ability to operate in parallel Styphon's House time-lines depends on not strewing portents and demonical visitations all over the place. As for Kalvan's Time-Line, find me a place that you can be sure won't be overrun by somebody's army in the next year and I'll move Paracop HQ there!"

"I admit that would be a search for Queen Griselda's Breechguard," Danthor said, with a more genuine grin. "But I remind you that the Assembly Hall is more than a place for talkfests among professors. We use it to publicize all activities on Kalvan's Time-Line, yours included. You have an interest as great as ours in keeping such a facility open."

"We do. We also have an interest in keeping everyone out there on Kalvan's Time-Line alive. What about letting the University use the Police

Briefing Room? It has the same facilities as your Assembly Hall and probably a bigger computer."

"And a lot of even bigger Paratime Policemen to intimidate our discussions!" the engineer ahead of Sirna growled.

Verkan Vall stared with elaborate care at the gray-sprayed ceiling. *And why that particular shade of gray*, wondered Sirna? It reminded her of a day-old corpse. Danthor Dras glared at the engineer. Sirna had heard the Scholar had once outstared a Sastragathi berserker. Looking at him now, she could believe the tale.

"I think the Paratime Police would hardly stoop to intimidation of First Level Citizens," the Scholar said. "I have a higher opinion of their competence and integrity than that."

Danthor Dras bowed in Verkan's direction. "Chief Verkan, I would prefer to keep our Assembly Hall if possible. I will accept your offer if necessary. Alternatively, could University funds make it possible to expand the depot's habitable space all around? Perhaps this is not a zero-sum game."

"Perhaps not, although it is Police property. I would have to check with our Legal Section on what we can accept. I'll do that as soon as I get back to First Level. My thanks, Scholar, and best wishes for success in your projects."

The Paratime Police kept strict control over outtime facilities, even on the Fifth Sector, where land was free for the taking. It made sense, thought Sirna, if the Paratime Police kept outtime bases small and few in number, they were easier to keep secure and under surveillance.

More scholarly mutterings using unscholarly language followed the Chief's retreating back, but he showed no signs of hearing any of it. Danthor Dras wore a genuine grin as he turned back to his followers.

"Sometimes it's necessary to concede on a small point to win a larger one. But I will never concede that the Paratime Police have the right to interfere with our operations on Kalvan's Time-Line. Their Chief's friendship with Great King Kalvan gives them nothing of the kind. We will defend ourselves against the Police as we would against Styphon's House itself!"

The cheering must have been heard all over the depot, let alone by the departing Paracop Chief. Fortunately everyone else was cheering so loudly that nobody noticed Sirna wasn't joining in.

II

"Then there is *nothing* more we can do against those fatherless Knights?" Warlord Sargos glared around Kalvan's tent as if ready to challenge any king or captain present to personal combat.

Maybe he was. Kalvan began to think that breaking a barrel of wine hadn't been the best idea. Sargos had grown increasingly belligerent instead of mellow.

"Not *nothing*," Harmakros talked with the air of a man trying for the twentieth time to persuade a stubborn child to go to bed. "We can't knock down the walls of Tarr-Ceros or besiege it for long enough to do any good. What else is there?"

Sargos emptied the last of a jug into his cup and looked into the ruddy depths. He seemed to find wisdom or at least a better-guarded tongue there.

"Nothing that will end the Knights for all time, I suppose. But is there anything else worth doing?"

"Yes," King Nestros said. He hadn't yet been officially proclaimed Great King, that would have to wait until his return to Rathon City, but he wore a gold-circled crown set with turquoise picked up from the Knights' baggage and hastily set into place by an armorer. "Anything that will keep them quiet for a year or two will be almost as good. United, with no enemies at our backs, we're their match. We proved it: now we know it, they know it and neither of us is going to forget it soon. Let us do something to make them remember it as long as possible."

Several faces around the tent wore, "Yes, but what?" expressions. It was time for the god-sent Great King Kalvan to take a hand. The rest had wrangled themselves into being ready to listen.

"Now, a lot of what we can do depends on how long we can keep the boats and barges in range of Tarr-Ceros," Kalvan said.

"Oh, demons fly away with those boats and barges!" Sargos growled. "If they won't let us destroy the Knights, what good are they?"

"If we have most of a moon, before the Knights' fleet returns from Xiphlon, we can destroy the Knights' lands," Kalvan snapped. "Alkides, do you think we have that much time?"

"With guns mounted in the right places, I suspect we can keep off anything short of all the galleys at once," the artillery office answered. "That's using mostly the Trygathi heavy pieces, that wouldn't be much good in the field anyway."

Sargos looked ready to curse the boats and barges again, but Kalvan fixed him with a sharp look. "Warlord Sargos, those watercraft are like herds or chosen warriors to the Princes of Kyblos and Ulthor. Would one of your chiefs thank you if you lost all his horses or a thousand of his best warriors including two or three of his sons?"

Sargos appeared to ponder the question and came up with an answer that at least kept him quiet. Kalvan signaled to Harmakros, who handed him a map of the area around Tarr-Ceros. It was a rough map, but it was a historical document—the first map here-and-now ever drawn on paper. There was also a second copy, on the more usual, not to say durable, deerskin.

"The Knights have left a belt of forest around Tarr-Ceros, between them and the lands that raise their food and horses. They've always relied on the forest to let their light-armed troops delay an enemy while the heavies move out.

"Now suppose we throw two forces around Tarr-Ceros. One is infantry, with light artillery support. They'll hold the forest belt, keeping the Knights *in* instead of enemies *out*. I'll wager half the Treasure of Balph it'll take even Soton a while to figure out what to do about that."

"Yes, yes," Sargos exclaimed. Eagerness crackled in his voice. "Our archers are without peer. Given time to hide themselves, they can hold the forest—"

"Boast about your archers when they've proved themselves!" Nestros snapped. "We of the Trygath are no children with the bow, as you yourself know—" Kalvan allowed them to go round about like that for a few minutes. By then, they'd mostly sobered up and were growing hoarse, at least, Nestros was; Sargos could bellow until the cows came home!

"Hold!" Kalvan shouted. "There will be enough Knights to go around, I am sure. To the archer who takes the most, I will personally give ten Hostigos gold Crowns and a weapon of his choice. General Alkides, can you move your four-pounders in that kind of wooded country?"

"With a little help from Galzar and a lot of help from men who aren't afraid to drag a gun." The two allied rulers couldn't promise their help fast enough.

Kalvan was starting his explanation of what the second force would do, when shouts of "Way, way, for a royal messenger!" and galloping hooves broke in on the meeting. Kalvan decided that royal dignity would be better served by going on with the briefing, even if the council hall were a wooded glen.

"The second force will be cavalry. It isn't intended to stand and fight. It's going to burn out every farm and village, run off every head of livestock, terrorize every peasant it can reach. If the Knights come out of Tarr-Ceros, they will have to fight their way through their own forest belt. If they stay in their fort, they will have to watch their peasants, crops, and herds ruined.

"The Knights get some of their supplies from downriver, but not all. It will be a lean winter and a lean year for the Knights. Soton will gladly march the Knights out in their breechclouts with clubs if all else fails, but they won't be nearly so formidable."

The picture made the others in the tent smile; everyone remembered the mountain of discarded armor and supplies. Someone was passing around the last cask of wine when the royal messenger poked his head into the tent. "Message for Great King Kalvan's eyes only."

Kalvan noticed that the man was pale under the spatters of mud, but thought it was only fatigue, as Kalvan broke the seal and unfolded the parchments. It was only when he'd read both the letters twice that Kalvan noticed everyone in the tent had backed as far away from him as they could. Harmakros was the first to find his voice, and even he sounded as if the wrong word could make his friend and Great King belch flame.

"It is not ill news of the Queen or the Princess, I hope."

"The Princess, no. It's from Uncle Wolf Tharses," Kalvan said through clenched teeth. "As for Her Majesty—she has brought the campaign against Prince Araxes of Phaxos to a successful conclusion." Conscious that curious eyes were still devouring him, Kalvan pushed the letter into his belt pouch, gulped half his cup of wine at once, and then spread the map out again.

"Now, General Alkides. What is your notion of the best crossing place?"

FⴲRTY-TWⴲ

I

The moment the meeting ended, Captain General Harmakros bearded Kalvan in his tent. "You may be able to pull the wool over their eyes—as you call it," he said, pointing back to the direction of the clearing where Sargos and Nestros were drinking the dregs from the last wine cask. "But I know you better. And what campaign against Phaxos is this that our Great Queen brought to conclusion? When we left Hostigos, we were at peace with Prince Araxes."

"Where's Prince Ptosphes?"

"Back there with those two. Sometimes he'll start re-fighting the Battle of Tenabra in his head, as if he could at this late date change the conclusion. I don't think he heard a word."

"Good. I don't want him involved. He'll convince himself that he should have volunteered to stay in Hostigos Town and carry that bag of guilt with him, too, all the way back home."

Harmakros fidgeted. "What is all this about?"

"There was some dust-up over the Royal Foundry expedition to Nostor. The evidence pointed in Araxes direction. Queen Rylla—who's had it in for Araxes ever since he disclaimed his oath to Hos-Hostigos last summer—took it upon herself to declare war on Araxes—"

"What!"

"My thoughts exactly. Of course, she didn't see fit to inform me of this little fracas until it was brought to a successful conclusion. If she'd taken a beating, we'd of probably only found out about it when we crossed the borders of Rathon into Hos-Hostigos."

Harmakros shook his head. "Rylla, what have you done? We should have never left her alone with Sarrask—he's got to be the brains, well excuse the term, behind all this."

"Not according to Uncle Wolf Tharses' letter. Sarrask actually advised caution! Not that my dear wife listened. Dralm Damn her!"

"What about Prince Phrames?"

"No mention of our gentle prince. I suspect his council was not welcomed. I don't even blame him for not sending the bad news; where I come from they used to kill the bearer of news like this. My lovely wife has turned our diplomatic relations topsy-turvy. We'll be lucky if Hos-Agrys doesn't join the Harphaxi Army in next year's campaign season. This certainly squelches any hopes of winning over the Council of Dralm."

Harmakros nodded his agreement. "What happened to Araxes?"

Kalvan looked down at the second parchment, for once glad it wasn't paper since it would have fallen apart under his wringing hands. "Let me quote the Queen: 'Once the Army of Hostigos had breached the walls of Tarr-Phaxos a sortie party went in and secured the person of Prince Araxes and the highpriest of Styphon's House he was holding under house arrest. We then had them both drawn-and-quartered and the body parts packed into one of the surviving cannon and shot like case shot at the carrion feeding outside the city gates. There was a great slaughter of buzzards and ravens. The former Prince—it could be said—cut a certain swathe through their collective body.'"

Harmakros shook his head. "That's our girl. The punishment was apt, since the Prince proved himself a traitorous cur, but it will be used by Styphon's House against us. Did she mention what the Harphaxi Army was doing while she burned Phaxos Town?"

"Only that the Royal Army of Hos-Harphax attended her like a nursemaid, but held itself back from any engagement. I would assume Phidestros made an appearance just to make sure the army did not decide to march straight to Harphax City."

Harmakros massaged his temples. "He knows our girl. She might have done it."

"I know, it scares me to death. I could have come back to Hostigos a widower and met an invading army, if her march through Phaxos had been any easier. She's had some difficulty finding an "acceptable" claimant to the princely chair so she's left our Sarrask of Sask in charge, as provost marshal, along with four thousand men—along with the 'prudent members of the Phaxosi Army, who had the wisdom to surrender and swear oaths to the Great Queen of Hos-Hostigos'—to keep the peace. Now, that's one for the books!"

Harmakros hooted. "Peace keeper Sarrask! I've heard everything now. Next you'll be telling me that men can fly."

"If I could, I know where I'd be going instead of playing nursemaid to these two knuckleheads, while we teach Soton a lesson in exceeding your grasp."

"Your Majesty, if you left Nestros and Sargos alone with their armies, they'd be at each other's throat in less than a moon quarter—the Zarthani Knights be damned."

"I know, Harmakros. It's going to be a long, hot summer."

II

Scholar Danthor's hand tapped the screen control. The picture changed again. Now it showed Prince Araxes' palace in Phaxos City.

Or rather, what had been the palace. Now it was a pile of blackened rubble, with charred beams and bits of furniture jutting up out of the tumbled stone. The gardens had been ploughed up, the ponds filled in with chopped down trees and corpses and the walls breached in a dozen places.

"Prince Araxes—the late Prince Araxes—was fond of his comforts," the Scholar reported dryly. "So he made Tarr-Phaxos strictly a military post and moved his court into the town palace. He was one of the first Harphaxi princes to do so. One imagines that his fate will hardly encourage many more imitators. Fortunately, he chose to hide in the keep of Tarr-Phaxos and thus spared himself, for a while, the fate dealt out to his family and retainers."

Sirna kept her eyes firmly on the screen. She didn't need to look at her neighbors to know what they thought of Rylla's disposal of the Phaxos problem. She could hear the gasps, hisses of indrawn breath and whispered denunciations.

Were some of them looking away, or feeling queasy inside? Sirna wondered. They probably didn't include anyone who'd seen pictures of Hostigos Town on time-lines where the Styphoni had overran it. The only pictures she'd ever seen matching those were from Mongol sacks or Third Reich Hispano-Columbian victories.

But those were the work of Styphon's House or people equally barbarous. This was the work of—

The picture changed again. Now it showed the Great Square of Phaxos Town, another of the late Prince's expensive public improvements. Armored Hostigi soldiers with red and blue plumes held back a crowd on all four sides. In the middle was a stout block of wood. On one side of the block stood a bare-chested man with a two-handed axe slung across his back. On the other side lay a half dozen shrouded bodies. Four Hostigi soldiers were lifting another body on to a litter. One soldier was putting what looked to be a woman's head into a bag bulging with what Sirna was afraid were other heads.

"The Great Queen," Danthor intoned, "gave orders that all immediate members of Araxes' family were to lose their heads. That is correct, that was a woman's head that soldier was carrying by the hair."

There was a collective gasp from the assembled faculty.

Sirna noticed most of the Hostigi were infantry, but a small mounted group occupied the middle of the west side of the square. One slim figure in silvered armor was bareheaded, long blonde hair tossed by the same breeze that whipped the pennons and standards.

Rylla. She had ordered this slaughter of the Princely House of Phaxos and all those nobles who wouldn't swear allegiance to the Kingdom of Hos-Hostigos. Forty men, at least—not counting the members of Araxes immediate family, their lives forfeit, their property already being divided among Hostigos supporters along with the gold looted from Styphon's temples.

When Rylla spoke of the need to punish Prince Araxes for letting his indecisiveness go on too long, could anyone have imagined this?

The screen now showed a close-up of a castle gateway, with men in Phaxosi colors filing out between two lines of Hostigi. The Phaxosi, Sirna noted, were disarmed, except for swords and daggers, but otherwise seemed to have all their gear and clothing. A few bandaged ones were being supported by their comrades.

"After eight days of shelling, the garrison of Tarr-Phaxos surrendered on promise of life, limb and personal property for all those not on Rylla's purge list. Rylla sent in a sortie party to deliver both Prince Araxes and the Styphon's House Highpriest the Prince was holding captive. Five of the officers went to the block and a Hostigi garrison is now installed."

"Was the agreement kept?" someone from behind Sirna asked.

"As of our last report, it had been. Of course, Rylla was given everything she wanted and I'm sure she has plans for those paroled Phaxosi troops. But I think what we have here is evidence of just how little one man can do to re-direct, or 'change' if you must use it—history. If Kalvan can't even control his own wife, how can he control larger events?"

"How do we know that she's not doing Kalvan's work while he's fighting Grand Master Soton?"

"Good question," the leonine countenanced Danthor, gave this particularly adept student a promising smile. "The Kalvan Study Team members included that in their report, after the Nostor Foundry debacle." He directed a sardonic bow in Sirna's direction.

Sirna tried to disappear into her chair. Dras had never been married; otherwise Sirna suspected he would have known the difference between marriages and historical events. Given a choice between trying to win a battle and try to change her ex-husband's mind on a matter where he'd made it up, Sirna would have pulled on armor at once! Although some marriages did resemble battlefields, even more than hers had—

She was surprised when she heard a voice that sounded like Aranth Saln say, "It's obvious the distinguished Scholar has never shared the Nuptial Cup."

Scattered laughter met this reply and Danthor Dras' face turned red. To regain control, he began speaking in a pontifical tone of voice. "The real damage done is in the minds of neutrals and would-be allies. We already have reports from our sources in the conclave of the League of Dralm. It is being asked out loud whether Kalvan is going to prove any different from Styphon's House? Must every worshipper of Dralm also march in Kalvan's train, wherever he may wish to take it? And so on."

Sirna mentally drowned the whole conclave of Dralm in a bottomless pit of bison dung. If Rylla had slaughtered a thousand Phaxosi peasants, but left the Prince of Fencesitters sitting on his sitting-down place, they wouldn't have said half as much. But a general house-cleaning of nobles who had advised their Prince to folly, even if they hadn't gone raiding themselves—oh, that was an abomination beyond belief.

Which Rylla should have known and, if she didn't know it, she should have listened to those who did. As much as you respect Rylla, you can't get around the fact that she has literally made a royal mess of things.

I certainly wouldn't want to be in Rylla's boots when her husband gets home!

The surrender of Tarr-Phaxos was the last picture. The seminar wound down as people drifted either out into the corridor or toward an improvised bar-buffet behind the display. Sirna headed in the latter direction. Missing lunch had given Sirna an appetite even worrying about Rylla couldn't take away. As Sirna came away with a loaded plate, she nearly bumped into Darlan Trov. She hadn't seen him come in, but she was instantly wary. It was a universal rumor that he was one of Hadron Tharn's advisers in some of the man's more questionable schemes. It was also a rumor that Darlan Trov had never bothered to deny.

"What do you think of Rylla's latest antics?" Darlan asked.

Sirna toyed with the idea of saying exactly what she thought and hoping Darlan would take the report back to Hadron Tharn. A pro-Kalvanist could hardly be trusted as a spy and Sirna would be out of a job she no longer wanted to do. She was still filing her reports, but they were so mundane—mostly Study Team internecine warfare—they put even her to sleep.

Except that Hadron Tharn had a long memory, a short fuse, and more influence than any other six Opposition politicians put together in University circles. If he pressed enough of the right buttons among his allies, he could probably find a majority on Sirna's thesis committee. Sirna wasn't quite ready to bring her outtime career with the University to an end, just for the pleasure of speaking her mind.

"Well, I agree that it was taking too hard a line with Prince Araxes, at least with Kalvan absent. But I don't agree that Kalvan hasn't made any difference. Did we hear or see of any atrocities against civilians?"

"There was that rape in Lower Town—"

"For which three Hostigi and two mercenaries were tried and hanged, as Danthor pointed out. If Rylla had wanted to, she could have gone through Phaxos like the Red Hand through Sask. She's learned something from her husband. I only wish she had learned more."

"You want to see Styphon's House overthrown, then?"

About as subtle as one of Roxthar's Investigators, and deserving the same sort of answer. "I think once the fireseed secret was out, Styphon's House was doomed. The only question now is how long it will take, and what will be left afterward. The faster Kalvan wins, the faster he or somebody else can rebuild afterward."

"That sounds as if you care about what happens to a bunch of Fourth Level barbarians."

For a moment Sirna knew exactly what had motivated Rylla, sympathized and would have done something equally drastic to Darlan Trov until she remembered that she was on the wrong time-line for that.

"As people, no. But a time-line that wracks itself to pieces so that nothing really interesting happens for a century—what good is that to the University? Could we even investigate it safely? You've been outtime enough to know the answer to that."

Darlan only nodded and turned away, his disappointment as naked as a tavern dancer. Sirna stabbed a meat roll with her fork, rejoicing in a subtle if small victory. *Gods, if you exist, try to teach Rylla a little subtlety too. Nobody else can.*

III

The sound of three cannon shots floated over the hill from the direction of Tarr-Ceros.

"Some sentry must be nervous," Harmakros said. Great King Kalvan and the Captain-General reached the end of the path they'd worn in the hillside. As if chained together, they turned and began walking back toward the other end.

We might as well sit down, thought Kalvan. *Anybody sees us, they'll suspect we have bad news, and rumors like that we need like a sortie by the Knights. Besides, I'm not going to sleep tonight no matter how tired I make myself.*

At the far end of the path, Kalvan noticed a convenient stump and sat down. Both his feet and his head were aching, but there wasn't enough wine left in the whole army to do much about either. He had to make do with lighting his pipe. On the far side of the hill from Tarr-Ceros, there was no need for a blackout.

Fingers of black smoke, from burning farmhouses poked up to the low clouds. While everything within five miles of Tarr-Ceros had been stripped and burned, the smell of fire still lay heavy in the air. Every once in a while a breeze blew the odor of black powder in their faces.

"At least we've got a new fortress on one possible Styphoni line of advance into Hos-Hostigos," Harmakros said.

"At the price of sending the whole League of Dralm into a tizzy. Besides, half the nobility of Phaxos will turn their coats right back the moment the Styphoni march. How useful is Tarr-Phaxos with them at its back?"

"We'll have to make sure it's well-stocked for a siege—" the Captain-General began.

"What with?" Kalvan exploded. "We left Rylla and Sarrask with just enough to stand on the defensive. Everything else went into this western campaign. We won, but now there's nothing left back home and we'll still have the Knights to deal with!"

"Not this year."

"Is that the best you can do, Harmakros? Hope that something will turn up in time for next year?"

"Another harvest certainly will. Or has Your Majesty forgotten the passage of the seasons?" Harmakros stepped back at the look on Kalvan's face. "Forgive me, Your Majesty. That was—"

"A salutary reminder that I badly needed." Kalvan sighed and pressed the heels of both hands to his aching head. His pipe dropped forgotten to the ground; Harmakros stamped out the coals just in time to prevent a grass fire.

Kalvan ended the silence by retrieving and relighting his pipe. "Now I think I'm going to try a salutary reminder on Rylla. Harmakros, do you want to be a Prince, or—"

"Stop, Your Majesty! Haven't we had this conversation several times— and isn't my answer always the same. I am already far above any station I dreamed myself in as a young man. But this is not the time, and Phaxos is certainly *not* the place for me—"

"But more than anyone else you have earned such an honor."

Harmakros shook his head. "Maybe, but running that Princedom is going to be a fulltime job. Araxes did more than ruin the Phaxosi econ- omy; he elevated his barons beyond their place. They will have to be reminded of that place and—believe me—that will take time, patience and some blood. I cannot both manage Phaxos and be Captain-General of the Royal Army.

"Who will then be Captain-General, Your Majesty? Certainly not Chartiphon, who is the best of men, but not fit for this new style war- fare. Phrames? He is still occupied with Beshtan bandits and errant merchants. Hestophes? He would be my choice, but only with more sea- soning. No, other than yourself, Your Majesty, I fear, there is no other candidate.

Kalvan reluctantly nodded his head in agreement. "Thank you, Har- makros, for this wise counsel. Who would you suggest we place on the Phaxosi throne?"

"A Phaxosi with some blood ties to the Princely house. A devout fol- lower of Dralm and one who is respected both within Phaxos and without."

"An excellent suggestion. I will leave his selection in your capable hands. I suspect you have a candidate in mind?"

Harmakros smiled. "Yes, but I need to check out some particulars and speak with him before I mention any names."

"Good. Now to the business at hand. I've thought about what needs doing back in Hostigos and what needs doing here. Harmakros, you can't do what needs doing at home, so that leaves you in charge here. Can I make it a friendly request, or do I have to make it a royal command?"

"With all due respect, I don't think Your Majesty is feeling particularly friendly toward anybody."

"I'm not." *And you know exactly why, but you're too damn tactful to say it out loud.*

"I don't want to be disrespectful, but I don't think you can leave without offending one or both of our allies. Warlord Sargos treats you like his magic Talisman and is afraid the entire horde will fall apart the moment you leave—and likely enough, I suspect he's right. King Nestros wants you by his side so that he can 'soak' up your wisdom, as he puts it. If you leave, it won't be a moon quarter before the entire Rathoni army leaves pack, baggage and camp followers. That is, if the two of them don't manage to start a blood feud before Nestros' can dodge out of his obligations. Maybe you don't see it, but it's only the worry that you might think less of either of them that has kept them working together. Remember the split between Sastragath and Trygath is more than geographical, it's a line bathed in blood. Only time and working together will erase it."

"Right again, Harmakros. Still, this campaign draws to a close. Prince Ptosphes left a moon quarter ago with the wounded and sick. We've burned fields, farms, barns, silos and driven all the farmers out of the area. There's not much more to do."

"You're right, but I'll let you explain it to our allies. I don't think they want to leave just yet."

"Then let them stay, as you said Nestros has already grown bored with this campaign. Sargos still has to figure out what to do as Warlord once this campaign is over. I wish him luck!"

"If you want to leave, I can stay and keep the Knights busy for another moon-quarter."

"Good," Kalvan clapped Harmakros on both armored shoulders, with a clang. Outside the fortified camps, armor was a wise precaution; oath-brothers had been swimming the river and slitting throats the last three nights. "I knew I could rely on you."

IV

Grand Master Soton sat in his private audience chamber at the heart of the great fortress of Tarr-Ceros and stared blankly at the stonewalls. Too many good men dead, he thought, and four more banners to hang in the Hall of Heroes. During his term of Grand Master he had now hung a total of seven banners, representing seven decommissioned Lances; more than any other Grand Master in the past two hundred years. *The Order will not soon forget me!* Those seven Lances together accounted for almost a quarter of the Order's strength . . .

Am I destroying the Order to salvage my own pride?

No, Dralm damn-it! I am trying to save the Temple of Styphon's House, and part of the Temple is the Order of Zarthani Knights—my part. Kalvan means to destroy the Temple and to do this he must destroy the Order and me. Kalvan is the enemy and must be stopped at any cost!

A gentle knocking at the plank door took his mind off Kalvan and these all too familiar thoughts. "Come in."

Knight Commander Aristocles entered the chamber. "Good news, Soton. The nomads are finally leaving—at last!"

"Finally, they leave! I hadn't expected the barbarians to stay even a day after Kalvan's departure. It's been almost a moon-half. They must be growing short of rations. Either that, or they have run out of farms and barns to burn."

"True. Sadly, with their passing they are now burning all the forests and stands of wood for three days ride in all directions!"

"There will be little produce to harvest, but we can bring in victuals by boat. The real cost has been to Kalvan in the one coin he cannot afford—time. There we have defeated the Usurper. Fall approaches and by the time Kalvan's tired army marches back to his not-so-grand kingdom, it will be too late in the year to mount a successful attack on Hos-Harphax or any of our other allies."

Aristocles pulled a flask of wine from behind his back. "Let us share a drink. A drink to the real victory—the salvation of Hos-Harphax, and the war against the Usurper!"

Soton gave Aristocles a goblet up from his desk and watched his old friend fill it to the top. Aristocles then poured another cup for himself. "To victory!"

"A costly one, for the Order. But a sweet victory all the same."

Grand Master Soton frowned. "Our Harphaxi friends owe us a great debt. I pray that Prince Lysandros and Captain-General Phidestros use the time, our blood has bought, wisely."

"Grand Master, we will be there to see they spend it wisely!"

"Yes, the Inner Circle will demand it." Soton paused, offering another toast. "To next year's campaign! And that this time next year, when we make a toast to our success, it will be in Tarr-Hostigos!"

"And to the Usurper's death!"

"Yes! And now a toast to absent friends." Soton held his goblet up in the air. "Thank you, valiantly departed Drakmos. You have a great Honor Debt—may the gods honor you in their Halls."

Soton set down his empty goblet down and paused to strike a flame with his tinderbox and light his pipe.

There was a knock on the door.

"Come in!"

Sarmoth peered into the room anxiously. "Grand Master. A messenger from Balph waits outside."

Soton drained his goblet. "Send him in."

A Styphon's House highpriest, still wearing his travel cloak, entered the chamber. He opened a courier's pouch and presented a folded parchment to Soton, "For you, Grand Master from Styphon's Voice."

Soton started reading, then looked up at the highpriest and said, "You may leave."

The moment the priest was out the door, Soton handed the parchment to Aristocles. "What does it say?" Soton, as the son of peasants, had never learned to read as a child, and while he had worked hard over the years to learn numbers and decipher many words, he was still a slow and halting reader. Aristocles was one of the few who knew this secret.

Aristocles looked down at the letter, which was written with bold scrip. "From a scribe's hand, not Archpriest Sesklos'. I suspect Anaxthenes dictated it. Would you like a summary, or do you want me to read it word for word."

"By Galzar's Mace, I know how wordy these letters from the Inner Circle can be. Please summarize it."

Aristocles read for a quarter candle, his lips moving as he went along. Finally, he looked up. "It says here that while Kalvan was away with the Army of the Trygath, Queen Rylla mounted an attack on one of Hos-Harphax's vassals, Prince Araxes. She had Araxes' killed and punished his princedom dearly."

Soton nodded. "This is valuable news. Was the Hostigi vixen able to draw the Harphaxi Army into this attack?"

"No," Aristocles answered. "The Harphaxi Captain-General wisely stayed above the fray."

"Good. We don't have time to rebuild the Harphaxi Army again!"

"Or the blood, Soton! There is good news, too. According to the letter, 'this brazen attack upon the Princedom of Phaxos has displayed the Hostigos' greed and vainglory to all the rulers in the Five Kingdoms. Already, Styphon's Union of Friends has received offers of gold and soldiers from many princedoms in both Hos-Agrys and Hos-Zygros. The streets of Agrys City are filled with protestors.'

"The letter goes on to say that Prince Lysandros furthermore has used Rylla's sneak attack to convene a formal meeting of the Harphaxi Electors to discuss the Phaxos Crisis. Maybe our wily Prince Lysandros can use this annexation of one of the Harphaxi vassals to further his own ends with the Electors."

"Or Lysandros will use it to convince the Regency Council it's time to get off their collective hindquarters!" Soton paused, and drew deeply from his pipe. "Each and every one of the Regents is more interested in feathering his own nest than in solving the Succession Crisis. Now Lysandros will have a credible threat—Rylla's invading army—to hold over their heads."

"And that," Aristocles finished, "is truly a crisis hot enough to light a fire under their hind parts!"

"Good news on an auspicious day," Soton said. "Our friend Lysandros ought to be on his knees thanking Styphon that Queen Rylla didn't take her army to Harphax City, or there might be a Hostigi usurper sitting on the Iron Thrown of Hos-Harphax at this moment!"

"Very true, Soton. And, now that all this political wrangling is over, we can get back to our real work; rebuilding the Order's military strength."

Soton sighed heavily. "Maybe it's over for you, Aristocles. For me it's just beginning. I'm afraid you'll have to begin rebuilding and repairing the damage Kalvan's forces inflicted without me. I must go to Balph and take council with the Inner Circle. It is time to make further preparations for the war against the Usurper Kalvan. I will need the Archpriests' help to convince Great King Cleitharses to mobilize the Ktemnoi Squares for next spring. Also, the Inner Circle has been balking at Captain-General

Phidestros' demands for more gold and victuals. I need to remind them that any credible invasion army against Hostigos will need many depots, well fed and well paid soldiers and more weapons and fireseed than have been assembled in living memory. Fortunately the Archpriests of the Inner Circle fear Kalvan almost as much as they do Archpriest Roxthar so that chore will not be too difficult."

"For this, they do indeed show wisdom."

"Call Sergeant Sarmoth, we have a trunk to pack. And a debt to settle with Kalvan—on a bill that is long overdue."

FALL

FORTY-THREE

I

The shutters of the royal bedchamber banged in the rising wind. Rylla heard the first few drops of rain splatter against them and rose up from her chair at the table, after first setting the inkwell on top of the letter she was writing to Kalvan.

As she pulled the shutters closed, the wisdom of her husband struck her again. Had she chosen to summon a servant, she would have had to conceal the letter. As it was, doing the work herself meant that no one but herself and Allfather Dralm would see the words until her husband broke the seal.

Of course, the idea of doing the work yourself could go too far. There was such a thing as royal dignity. Likewise, one did not honorably turn faithful servants out to starve.

With the sound of the wind and rain shut out, the room was silent and appeared even emptier than usual. Rylla hoped that the rain would not fall too heavily. The crops were standing tall and promised a fine harvest. The rains that had plagued Kalvan in the west had fallen only moderately here in Hostigos.

Rylla forced her eyes away from the bed unshared for far too long, and back to the parchment. Her quill marched busily across it, and the words followed:

439

—none suitable for the rank or duty of Prince of Phaxos. It seems that even the lesson we taught them has only made the nobles of Phaxos cease opposing us; they have not ceased to quarrel with one another.

So I had the choice of leaving Phaxos in chaos, as you left Nostor during the Winter of the Wolves, to be a fearful lesson. Or else I could end its existence as a Princedom and join it to Hos-Hostigos as a Royal Province. The proposed Proclamation of Union I have enclosed will set forth the reasons why I chose the latter.

The Proclamation of Union was being drafted as she wrote under the oversight of her father, who had returned with the sick and wounded several days ago. Ptosphes knew better than she, how to couch the Proclamation in words that would not offend those Phaxosi with whom there was no quarrel, and tell the rest exactly what the Hostigi thought of them.

The door flew open. Rylla started up, ready to blaze at whoever had entered without knocking or even asking permission. She saw Lady Eutare, the only one of her attendants who had permission to enter without asking permission. It had made for some jealousy among the other ladies-in-waiting, but the Beshtan noblewoman had done better service to the Realm than any of the others.

First, Lady Eutare had foiled a plot to betray an important castle to the Harphaxi and spirited away a considerable sum in gold and silver. Second she had caught Prince Phrames' eye so that he now considered himself all but betrothed to her. That made things easier between him and Rylla; they had been feuding ever since her decision to invade Phaxos. Lady Eutare was someone they both cared about.

It was high time that Phrames started begetting a family of his own. Demia would need playmates of a suitable rank before long. In time, she would need a husband from a stock worthy of her, and what better stock than Phrames?

"Yes, Eutare?"

"The King has returned!"

Rylla sat down again, because her legs would no longer support her. Her stomach felt uneasy and her mind was unsettled. *Please, Allfather Dralm, make this homecoming a joy, not like the battlefields I left in Phaxos.* Kalvan had never been truly mad at her before, but the absence of letters from him since her return from Phaxos did not bode well.

After a moment, she saw something in Eutare's eyes that made her uneasy. "Is he wounded or sick?"

"No. No. But—Your Majesty, he rode in with barely the escort of a messenger, on horses that looked ready to drop in their tracks. Those who saw him dismount say he wore a visage fit to frighten Styphon's demons."

Rylla frowned. "He is probably half-witted with fatigue. Well, he can sleep soundly tonight. We can celebrate his victory tomorrow."

"But, Your Majesty—"

"Would I be welcome when you sat down with Prince Phrames?"

Lady Eutare flushed. "As you wish, Your Majesty." She appeared to want to say more, or at least delay her departure, but Rylla's tone brooked no argument.

As Rylla turned back to the letter, footsteps sounded on the stairs and a familiar voice made her heart leap in her chest. "Is the Queen at home?"

"Yes, Your Majesty."

Then the footsteps coming up the stairs faster, grew louder as Rylla sprang up and ran to the door—

—to stop as though she'd run into a quickset hedge, as Kalvan stalked into the room. He was muddy and saddle worn, wet and stinking, but none of these would have mattered under other circumstances.

With that look on his face, Rylla could no more embrace her husband than she could have an Archpriest of Styphon.

"Kalvan, what's wrong?" He slammed the door closed behind him.

"What the Styphon did you think you were doing, with that butchery in Phaxos?"

"BUTCHERY!" She hadn't intended to shout, but his tone pricked her like spurs into a horse's flanks. "I call it burning out a nest of enemies and guarding your back!"

"Dralm damn-it! Stabbing *me* in the back, is more what you've done! You've just given every prince in Hos-Agrys and Hos-Harphax good reason to distrust us. Do you know what the League of Dralm—"

"I don't know anything about the League of Dralm, and I don't care either. If Allfather Dralm really favors them, let Him give them the sense to see that we're on his side. If Dralm won't do that, who the Styphon cares about the League?"

Kalvan threw his gloves down on the table. "We'd better care about what they think, whether Dralm does or not! Do you want the Harphaxi Electors withdrawing their opposition to Prince Lysandros for Great King of Hos-Harphax?"

For the first time Rylla felt a twinge of fear for something else than her husband's ravings. "They wouldn't—"

"They would. One rumor I just heard along the road says they're meeting right now. There were always plenty of Harphaxi princes and priests who said the League shouldn't intervene in the affairs of a Great King-dom, even if it was about to elect a Styphon-worshipper."

"I suppose they wouldn't want to set a—*precedent,*" she said using a word from Kalvan's native tongue. She would have uttered a Sastragathi snake-spell if it would have changed the look on her husband's face!

"No. It would be a gift to the Styphoni. Now you've gone and handed the Council of Dralm an even better reason for staying out of the Har-phaxi election. Half of them will now be thinking: We need a strong Great King on the Iron Throne, to balance Kalvan's empire-building."

"Empire-building? I only defended what any respectable Prince or Great King would call his honor—"

Kalvan went off like a barrel of fireseed with a short fuse. "Defended? Is that what you call it? If my 'honor' needs defending, in the future, let me do it! What you've really done is tarnished my good name. Your invasion of Phaxos, behind my back—"

"How could I do anything behind your back! You were not here to answer Araxes' latest insult."

"Did I tell you specifically, not to leave Hos-Hostigos?"

Rylla shrugged her shoulders. Maybe she had acted against her hus-bands' words, but she was no horse to be led around in circles and given commands—not even by her beloved.

"Yet, you insisted upon invading Phaxos, which very likely undid every-thing I did in the west. I've half a mind to call Harmakros straight back and—"

"Isn't he with you?"

"I left him to command our army in the west with our allies to finish wasting the land around Tarr-Ceros. With luck, that should keep the Knights out of the field this year and next in spite of what you've done. When Harmakros returns, though, he's going to help me select the next Prince of Phaxos—"

"Who says so?" Rylla replied indignantly.

"The Great King of Hos-Hostigos says so. Or—" Kalvan's eyes wandered to the table and the paper letter setting upon it. Before Rylla could do more than pray for her patience, he'd crossed the distance to the table, snatched up the letter and read it.

Rylla had thought his visage was frightful before. *Now* she would have run from the room if that would not have been regarded as cowardice. For the first time in their marriage, she stepped back from her husband, to give herself room and time to draw her dagger if all else failed.

Kalvan said nothing and took only a single step, and that was to lean backward. But he picked up the letter in both hands, and tore it down the middle, then tore each piece in two. The four fragments of paper fluttered to the rug.

"Harmakros will rule Phaxos, until *I* find a Phaxosi nobleman we can trust to make Prince. There's little for him to do in the Sastragath and he will be returning soon."

"And how will they do under Harmakros in the meantime?" Rylla snapped off the question like a pistol shot. "Do you remember the Captain-General's wasting of Nostor and the massacre at the Sevenhills temple-farm? Do you think he will be gentle in wasting the Knights' lands? What does he have that will make his rule better than ours?"

She nearly flung an unforgivable accusation at her husband, concerning him and Harmakros. She stopped short of that folly, first because she knew it was nonsense and second because she feared driving him to say something equally unforgivable.

Having rejected vile insults, she still found no gentler words. She was standing, shaking like a tree in a high wind and hissing like an angry cat, when footsteps sounded once more on the stairs.

Prince Ptosphes entered, with an air of noticing nothing so carefully wrought that it defeated his own purpose. "I heard that Kalvan had returned. The Proclamation of Union has been drafted. I have here the—"

"There won't be any Union," Rylla stated.

"Oh?" The Prince looked like a man who was trying to navigate his horse through caltrops that were strewn before him.

Rylla wanted to scream at her father not to play the witling when she wanted an ally. Instead she managed to say without stammering, "The Great King thinks that Duke Harmakros would serve well as ruler of Phaxos, until We find a suitable candidate for Prince."

"The Great King thinks that Harmakros can be trusted to wipe his backside without being told how!" Kalvan bellowed.

Rylla was quite sure they heard him outside the chambers, probably outside the keep, possibly on the Harphaxi frontier!

The bellow won Kalvan the undivided attention of both wife and father-in-law. "May Dralm be my witness, I'm just sorry I didn't leave your father here to watch over you and that moron Sarrask. Prince Ptosphes might have done something to prevent this idiocy!"

Ptosphes turned bright red, while he turned his head right and left as though seeking a place to hide.

"Are you calling me a fool as well as Sarrask, since he only did my bidding!" Rylla screamed. She knew she had been as loud as Kalvan but didn't care.

"Well, you Dralm-damned behaved like one, kicking a stone because you've stubbed your toe on it! Butchering the Phaxosi nobility like a herd of sheep. And what about Araxes family—what did they do?"

"Did you want his sons to slink about the Six Kingdoms," Rylla yelled, "seeking vengeance and trying to raise armies that someday our children will have to fight?"

"Of course, not. But to kill them in cold blood—*How could you?*" The vein in his forehead was throbbing.

"I did what I had to do, for Us, for Hos-Hostigos. And if you don't understand that, you don't understand anything."

"You didn't do it for Hos-Hostigos, you did it for Rylla. And your appearance to others. It wasn't my pride you were avenging, it was your own!"

She brushed the tears of anger out of her eyes.

"And now having thrown away half our friends in the League of Dralm—"

"Friends, like Primate Xentos! I couldn't take away half of something that never existed." Rylla was relieved to discover that she could speak instead of scream, even if her throat was suddenly raw.

Her father took hold of her arm. "Your Majesty, with all due respect I think there is a chance that the Great Queen has spoken truly. I think we should consider this at another time, after you have rested from your travels and taken refreshment."

Ptosphes' tone could not have been courtlier, or his grip on her arm gentler, as he maneuvered her to the door. Yet, Rylla knew that if Kalvan had made a move toward them he would have faced the Prince's drawn sword, and that if she had resisted her father would have dragged her bodily out of the room.

So, she let him lead the way, and they were halfway down the spiral stairs when they heard the door slam behind them. It echoed up and down the stairway like a cannon shot.

Rylla swallowed, and then slammed her clenched fist so hard into the wall that it was bloody when she drew it back. Ptosphes gently uncurled her fingers, as he had when she was a child with a minor cut she had brought to him for healing.

"We'd best see Lady Eutare and have her bandage this. Otherwise, Dralm-only-knows, what tales will run through the castle about how you gained this injury!"

II

Verkan Vall walked through the entryway into the great room of Tortha Karf's palatial Hostigos townhouse. "Very nice, Tortha."

"My home away from home," Tortha responded. "No rabbits, either! And all the comforts of my former quarters in Xyphlon, I hope?"

"We had a team in Xyphlon City for five ten-days establishing your cover, creating the Trading House of Tortha, implanting pseudo-memories on your last living relative—a sister named Horthvarga, no less—and generally casing the place. The Mexicotál siege, though doomed to fail, has everyone upset. It hasn't helped that the Mexicotál have built their own local Pyramid to the Sun outside the City, where every day their human-skin accoutered priests are taking human sacrifices and hearts from local captives and prisoners-of-war. It's enough to make you want to drop a thermo-nuclear on their capital city."

"I hate to admit it, but that bunch has this Styphon's House racket beat all to Regwarn and back."

"Ahhh, good to see you picking up the local references, Tortha. As well as losing all First Level objectivity. I remember how you used to lecture me on the subject."

Tortha harrumphed. "I'm not the only one. Besides, these Hostigi folks grow on you. What brings you to Hostigos Town."

"I had promised Kalvan to bring him some guns from Greffa in exchange for all that fireseed I took with me. I did too, but the trading party's about five days down the road. I took my prerogative as chief trader to ride on ahead. I thought I'd meet with my old trader friend before stopping into the palace and seeing Kalvan."

Tortha nodded as he removed his tobacco pouch and a new carved ivory pipe. "I like the way you stay in character."

"Where'd you get the pipe? Isn't that Kalvan's face carved on it?"

"Bought it off a Zygrosi trader. Some whaler carved it out of a walrus tusk—scrimshaw. I've ordered a bunch more, when he returns from his last trading mission before winter sets in. I intend to give them out as presents at Year-End Day. Don't mention them to Dalla—I've got a pipe with Rylla's face carved on it for her."

"Word. By the way, Dalla came along this trip. She'll be here in a few hours. She wanted to air out our townhouse."

"I guess you won't have time to visit the baronial mansion in Beshta this trip?"

Verkan laughed. "You mean my drafty, falling-down castle. Tarr-Verkan, Dalla's taken to calling it. I think it formerly belonged to one of Prince Balthar's cousins, from the cheap side of the family!"

Tortha joined in the laughter. Balthar had been legendary as a miser long before his well-deserved death at Tarr-Beshta at the hands of Rylla's giant bodyguard, Xykos.

Verkan sobered up. "I've got more bad news."

"What now?" Tortha asked. "Living in Hos-Hostigos is like being at Paratime Headquarters under Code Yellow all the time. Or is this Code Red?"

"No, Code Yellow, it seems that Captain-General Phidestros has besieged and taken an important Beshtan castle, Tarr-Veblos."

"The Harphaxi strike back!"

"Well, Captain-General Phidestros had to do something before he lost his job. After last years drubbing at Chothros Heights and Rylla's successful invasion of Phaxos, in the heart of Hos-Harphax, the Harphaxi princes and people were losing morale. The top command knew Phidestros really wasn't in a position to stop Rylla, but Lysandros was going to have to do something or risk the Election of someone else as Great King. Phidestros was smart enough to realize that he had to make a face-saving move before returning to Harphax City, or face a further erosion of morale in the Royal Army as well as a loss of confidence in his leadership.

"Phidestros pulled a fast one on Prince Phrames. He moved his cavalry close to the Beshtan border, keeping Phrames and his army busy worrying about invasion sites. Meanwhile, Phidestros sent off a smaller force of mounted infantry and artillery to besiege Tarr-Veblos. The tarr was undermanned, after Phrames pulled most of the Beshtan Army out of their prepared positions and into Arklos to protect Rylla's flank from the Harphaxi Army, and vulnerable."

"Why didn't Prince Phrames reinforce his tarrs?"

"By the time Phrames got back to Beshta from Arklos, Phidestros' large cavalry force was preparing for what appeared to be a large scale invasion. Phidestros was smart enough to stay far away from Tarr-Veblos and Phrames never reinforced the skeleton garrison. So while Prince Phrames is shifting his army up and down the border, Phidestros' second force hit Tarr-Veblos at night, with a company of—I guess you'd have to call them mountain troops—who repelled their way into the castle, killed most of the sentries and took the outer courtyard. They opened the gate and the rest was history, what with Phidestros' artillery firing point bank on the inner bailey and keep. Phrames has been trying to re-take the tarr, but Phidestros already had his army in the area and lots of reinforcements, so I think Tarr-Veblos is going to stay Harphaxi, at least, until next spring."

Tortha whistled. "He pulled a Kalvan."

"Kalvan doesn't have any corner on military genius and Phidestros, as it turns out, is a first rate commander."

Tortha tapped the residue out of his pipe into an ashtray, and then refilled the bowl. "When will word of this debacle reach Hostigos?"

"Any hour. I'm surprised word hasn't reach Hostigos Town already."

"I'd have heard the fireworks shooting out of Tarr-Hostigos, if the news had reached Town."

"By the way, how are the Royal couple these days?"

Tortha's face took on a worried cast, as he paused to strike a spark on his tinderbox and light his pipe. "Not very well. Kalvan came back way ahead of schedule from Tarr-Ceros without any escort but a few Lifeguards I suspect he couldn't shake. The story I heard—you know we've resisted leaving any telltales in Tarr-Hostigos—"

Verkan nodded. "We don't eavesdrop on friends. Although, there are occasions—like this—when it would be a help."

"Anyway, after Kalvan got back, they went to it with everything but the Great King's ceremonial halberd. Apparently Prince Ptosphes had to come in as peacemaker. I don't know if it did any good. Rylla came out of it with hurt pride, a bandaged hand and her back so stiff you could use it as a bridge. I doubt Kalvan had anything to do with the injury, since Ptosphes is still lodging at the Tarr. Kalvan's been drinking heavily and staying out of the common quarters. Everyone at Tarr-Hostigos is walking on tippy-toes."

"Someone is going to have to have a talk with that boy."

"You might try, you certainly got enough talks from me during that first companionate marriage with Dalla! You should have picked up something along the way."

Verkan covered both his ears. "Will I *never* live that down? And you, a lifelong bachelor! It's a wonder we ever got back together."

Tortha grinned. "Let me get out a couple of goblets of Ermut's Best. You got me there. Let's take a drink to me minding my own business. At least I learned enough to not bother poor Kalvan with my words of wisdom about Queen Rylla!"

"I'll offer a toast to that!" Verkan took the offered goblet and took a drink. "To minding your own business. I think I may take some of that advice for myself and not try to tell Kalvan how to patch up his break with Rylla"

"He'll appreciate it, I'm sure. He's already got Prince Ptosphes hovering over him like an old hen!"

"Of course, I can't make any promises for Dalla."

"Ha! No sir, Chief. Dalla and Rylla will soon be up to no end of mischief!"

"You can say that again. After Dalla arrives, Kalvan's going to need all the help he can get!"

III

As Duke Skranga puffed his way up the keep's stairway to the third floor, he noticed he was absent-mindedly tugging his already sparse beard. He mentally admonished himself and brushed away the few tufts of red hair that had fallen out. *By Hadron's Forked-Tongue, if I keep losing hair, my chin will be as clean of hair as my crown!*

Skranga knew only too well what was really bothering him. He had never liked being the bearer of bad news—especially to his King. More than one Great King had be-headed messengers with tidings no less worse than his own. While it was true that King Kalvan was usually above such base conduct, it was also true that Skranga had no family or interest to protest any action the Great King might make on his person. What a fool he had been not to take Kalvan's gold long ago and run off to distant Hos-Zygros instead of lingering about in Harphax City.

On the other hand, the best he could have come to in Hos-Zygros—a most frigid and inhospitable place—was a genteel anonymity, where he would be fair game to ruthless lords and the bandits who prey on the strangers no one will miss. No, he had—for once—done the right thing, no matter how onerous the duty occasionally became. After all, he had almost a hundred agents and intelligencers on his payroll and knew more about the comings and goings in the Six—no—Seven Kingdoms (counting the new kingdom of Hos-Rathon) than any man outside of Balph. This was the work he was born to do.

Upon entering Kalvan's study, he noticed how haggard the Great King appeared and the bruise-like shadows under each of his eyes. Apparently the rumors were true and the Great King had been evicted from the royal bed-chamber by Rylla. It might be a good time to start reviewing possible candidates for the royal couch; it would not hurt, despite his loyalty, to have an ear only a heartbeat away from the Throne. Besides, his agent would be guaranteed to be discreet; someone else's might do the Kingdom harm. He mentally reviewed his latest conquests and decided there was no end of possible candidates; most fair enough to warm a man's heart as well as slake his hunger.

Kalvan rose from his desk and pointed to a horsehide-covered chair. "Sit down, Duke Skranga. And, by Dralm's white beard, may your news be good news!"

A closer look at the Great King revealed blood-shot eyes, which bespoke a bad hangover—a condition Skranga knew well like a shrewish wife that beat on one's head when one was having a good time.

Skranga resolved to let this badger out of the bag very slowly. "Your Majesty, I have been in contact with most of my intelligencers as you requested in regards to the Phaxos matter."

"Yes?"

"We have some very good news. Xentos, as Primate of Dralm, was able to use his influence to defeat a resolution put before the Council to place Hos-Hostigos under a Ban of Dralm. It was a close vote and, while a Ban of Dralm would not have hurt our trade overmuch, it might have cost us heavily in support by those Princes who covertly aid our struggle against the False God Styphon."

"Skranga, you are prattling. It's not like you, so get to the point."

Skranga took a deep breath. "It appears the Princes of Hos-Harphax are beginning to fear *your* ambitions more than they fear Lysandros and his ties to Styphon's House. In Hos-Hostigos your recent success against the nomads far out-weigh any concerns over who sits upon the seat of Phaxos. However, I also understand, from a reliable ear, that Prince Balthames of Sashta has been secretly talking with a merchant known to be in Styphon's employ."

"That ingrate! I suspect that half his boyfriends are on our payroll. Is this true?"

Skranga nodded.

"Good. Perhaps one of them can slip him a potion some cold winter night."

"Your Majesty, I suspect the fog of recent events has clouded your usual good judgment. The assassination of one of your Princes, following so close upon the war in Phaxos, might add fuel to the rumors about your ambition to become Great King of All the Kingdoms—"

"Enough! You make excellent sense. I'm not myself this morning. But we are going to have to do something about Balthames before he betrays us as his brother, Balthar of Beshta, did at the Battle of Tenabra. Do you have any ideas?"

"Yes. As I understand it this merchant, one Kythames, has been acting as the go-between for Prince Balthames and one of Lysandros' agents. Kythames has rather exotic tastes in female flesh. I have a most unusual Ruthani maiden, purportedly from the Sea of Grass, who has been known to make men so lovesick they leave their families or even kill themselves upon her leaving . . . I will use her as a hook to catch this Kythames and, when he is under her spell, I will have her obtain evidence from him that will damn Balthames in anyone's eyes."

"Excellent. But don't tell me any more details. Since neither Balthames nor his brother ever had any issue, I can make a gift of Sashta to Captain-General Harmakros. It would be a fitting reward for his loyal service and friendship to the Throne."

"I agree, Your Majesty, although it might be wise for him to legitimize his bastard, Aspasthar, now rather than when he takes the seat of Sashta. You might suggest this to him. I suspect that Harmakros is not anxious for a fall marriage and would like to guarantee the succession of Sashta in favor of his only son."

"Good advice, Skranga. I'm glad someone in Hos-Hostigos is still thinking clearly! What are your suggestions regarding the issue of succession to the Seat of Phaxos?"

"We must walk very carefully there, Your Majesty. Rylla, in an excess of zeal, not only had Prince Araxes put under the headsman's axe, but also all the members of his immediate family."

The sudden drawn cast to Kalvan's face suggested the King might suddenly lose what little food he had consumed at first meal. Skranga waited until Kalvan appeared to have composed himself before continuing.

"There are about a dozen possible claimants to the Seat of Phaxos, but few would be in the Throne's best interest. Alas, with the unhappiness accompanying the conquest still in people's minds, I urgently suggest that we place someone on the Seat with blood ties to Araxes. Fortunately, we have one such claimant in Hostigos, a mercenary captain who goes by the name of Hyphos. He has served Your Majesty faithfully through three campaigns and is a devout follower of Allfather Dralm. For this 'disloyalty' he is not held in much regard in Phaxos, which will further bind him to the Throne now that Phaxos has become part of the Kingdom of Hos-Hostigos."

Kalvan nodded. "It's not like we can give it back to Hos-Harphax."

Skranga laughed like a barking dog.

"This must be the same Captain Hyphos that Harmakros recommended before I left Tarr-Ceros. The Captain-General says he's a good commander and that he is loyal to the Throne. I'm not personally familiar with him."

"Captain Hyphos is a forthright soldier from all appearances and one who speaks his own words, although not with the earthiness and directness of our friend Prince Sarrask. He has no great love for Araxes, who has always held his family in contempt, for Hyphos' father—a lowly baron—was only related to Araxes by blood through the sister of his late mother.

"Baron Hyphos would not be in contention for the throne now had his father not died last year of pleurisy and his older brother not perished at the Siege of Phaxos Town. There was little love lost between the two brothers and word has it he died an honest soldier's death."

Kalvan nodded and said he would have General Klestreus do a counter check on Skranga's intelligence information. "It wouldn't do to put a man on the Phaxosi throne who had a blood debt to his Great Queen because his brother had died at her hands, no matter how far removed."

Skranga nodded sagely, even though he didn't like the idea of the fat fool Klestreus looking over his shoulder. "You are wise to move cautiously in this matter and others, Your Majesty. There have been far too many changes in the Great Kingdoms since your arrival, and if there is one thing Princes and lords do not like it is change. I pray Your Majesties have no plans for any new Great Kingdoms, such as the new kingdom of Hos-Rathon!"

"Not at the moment." Kalvan's scowled.

"Good. Few of the Throne's allies have happily accepted a Trygathi Great Kingdom. Now there are rumors you have promised Ranjar Sargos the Throne of Great Kingdom of the Sastragath."

"Balderdash! More of Styphon's work. Do what you can to put a stop to these rumors, and put out the word that we are planning to put a rightful claimant upon the Seat of Phaxos. Furthermore, let me add your advice about the Phaxosi succession is both welcome and valued. I will have our Treasurer make a deposit of five hundred Crowns into your account as further measure of my appreciation."

Skranga left Kalvan's audience chamber with the feeling that today had somehow magically turned into the best of all possible days, and that His Majesty was the finest Great King since Erasthames the Great!

F⊕RTY-F⊕UR

A s of late, thought Archpriest Anaxthenes, there have been far too
many emergency Council meetings. Of the thirty-six Archpriests
of the Inner Circle, only thirty-one were in attendance today. Of the five
Great Temple Highpriests, only Archpriest Theomenes of the Great Temple of Ktemnos was here; this Council having been called too quickly for
the others to have time to travel to Balph. The other absence was explained
by sudden death, although whether by poor health or misadventure no one
knew.

Nor was anyone particularly interested in finding out; not in these times,
when the number of white-robed priests were increasing daily. Investigator
Roxthar and his followers were insinuating their way into every arm of Styphon's House, although, so far, they had made no inroads into the Inner
Circle. *Give them time*, Anaxthenes thought cynically. They already had
their allies and stooges, such as Archpriest Dracar. The Investigators even
had allies in the Temple Guard. The Order of Zarthani Knights was the
only body left that had any independence from Roxthar's Investigation, and
mostly because they were situated at the frontier—far away from Balph.

There was a murmur of voices in the Hall as the assembled Archpriests
questioned each other about the reasons for this meeting and the disastrous

Siege at Tarr-Ceros. Anaxthenes, nor anyone else but Roxthar's allies, knew much about the Council's agenda. Styphon's Own Voice Sesklos had called the session at Roxthar's insistence.

Anaxthenes had lost many of his sources as the Investigation purged his informants and allies from the ranks of Styphon's House. The yellow robed highpriests were disappearing from Balph at an alarming rate, the smarter ones leaving for places as far away from the Holy City as they could get. The rest were victims of the Investigation. If Roxthar continued to purge Styphon's heretics from the priestly ranks, in a few years there wouldn't be enough priests left to man the Temples. Most of Roxthar's Investigators were not True Believers, as far as Anaxthenes could tell, but ambitious underpriests who saw Roxthar as their means to ascend the Temple hierarchy. Many of the Investigators reveled in their power to terrorize their superiors. *What happens*, he asked himself, *when the Investigation begins to investigate the Investigators?*

Now, Anaxthenes knew only rumors: Grand Master Soton had been shot and killed at the Battle of Drynos. Tarr-Ceros, the great Zarthani fortress, had fallen to the nomads. Now the great nomad horde was threatening to turn and attack Hos-Ktemnos. Kalvan was reported to be leading the invasion and planned to storm Balph itself. Now Rylla and her army were before the walls of Tarr-Harphax ... And so on and so on.

He didn't know enough to credit or discredit the rumors; although, based on general knowledge of Kalvan, he doubted the Usurper was leading any army into Hos-Ktemnos. Not with the Army of Hostigos split into two armies, and the False Queen Rylla leaving part of her army behind in Phaxos ...

The voices suddenly stilled as Sesklos, still wearing the red robe of Primacy, entered the hall and took his seat at the apex of the triangular table. Moments later Roxthar, bladelike in his white robe, entered to sit directly opposite Sesklos at the foot of the table. Anaxthenes noted the empty seat next to Roxthar and wondered why it was being held vacant.

What new surprise is the Holy Investigator about to spring upon us now?

After a short prayer to Styphon and his usual introductory preamble, Supreme Priest Sesklos rose up and began to speak. Anaxthenes, seated to his right, was close enough to see that Styphon's Voice was reading from a parchment. He wondered who had scripted it. He knew it had never passed his eyes.

"My fellow Archpriests, the city is rife with rumors and reports of defeat and invasion by our enemies. Know this, that while some be true, most are false."

There were a few hoots of derision, but when Archpriest Roxthar nodded the room fell quiet again.

Sesklos continued on in this vein for sometime in his quivering voice, explaining that the rumors were being spread by allies and dupes of the Usurper. It had been decades since old Sesklos had spoken more than a few sentences, and already the assembled archpriests were fidgeting in their seats. Finally, he finished, "Here, to report in person, on the nomad problem is Grand Master Soton." Hardly a heartbeat had passed before the Grand Master entered the Hall and stood beside Roxthar. Roxthar stood up saying, "I will let the Grand Master brief the Inner Council on the war against the Daemon Kalvan."

The Grand Master stood before the seat next to Roxthar, dressed in the Order's black robe emblazoned with a silver sun wheel on his breast, the insignia of the Order of the Zarthani Knights. Soton's face was more lined than Anaxthenes remembered, maybe because it was discernibly thinner. Soton was known as a commander who ate his troops' rations and suffered along side them when times were bad.

Grand Master Soton nodded to the Holy Investigator, to Styphon's Voice and then to Anaxthenes. Dracar, who in past times would have been livid at such a slight, was still staring at Roxthar, like a bird hypnotized by a snake. Soton told of the nomad invasion from across the Great Mother River and how he and his Knights had chased the barbarians through the Sastragath into the Upper Sastragath and finally into the Trygath. The Knights had dislodged most of the resident tribes and clans along the way, swelling the ranks of the nomads until they counted over two or three hundred thousand warriors.

"Our original plan had been to keep pushing the tribesmen until they moved into Hostigos and let them strip and tear the false kingdom to its bones. Here we failed. We did not expect Kalvan, who has never to our knowledge fought in the wilderness of the Trygath, to be able to mount such a hasty and formidable army. Nor did we plan on him allying himself with King Nestros—"

"You mean the new False Great King Nestros!" Archpriest Dracar cried. He was all but foaming at the mouth, while Roxthar was smiling. "We have been working for a century to make the Temple's participation mandatory for the crowning of Great Kings throughout the Five Kingdoms, and have been successful in both Hos-Ktemnos and Hos-Bletha. We have long hoped to crown the first Great King in Hos-Harphax. Now Kalvan has put all this work, and even the Temple itself, into jeopardy!"

Once he was certain that Dracar was finished, Soton began again as if the Archpriest had never spoken.. "Yes, Nestros' elevation was a demonically brilliant idea of Kalvan's, and one we did not anticipate. It completely pulls him out of our sphere of influence and forces him into a continuing alliance with Kalvan. Of course, the Temple could offer Nestros' absolution—"

"NEVER," Dracar shouted. Half a dozen other Archpriests shouted along with him until Roxthar silenced them with a sudden hand movement.

"The traitor and Usurper Nestros has sealed his fate," Roxthar declaimed. Anaxthenes shivered. He was sure that Hadron's lair in Regwarn held less promise of pain than the Investigator's offices in the Temple basement.

When Soton had the assembled Archpriests attention again, he continued. "Nor did we expect the Usurper Kalvan to defeat the nomad horde. Very quickly our own army went from being hunter to quarry. So we left a rearguard at the Drynos, which cost the Order four Lances of Styphon's best soldiers. However, our sacrifice did delay Kalvan and the barbarian horde long enough so that the remainder of our force could retire in safety at Tarr-Ceros. Had Kalvan and his allies been able to defeat our main body—I would not be here today and the nomads might have already advanced into Hos-Ktemnos."

There was a collective sound of in-drawn breath and nervous shuffling throughout the room.

While verbally Soton glossed over an action that had meant the end of four of his precious Lances, Anaxthenes saw the pain of it was writ clear upon his face. "True, at first glance, this appears that we have suffered a great disaster, in actuality we accomplished most of our original mission— although at a much higher cost than we had anticipated. First, we stopped Usurper's invasion of Hos-Harphax, an action that would have led to the loss of our only trusted northern ally. Secondly, we have bought ourselves time to prepare for the invasion of Hostigos, time in which Kalvan wasted most of his energies trampling through the Trygath placating his new allies. Not training more troops and influencing princes and barons in Hos-Harphax and Hos-Agrys.

"Furthermore, in his absence, his wife has invaded a neighboring Prince-dom thereby incurring the legitimate wrath of princes and nobles throughout the Five Kingdoms. Even the False League of Dralm has con-demned Hostigos for this unjustified invasion."

There was the tittering of laughter among the assembled archpriests.

"The False Queen Rylla has unwittingly wrought a miracle that even Styphon Himself might have found difficult; she has forged a consensus out of the collective Princes of Hos-Harphax. We have just learned a few candles ago, from a swift packet ship, that the Harphaxi Electors met in a special session and abolished the Regency Council, proclaiming Prince Lysandros the new Great King of Hos-Ktemnos!"

There was a spontaneous burst of applause that rang the rafters.

"For the first time in the history of Hos-Harphax, an Archpriest of Styphon's House will lead the ceremony of coronation." Soton pointed to Anaxthenes. "Since Styphon's Own Voice will be unable to make such a long journey, our own First Speaker Anaxthenes will represent the Inner Circle and perform the coronation of Great King Lysandros the First."

Anaxthenes was in shock. *Is this an honor, or just Roxthar's way of getting me out of Balph while he works more mischief?* Since even the Investigator looked surprised by this news, he wondered if it was Soton's idea. Clearly, whatever the reason, his star was once again on the ascent. Several of the other archpriests were looking at him in wonderment.

"Already promises have been made to Great King Lysandros by princes of gold and soldiers for a counter-invasion of Hostigos."

This time applause was even louder. Grand Master Soton appeared to be a miracle worker; there was a visible lightening of the tension inside the Council Hall. Even Anaxthenes was beginning to wonder if the Usurper Kalvan was invincible any longer.

"Next year we shall put the war on Hostigos soil and let the blood of *her* sons fertilize the fields! This war will drain the treasure from our counting houses, but we shall fill them again with Kalvan's wealth and stolen gold."

There had never been any doubt as to Soton's professional commitment to this war; now, there would be no doubt to his personal commitment as well. Kalvan had given the Order grievous losses and had shaken Soton to his very core. Anaxthenes now knew that Soton, like a wolf at a bear's throat, would not stop his attack until death alone stilled his limbs.

From the hungry look on Roxthar's face it was obvious that Soton had told the Holy Investigator exactly what he wanted to hear.

Roxthar rose and put his hand on Soton's shoulder. "We shall destroy the False Daemon Kalvan. Force him back into his lair and destroy him and all his kin. There shall be no more Kalvan, no Hostigos, when our work is done. The land shall be soaked in blood and tilled with iron. We shall forge a Grand Host of Styphon's allies next spring and destroy this Kalvan and his tools. What heresy the Grand Host overlooks, my Investigator's shall uncover."

Soton didn't look happy at this prospect, but controlled his disgust, which made Anaxthenes wonder if the Grand Master had not made his own deal with Roxthar, much as so many others had been forced to do in these new times.

"When the Holy armies are finished," Roxthar's harsh voice rose in a crescendo. "There shall be no more Kalvan, no more Hostigos, no more Rathon, no more Dralm! Kill Kalvan! Kill Kalvan! Kill Kalvan!"

Suddenly all the voices in the room, including his own, added their weight to Roxthar's chorus, "KILL KALVAN! KILL KALVAN! KILL KALVAN!"

The End

CPSIA information can be obtained
at www.ICGtesting.com
Printed in the USA
LVHW112148130520
655551LV00006B/35/J

9 780937 912065